HERE'S HOW WE SURVIVE

THE (LOVE) STORIES FOR 2020

CHARITY TAHMASEB

COLLINS MARK BOOKS

COPYRIGHT

CONTENTS

AUTHOR'S NOTE

In late 2019, I conceived of a project where I'd post a story on my blog each Friday for an entire year. Since we were heading into what was bound to be a contentious election here in the US, I thought we could all use a little compassion, kindness, and love.

I had plenty of previously-published stories to post and several others that had garnered lovely personal rejections but hadn't found a home. During the year, I figured I could leisurely write new stories to fill in the blanks.

Then 2020 actually happened.

We really had no idea, did we?

In the decades to come, 2020 will be a year historians will study. Like the Great Depression, WWII, and other eras of change, they'll examine what people did, what they believed, and how they got on. We'll tell stories about this year. As hard as it is to believe now, some stories may end up flavored with nostalgia.

Right now? We're all trying to survive.

Stories help us do that—the ones we tell ourselves and each other. We fall into a fantasy or a romance or a thriller as a means to escape and emerge renewed. Stories help us find our way in dark times, bolster us, and even transform us.
Stories make us better people.

During this year, there were so many things we all had to set aside. I certainly didn't write as much as I'd hope to. Yet, through everything—a bout of COVID in April, a sprained ankle in June, my daughter's car-parade high school graduation, and all the rest—this project kept me going.
If I kept one creative promise for the year, it would be this one. I'm gratified that I managed to do so.

Thank you to everyone who has come along on this journey with me— whether that was in 2020 or in the years to come.

December 2020

JANUARY

January's stories were a mix of sibling love, surprising friendships, and cautionary tales of workplace romances.

GRETEL AND HANSEL

FAIRY TALE RETELLING

Hansel wanted to go back.

Even after endless weeks in a cage, even after Gretel scrubbed and swept and scoured for the witch, even after she pushed the frog-skinned crone into the oven, Hansel wanted to go back.

They stood at the edge of the forest, where the grass grew wild and sharp; brambles grabbed at their skin. The trees above reached their branches toward the ground as if they might scoop the two up and carry them away.

"She's dead," Gretel said to him.

Hansel stared into the woods.

"I killed her."

He shook his head, the movement so slow that at first, Gretel didn't take its meaning.

"You didn't kill her," he said, his words as dead as the witch should've been. "She's alive."

Could she be? Gretel stretched her hands in front of her, palms skyward. These hands. They'd shoved from behind. They'd murdered. The crunch of bones, the sizzle of hair and flesh. The thick smoke that had filled her mouth and throat, the plumes laced with the stench of rancid meat.

No one could live through that. No one, perhaps, except a witch.

"Why do you want to go back?" she asked.

A smile lit his face, the same sort of look she'd seen their father cast toward their stepmother, the same look Millie gathered from men in the tavern. True, some men reserved that gaze for the pint of ale they held in their grip. When Hansel licked his lips, Gretel hoped he wouldn't answer.

He didn't.

Every year, on the anniversary of their escape, Gretel would find Hansel at the edge of the forest. She'd stand with him while the sun dipped below the horizon, the slanting light flickering against the trees. The branches appeared to elongate as if beckoning them to step inside the wood.

Every year, she took his hand—a limp, clammy thing—and tugged him from the edge. With each step, her legs ached. Only the feel of Hansel's hand in hers kept her steady on the path home.

But maybe she was wrong. Hansel lived as if his heart, his soul, still resided deep in the woods, in a gingerbread house. She'd catch him licking his lips, and she knew. She'd tasted the sugar too. It had left them both empty—she without her brother, he without his heart's desire.

The year they turned sixteen, Gretel climbed the path to the woods only to find Hansel's spot empty. Pulse fluttering in her throat, she bent low. Her fingers skimmed the dust trail. In the dim light, she barely made out a boot print. It was enough to go on.

Gretel scampered down the path, grabbed her cloak from the hook inside the cottage door, and raced back up the hill. Before she could catch her breath, before she could gather enough courage to venture into the woods, a hand gripped her wrist.

"Stay back, girl. Don't go after him."

The voice was lilting, filled with sorrow and knowledge. Not her father, then. Gretel turned to confront Millie from the tavern.

"I have to," Gretel said. "He's my brother."

"He hasn't been yours for a very long time." Millie tugged on her wrist, a gentle, coaxing move that had Gretel stumbling forward. "It's too late. Once the witch has you, she doesn't let go."

"Yes, she does." She wrenched her wrist from Millie's grip and held up her hands for the woman to see. "I did it once. I can do it again."

Gretel pulled her cloak tightly around her and plunged into the forest.

Brambles wielded their thorns like daggers, their sharp points shredding her cloak. Branches grabbed at her hood. Eventually one plucked it from her head, the force choking her until she undid the drawstring.

On she ran until the woods opened onto a stream. The stream led to the gingerbread house. Gretel halted, letting the fringe of trees around the clearing conceal her.

The path to the house was covered with brittle, the air perfumed with spun sugar and melted chocolate. Even from this distance, desire churned in Gretel's belly. Yes, she'd tasted the sugar. Yes, she'd thought of returning. But after that unbearable sweetness, the cream curdled in her mouth, the sugar scorched her tongue. She'd purged, not far from here, next to the stream while Hansel had continued to consume the treats as if they were the only thing that could sustain him.

The witch stood in the entryway to her house, but this was not the frog-skinned crone of Gretel's memory. The witch glowed like spring itself, her skin the color of a pale crocus stem, her hair flowing, as white as lily of the valley and as soft as spun sugar.

Hansel lounged against the rail, a candied apple in his hands, the fruit so big and bright it glowed in the night. The witch curved a finger beneath his chin, and with no more than that, urged him inside.

Gretel threw herself forward, but the rock-sugar fence that surrounded the house barred her way, new segments sprouting across her path. She flung herself against the fence, again and again until her palms stung. She watched the blood, black in the moonlight, drip between her fingers and onto the ground.

"I've failed him," she said, to the forest, for every creature to witness.

"Whoo?" came the soft call of an owl.

"Me. I have failed my brother." Gretel studied her bloodstained hands. Certainly, this was proof of that.

"Whoo." The call came again, a lullaby rather than an admonishment.

One by one, feathers dropped from the night sky, floating downward until they landed on Gretel's palms. Each feather soaked up its share of blood before disintegrating. When a lone feather landed against her cheek, she sank to the forest floor and fell asleep.

The blaze woke her hours later, the gingerbread house lit with flames. The odor of burnt sugar and charred sweets filled her nose, her mouth, her throat, the stench so caustic it felt as if a noose had tightened around her neck.

"Hansel?" She called his name, again and again, her cries too thin to cut through the thick smoke that billowed from the house. "Hansel?"

Near dawn, the fire burned itself out, the rock-sugar fence a slag that oozed its way through twigs and leaves. Only the witch's oven remained, squat and low to the ground. It was from here a figure emerged, movements tentative as a newborn calf.

Gretel leaped across the slag and ran to her brother.

Hansel took her by the shoulders, his fingers thin and tight. "I had to go back. I had to be the one to kill her." He shook her as if that would help her understand. "Me, not you."

His blond hair had turned ashen. If she brushed it from his eyes, Gretel thought it might crumble to dust against her fingertips. He reeked of burnt sugar and acrid smoke, but when she turned his palms skyward, they were clean and pink, like a child's hands.

She took him by one of those hands and led him to the path that would take them home.

Gretel and Hansel first appeared in the August 2016 issue of Deep Magic.

LUCKY

CONTEMPORARY

"You're lucky you didn't bleed out."

He says this as if I'm the one who built the explosive, dug the hole, ran the wires, and then—after all of that—pulled the trigger myself.

"Lucky," he says, again, in case I didn't hear him the first time.

I did, of course, through the haze of whatever is running through my veins. Morphine, maybe? I don't know. Do they still use morphine? Whatever it is, whatever opiate fogs my thoughts, it is lovely and seductive. It tastes like temptation and blood. I'm glad—no, lucky—I don't know its name.

I won't be able to ask for it on the outside.

He sits at my bedside, easing back the sheet that covers me, the stethoscope barely there against my skin. He's warmed it, I realize, warmed it against his palm. He probes, and while I'm naked, I'm also bandaged clear up to my armpits. Not that there's any modesty in an Army hospital. Not that there's any modesty in the Army.

My breasts are bound, like those of women warriors of old. Through the fog, I can see these women. They are fierce, with hair like coiled snakes. Their armor shines in the sun. Their weapons glint in the moonlight.

Were they lucky as well? Did they ever bleed out?

My gaze flitters down. The bandages are white and pure. They are armor in their own right.

"They didn't have to amputate," he says.

At first, I think he means my breasts. I blink, the fog of morphine, of war, of my own thoughts too thick for me to make sense of his words. Then I understand.

"I know." What I don't mention is I can see my reflection in the window. I can count the number of legs I currently have.

"An infection, though."

"Try not to sound so hopeful."

He grimaces. "Katy-bird—"

"Don't 'Katy-bird' me."

"You shouldn't be here."

"*You* shouldn't be here."

He's not my doctor. He's not even assigned to this ward. He's breaking all the rules—Army rules, medical rules. But he's my brother, which is why everyone glances away when he does.

"I could send you home." He delivers the threat in the way only a big brother can.

I stare at the window. There is no view. Even my reflection has faded. All I see is the glint on the glass that looks like the blade of a sword.

"I don't want to leave them."

"Them," he says. "Your platoon?"

I want to nod; I want to shake my head. It's my platoon—yes, of course, it is—but it's so much more than that.

"I don't want to leave me."

Now he stares at the window as if he, too, can see the images of warrior women in its reflection. His nod is thoughtful, the sigh heavy— the sound only an older brother can make.

He threads the stethoscope through his fingers and then pockets it. He touches my cheek.

"You're sure?"

Something shifts in his tone. All at once, he is not a doctor, not my older brother. He is simply Scott, and he looks as confused as the morphine is making me feel.

"I can't leave."

He nods as if I've explained my entire self in those three words.

People leave all the time—wounded or killed in action or by their own hand. I don't want to leave, not now, not ever. Here is where I can see the warrior women.

He kisses my forehead. It's tender and filled with the warmth of absolution. At the doorway, he pauses, one last time.

"You're still damn lucky you didn't bleed out."

For a moment, everything else fades—the war, the morphine, the glint of swords on the glass.

Yes, I want to tell him. *I know.*

I'm lucky.

Lucky may be my story that has racked up the most personal rejections, ever. It even snagged an honorable mention in Glimmer Train's Very Short Fiction contest. Sometimes those stories everyone seems to love (but nevertheless declines) can be the hardest to sell.

DRAGON'S BANE

FANTASY

Something is different in this part of the forest. Even the ground beneath Kit's feet feels unsubstantial to her sneakers. Like the solid earth might crumble away at any moment, and she would plunge into nothing.

Everything in her world feels like that right now—a slow and steady crumbling—all her plans, the heart that beats in her chest, even the lease on her studio apartment. Worst of all, her one bit of solace, the forest, spins around her, nothing solid and sure.

Except when she stumbles upon an old log. She's been here before, in this part of the forest, but how is it she's never seen this particular clearing, with this particular log?

The log is huge, reaching halfway up her thigh. The surface is rough even through her jeans, the bark baked warm by the sun.

Kit pulls out a thermos. Before her trek into the forest—ostensibly to think, but really, it was running away—she brewed hot cocoa. The real kind, in a pan on her two-burner stove. She measured out the cocoa and the sugar, adding a dash of vanilla and cinnamon.

Now she uncaps the thermos, and the aroma rides the crisp autumn air, filling it with rich chocolate and a hint of wood smoke. Kit inhales, and for that single moment, everything is okay.

Then the log beneath her rumbles. It's a rolling, tumbling, undulating motion that makes her think of a rollercoaster—and sends her plummeting backward and onto the ground.

She lands hard, breath leaving her in a whoosh, hot cocoa sloshing in the thermos. Somehow—*somehow*—she holds onto it, holds it steady and upright.

It's then she finds herself staring into a pair of huge amber eyes. They are the size of Kit's head—at least—and they glow with intensity. Beneath those eyes, she spies a snout and a pink, forked tongue.

She follows the elegant line of a neck to the large hump she earlier took for an old-growth log.

"You," she says now, testing her voice in the still air, "are a dragon, or I'm losing my mind."

The creature snorts, the scent of wood smoke with a hint of brimstone infusing the space around her.

"Although, I suppose there are worse ways to lose your mind."

The dragon snorts again as if in agreement.

"I'm Kit." She doesn't hold out her hand. One, she's still clutching the thermos. Two, she's not certain dragons shake hands.

The dragon bows its head in acknowledgment. Then, like a whisper, a word lights in Kit's mind.

Taggledorf.

"It's nice to meet you, Taggledorf."

The dragon thumps its tail once, and the earth shakes.

But this time, it doesn't feel as if the ground will crumble beneath her.

KIT VISITS THE SPOT OFTEN. Taggledorf doesn't always appear. Even when she—it's a long and complicated bit of pantomime to determine that Taggledorf is a she—doesn't, her presence is there. The air holds that scent of wood smoke. Sometimes there's brimstone.

But everything in that particular clearing grows a bit lusher, smells a bit richer. Hummingbirds flit and dragonflies buzz. In the winter, there is enough warmth radiating from Taggledorf's back that Kit can spend hours in the cold.

She brings the man she wants to make her husband to this spot. She does not expect Taggledorf to appear, but yes, it's a test. Her heart is still tender and cautious. While this man fills her with certainty, so did the other, the one that had her fleeing to the forest in the first place.

When she returns alone a week later and finds the clearing alive with forget-me-nots and wild roses, she has Taggledorf's answer.

She weaves a crown of roses for her friend, and when Taggledorf does appear, a bit shy, Kit places the wreath on the dragon's head.

"We will always be friends," she says.

SHE BRINGS her children to this spot, spreading a soft, flannel blanket across the clearing. In summer, they drink lemonade, in winter, hot cocoa. Taggledorf makes her scales shimmer and shine. The children spend hours slapping the scales with their chubby hands, squealing and shrieking with delight.

One time, the warm sunshine lulls Kit into a nap. She wakes, heart pounding and terrified, only to find that Taggledorf has corralled both children with her tail.

"Thank you, my friend." Kit sighs and leans into the old-growth that is and is not Taggledorf's midsection. "Thank you."

KIT DISCOVERS that Taggledorf loves stories. It's when she reads to her children that the dragon's scales glow and hum. Picture books and Mother Goose, eventually graduating to chapter books. Her children sit on the dragon's back and take turns reading aloud.

When they've moved on—to novels and textbooks and quantum mechanics—Kit takes to reading in the clearing any time she can. The heat against her back tells her which stories are her friend's favorites.

When her eyesight dims, and her hands no longer can hold an e-reader, never mind a paperback, she plays audiobooks for them.

In the sunshine, they rest, safe in the knowledge that nothing changes as long as the story goes on.

IT HAS BEEN months since Kit has visited the clearing, maybe even a year, but she doesn't want to think hard enough to count. Today is perfect for a trek—her last trek to her clearing.

The spring air is warm, but the path is still clear of summer growth, those brambles and branches that might trip her up.

Even so, the walk is long, much longer than when she pushed a double stroller along the dips and ruts. By the time she reaches the old-growth log that isn't a log, her legs nearly give out beneath her.

"No stories today, my friend. I only want to rest, with you." She sinks against her friend, knowing Taggledorf will cushion her fall. "I have no wish to be found until ... after."

She snuggles against the dragon with the full knowledge that stories go on, but hers ends now.

And thanks to Taggledorf, it was a good one.

THE GIRL SMELLS FAMILIAR. This is the first thing Taggledorf notices. The second is the salt, so strong it has chapped the girl's cheeks and flavors the air.

Grief is something that can fill your mouth. This is something Taggledorf knows. It is something this girl is learning.

The girl settles next to her, back against Taggledorf's midsection, the very place where *she*—the other she—sat for so many years. The girl's body shakes, and Taggledorf lets the fire that always burns in her belly flare a bit—enough warmth to comfort and soothe while she ponders this girl.

She feels right.

Not everyone does, of course. That is the dragon's bane. So many of her kind have abandoned friendship, opting to gradually become the landscape they occupy.

But Taggledorf knows that despite the grief and goodbyes, a good friend is a story unto itself.

So she opens her large amber eyes and stares at the girl.

The gasp has more delight than fear.

The fingers are gentle against Taggledorf's snout.

"I miss her," the girl says.

Taggledorf nods. She does too.

"I'm Carly." The girl doesn't hold out her hand. She already knows that dragons don't shake hands.

Taggledorf blows a stream of smoke into the air. In it, is the sound of her name.

"It's nice to meet you," Carly says.

The dragon thumps her tail once, and the earth shakes.

And for now, at least, it doesn't feel as if the ground will crumble beneath either of them.

Dragon's Bane was written specifically for the (Love) Stories for 2020 project.

RULES FOR VISITING HADES

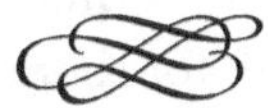

CONTEMPORARY, SPY VS. SPY

Berlin, May 2005

I knew he stood behind me before I caught his reflection in the window of a passing Mercedes. That sensation started at the base of my skull. The skin of my throat tightened. My heart thrummed— like it hadn't in years.

I'd come back to Berlin to stare at the spot where Checkpoint Charlie once divided a city, a country, a world. Just me and all the other tourists, many of them so young they confused Berlin's wall with Pink Floyd's.

You are now leaving the American sector.

"So," he said, at last. "Do you miss it?"

"What?"

"The cold war."

Of course. Why not ask Persephone if, during spring, she missed Hades?

"Do you?" I asked.

"It was easier to tell who the good guys were."

Peace through superior firepower.

Only then did I turn to look at him. "Do you think so?"

"Don't you?"

I didn't know what to think. What did you say to a man who looked like Cary Grant and spoke Russian with all the poetry of Pushkin?

"I knew the world was changing," he said, "when I woke on January first, 1990 with the most amazing hangover."

I knew months before The Wall crumbled that my world had shot off-kilter. A missed phone call. A missed meeting. A missed drop. Patterns. We were taught to look for them, piece them together, create a whole from a few lone indicators.

In those days, it was never a matter of who would betray whom, but when you played that card. I'd always wondered if I played mine too soon. Seeing as I wasn't part of that amazing hangover, I knew. I'd been too late—a spy who didn't know to come in from the cold.

Welcome to the new world order.

I found, after years, a cold sort of comfort in the old myths, about Persephone, about Orpheus and Eurydice. Clearly, there were rules for visiting Hades:

- If you find yourself caught there, don't eat the food.
- If you're leading someone out, don't look back.

I did both.

On any given day, Vienna, or Prague, or Berlin could look a lot like Hades. And Persephone's pomegranates were always in season.

"So," he said. "Do you miss it?"

"I do."

"Then will you have a drink, for old time's sake?"

"You drink?" I asked. Amazing hangovers notwithstanding, he'd long ago lost his taste for alcohol. I still had my sources. And that much I knew.

"Occasionally," he said. "I've always had a fondness for White Russians."

A blush curdled beneath my jaw and spread across my cheeks. It'd been a long time since I'd seen twenty-five, but you wouldn't know it by the way he looked at me—a look that worked on a thousand women, myself included.

"And do you still drink?" he asked.

"Occasionally," I echoed. "Cosmopolitans, mostly."

"All things American." He laughed. "I'm not even sure what's in one of those."

"Vodka."

"Oh, of course," he said. "American with a twist."

"And cranberry or pomegranate juice," I added, just to be perverse.

"Which do you prefer?"

I thought for a moment. "Pomegranate."

He offered his arm, a gesture reminiscent of Vienna, Prague, and even Berlin.

Gentlemen, we have détente.

I'd always believed that Persephone, like Eve, chose to taste the fruit. Now I wondered. Perhaps the fruit chose her.

I took his arm. We turned from Checkpoint Charlie, left it behind us. This time, I didn't look back.

Rules for Visiting Hades first appeared in the Flash for Big Cash Contest Anthology, March 2007. Hades placed third, and I won $50. So I guess you could say I flashed for moderate cash.

MOVING DAY

FANTASY

She stands in the center of the apartment, waiting for the landlord and the final walkthrough. She blinks as if she's not used to seeing the space so empty. I'm not used to it either.

She is moving out today, and I tell myself that this is for the best, that I couldn't be prouder.

The walls feel bare and vulnerable, mottled with shadows from where she hung her art. At first, she only painted tiny pictures, full of sickly greens and mustard yellows and dank purples. They were bruises, these paintings.

I was so glad when she replaced them with her recent work—that of cupped hands, upturned faces, and hope.

I will miss the paintings. The landlord enters with a clipboard. He is small-hearted. He loves neither his tenants nor the spaces they occupy. He only wants to cheat her out of the security deposit. I've seen this all before.

He wrinkles his nose, his face scrunched in a poorly disguised mask of disappointment at the scents that swirl in the air. Lemon. Pine. Murphy's Oil Soap, which has always been my favorite. The space is pristine.

True, for the first two months, she barely unpacked. She slept in the closet, hidden beneath a pile of blankets. In the kitchenette, she boiled water for ramen and spread peanut butter over bread. This was subsistence living, and I ached for her.

But that was before.

In these last few months? The aroma of curry and chocolate filled every pocket of space. She decorated earnest, braiding rag rugs that warmed the tile in the kitchenette and the bathroom. I'm always surprised at how little it takes to turn beige walls and gray linoleum into a home.

The landlord halts, fingers exploring a depression in the drywall. He snakes his hand back and forth—always finding fault, this one.

"What happened here?" he asks. His gruff voice is tinged with a hint of triumph.

She presses her lips together and shakes her head.

"Almost looks like someone got thrown into the wall."

He laughs.

She doesn't.

The landlord marks something on his clipboard.

That was the beginning of *after*, the last time she unlocked the deadbolt.

The pounding on the door continued, of course. Daily at first. Then every other day. Then once a week. Then, all at once, the pounding stopped completely.

I think we both exhaled.

Soon after, fresh colors crept into her paintings. She started taping brochures to the bathroom mirror—of students with backpacks, lounging by fountains or gazing studiously from their seats in a lecture hall.

"I'm going to have to charge you a hundred for the wall," the landlord says now.

She glances toward the ceiling, rolls her eyes. We both know he isn't going to repair the wall.

I so want to hold onto a memory of her. The landlord won't let her leave the braided rugs. This is all I have, this dent in the wall. The memory of her strength. I'm glad he won't be fixing it.

She turns over the keys, but in the hallway, she pauses.

"I think I left something in the medicine cabinet."

She dashes inside and stands in the center of the room, arms spread wide. She spins in a slow circle, taking in the kitchenette, the tiny balcony, the dining alcove.

On her way out, she lets her fingers linger over the deadbolt, taps it once, twice, three times.

"Thank you."

She has never slammed my door and doesn't now. The sound of her footsteps fades down the hall one final time. I exhale into the empty space, my ventilation system rattling as if I could tell her goodbye.

I'm so very proud of her.

I've always wanted to write a flash fiction story from the perspective of an inanimate object. Moving Day turned out to be that story.

FEBRUARY

It was all about love in February—romantic love, star-crossed love, a bit of unrequited love.

INCRIMINATING EVIDENCE

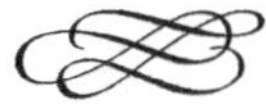

POST-APOCALYPTIC

"You won't tell anyone this."

I don't remind Magnus that I can't. Besides, his is a knee-jerk sort of question, the one he always asks at the start of a counseling session.

"You're the only one I can talk to," he says.

I nod, doodling on a piece of paper, its edges so charred that the smoky scent reaches me. It contains a list of names that, depending on whose fingers clutch the paper, could be almost anything—a death warrant, a hit list, a who's who of the most recent rebellion.

But since a Sage last held it, I've taken to desecrating it with doodles —mostly hearts and flowers—and mostly adorning Magnus's name. No, I shouldn't have a crush, but then I shouldn't be dispensing advice without a license, either.

Such are the times we live in.

"I need to fire my second," he says.

I crook an eyebrow at this. True, I am a rebel confidant, for lack of a better term, but I normally deal with Oedipus or Electra complexes, abandonment issues, and learned helplessness. (You'd be surprised how many revolutionaries aren't quite sure what to do after the coup.) But firing one's second in command? Purely an operational decision.

"He's a good friend," Magnus says.

Ah, the crux of the problem. I give a single nod, one that means: *Go ahead.*

"But I fear his loyalties may lie elsewhere." Magnus stares at me, his gaze holds both pleading and defiance. Has his second, Orlando, confessed to me? Magnus wants me to confirm. He wants me to deny. He wants something I can't give him. I can no more tell Magnus this than voice his doubts to Orlando.

Magnus strokes his chin. "It worries me."

Now I nod. It should and greatly.

"Do you think I should consult the Sages?"

I tilt my head to one side and give a little shrug—the maximum consideration the Sages deserve.

Magnus laughs, a big boom that fills the room and warms my heart. Still, I must swallow the bitter anxiety that floods my mouth. He is strong, I tell myself. This strength will be his salvation, not his downfall.

"Yes," he says, still laughing. "I know you've never set much store in their advice."

I have my own reasons for disregarding the Sages. That they dispense worthless advice is secondary.

"Of course..." A slyness crosses his face, the look both playful and seductive. "They led me to you."

Well, there's that.

He taps his fingers against a pillow as if counting off options. My office is rudimentary, at best. A scavenged door for a desk, propped up on crumbling cinderblock. Crates double as chairs. A fire in the hearth makes it warm enough for year-round use. But the pillow? Velvet with silky fringe in a deep emerald green. It harkens back to long-ago days. Most of my clients can't help but fondle it. When they do, their fears pour from them.

"It's the betrayal," Magnus says, his fingers entwined in the fringe, which might double as strands of hair by the way he strokes it.

I stare at his hands until the heat in my face forces me to glance away.

"We expect it. Don't we? We always look for the betrayal."

I turn back to him.

"But it's never easy."

I blink rapidly, in a way that I hope conveys understanding, not flirting.

"You would caution me against haste," he says.

I give an emphatic nod.

"Rash judgments?"

Yes, those too. I can't help but smile. Are all client relationships destined to be so intimate? Or is it only that one client, the one you end up needing more than he needs you?

Magnus closes his eyes. His lashes are childlike and startling against the scarred terrain of his cheekbones.

"Just saying it out loud." He exhales, the force of his breath ruffling the pillow's fringe. "You can't imagine what a relief that is."

No. I can't.

He opens one eye and peers at me. I've always envied those who can do that. I need both eyes to see the world, and even then, I doubt I see it clearly—or at least not like I should. But it's this gesture that decides things—his absolute trust in me. My world is a complicated tapestry with so many threads. But tug Magnus from the weave?

My whole existence would unravel.

I glance down at the list of names. The Sages may dispense worthless advice, but their sources are impeccable. I start to tear my scribbling from the rest of the page, but there's no hope for it. I've entwined myself so thoroughly with Magnus, at least in doodles. I shove the charred and adorned sheet at him before I can change my mind.

Perhaps devotion can soften betrayal.

Even as his mouth turns grim, his eyes remain soft, dart toward the top of the page, then toward me.

"I know you'll never tell," he says.

I won't. I can't. Long ago, on my fifth day—as the tradition goes—the Sages sliced the tongue from my mouth.

He carries the paper to the hearth and lets it drop into the flames. Evidence of betrayal—of devotion—evaporates into smoke. I join him on the walk from my office. At the threshold, he presses a finger against my lips and kisses my forehead. I dare to yearn for more—that kiss traveling my cheek, brushing my mouth, lingering there.

But there's no hope for it. Already the warmth of his lips is a memory.

"Ah," he says. "My perfect confidant."
Yes, it's true. I am the perfect confidant.
When he leaves without a backward glance, I know this:
That's all I'll ever be.

This odd little tale of post-apocalyptic unrequited love first appeared in Fantasy Scroll Magazine.

STEADFAST

ROMANCE

*P*oppy fell the moment Carlos showed her his feet. She'd never met a man—or rather, a civilian man—with feet uglier than her own. But ballet slippers weren't any kinder to toes than combat boots were.

Before she saw him, she'd planned on making a tactical retreat from the reception. It'd been a mistake to take leave for this wedding, an even bigger one to wear her dress uniform. Coming home never worked. Hadn't she learned that by now? Too many awkward questions, too many *thank yous.*

What made her pause at the ballroom's entrance, Poppy couldn't say. She didn't see the groom twirling his bride or the bridesmaids in clouds of chiffon floating across the parquet.

Only Carlos.

With uncommon grace, he crossed the room. He navigated the maze of chairs, tables, and guests like a man intimately familiar with each muscle of his body. When he landed in front of her, he didn't speak but merely held out his hand.

"I don't dance," she said.

"Everybody dances."

"Not me. I march."

He tipped his head back and laughed. "I can dance well enough for both of us."

And yes, he could. Demanding to see his feet came several glasses of champagne later.

"Stay," he whispered the next morning. "Spend the week with me. You can come to rehearsal. I'm dancing the role of the steadfast tin soldier."

She laughed at the audacity of it, of burning a week's worth of leave in New York City, with this beautiful man whose world was so different from her own.

"Do you know *anything* about being a soldier?" she asked.

"That's why I need you. You can be my technical advisor."

"No one will believe that."

Everyone did. Or, rather, they indulged their principal dancer. She taught Carlos how to drill with a wooden rifle. During breaks, he taught her how to hold herself so he could lift and spin her around.

With Carlos, she could dance. With Carlos, she was weightless.

At the airport, he tucked a necklace into the palm of her hand, the pendant an exquisitely engraved poppy.

"We both have demanding mistresses." His words were so soft she barely heard them above the clamor of traffic and travelers. "You don't need to come home to me. Just come home."

She wore the necklace every day in Afghanistan. Poppy no longer regretted attending the wedding, or even wearing her uniform. Her only regret was never seeing Carlos dance on stage.

They wrote letters, the old-fashioned kind, hers torn from a notebook, the paper encrusted with sand and dotted with dirty fingerprints, his on the back of paper placemats, or cleverly crafted in the margins of playbills.

Then her world erupted in fire. When the burn subsided to mere embers, it was too late and Walter Reed a world away from New York City. Still, Poppy vowed: she would see Carlos dance.

Sleeping Beauty gave her the chance.

She had flowers delivered to his dressing room—white roses laced with red poppies. That way he'd know. That way, if he didn't want to see her, he could hide until she abandoned her vigil at the stage door.

Poppy waited there, her head still buzzing from his performance, her weight sagging into the crutches, her foot heavy in its cast.

Her cheeks flamed when she caught sight of him emerging from the door, her skin hot against the December air. He scanned the alleyway behind the theater. The moment his gaze met hers, he froze.

"Bet my feet are uglier than yours now," she said.

He exhaled and laughed. It was only then she saw the poppy tucked in his lapel. He took in her crutches, her foot in its cumbersome cast. His eyes grew somber.

"My steadfast soldier."

"I'm home," she said.

He moved close, fluid and graceful, and cupped her cheek with his palm. "So am I."

All at once she was weightless.

Steadfast was first published at Flash Fiction Online (and was nominated for a Pushcart Prize as well). It was my attempt to retell Hans Christian Andersen's The Steadfast Tin Soldier. So I did, with a gender flip and an unapologetic happy ending.

THE BURDEN OF SO MANY ROSES

YOUNG ADULT

The road to popularity at Fremont High School is paved with rose petals. Or, to be exact (and I usually am), petals from three-dollar roses. This year, I have a three-part plan to conquer those roses:

- Money (Christmas, babysitting, minimum wage from the Sub Shoppe)
- Handwriting samples (AP World History projects, chemistry lab, Spanish class)
- Selection of boys (valedictorian, quarterback, swim team captain)

They're all going to send me a rose on Valentine's Day—even if they don't realize it.

The problem? Girls from the cheerleading squad run the rose booth. I must make sure no one sees me take more than a few notecards. But a sweater with big pockets and a little misdirection work wonders. I slip in before school and give Sienna my biggest smile.

"For my best friend," I say, a lie, of course.

One, that rose is totally for me. Two? Maybe next year at this time, I'll have a best friend—or any friends, for that matter. First, I must tread the rose-petal path.

"Aw," Sienna says. "That's so sweet. Some girls don't get any roses."

Not that Sienna would know. She's never been one of *those* girls. The thing is, everybody knows that girls buy for each other. It doesn't make you popular. It doesn't make guys think you're hot. All it does is make you look desperate. I will not be that girl. Not anymore.

That night, I neglect calculus in favor of perfecting Marcus Hanson's blocky boy letters and Toby Preston's lazy scrawl. In the end, I spend fifty-four dollars for eighteen roses. I can always stash a few in my locker if lugging around so many roses turns out to be too much. On Valentine's Day, I choose a pink sweater. When I walk into school and see Sienna wearing a similar style in a similar shade, I know it's perfect.

This day will be perfect.

All morning, roses flood the classrooms. It's a record sale, the principal announces over the PA system, with the proceeds going to Operation Smile. We are, she tells us, a most generous group of young people. Some more than others, I think.

More roses arrive, but by the time class ends, not a single one is for me. Next class. I'll practically drown in all the roses. But by lunch, I trudge to the cafeteria empty-handed. Sienna, at the cheerleading table, has a stack of roses—red and pink and creamy white. She plucks one from the pile and hands it to a freshman girl passing by.

Oh, to be Sienna. To have roses to spare.

During chemistry, the collar of my pink fuzzy sweater chokes me. My armpits produce massive amounts of sweat. I blow an easy pop quiz. Then, I have the best thought.

All my roses will arrive during last class! I'll stagger to my locker under their weight. When I pass Sienna, she'll give me a secret smile, the sort only shared by girls who struggle under the burden of so many roses.

When the last bell rings, I stay rooted in my chair, convinced there's been a mistake. Not a single rose! Mrs. Meyer clears her throat, then asks:

"Are you okay?"

I nod, but I'm not okay. I'm out fifty-four dollars. The path to my locker is strewn with other people's rose petals. My books make my arms ache. I dial the combination, but don't lift the handle.

"Hey, Emily."

I turn. Toby Preston stands to one side, pink-cheeked and adorable.

"This is crazy," he says. "But back in sixth grade, I never gave you this." He pushes an envelope at me. "It was stupid, because we had to give everyone a valentine, but I didn't want anyone to know I liked you."

I hold the valentine like it's made of spun glass. This is better than a rose.

"Would you like to go somewhere?" he asks. "Coffee shop, maybe?"

Oh! Even better. Who needs roses anyway? I nod and open my locker for my coat. Out spills a rose. Then another. They tumble out, cover the linoleum, bury me up to my ankles.

Toby's cheeks blaze red. His Adam's apple bobs once, twice, so hard my throat aches in response.

"I guess coffee's out of the question," he says. Before I can stop him, he sprints down the hall.

A custodian helps me clear away the roses. She loans me a pair of work gloves, but the thorns find my skin. One pricks my cheek, and I can't stop the blood tear that rolls down my face.

"Seen this before," she says after I shove the last rose to the bottom of the dumpster.

"Really?"

"It happens. Every few years or so."

"*What* happens?" I want to know why and what it all means.

Her eyes are kind, but she shrugs. "I think that's up to you."

I leave school empty-handed.

A block from home, I spot a little girl at a bus stop. In the center of the road sits a smashed shoebox. Red construction paper hearts flutter in the wind. Tires grind Red Hots and conversation hearts into powder. Her sobs fill the air but do nothing to stop the cars from plowing through her valentines.

"They're all gone," she says, "I don't have any left."

Neither do I. Then I remember Toby's valentine. I pull it from my backpack. The wind nearly steals it, so I hang on tightly. Then I wonder if I can let it go.

"What's that?" the little girl asks.

"It's yours." I kneel at her side and hand it to her.

"Oh! It even has my name on it! Right here. It says *Emily*."

"See? It was meant for you."

She skips down the sidewalk, clutching Toby Preston's valentine to her chest. I turn for home. Only when I reach the front porch, do I feel it.

I am one rose lighter.

The Burden of So Many Roses was first published in Kazka Press as part of their monthly contest. The theme was an undelivered Valentine. It's one of those Valentine's Day stories for when you're not feeling Valentine's Day.

THE GOBLIN AND THE PIXIE

FANTASY

Everyone knew that pixies were cruel. Those teeth. Their words. A conversation with one was like dying from a thousand tiny cuts. You might think: *one or two scornful remarks won't matter.* But they added up, faster than you could count.

That was why Renate kept her distance. That, and because she was a goblin. And not one of those flashy lime green ones, or one a delicate shade of violet. She was brown, like the bark on the trees of the forest she called home.

Practical, but dull.

But the pixie? Oh, he would dazzle you—lithe, sultry. His talent was the piccolo, as Renata soon learned, but he could sing and dance and execute all manner of acrobatics. His wings were a glittery sapphire while his skin was the icy hue of a January sky.

He was so beautiful, his features elegant and lovely, even those razor-like teeth. Renata felt a bit chagrined for her admiration. It was shallow, wasn't it? It made *her* shallow, didn't it? She didn't even know his name. Pixies seldom confessed such things, not even to a lover. If you knew a pixie's name, the saying went, then you knew their entire heart.

But never, in all the annals of history, had there ever been a goblin-pixie pairing. So Renata dreamed her unattainable dreams safe in the knowledge they were only that.

Until the day the pixie fluttered down from the sky and landed on the forest floor in front of her.

His feet barely whispered against the carpet of fallen leaves. His wings hummed, and the sound was warm and soothing, like a lullaby.

"Why do you stare at me all day long," he asked.

Renata knew she didn't have quick wit—if this were a conversational trap, then she would walk right into it. So she saw no reason to be dishonest.

"Because you are the most beautiful being I have ever seen."

With those words, heat burned her cheeks, her skin so hot she might set the forest aflame.

The pixie tilted his head. "Do you like how I play the piccolo?"

"I do, very much."

He twirled, a perfect pirouette, and landed gracefully. "And my acrobatics? What do you think of them?"

"They are lovely."

For a long moment, he scrutinized her. Then, he nodded once and took flight.

Odd things happened after that. Sweet music—that of a piccolo—accompanied her trek through the forest. The tune changed depending on what she was doing. Slow and thoughtful for rooting out mushrooms. Lively and quick for picking berries.

When she was helping a doe birth twins on a slushy spring morning, a warm buzzing sounded above her, shielding her and the doe from rain. Renata glanced up, but all she could see was the furious beating of pixie wings.

On clear nights, when she peered into the sky, her name would sparkle among the stars.

She searched for hidden cruelty and found only kindness.

The next time the pixie landed before her, stepping lightly across daisies and buttercups, Renata could do little more than clutch her hands beneath her chin.

"Why do you always brighten my day?" she asked.

"Because you brighten mine."

"Me?" This she could not fathom. "How?"

"You know which of the forest's bounty is edible, and which is not."

"Don't pixies know this?"

He flushed, a delicate pink spreading through his entire body. "It's a good thing pixies have strong constitutions. I only know what to eat from watching you."

"I can teach you." Such boldness! Renata almost swallowed back the words.

But he inclined his head and continued. "You care for the forest creatures. You care for our home when the rest of us enjoy it, use it, but far too often disregard it."

"I love the forest and everything in it." It was as close as she dared come to confessing her feelings for him.

He took one step closer. "And you have the eyes of a doe and the skin the color of a wise oak tree. You are beautiful."

She was about to protest or shake her head when he took another step forward.

"I am Simon."

Oh? *Oh.*

"You know I'm Renata."

"I do. May I kiss you, Renata?"

She didn't think twice, although perhaps she should have. She knew of the teeth, of the cuts, of the pain. Kissing a pixie was something a steadfast, ordinary goblin like herself should never do.

Renata stepped forward.

She closed her eyes.

The kiss was warm, steeped in magic and honey. When the quicksilver taste filled her mouth and blood ran down her chin, Renata gasped. She felt no pain, had no cuts.

It wasn't her blood.

It was his.

Simon had sliced through his own lips as to not injure her.

But a steadfast little goblin such as herself had a salve for that. She tended to his wounds, and by nightfall, he was healed enough to play the piccolo.

It took until winter, with the snow piled high around Renata's little cottage, until they discovered a way to kiss without incident.

Neither one minded.

The Goblin and the Pixie was written especially for the (Love) Stories for 2020 project.

MARCH

For March, it was all about strange and surprising connections, unexpected friendships and traditions.

KEEPING TIME

FANTASY

The mantel clock kept its own time. It was fussy, too, in the way old clocks sometimes are, refusing to work when wound in a way it found unacceptable. Because of this, in each generation, the task fell to either the youngest or oldest member of the household.

Maisey was five when her grandmother showed her how to wind the clock. She bounced on the balls of her feet, her fingers itching for their turn. She'd warm the brass key in her palm, the way her grandmother did. Every evening they'd clean the old clock with a soft cloth and lemon-scented polish.

"Pay attention," her grandmother would say. "It will soon be your turn."

"When, Grandma, when?"

Her grandmother chuckled. "Not soon enough for your father."

But when Maisey's turn finally came, her feet no longer bounced. After the funeral, she dragged a chair through the gathering, cutting off words about her grandmother—some soft, some less so—and clambered up to reach the clock on the mantel.

"Maisey!" Her mother's voice cracked, its edges so sharp that, if it were a real thing, you could cut someone with it.

"I promised Grandma," Maisey said.

In the middle of murmured condolences and her mother's sobs, she pulled out the key and wound the clock.

When her father retired, Maisey offered the key to him. But he had too many golf games—and then, too many back problems—to bother with an old clock. Her mother spent so much time canning tomatoes (which no one ever ate) and volunteering (which gave her a headache) to remember the old timepiece gathering dust on the mantel.

So Maisey dug out a chain from her jewelry box and hung the key around her neck. The clock ticked on, grateful for the gentle touch of Maisey's fingers. When she packed the car for college, she placed the clock in last, belting it into the front passenger seat.

She went through three roommates until the campus housing department found one who didn't mind the faux mantelpiece taking up half their dorm room. After one too many broken hearts, Maisey let each perspective boyfriend wind the clock at least once. In the end, she picked the man with the lightest touch and most nimble fingers. She learned there were advantages to this well beyond winding clocks. When she graduated, she took him, the faux mantelpiece, and the clock.

Together, they built a life.

When at last her granddaughter was born, a girl whose eyes shined each time she heard the clock tick, Maisey knew her own time was drawing near. These days, she polished the clock more often, fussed over its placement on the mantel.

"We need to spruce you up," she'd say. "Can't have you looking your years—not like me."

The wood casing gleamed in the light. When little Tessa pressed a finger against its side, she gave Maisey a delighted smile.

"Oh, Grandma! It's warm."

It always was, this old clock, warm and constant.

"You have always been my loyal companion," she told it on the day she loosened the chain from around her neck.

Einstein once said, "The only reason for time is so that everything doesn't happen at once." But what if, for the briefest moment, she could defy that rule—and even Einstein himself—by passing on the key before passing on herself? When Tessa turned five, Maisey presented the key to her, chain and all, and hovered while the little girl wound the clock for the first time.

And yes, there it was, her life, all of it, from her own grandmother's death, the scrape of the chair across the floor, sharp braces against her lips, the whisper of taffeta prom dresses, textbooks weighing down her arms. Timothy on bended knee, the mantel and clock behind her, as if peering over her shoulder. On it went, in one great wash through her blood—all of time, all her life, all at once.

"What now, Grandma?" Tessa asked.

"Keep it well, my dear," Maisey said, "keep it well."

That night, the clock stopped ticking.

The afternoon of her grandmother's funeral, Tessa dragged a chair across the floor and scrambled up to the mantel. She turned the key once, twice. Tessa inhaled lemon-scented dust, then held her breath. Behind her, the air shook. She turned, saw her mother, whose body trembled with sobs. Tessa jumped from the chair and threw her arms around her mother.

From the mantel, something shifted inside the clock. A single tock shuddered through its wood casing. Then, once again, the old clock started keeping its own time.

Keeping Time was first published by Kazka Press. It was subsequently produced in audio by The Centropic Oracle.

THE GIRL WITH THE PICCOLO

FANTASY

No one thinks about the empty note casings after the nightly revelry. Someone has to pick them up, right? That I spent four grueling years at the Acoustic Academy at Stormy Point for the privilege is something I try not to think about.

True, it takes only a breath or two to chase the notes into my sack. Still, patrolling the DMZ (Disharmonious Zone) feels anti-climactic. I didn't sign up for this. But now, with the sun nearly cresting the horizon, I can't say what I did sign up for.

I holster the piccolo and continue the patrol. When I first enlisted, I wanted something shiny, something big and brassy, a trumpet or a trombone, or—if I dared to dream—the saxophone. (Really, who doesn't want the sax?) The supply sergeant gave me a once over and puttered around her inventory on grizzled wings.

"Here you go, sweetie," she said, dropping a piccolo into my outstretched hands.

My own wings sputtered, and I sank to the ground in disbelief.

"None of that," the supply sergeant barked. "Remember, everyone underestimates the girl with the piccolo. Don't let them."

Perhaps I have. Let them, that is. This might explain why that piccolo and I now do border patrol.

Through my viewfinder, I scan the tree line on the other side of the

DMZ. I catch sight of my enemy counterpart. She is a brilliant pink, where I am midnight blue. Her wings drip with glitter. Mine sparkle with stardust. I wonder how she can breathe a single note through her piccolo with all that tinsel in the air.

Through the lens, I see her eyebrows furrow. When her viewfinder is level with mine, I stick out my tongue. This, sadly, is the highlight of my evening.

I near the border, my bag overflowing with spent notes. I swipe the residue from a tuba casing. The tubas are so wasteful. I can fuel my piccolo for a week on what they leave behind. Across the way, the pink fairy dips and swoops; I suspect she's doing the same thing I am.

A shift in the air makes the fine hairs on my wings stand on end. I shoot skyward just as a full marching band crowds the path alongside the meadow. Stardust fills the air. I could reach out and pluck notes as they float past me. I might. Except. This particular band? Doesn't include a piccolo player. Underestimated? Try forgotten. Typical. They can play on without me.

I turn to fly away when the stench of rotted nectar hits me. I blink back tears. The aroma clogs the back of my throat. The players are drunk, spoiling for battle, and a wing's breadth away from the DMZ. From above, I watch the band weave along the path, each rousing measure inching them closer to treaty violation. I cast a look for the security forces. Certainly, someone is on the way.

Or not. I blow a few quick notes into my piccolo, an alert that may not reach its intended recipients, at least, not in time. Frantic, I peer through my viewfinder. The stricken face of my counterpart stares back at me, a hand on her own piccolo. A few breaths and she will bring in her own band—and they will not be drunk. They will be deadly, armed with wing-piercing notes. They will tear across the meadow, swoop into the DMZ, reigniting the Fairy Wars.

All on my watch.

I pull out my piccolo. Next, I take a quick peep through my viewfinder to make sure my pink counterpart is watching. She is. I mimic holding a baby, of rocking it to sleep in my arms. Certainly, this movement is universal. Pink fairies come from somewhere, yes? I peer through my viewfinder again. Nothing but a pair of pink fuzzy eyebrows, drawn into a frown.

I rock my imaginary baby again, then hold up my piccolo. I run my fingers across it while holding my breath—one false note will bring my plan crumbling down. I check my viewfinder again. One of those pink eyebrows is raised. In question? Understanding? This time, I waltz with my imaginary baby before checking the viewfinder.

I hope her smile means what I think it does. I hope this isn't a ruse. Without her help, I will be tried for treason, assuming, of course, I survive the ensuing battle.

I hold up a hand for the countdown ... three ... two ... one. Fairies have many lullabies, but only one in three-quarters time. When pitched just right, it soothes the most colicky baby, sends mortals into a deep sleep. As for drunken fairies ...

Her piccolo plays counterpoint to mine. At first, my comrades show no sign of stopping their rampage. In fact, the tuba player bursts through the ranks, intent for the DMZ and the meadow beyond.

Before he can reach the DMZ, his pace flags. The tuba slips from his grip. His wings falter. By the time both are on the ground, he's snoring. The rest of the band drops off, in twos and threes, notes scattered everywhere. My own notes, and those of the pink fairy, play in the sky, creating an iridescent lavender that prolongs the night.

At last, I need a breath—and so does she. I alight on the tuba. From this vantage point, I can peer across the meadow. Through my viewfinder, I study my enemy counterpart. How many times has she fogged my view with pink glitter? How many times have I stuck out my tongue? This time, before she can look away, I salute. Then, I shoot skyward. Someone else can clean up all these notes. After all this time, I realize what the supply sergeant meant.

Never underestimate the girl with the piccolo.

That goes for both of us.

The Girl with the Piccolo was first published by Kazka Press. It subsequently appeared in Evil Girlfriend Media and was produced in audio by Cast of Wonders.

INSIDIOUS BEASTS

FANTASY

I straddle the roof of my cottage, or rather, the part of the roof that remains. From my perch, I peer through the giant-sized hole and into my bedroom. The quilt is downy white, and part of me wonders if there's any harm in simply dropping through that giant-sized hole and landing in its softness.

If there's any harm in delaying what I must do today.

Above, the sky is clear, a startling blue that's the color of forget-me-knots. Still, the air is sticky against my cheeks, and I taste the promise of rain on my tongue. Beneath the heat—and the late-summer storm that's certain to roar through our valley—I sense the chill of autumn.

Yes, there's great harm in delaying what I must do today.

With a finger, I test the ragged edge closest to me. A telltale red stains the thatch as if some giant creature cut its lips while taking a bite out of my house.

How—and why—did I sleep through that?

I woke to the sunrise touching my eyelids, birdsong in my ears, and a gaping hole above my head. That I don't know, can't remember, makes my stomach clench with foreboding.

"I can guarantee a lot," comes a voice from the path below. "But, I never claimed my materials were giant-proof."

Master Rinaldi stands at my front gate, fingers curled around the latch as if he's merely waiting for an invitation to lift it.

I don't grant him one.

"A giant did this?" I ask.

"What else? Insidious beasts. They're taking over the forests, the hinterlands. You should move to the village. This is no place for a woman on her own." He waves a dismissive hand at my cottage, which up until this morning, was a fine place for a woman on her own.

"Giants eat thatch?" It's a ridiculous question. I know they don't. We both know that.

He raises a suggestive eyebrow. "Perhaps it was searching for the treat inside."

I ignore this. "You wouldn't happen to have more thatch, would you, Master Rinaldi?"

I gauge the hole in my roof. The laborers I hired earlier this summer would all be in the fields, working to bring in the harvest. I could, perhaps, tackle this job on my own.

Perhaps.

When Master Rinaldi doesn't answer, I turn my attention back to him. His gaze roves my legs, clad in breeches. There's a calculating glint in his expression, one I've seen him wear in the marketplace.

Master Rinaldi knows weaknesses and how to drive a bargain. He is also blessed with a lovely wife and ten children, all strong and healthy. He is someone who has everything a man could want.

And yet, his eyes—and hands—roam.

If I wish more thatching for my roof, I suspect there's an added cost, one that doesn't involve the silver coins in my purse.

"So late in the season?" He shakes his head as if my plight is the saddest thing he's seen in a month.

"I could try Master Carr," I say, hedging my bets.

Master Rinaldi merely smirks.

The trouble is, Master Rinaldi's supplies are the best—sweetest smelling, free of vermin, such as night loshes and murdocs. During the winter, too many families have slumbered beneath an infected roof only to never wake in the spring.

If I'm to make it through the winter, I may have to pay the price he's asking.

The rumble starts so low and—to paraphrase Master Rinaldi—insidiously that I barely register it. The soft tremble travels the framework of my cottage until the shaking reaches my ribcage and bits of straw float to my bedroom below.

A shadow looms on the horizon—a giant-sized one, to match the hole in my roof.

Master Rinaldi falters. He steps away from my gate only to stop and double back. He doesn't want to be here. But with me stranded on the roof, he has no wish to appear cowardly.

"Mistress Benton, I implore you. Pack what you can carry and leave with me now."

The earth shudders with the giant's approaching footfalls. I clutch the roof, the rough thatch cracking against my palms. Master Rinaldi stumbles, his gait haphazard, on a path that takes him away from me and toward the village.

"It's coming back," he says. "For *you.*"

Could I scamper down from the roof, grab a few precious belongings, and race for the village? Then what? Secure a room at the inn until my silver runs out? Throw myself on the mercy of the village elders? Of Master Rinaldi?

I shake my head, resolute in this.

"You're mad," he calls up to me. "A fool of a woman."

Yes. Likely I am. But I'm a woman with a home of her own—a rare thing in these parts. If I leave, someone—a man—will claim this land. If I stay and die, then someone—a man—will claim this land.

No matter what I do, the outcome is the same.

So I choose to stay.

Without a glance over his shoulder, Master Rinaldi lurches down the path, his stride chaotic under the onslaught of the giant.

I hang onto the roof with all my might and wait.

As the giant grows closer, the steps grow lighter. It's as if it knows the power in its footfalls and is now treading lightly.

And as the giant grows closer, I see that it—or rather—she is wearing a shift the color of forget-me-nots. Her feet are bare, her hands clenched in fists. Her hair, plaited into braids, is alternately gold, silver, and ebony.

She is awe-inspiring, and I can't look away.

When the giant reaches my cottage, she kneels. This does not put us at eye level, although it comes close. Her eyes are the same color as her dress, and I think that may be why she wears it. I don't know if vanity extends to giants, but I don't see why it can't.

She unclenches her right fist. In her palm rests the tangle that once was my roof. Interspersed in the straw and reeds is the inky black remains of a murdoc.

I press a hand against my chest and pull in a deep breath, just to reassure myself I still can.

"Is that why I didn't hear you?" I ask.

The giant blinks her great blue eyes in what I take as *yes*.

"Has it been there all summer?"

Now a single tear rolls down her cheek. It lands on the packed earth of my walkway and splashes so high I can taste the salt of it on my lips.

How far gone was I? How close to death? My heart thumps with latent fear, and then my pulse sparks with anger. Convenient of Master Rinaldi to show up this morning of all mornings.

So convenient that, for a moment, I don't have any words.

"How ... insidious." I say, at last.

A smile tugs the corner of her mouth. Oh, yes, she knows all about Master Rinaldi. The giant crumbles the tangle of straw in her fist, obliterating whatever remains of the murdoc. The wind steals the vestiges of straw and beast, lifts them high into the air, and carries them away.

Only then do I feel my breath return in full force. Only then does it occur to me to worry for someone other than myself.

"Are you hurt? Did the murdoc hurt you?"

Her smile has revealed something I missed previously. The blood. Scrapes and cuts, yes. She hurts.

"I have a balm, but it's." I point at the hole in my roof. I sigh. "It's down there."

She holds out a palm, and without hesitation, I step onto it.

I find the balm and a soft cloth, and I gesture for the giant to return me to the roof. From there, I lean forward, dab the healing balm—a recipe of my grandmother's—against the wounds.

The giant laughs. In relief? Delight? It's hard to tell. The force of it nearly knocks me to the ground.

Then she opens her other hand, and there is thatching, fresh from someone's storehouse. I suspect Master Rinaldi's.

Honestly? He owes me.

Together we make short work of repairing my roof. Near sunset, when the task is done, I pour us each a serving of mead, her portion in the largest bowl I own. She takes dainty sips but still manages to finish the drink almost immediately.

It is nearly dark now, I have a giant on my door stoop, and I'm not quite sure what happens next.

The giant pulls a piece of parchment from her pocket and unfurls it. The script is precise, but the letters so large I must back up to read the message.

My name is Martine.
I can speak, but my words are loud, and I don't want to scare those
around me.
If I'm showing you this note, it means I wish to be your friend.

"Martine," I say. "That's a pretty name."

She smiles, her teeth so white and fierce that for a moment, I can't collect my thoughts.

"I'm Benton," I add, my heart pounding a strange beat. I'm not frightened. I'm not nervous. I want to name this thing I'm feeling, but suspect it's nothing more than a spark of hope. I don't want to extinguish it by staring at it too hard. "My mother wanted a boy and saw no reason to change the name when I wasn't."

Martine lifts an eyebrow, a wry gesture that makes me laugh.

"Do you have a place to stay?" I ask.

Where *do* giants stay? Does Martine have a family? Who are her people, and why is she alone?

She gives a slow shake of her head, and another tear trickles down her cheek. The heartbreak and sorrow that rolls off her might flood this valley.

"You can stay with me."

Those blue forget-me-not eyes widen.

"I own the land from that corner of the forest, through the meadow, and all the way to the stream. Is that enough room?"

She claps her hands together, and the force of it reverberates across the land. Certainly, the villagers are trembling in their cellars at this very moment.

"Stay," I say to Martine.

In time, I'll learn of her heartache. Perhaps I can help her find her people, assuming she is lost, of course. Or perhaps she's like me—a woman on her own.

"Stay, and be my friend."

When Martine nods, that spark of hope kindles into flame.

And no matter how insidious Master Rinaldi is, I must admit that he is right in one respect.

This is no place for a woman on her own. But for two?

It's perfect.

Insidious Beasts was written especially for the 2020 (Love) Story Project.

A MEASURE OF SORROW

FANTASY/FAIRY TALE

A wolf seduced her sister, and a witch wrapped her bony fingers around her brother's heart, so when a giant came for her, she told him she wouldn't go.

He plucked a rose petal from the bushes that grew around his castle, and that was her bed. When the day grew hot, he offered dewy raspberries to quench her thirst. When she refused, a single tear fell from his eye and splashed at her feet. The salt on her lips tasted like sorrow. She was drenched, but unmoved.

Only when he left his almanac out—quite by accident—did she creep from the threshold of her cottage. It took all her strength to turn the pages, but turn them she did. The letters were as tall as she was, but read them, she did.

He caught her reading. If he wanted, he could have slammed the book shut, trapped her—

or squashed her. He didn't.

He looked to the book and then to her. "Will you come with me now?"

"I am not a pet."

"Of course not."

"Or a meal."

He blew air through his lips, the force of it ruffling her hair. "You are much too small for that."

"Then what am I?"

"I need someone to tend to the mice. They are ailing. And the butterflies. My fingers are too clumsy, and I cannot mend the rips in their wings."

"So, you have work for me?"

"Good work, with good pay. You can keep your family well."

"They would feed me to the wolves."

"Then how am I any worse?"

How indeed? Did she trust this giant and his promises of mice and butterflies?

"Will you?" He extended a hand.

She stepped onto his palm, and he lifted her higher and higher—even with his mouth, his nose, his eyes. Then he placed her gently on his shoulder.

"What made you change your mind?" he asked.

"The almanac. Will you read to me sometimes?"

"Would you like that?"

"Very much."

"I shall read to you every night."

Mice and butterflies filled her days. On the back of the Mouse King she rode, clutching the soft fur about his neck, racing through the castle to tend to mothers with large broods, crumbs and bits of cheese tucked in a canvas sack. With thread from a silkworm, she repaired butterfly wings, her stitches tiny and neat.

The giant peered at her handiwork through a glass that made his eye all that much larger. When he laughed his approval, the sound rolled through the countryside. And every night, when he reached for his almanac, she settled on his shoulder and marveled at how someone so colossal could speak words with so much tenderness.

Even when his bones grew old, and all he could do was move from bed to chair, he read to her. When his eyesight grew dim, he recited the words from memory, so strong was his desire to keep his promise. Until, at last, the day came when the stories stopped.

A thousand butterflies fluttered into his room. Mice came from fields and forest alike, led by the Mouse King. They bore the giant outside, where they laid him to rest beneath the rose bushes.

It was there she learned that all her tears combined could not rival the sorrow contained in a single giant teardrop.

A Measure of Sorrow first appeared in Luna Station Quarterly and subsequently in Evil Girlfriend Media.

APRIL

April was all about fairy tale retellings.

CRYING WOLF

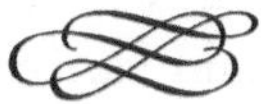

FAIRY TALE RETELLING

Everyone warned her, of course. Never go near the wolves. They would trick you, seduce you—this last always spoken in a hush. As if seduction were a bad thing.

Red knew otherwise.

He sat, so very still, so very perfect, like a gentleman, really. Better, actually. More refined with his silver-gray fur, more honest with those rows of teeth.

She'd prefer a wolf at her door rather than the parade of unrelenting suitors that wore a path to her front gate.

When Red stepped close, she saw the problem. The swelling in his jaw told here where, the soft whimper that it was bad.

"You'll have to open," she said.

And he did.

She held up the pair of pliers. A crude instrument for such an elegant creature, but it couldn't be helped.

"This might hurt," she added.

Yes, it would.

His fur held the scent of ripe blackberries and pinesap. Beneath that, she caught the fetid odor of infection. The tooth was near the back of his mouth, and his breath was hot and gamey.

His canines brushed the nape of her neck, flirted with her collar-bone, the feel of it like a whisper.

"Hard and quick," she said.

A moment later, she yanked the tooth free.

Red held still. She didn't leap back, didn't wince. All she did was clutch the pliers tight in her fist and close her eyes. That way, she didn't have to see how much his jaw trembled in the aftermath.

He moved first, stepping back with a graceful sweep of his tail. He inclined his head in gratitude and vanished, the forest swallowing him up once again.

For a week, Red kept a stew simmering on the stove, let the chunks of meat cook until they disintegrated upon the first bite.

For a week, she left a plate of that stew near the woodpile at the edge of the forest. Every morning, the plate was licked clean.

For more than a week—months really, and into the New Year—fewer and fewer suitors found their way to her cottage door.

Such were the benefits of friendship.

Crying Wolf was first published in Daily Science Fiction. Little Red Riding Hood is one of my favorite fairy tales to retell.

THE SECRET LIFE OF SLEEPING BEAUTY

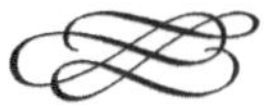

FAIRY TALE RETELLING

"Try it," my cousins say. They are the perfect princess trifecta, all in pink, peach, and plum.

I hesitate. I don't trust myself. Not around things that are sharp. My mother, the queen, has banned all things pointy—embroidery and knitting needles, even crochet hooks, but the object in the corner of my room is different.

"Come on," Plum says. She holds up her cell phone, ready to take a picture while the other two urge me forward. "You know how she is."

I do. So does my mother, who always intones, "Never trust a woman whose only goal is to look as young as her teenage daughters."

My aunt's gifts have a way of backfiring. Last year, she gave me an elixir that makes your lips red like cherries and your cheeks glow like apples. I refused even to try it, but my cousins guzzled it down. At that evening's ball, fruit flies swarmed around them the entire time.

What I really want for my birthday is a baseball bat and glove. I want to round up the pages, cajole the scribe into keeping score, and play until the sun hovers low in the sky and it's too late to bathe for a formal dinner, never mind the ball afterward. But my cousins tremble; if they don't get proof that I've at least *touched* the present, their mother will rage. Pity compels me forward. Besides, compared to last year, a spindle is downright practical. I reach out. Plum's cell phone camera clicks.

Three seconds before I hit the stone floor, I think: *my finger is going to hurt all day long.*

Chaos roars around me, but I can't wake. A narcoleptic slumber is no way to spend your sweet sixteen. My mother thunders at my cousins, and they cower, all quivering tulle and satin.

My finger still hurts.

The sobs subside. Yawns fill the air. Courtiers sink to the floor. Page boys slump against the wall. My cousins, too, sleep. My mother tucks a blanket around me and kisses my forehead before taking to her own bed.

For one hundred years, we lie dormant. This wouldn't be so bad except my cousins, they snore.

Heavy boots stomp. A sword rattles. The door crashes open. The scent of blood and sweat fills the room. Something looms above me, something I think means to kiss me.

I worry about one hundred years of neglected dental hygiene. But really? He's the one with dragon breath. Volumes have been written about epic first kisses. This one? I'm not sure it rates a Facebook status update.

My eyes spring open, that kiss the living embodiment of caffeine. A boy I don't recognize kneels by my bed. I worry about being nearly one hundred years older than he is. We will have to rename the village. Cougarville has a nice ring to it. First, we should probably get to know each other.

"What's your name?" I ask.

"Charming."

I blink. I'm sure he's many things. Clearly, he has mad skills in the sword-wielding department. But I was on the receiving end of that kiss. Charming?

Not so much.

"Shall we marry at sunset?" he asks as if he already knows the answer.

Shall we ... *what*? He squeezes my hand. Pain shoots through my finger, and I yank free. Marry? For real? I'd rather swing a baseball bat ... or a sword. And Charming does look tired. (I hear dragon-slaying is kind of stressful.)

After all this time, the spindle still sits in the corner of the room. I point to it.

"Can you bring me that?" I ask, all princess-y innocence. I should feel bad about this, but I don't.

Charming only manages a step, spindle in hand, before he crashes to the floor, armor clanking loud enough to wake the dead. But everyone sleeps on, and Charming's snores blend with my cousins'. It's a fairytale match. They can fight over him once everyone wakes up.

I fashion a new notch in his belt, and then I attach the scabbard and blade around my waist. I pull on my own boots and pick up his shield. It feels good in my hand. I tuck a pillow beneath Charming's head and leave the room.

My finger no longer hurts.

In the master suite, I pause next to my mother. A serene smile lights her face. I tuck the comforter around her shoulders and whisper, "I'll be back."

After I've slain a few dragons.

The Secret Life of Sleeping Beauty first appeared in Unidentified Funny Objects, Volume 1 and in audio at Cast of Wonders.

A MOST MARVELOUS PAIR OF BOOTS

FAIRY TALE RETELLING

It was during the wedding feast, when the air was heavy with roast goose and red wine, that Mirabella realized they'd all been duped by a cat.

Her new husband, the Marquis of Carabas, was sitting to her right, his teeth tearing goose flesh, grease coating his lips. She shuddered and pushed away thoughts of the marriage bed. Her father, the king, was well into his cups and tore at his food as if to mimic his new son-in-law. He slapped the marquis on the back and praised heaven that—at long last—Mirabella had found herself a husband.

At long last, indeed.

Near the end of the table, the cat was lounging, booted hind legs crossed. With a paw, he wiped goose fat from his whiskers. Mirabella fixed her gaze on him until he raised his yellow eyes and took in her full measure.

Then, the creature winked.

She sat back, a flush heating her cheeks, traveling her neck, and ending somewhere near her décolletage. She sighed, not in the mood for wine, song, or her new husband. True, the marquis was handsome. A point in his favor, to be sure. A goose leg slipped through his fingers, and he stopped its descent with one meaty hand. Mirabella cringed and again shoved thoughts of the marriage bed from her mind.

She turned to her new husband and asked, "More wine?"

Without waiting for an answer, she filled his goblet to the rim. He'd barely spoken since they'd exchanged *I do*. Come to think of it, the lad—for he was hardly older than she—seldom spoke more than a word or two at a time. Mirabella leaned forward and, once again, trained her gaze on the cat. This time when he winked, she didn't flinch.

Oh, there was no Marquis of Carabas. She's stake her somewhat tarnished reputation on it. Certainly, if this lad were nobility, he would've curried her father's favor long before now. Not only that, but he was untouched by palace gossip, which was rife with rumors about her improper relationship with her tutor. In her defense, the relationship hadn't been at all improper.

Well, maybe a little bit improper.

But thanks to some rumors and a fast-talking cat, her father was now praising the heavens and had shoved this lad into her arms and her bed. Would he care to know the truth about the marquis? Of course not. A married daughter was one less burden, especially a daughter with a somewhat tarnished reputation.

The splash of wine against her chest forced a gasp from her. The red liquid soaked into the bodice of her gown, the spot resembling a sword wound. Her new husband stared at his empty goblet as if the wine had sprung forth of its own accord. Her father pounded the marquis on the back, his hearty laugh filling the banquet hall. And, at the end of the table, that damn cat winked.

HER NEW HUSBAND'S snores filled the bedchamber. From her vantage point on the balcony, Mirabella could see the outline of his form on the duvet. Make no mistake, it was a fine form, despite the drool.

"You admire my master, then, Princess?"

Ah, that damn cat.

"There is more to admire in a man than form or face, Master Cat."

The cat trod along the balcony's edge, feet whisper-soft against the stone, even with the boots.

"What is it you wish?" he said.

"I fear my wishes matter not to man or cat."

"I did not ask that."

Mirabella glanced into the bedchamber. Yes, assuredly, her new husband would not wake until noon, if then. "Tonight's wish has already been granted."

Could cats grin? Well, this one could, and did, twirling long whiskers with a paw. "And tomorrow's wish?"

Yes, the crux of the matter.

"I cannot simply un-marry, Master Cat, and I doubt my new husband will appreciate his rival." She gestured toward the telescope at the balcony's far end. She had yet to peer at the night sky this evening—or rather, morning. Of course, at this moment, the only view was of a cat's tail, which was swishing in front of the lens.

Still, the urge to lean over the telescope remained. For a few hours, she could pretend that Sebastian was still at her side, imagine his fingers lighting on the back of her neck, hear his ardent whisper. "Do you see it?"

The night spent with her tutor fueled court gossip even now. That the two of them had gazed at the stars and not into each other's eyes was of little matter. As she ran a hand along the telescope, the skies were clear, but her mind was clouded with thoughts of the upcoming tour of the kingdom. The grand celebration of her marriage meant visiting people she didn't much care for and receiving gifts she certainly didn't need. But the real question was: pack the telescope or leave it behind?

"You'll be traveling light," the cat said.

"Unlikely, Master Cat. Have you never seen a royal entourage take to the roads?"

"I have, Princess. It's all part of the plan."

"What plan is that?"

"Do you not wish to see your Sebastian again?"

Her hand stilled on the telescope, her fingers ice. Damn palace gossip, and damn that cat besides. How could he know her heart?

"You keep a great many unsent letters beneath your bed."

Oh. That was how.

"Would you like to be free? Study with your tutor in peace?"

Mouth dry, Mirabella nodded.

"Then, trust me."

"I shall do no such thing, Master Cat."

"But what if you could un-marry, Princess?" the cat asked. "Would you trust me then?"

"What God has joined together, let no man put asunder," Mirabella replied. "Even cats know this."

Ah, yes, cats could grin. "Oh, Princess, have you not noticed? I am certainly no man."

THE CARRIAGE BUMPED OVER NEVER-ENDING ruts. A week on the road, and the only sign of the cat had been this morning when he had slipped a wineskin into Mirabella's hands.

"Hold it beneath your cloak," he said. "Just so."

Only thoughts of her studies, of Sebastian, compelled her to comply. She cradled her burden and settled in for another long day.

A cry rose up outside the carriage.

"Brigands!" a guard shouted.

Swords clanked, and then the carriage door flew open. The cat sprang past her, a single claw piercing the wineskin. Red bloomed beneath her hand, the wine soaking her gown. The marquis took one look at the stain spreading across her bodice and crashed to the carriage floor, face-first. Never mind that she reeked of her father's finest vintage (come to think of it, so did the marquis); she was, in everyone's view, fatally wounded.

And with death came freedom. Un-marry, indeed.

Before she could leap from the carriage, a paw tugged on her sleeve.

"You'll need this, Princess." The cat proffered a dusty cloak, ragged along the hem. He dropped a small canvas sack at her feet. "And, of course, you'll need these." He pulled the boots from his hind legs.

He crouched, then sprang through the carriage window, and Mirabella swore his final sentence was more caterwaul than words. She pulled on the boots, the leather kissing her legs, the soles cupping her feet. She held one leg extended, turning it to study the boot. How was this possible?

No matter. They fit. She jumped from the carriage. The boots carried her through sword clashes and rearing horses. No one called out. No one stopped her. Except for a cat that wove between her ankles.

"Master Cat?"

His tail twitched, and he blinked slowly, but that was all.

She nestled him in her arms, the cloak shielding them both, and took to the road.

That night, she tugged the boots from her feet and placed them far enough from her campfire that no spark would reach them.

"Master Cat, would you like to take a turn in your boots?"

Within moments, the cat was standing before her in all his booted glory. He surveyed their surroundings.

"Seems safe enough," he said. "I shall fetch dinner and return shortly."

Mirabella pointed to the pot simmering over the fire. "I have dinner."

"I shall fetch us a decent dinner, then."

She huffed but couldn't argue. Her skills with a telescope far surpassed anything she could manage with a cook pot.

"I shall almost regret finding Sebastian," she said to him later, over stew and a loaf of hard-crusted bread from a nearby village. "I will miss these marvelous boots."

"Why not commission another pair?" the cat asked, strutting about, the leather boots glowing warmly in the light of the fire.

"How will I do that, Master Cat? I will be a scholar and a somewhat impoverished one at that."

"Haven't you guessed, Princess? Who do you think gave me these boots to begin with?"

"Not the marquis?"

"Hardly."

"But then—"

"Princess, you know their creator. Intimately, if I dare say so."

"But ... Sebastian is a scholar. He studies—"

"The mysteries of our world—and he has mastered a few."

Mirabella sucked in a breath and blew out a stream of air rather than harsh words. After all, what was there to say?

With a paw, the cat twirled his whiskers, and then strode off into the night. So, it had been Sebastian all along.

And, of course, that damn cat.

A Most Marvelous Pair of Boots was published in the first issue of Timeless Tales magazine.

CHEATING DEATH

FAIRY TALE RETELLING

The first time I saw Death was the day my brother came of age.

I followed him into the woods because I knew he'd meet his godfather there. My feet whispered against the thick carpet of pine needles. I ducked behind a tree, my fingers clutching bark, and waited.

Like all good godparents, Death gave my brother a gift.

He whispered in my brother's ear, pointed his scythe at a patch of herbs, and nodded once.

That was all it took. My brother left the woods a talented physician while I was a mere midwife's apprentice.

I remained rooted among the pines, certain there was something to glean by the mere presence of Death. I wasn't afraid, mainly because no one ever noticed me.

No one noticed you when you were one of thirteen children, stuck somewhere in the middle, especially if you were a girl, especially if you were disappointing. By disappointing, I mean ugly. Or, at least, not pretty. But truthfully, this was something I didn't mind as I never needed to look at myself. Women in labor and newborn babes didn't mind either.

I combed the forest for that magic herb. Soil stained my nails. Dank leaves soaked my skirt. I tore my apron, and pine sap matted my hair.

I searched until the moon rose high above the canopy of trees and a shadow fell across the glimmer it made through the forest.

I looked up into the vast emptiness of Death's face.

He reached out a hand. "Come, my child."

My heart squeezed in my chest, the air thick and cold in my throat. I'd been trying to cheat him, hadn't I? Find the herb, use it to start my own practice. I shut my eyes, resigned to my fate.

"I only mean to take you home," he said.

With a rush, I knew it was true. So I took his hand, surprised by its warmth.

"I want to be a physician," I told him.

"Yes. I know." His voice was sonorous and sad. "I cannot grant your wish."

Something about our slow, comfortable gait, my small hand in his, made me bold. "It isn't fair."

"Perhaps not, but know this: I am Death, and in the end, I make everyone equal."

The words left me with little comfort.

My brother treated the Lord Mayor, nobles, and anyone with enough coin in their pocket to pay for nearly foolproof cures. True, not all his patients survived. Those who did enjoyed robust health.

I walked women through labor, coaxed infants to feed, scrubbed blood from my hands and tears from my face when neither mother nor child survived.

The second time I saw Death was when the King took ill. Frantic servants rushed in and out of the palace, a carriage flew through its gates and returned with my brother.

Death waited patiently outside, pacing the path along the moat.

When the King miraculously recovered, Death remained in our village. No one took notice of him except for myself. When I passed him on the road, he'd execute a stately bow as if I were a grand lady.

Then the princess took ill, and the King sent for my brother once again. When she recovered as miraculously as her father had, that's when it struck me: my brother had cheated Death.

And Death wouldn't leave our village until he'd collected his due.

My brother left the palace as grandly as he entered, in a horse-drawn carriage. The next morning, when most were still asleep, he crept from his home, and I followed him into the woods.

I knew he'd meet his godfather there.

My brother begged, pleaded, cries filling the forest and tears bathing his face. And no, that was not something a sister should see. I sank to the ground beneath a tree, the bark rough against my shoulder blades, and shielded my eyes.

I stayed like that, the morning dew giving way to the afternoon heat and then the evening's chill. When the moon rose above the canopy of trees, my brother was gone, but Death was not.

He held out his hand, and this time, while my heart raced, I didn't hesitate. Again, the warmth startled me. He led me through the woods until we came to a clearing.

With his scythe, he pointed to a patch of earth, one covered in a leafy herb. By the time I filled my apron pockets, Death had vanished.

I stood in the dark, not knowing where I was or how to reach home, panic fluttering in my chest. The scent of the herb rose, sharp and tangy, assaulting my nose with both its odor and its promise.

"Thank you," I called out.

A breeze stirred the air, raised the fine hairs on the back of my neck. The moon peeked out from behind a cloud and lit the trail home.

It was then I knew what I needed to do, what path I needed to take.

I have my own apprentices now, three to be precise. When the princess birthed her twins, they called for me. I took no royal coin for my efforts. Besides, all I truly need grows in that little patch in the forest, and I can always find it by the light of the moon.

I haven't seen Death since. I suspect that when I do, he'll offer me his hand, and its warmth will surprise me. He'll help me to rise one last time and say:

"I am Death, and in the end, I make everyone equal."

Cheating Death was first published in Corvid Queen.

MAY

May was all about odds and ends, those strange little stories that sometimes pop into my head.

THE POTATO BUG WAR

HISTORICAL, WWII

Her students collected so many potato bugs that Emilienne had to dash back to the vineyard for an extra wagon and a pram, all under the glare of a German soldier. The pram squeaked its protest, the wheels jolting along ruts while Henri's words rang in her head:

Make it a game. Let the children have some fun.

So Emilienne handed each of her charges a jar and sent them into the potato fields under the hot Burgundy sun.

"Whoever collects the most wins a sweet!"

The children scampered through the fields, hands greedy for the tiny bugs. The damage was minimal—for now. But a blight was a blight, the potato crop at risk. As Henri put it:

Can't deprive les Boches of their pommes frites, can we now?

Her students bent and plucked. One girl stumbled across the furrows, jar clutched to her chest in triumph.

"Mademoiselle! Look how many I've collected!"

The girl ran off with another jar but turned before resuming her spot in the field. "Will it be enough?"

Emilienne patted her skirt pocket, the one with the sweet. "We'll see."

She arranged the jars in the wagons, glass scraping against metal, sun baking the striped creatures inside. They crawled over each other, all in search of an opening that was no longer there.

So many bugs, and yet, she wondered. How many did the Germans expect them to collect? Would it be enough? How much *was* enough when it came to potato bugs?

In the end, she awarded the sweet to the industrious little girl. The child's two older brothers lugged the wagons into town while Emilienne pushed the pram. The jars rocked and clattered, her strange, many-legged babies squirming. Sweat trickled down her spine, and a taste, like rusty grit, filled her mouth.

At the turn-in point, a lone soldier waited. He was no more than a boy, this German, this Nazi. In her head, she heard Henri:

Poor bastard probably has to count them all.

"What will you do with them?" Emilienne knew better than to start a conversation. She wasn't a collaborator. And no matter how much her belly rumbled at night, she wouldn't accept those kinds of favors.

Still, she wanted to know. As if the fate of these potato bugs mattered to her, to Burgundy, to the war.

"Drown them." The boy grimaced as if he, personally, was responsible for the task.

Poor bastard, indeed.

In the end, she relinquished all but one jar. It was such a foolish thing to do, hiding it there beneath the pram's tattered cushion. Would they line up a firing squad? Shoot her? Perhaps, but only after the Gestapo had their turn.

Tell me, Fraulein, why have you deprived the Reich of these potato bugs?

Yes, why had she? Emilienne couldn't say. That didn't stop her from gathering potato leaves from the field. That night, in the wine cellar, she stabbed the lid with an ice pick. She shoved handfuls of leaves into the jar and fed her hungry, many-legged babies.

That summer, whenever she overheard the Germans complain about the harvest, Emilienne thought of a jar, hidden in the wine cellar, and swallowed a smile.

It was enough.

This strange little story was first published in Pulp Literature, Issue 19. And yes, the Germans really did send French citizens into the potato fields during a blight to collect potato bugs.

WHAT LITTLE REMAINS

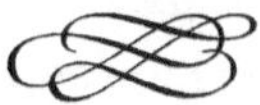

POST-APOCALYPTIC

In the mornings, I slip out the broken window so anyone still living in this building will not hear me. Footfalls echo in the empty hallway, and since debris blocks the stairwell to the roof, no one climbs to the top anymore.

Except me. But I take the long way.

I slide along the tenth-floor ledge, rough bricks scraping my shoulder blades, heels locked against the building. My fingertips inch from brick face to mortar. It's this I concentrate on. To think of the fall is to wish for it.

In the mornings, mist hides the city and dampens the stench of rotted wood and flesh. In the mornings, I inhale the scent of damp soil from the rooftop garden and the sharp odor from the volunteer tomato plants. When I was little, I always imagined the plants with tiny flintlock rifles over their shoulders, marching from one garden to the next. I know better now. But as I tug weeds from around their stems, I like to think we're both fighting a good fight.

This morning, when I pull myself onto the rooftop, my foot strikes a rake. The handle flips up and plops back onto the tarpaper shingles. I freeze, certain that yesterday I left the rake leaning against the stairwell to the floors below. I take a cautious look around.

In the garden itself, a set of footprints, much larger than my own, crosses the expanse. Tiny hairs prickle on the back of my neck, like someone has come from behind and blown a stream of air against my skin. I remain stricken.

By the time the sun touches my face, my feet ache, and my calf muscles knot, so when I do move, my gait is hobbled. I study the outline of the footprints. Some sort of heavy work boot—the depression is deep and the soil crushed. Yet my spindly volunteer tomatoes stand proud, all green except for a faint yellow blush. No one has tugged on a carrot or dug a potato. The soil is moist. The watering can sits on the east side of the garden, not the west, where I left it yesterday. And then, of course, there's the matter of the displaced rake.

Only when the sun warms the top of my head do I notice them. My heart jolts. I grip the rake, certain I'll snap the ancient wood in half. There, on the roof's edge, is a perfect set of fingernails—the press-on kind, that, once upon a time, were advertised on TV. They are such a brilliant red, they make the brickwork around them look dull and dowdy. They are so pristine and lined up so exactly, I'm surprised they're not attached to some starlet hanging on for dear life, waiting for the man in those heavy work boots to clomp across my garden and rescue her.

I whirl around, certain he's here to do just that. The roof is empty. A breeze rustles the leaves of the tomato plants. They bow their heavy heads and whisper to each other. They will not tell me what they know.

ALL WEEK, I sneak up to the garden earlier and earlier, until there's a danger I'll miss the ledge in the dark. Fresh footprints greet me each morning. Mid-week, someone clears the scum from the top of the water in the rain barrel. Weeds gather in wilted piles along the edges of the garden's cedar container. Most unsettling, every day I find a set of press-on nails in the same spot. Today they glow sparkly pink, glitter catching the early morning light.

Something compels me to search for the starlet. I kneel at the ledge, stretch out a hand. It's silly, but at the same time, I'd want someone to reach out for me. Today, the sun strikes my face at the same moment my fingers reach the air beyond the ledge. A burst of light blinds me. Wind kicks up dust, and I duck my head.

Warm hands with sharp nails grip my arm. I jerk backward and tumble across the roof. Someone tumbles with me. After the noise and light, all is quiet except our haggard breaths.

"I'm through!" the girl next to me says. "And look! My fingernails. I thought I'd lost them for sure."

Her clothes flow with her every move. Her hair is tall, so tall, maybe taller than her head—well, at least the bangs are. Brilliant blue is smeared across her eyelids. Dark pink streaks her cheeks. And her lips are as red as my tomatoes should be. I touch my own face, but brick dust and mud can never compare.

"Are you an actress?" I ask.

"What?" She shakes her head, but her hair barely moves. "No, silly. I just live—" Her brow creases and she scans the rooftop. "Well, here, but not here." Her gaze travels until it reaches the garden. "Oh, how strange. I keep wondering how my grandmother's garden changes. But it doesn't. I'm just seeing yours."

"Thank you for pulling my weeds," I say.

She laughs. "But then I get in trouble for not pulling my grandmother's. And I always put my nails there." She points to the ledge. "So I won't ruin them. I thought the wind was blowing them away."

The air shimmers above the nails. Something bright flashes from the space beyond but vanishes before I can even grasp what it might be.

"I'm Shelli, by the way, with an i." She stands and her clothes flutter, their colors startling, like the blue jays and goldfinches you still sometimes see.

Her feet are tiny, her shoes so clean and bright. They do not have the heavy soles that crisscross my garden and trample the soil.

"I'm Kit," I say, "with an i."

Shelli laughs, but as she walks the rooftop's perimeter, her features grow somber. "This isn't all like my grandmother said it would be."

"She's been here?"

"A long time ago." Shelli shields her eyes with a hand and peers out over the ledge. "Is this the end of the world?"

"No, unfortunately."

She scrunches up her face. "The future, then?"

I shrug. That glimmer catches my eye again. I wonder what it is about my rooftop that makes the air do that. I wonder what it is about my rooftop that brings strangers to me.

"I'm from 1999," she says. "What year is it here?"

Some claim to know the year, but no two claims match. I've since stopped caring, so all I do is shake my head.

Shelli leans forward where the ledge is still waist high. "I go to school ..." She points. "There."

I follow her gaze and her finger to the charred remains, where wisps of smoke rise in the morning mist. "I used to go there," I say.

Her mouth turns down, but she is still so pretty. I want to work in her grandmother's garden, have shiny, tall hair, and fancy nails—a different color on each finger. I do not want to stay on my rooftop. I do not want to use everything I have to coax tomatoes from the soil. I want to go to a place where hope still lives.

"I don't know how to bring you back," she says, as if reading my mind. "I'm not even sure how I got through."

"That's okay." But the words leave my mouth with a sigh.

Her gaze darts from black-streaked buildings to my garden and then to me. "It's not really okay."

She's right, of course, but I don't have words to tell her that. "I want to show you something," I say instead and point to the heavy footprints in the garden. At the sight of them, it feels like a boot is crushing my heart. "Someone else is slipping through."

Shelli kneels at the garden's edge and traces the impression as if that will tell her what we need to know. She says, "Be careful." And I think that maybe it has.

Before I can respond, all the air around us is sucked away. I duck my head, bring a hand up to cover my nose and mouth. Soil and dust swirl around me. Grit stings my eyes. Then, all is quiet. Shelli is gone. Only her pink, sparkly nails remain, not clinging to the edge, but at my feet in a little pile. I scoop them up and hold one against my finger.

Oh, so pretty.

～

TODAY, I find the tomatoes crushed, their seeds and pulp spread across the garden, their juice soaking into the soil. I tunnel my fingers beneath the dirt, excavating tiny bits of green flesh in hopes of saving it. My efforts only drive the dirt deeper into what little remains.

I gather the tomatoes anyway. Perhaps with water from the rain barrel, I can rinse the bigger chunks clean—or clean enough. Perhaps ...

The slap of the rake handle against tarpaper shingles forces my gaze up. At first, all I see are big, white boots, with heels so enormous, they could smash my largest tomatoes with one step—and probably have. His clothes do not billow. They are sleek and stiff, an exoskeleton that encases him from foot to head. The man before me is not from the past, not like Shelli. If he's from the future, then I think humanity may be better off among the remains. My gaze darts to the building's edge and the nails there—a set of brilliant blue. Only today, one nail points toward the rooftop stairwell.

"You don't belong here," I say to the man.

His image flickers then solidifies again.

"This isn't your world."

More flickering, but he stubbornly stays on my rooftop. Not only that, but he takes a step forward, followed by another.

I dodge his steps, like a mouse out-maneuvering a feral cat. The toe of one boot catches me and sends me flying toward the building's edge. I roll, palms scraping tarpaper and grit. I grip the ledge, stop my descent, heart thudding against the brick, lungs inhaling dust. When I open my eyes, bright blue nails greet me, pointed toward the stairwell. I scramble to my feet and dash for safety.

Shelli flings open the door and pulls me inside. "Thank God! You're okay."

"You too."

We cling to each other in the shelter of the stairwell.

"He can't open the door," she says.

"Did he try?"

Shelli nods and I clutch her tighter.

"What do we do?" she asks.

I shake my head. What can we do? He's already destroyed my garden. Once the noon sun strikes the rooftop, cowering in the stairwell won't be an option. We'll broil in here, and with the stairs blocked, there's no way down. Perhaps the two of us could rush him, using our combined strength to push him over the ledge.

I open my mouth to voice this idea, but can't force the words from my throat. So little remains—of my garden, of this world—that I don't want to take one more life, even one that doesn't belong here.

In front of us, the man crouches, lifts a handful of tomato and soil to his face. He pushes back his visor and inhales as if it's the most wonderful thing he's ever smelled. Then, he turns toward us. Sorrow washes across his face. His mouth moves. After a long moment, I piece together his words.

I'm sorry.

Oh, and so am I.

"He's trapped," I say to Shelli. "He's not in this world, or his own, but in between."

She nods, but her eyes are huge, the beautiful blue around them caked and creased. Dark smears travel down her cheeks. I venture from the stairwell, Shelli gripping my hand.

"You need to get back," I say to the man. "Right?"

The sorrow fades, and he nods. He steps from the garden, trailing mud and tomato innards. I try not to cringe at the destruction or his approach.

"There must be a way." I glance toward the now-empty ledge. "Shelli! Your nails! They're gone."

I creep forward and take the man by one of his stiff, gloved hands. His fingers swallow mine whole. The safety of the stairwell is too far away; he is too strong. But he trots by my side like a compliant puppy.

"Where, exactly?" I ask Shelli.

She bends over, hair sweeping the bricks. "Here, where this dent is." She peers at me through the strands of hair. "My grandmother told me to stand here and wish upon a star. Funny how it's lasted all this time."

We position the man at the ledge and stand across from him. An urge hits me, like I should salute. Instead I stretch out my hand. A smile lights his face that makes him look like an action hero. He shakes my hand, then Shelli's.

Then, it's as if the wind steals him. When the dust settles, speckling my arms and face, nothing remains except for me, the crushed tomatoes, and one of Shelli's bright blue fingernails.

❧

FOOTPRINTS no longer mar my garden. The rooftop's ledge looks lonely without Shelli's colorful nails. I may have salvaged a tomato plant. A week has passed, and it seems to have a hold on the soil, if a tenuous one. I am its fiercely protective mother. I spend hours on the roof, chasing away chattering crows, providing sips of water from the rain barrel.

This morning when I crest the rooftop, something bulky sits on the opposite ledge. I creep forward slowly, still on all fours. There, in the spot where Shelli's nails used to clutch the edge, a basket of tomatoes sits, along with packets of seeds. Beneath those, I uncover a set of press-on nails, the very shade of the tomatoes.

The sun hits the ledge, warming the tomatoes, making their skin glow. The nails dazzle my eyes. Together, they are the color of blood and hope.

And oh, so pretty.

Sometimes a character and her voice arrive in my head and I'm simply there for the dictation. This would be one of those stories.

THE SHORT SWEET LIFE OF MY INVISIBLE PROM DATE

YOUNG ADULT/FANTASY

Geppetto carved Pinocchio, Pygmalion, his statue. So I knew it could be done. True, Victor Frankenstein had his monster. This was something to consider since I had no intention of attending zombie prom. Still, it was his example I started with.

After all, the perfect prom date doesn't just build himself. Forget frogs, and snails, and puppy dog tails. That might be the stuff little boys are made of. The perfect prom date?

Hardly.

When it came to raw material, my high school left much to be desired. Even so, there was enough there that I could make do. I began the culling in March with Magnus Reynolds. His GPA was only second to my own—a close enough match. Since cutting open his head and extracting his brain wasn't an option, I went with the next best thing.

True, there's that dent in my front left bumper, and granted, it might technically be theft even if the mailbox contents have somehow spilled across the road. But I doubt his parents will miss a report card that resembled every other one.

Up next was Sam Collier. Now here was a rare find! A boy who simply didn't know how hot he was. Considering the ego-driven pretty boys at my high school, Sam should be classified as endangered. Which is why I truly regret the mishap with the Bunsen burner during physics lab. Still, the lock of that perfect blond hair was worth it. It's amazing what people don't notice when a table's on fire.

For the last ingredient, I had to truly get creative. This was my riskiest move, humiliating if I got caught, chancy when it came to the item I needed. Under the cover of steam, I crept into the boys' locker room, waiting until the pound of water in the showers drowned out my footsteps. I rushed from locker bank to locker bank, ducking behind a garbage can to catch my breath and quiet my pounding heart.

I grabbed the first item my fingers encountered, then I bolted, sneakers skidding on wet tile. I clutched the crumpled material in my hand and didn't stop running until I reached the girls' bathroom. I crashed into the last stall and slammed the door behind me. Only then did I look at my prize.

A jockstrap.

Still. It fit the requirements. Anyone who has a passing familiarity with boys can tell you: sweat is an essential component of their makeup.

I was at the florist when I discovered my date's name. I was buying the Dreamy Pink Wristlet (for myself) and the Dashing Boutonniere (for him), when the cashier said:

"Owen."

"Who?" I asked.

"I said, you owe, um, fifty-five dollars and eighteen cents."

Oh-um? *Owen.* Not only was it the perfect name, but it could be our private joke. All couples need at least one of those.

The night before prom, I gathered everything together: the tux I rented from The Men's Warehouse (including socks and shoes, size II), a white T-shirt, a pair of boxer briefs (no date of mine was going commando). In my closet, I set up the altar.

Anyone who's read Mary Shelley's *Frankenstein* knows Victor's downfall was his pride. He played God. They don't call it the miracle of life for nothing. After all, didn't Pygmalion pray to Venus? I needed divine intervention, and I wasn't too proud to ask for it.

On my altar, I placed the report card, the lock of hair, and even the jockstrap. I sprinkled peppermint leaves (for fresh breath) and honey (for sweetness), then I lit candles (heart-shaped, of course). As the scent of pine, sandalwood, and cinnamon drifted across my face and through my hair, I prayed.

Now, it probably doesn't surprise you that there isn't a patron saint of prom. That night, I prayed to Saint Raphael, who is the patron saint of lovers, young people, and happy meetings. If that doesn't describe prom, then it probably should. When I was done, I blew out the candles and slipped into bed. That night, I dreamed of Owen.

In the morning, everything was gone! The tux, the shoes and socks, even the jockstrap, if you can believe that. The aroma of burnt cinnamon lingered in the air, and something told me I'd messed up horribly. I would not be going to prom. I would not have the perfect prom date.

Miracles take faith, I told myself. For the rest of the day, I shoved the worry from my mind and acted as if all were well. I kept my mani/pedi appointment and the one for my up-do. The stylist even added sparkly rhinestones for free when she saw how badly my hands shook.

By seven that night, I was ready, even if no limo sat in our driveway. Not yet. Owen was nervous, too, I told myself, so he'd be a little late. It was his one (adorable) flaw.

"Honey?" My mom's voice was soft. "Are you sure you're okay with this, being at prom alone?"

I rolled my eyes. "I won't be alone."

"Tori—"

Just then, that flash of black appeared, the limo long and sleek. I caught the shimmery sight of Owen as he took our porch steps by twos.

"Bye, Mom!" I called out. I burst through the door and left her standing in the living room, her mouth a perfect o of surprise.

Of course, a perfect prom date deserved such a reaction.

I quickly learned that to see Owen, you couldn't stare straight at him. He teased the corners of my eyes. I caught his grin—warm and charming. His height—at least three inches taller than I was. I worried people would stare and not see the real Owen, not see what I did—the wonderful boy who was the perfect prom date.

The kids at my school might be rude, but none were outright gawkers. Still, I was careful. As much as I wanted a photo, I sensed the flash might harm Owen, burn away the delicate work of miracles. We spent our time dancing in dark corners. Light from the glitter ball fell across us. My skin glowed, but Owen's shimmered like something otherworldly.

And he was the perfect date. We danced, but not so my feet got sore.

When I was thirsty, he fetched me punch. He was on such a mission when prom queen Sierra Blakely drifted by.

"I don't think I know your date," she said.

"He doesn't go to our school."

She glanced around. "Well, where is he?"

I nodded toward the punch bowl. At this distance, I could just see the sleeve of Owen's tux. In his hand, the cheap plastic cup looked like a crystal goblet.

"I don't even have to ask," I told Sierra. "He just knows when I'm thirsty."

"Oh."

Her expression was wistful, or maybe sad. She'd gone with Trevor Radke. Sure, he was cute, and a football player, but he made all his friends call him Rad-Man. That was just all kinds of awkward.

We left prom early. Anyone with a passing familiarity with miracles and fairy tales knows not to mess with the deadline. We needed to be back in my room before midnight. Even on the ride home, I could feel Owen waver, his shimmer fading, and the best night of my life coming to a bittersweet end.

By the time we reached my room, he couldn't stand without help, so I arranged his tux on the hangers and hung it on the back door of my closet. Then I placed the shoes neatly beneath. My perfect night needed its perfect ending. I wasn't ready to let go, not quite yet.

I lit the candles again and switched off the overhead light. That helped. Then I wrapped the arms of his tuxedo jacket around my waist and placed my hands on the jacket's shoulders.

"Thank you," I whispered, "for being my date."

I kissed him then. Everyone knows the perfect prom ends with a perfect kiss.

And it was.

Maybe it was that perfect kiss, or the candles, but something happened then. I couldn't see Owen, not even a teasing shimmer from the corner of my eye, but all at once, those strong arms took form and pulled me closer. Owen held me like he never wanted to let me go. The scent of burnt cinnamon filled the air. As to what happened next?

Well, as anyone with a passing familiarity with prom knows, sometimes it ends with more than just a kiss.

~

A YEAR LATER, and prom remains my most cherished memory from high school. Beating out Magnus Reynolds for valedictorian is a close second. Even so, perfection has its price, and miracles have a way of spawning some of their own.

True, I worry. I know all about Rosemary and her baby. But Owen was nothing but sweet, and the same goes for his son. (Yes, I can tell. A mother *knows*.) But when you get right down to it, Owen Jr. doesn't need much: no burping or changing. He doesn't need more from me than merely my presence. This makes me tired, but I'm also a single mom taking a full load of college classes and working a part-time job. Mothers will sacrifice anything for their children, and I will make sure Owen Jr. has everything he needs.

Although, when I think about it, I suspect he'll only need one thing:

A date to prom.

This strange little story, with a possibly unreliable narrator, first appeared in Mad Scientist Journal, Winter 2014.

THE LIFE EXPECTANCY OF FIREFLIES

CONTEMPORARY

After it was all over—after the handcuffs, the crime scene tape, and a noose crafted from a silk Armani tie—I think all of us would agree that it was Benji's neck tattoo that caught our attention.

Of course, even here in the suburbs, we had our share of tattoos—the tramp stamps, the biceps circled in barbed wire, even a few full sleeves. But Benji's tattoo was something else. Interlocking coils traveled his right shoulder to collarbone, across the hillock of his Adam's apple, ending at last in a bloom below his left ear. You could imagine him leaning his head back, his throat a vulnerable canvas for the tattoo artist.

Within months, most women in the neighborhood had confessed to running their tongue along the intricate lines, as if the ink were something you could taste. By Benji's second spring in the house at the end of the street, it was a rite of passage. Every housewife, single mom, and career woman had taken her tongue to Benji's neck.

Except me.

I wondered if that's why, in the evenings, he chose my porch. Not that he relaxed. Even when he tipped his head back, the cropped salt and pepper hair brushing the whitewash, his form melting into the steps, the man vibrated with tension. It filled the air around him. It made some women think of sex and sin and sweat, his bare neck an invitation to lap up the ink.

It made me clutch my cell phone, my thumb on the speed dial, my feet pushing against the floorboards while I sat in the porch swing. I took short, choppy breaths. Once, my jittery thumb hit 911. When the police cruisers arrived, all sirens and lights, all I could point to were the fireflies in the bushes, the dark house at the end of the street, and the porch steps, now vacant.

Only when my porch was empty did the air feel still enough to breathe. I'd spend those moments catching fireflies and letting them glow between my fingers. Only then was I glad that Benji had chosen me.

Benji filled our days. He helped carry in groceries (and, in some cases, left several hours later). He mowed lawns—usually shirtless. He drank gallons of freshly-squeezed lemonade and martinis expertly shaken. He rescued kites from trees and organized the neighborhood kickball tournament.

And in the dark house at the end of the street, he was cooking methamphetamine.

After it was all over, you wouldn't have recognized Benji, not from all the descriptions: the creeper, the peeping Tom, the loner with bad teeth, the guy with the Satanic neck tattoo.

Only my story didn't match. The police interrogated me, but it was a half-hearted attempt, their gazes filling the room with pity. They released me in less than an hour, even though I had the receipt for the tie in my purse. Even though moments before the police shackled his wrists, Benji turned toward me, ran his fingers along the tattoo, then blew me a kiss.

Half an hour earlier, I'd handed him the box wrapped in silver paper, the one that held the silk Armani tie. Twenty minutes after that, I dialed 911. For real, this time. No one knew how Benji smuggled the tie into his jail cell. We all could imagine the second, permanent tattoo.

Most nights, I think he wanted to end it. Most nights, I think he wanted me to be the one to do it. This was why he chose me, chose my porch.

But on summer evenings, I stand there, gaze locked on the dark house at the end of the street, and doubt fills the night. I catch fireflies and let them burn between my fingers until they wink out, one by one.

My porch is empty, the night still, and the air impossible to breathe.

This strange, dark little piece garnered many personal rejections until it was published in Fine Linen Magazine.

CHICKEN FAT AND WHIPPED CREAM

YOUNG ADULT

I stand in the center of the gym, the air thick with the scent of dusty basketballs and sweaty tube socks. Strains of the chicken fat song fade, but a few girls defiantly sing-whisper the chorus:

Give that chicken fat back to the chicken and go, you chicken fat, go!

I am trapped in a great mass of girls, all in identical powder blue, one-piece gym suits. The elastic pinches my waist. The polyester shorts scratch and come with an automatic wedgie. No one dares tug. That would only bring on another chorus, one of:

Gro-oss, she's digging in her buh-utt.

Some crimes require extra syllables.

But really, this class is the crime. *Slimnastics*. It's not a real word. It's not a real sport. There's no such thing as an Olympic slimnast. In the past three weeks, we have learned all the steps, sung all the words.

None of us are slimmer for our efforts. Ms. Binkly, the gym teacher, is talking now, not that anyone is listening. The faintest lilt of the chorus sounds behind me, but I resist the urge to turn, to look, to act too interested.

Ms. Binkly's most striking feature is a Marine Corps style haircut. Maybe we don't always listen, it's true. Here's the thing:

No one ever talks back.

I stare at the ceiling, an ear toward the front. Something about her tone bothers me. It's not the sound of a unit wrap up with warnings about the upcoming quiz. And really, how would you test a knowledge of slimnastics?

In the Chicken Fat song, where does the chicken fat go?

- To KFC.
- The principal's thighs.
- Back to the chicken.
- All of the above.

No, what she's saying now strikes us all breathless. If we'd actually exerted ourselves during the chicken fat dance, we'd all be doubled over. Instead, we stand absolutely still in cold horror. How do you test slimnastics? By making your twenty-five apathetic students choreograph and then perform their own routine.

In front of everyone.

Ms. Binkly places a stack of records on the floor. She claps her hands together. "All right, ladies! Break into groups, grab a record, and star in your own routine!"

She leaves us with that and retreats to her office. In a few minutes, the odor of sulfur will seep from beneath the door, followed by smoke.

Girls flock forward, pounce on the stack of records. I know enough about the pecking order not to get pecked. I step back and wait for the leavings.

I am left with a girl named Brianna and a single, dog-eared album on the gymnasium floor. We're not friends, Brianna and I. Allies might be a better word, like the US and Russia during World War Two. We definitely have a common enemy, and we both need to maintain our GPA. We inch forward, shoes squeaking on the floor.

We stare at the woman on the album cover. She's naked—or would be, if not for the mound of whipped cream she sits in. The album is called *Whipped Cream and Other Delights*. Brianna and I are young enough not to truly understand what these other delights might be, but old enough to know they don't always involve food.

"This is hideous," Brianna says.

She means everything. From the social doom of the album cover to the fact the only empty record player is the one next to Ms. Binkly's office, where we end up ten minutes later, sucking in secondhand smoke while tripping through the opening steps to our routine. Our song of choice?

Whipped Cream.

Brianna and I are both smart enough to relish this bit of irony.

On performance day, Brianna skyrockets her hand into the air, and Ms. Binkly calls us to the front.

"Going first means a better grade," Brianna says to my frown on our way to the center of the gym.

She's right, of course. It's this sort of cold logic that will make her class valedictorian in five years' time. But now, as we churn our arms like egg beaters, I realize that slimnastics really does have a test.

What is Whipped Cream?

- A garnish for desserts.
- A song by Herb Alpert & Tijuana Brass.
- A form of public humiliation.
- All of the above.

Chicken Fat and Whipped Cream was first published in Easy Street Magazine. It may, or may not, be based on actual events.

JUNE

June was all about paths and predicaments, of finding your way out or
back home again.

KNIGHT AT THE ROYAL ARMS

PARANORMAL

he lobby of the Royal Arms Hotel is so very quiet, and I can taste the hunt in the air. Not that I'd planned on hunting. I only stepped inside out of the rain. Still, the thought tempts me. I don't know what sort of shadow creature lives in this space, but considering the marble floors and gilt-edged mirrors, the prize might be worth the effort.

The glimmer has lulled the concierge to sleep. He slumps over his desk, snores rattling loose paper. The doorman has sunk to the floor. With the sun about to set, that leaves me, the creature, and possibly another tracker as the only ones awake. I take a few steps further in, boots skidding against the marble, not fully committing to the hunt. Not yet.

There *must* be another tracker. Someone must have a claim on this space, and I know I shouldn't venture any farther. But there's no denying DNA, and the shadow creature that resides here is calling to me. So I blow a goodnight kiss to the concierge and find the stairs.

IN THE THIRD FLOOR HALLWAY, I breathe in dust, fingertips investigating the textured wallpaper. I remain silent and try to gauge whether that creaking floorboard gave me away.

Something always gives me away—a floorboard, the squeaking soles of my boots, a rather clumsy entrance that involves breaking glass. That's all fine when I'm prepared to hunt. Tonight I only wanted a peek.

Behind me, something rasps, brief and brisk, like sandpaper against skin. Mist fills the far end of the corridor, swallowing the glow from the sconces. I squint, but the shadow creature hasn't reached its full, solid form. For this, I am grateful. I race, carving a zigzag path along the corridor. I rattle one doorknob, then another, all of them locked.

At this point, the creature is still mostly vapor. You could poke your fingers through it. But then, you can poke your fingers through a thundercloud. That doesn't make the lightening less deadly.

I sprint down the hall, intent on the last door. I try the knob, then spin, my back against the textured wallpaper. No stairs, not even a fire exit. That's got to be a code violation. At the end of the hall, strands of gray mist probe tentatively. Something that resembles a claw solidifies and holds its shape long enough to tear a hole in the carpet.

Frantic, I try the door one last time. Three things happen. The creature surges forward, filling the hallway with its girth, the door flies open, and I tumble inside. I kick the door shut, my boots and the creature simultaneously slamming against the wood. The door frame shakes but stays put.

The room is dark, curtains drawn. My own ragged breathing fills the space, as does someone else's. I'm staggering to my feet when the lights blaze on. I flinch, cover my eyes with one hand, and attempt to protect myself with the other.

"What the hell?" a voice says.

And then I know: I'm really in trouble.

I grope for a chair and whirl it so it becomes both a shield and a weapon.

"I was here first," the voice says. The tone is strong, authoritative, but a hint of fear invades the arrogance. We all carry that in our voice, those of us who hunt. You can't touch the shadows without them touching you.

"Says who?" I counter. True, I hadn't planned on hunting tonight. Now that I'm here? Why let the opportunity slip by?

"Luke Milner," he says. "Tracker number 127."

"I know who you are." Or at least *what* he is. There are so few of us that we know each other by reputation, if not by name and face.

"I've been tracking this creature for weeks," he says. "It's on record, claim 5867. Feel free to check."

"Oh, I will." I roll my eyes.

"Plus, you totally fell in here." He shakes his head. "You don't even know your way around."

I grip the chair harder. "Oh, sure," I say. "I fell in here. I also flushed out the creature. In what? Less than an hour? How long have you been tracking it again?" I make my voice go all sweet, which is perfectly awful of me. But I can't help it. I dislike most other trackers. Like I said before, it's in my DNA. As a damsel in distress, I have good reason not to like or trust nearly everyone.

"Know the way back out?" Here, Luke Milner offers up a perfectly awful grin, providing me with yet another reason for my aversion.

While logic dictates that if you can find your way in, you can certainly find your way back out again, shadow creatures have a way of erasing that sort of logic. I do have a knack for flushing them out—and an annoying knack for getting stuck in various labyrinths for days. Normally I don't go in without a plan and a week's worth of supplies. The hotel room is covered with that same velvet wallpaper as the hall, all fleurs-de-lis and scrollwork, which makes the space feel elegant despite the freeze-dried meals and canned goods that line the dresser. Luke even has an adorable little camp stove. Plus that queen-size bed? Big enough for two. Not a bad setup, and I can't help but be a little impressed.

He waves his hands as if he can halt both my gaze and my thoughts. "Oh, no. Don't even think about it. My claim. My creature."

"Which you can't seem to flush," I remind him.

The trashcan overflows with wrappers and bottles. A room service tray holds a pot of coffee and pitcher of cream. One whiff tells me it's starting to turn. He's been here for a while without any luck. It's hard to catch a shadow creature on your own; it's even harder to trust another tracker. He can't leave the hotel without risking a claim jumper. But why stay if you can't draw out the creature to begin with?

"You saw it then?" he asks.

"Claws. Sharp. Not sure what it is, but it's big." I shrug. "Maybe a dragon."

He pauses as if considering this—and me. "What makes you so special, then?"

It's a fair if somewhat passive-aggressive question. "I come from a long line of damsels in distress."

Luke snorts.

"Shall I step into the hall and demonstrate?" I gesture toward the door. All hunts require bait. Usually, that's me. I survey the room again. This Luke Milner doesn't seem to have anything that resembles bait.

"You don't look like a damsel in distress."

True. I keep my feet in boots. You try running around in satin slippers or high heels. Tulle and lace and all the rest? Highly flammable, especially in the case of dragons.

"It's in the blood," I say. "Did I not fall in here exactly when I needed to?"

"I was opening the door."

"See? You must have some latent knight-in-shining-armor blood running through your veins."

Luke makes a face.

Okay, *very* latent. But it's there. He's too well-stocked and prepared to be anything else. In theory, I should like that in anyone. Plus, he has that knight-in-shining-armor *look*, wavy hair and features chiseled in all the right places. His eyes might glint with humor if he weren't so surly. Something tells me Luke Milner is often surly.

I've never had any luck with knights in shining armor. They're always too little, too late, and I always end up bound ankle and wrist, eyebrows singed.

Luke narrows his eyes to slits. I cross my arms over my chest, prepared to wait him out. He glances away, but in the mirror, I catch his reflection—all sour milk and resignation.

"Do you have a name?" he says at last, "or do they just call you CJ?"

"C ... J?"

His smirk provides the answer. CJ. *Claim Jumper.*

"I'm Posey Trombelle," I say, putting some teeth into my name. "Tracker number 278."

"Posey?" He makes another face.

"It's short for Poinsettia. I was a Christmas baby."

His expression goes blank. When he doesn't respond, I add, "My sister was born in February, on the fourteenth. Trust me, she got it worse."

"Well, what do you suggest we do ... Posey?"

"What were you about to do when I fell into your room?"

"Go out," he says. "Reconnaissance."

I raise an eyebrow. Because that? Fairly obvious.

Luke rubs his hands across his face. A growl begins in his throat, but the sound is all frustration without any bite. "I have a theory," he says, "that there's more treasure to be had by not slaying the creature—"

"Because most of it is in the lair," I finish.

Oh, of course! How clever. Once you slay the creature, access to any treasure in its lair vanishes. I can't help it. I like the way he thinks. Maybe this Luke has more knight in him than his sour-milk expression suggests.

"You figure out how to do that," I tell him, "and they'll have to call you Sir Luke."

LUKE STARES at the document on the coffee table, pen clutched in his hand.

"You can't do this without me," I point out.

His knuckles go white.

Granted, a handwritten agreement on hotel stationery pales when compared to a notarized contract. Under the circumstances?

"In fact," I say, tapping three paragraphs down on the paper, "you can't get a better deal than this."

No one would intentionally draw a creature to them, but I've signed on to do just that. Of course, I'm uniquely suited for the task. But while Luke searches out the lair, I must fend off the creature. While I often find myself in precarious situations, I seldom walk into them of my own volition. At least not while leaving myself wide open for betrayal. I occupy the creature, and he runs off with the treasure. I try not to think about that scenario too much.

At last his grip loosens on the pen. He scrawls his name across the bottom of the page, nearly obliterating my own.

Next comes a grappling hook and some rope, which Luke secures at my waist. He threads a whistle onto a length of nylon cord. He ties the ends and then places the whistle around my neck.

"Last resort," he says. "If you need me—"

"Just blow?"

He cringes. An angry flush covers his cheeks. Before he can turn away, I touch his arm. "Hang on."

From the depths of my cargo pants pocket, I pull a bandana. "A knight shouldn't venture out without a token," I say and tie it around his arm. As tokens go, one-hundred-percent cotton is no substitute for silk, lace, and embroidery. However, the bandana *is* pink.

"Seriously?" Luke eyes the bandana. His fingers twitch over the knot like he might undo the whole thing and toss it on the floor. Instead, he presses his palm against his jeans and sighs.

"See if it doesn't bring you luck," I say.

"I don't believe in luck."

"You should." I give him a two-finger salute and slip out the door.

I TAKE soft steps down the hallway, retracing my original path. I even zigzag, fingertips brushing the textured wallpaper on one side of the corridor and then the next. The ventilation system breathes to life, its steady, mechanical hum the only other sound.

At the corner, I pause. Things are too empty, too quiet. The space around me feels thin, like something else is using up all the available oxygen. Something large. The elevator lobby is the perfect place for an ambush. At least, it's where I'd set one up.

The marble floors in front of the elevator sport a faux Persian rug, a Queen Anne side table, and chairs upholstered in the most amazing shade of canary yellow. The space is pristine. I sniff the air. No lingering scent of sulfur, no rot. What about some slime, a tuft of fur, or even a scale on the floor? Nothing? I taste the air one last time, not trusting this good fortune, but my feet are already moving. To hesitate is to lose this chance.

I rush to the elevators, push the up and down buttons, then retreat to the safety of the stairs.

No sensible tracker uses the elevator—not if they can help it. It's the equivalent of stepping into a lunchbox. Still, it's a handy ruse. A damsel in distress inside an elevator? There's no better bait.

The elevator bell chimes. The doors whoosh open. Dark mist spills out, and a roar echoes against the walls, the sound hearty. The creature must be on the verge of transforming into something solid—and deadly. I'm half a step inside the stairwell when mist curls around the handrail and engulfs my fingers. I glance at the gleaming claws clicking against the lobby floor, then behind me to the creature forming on the stairs.

Here be dragons. Not one, but two. And here I am, right between them.

I cast my gaze upward, searching for a handhold, a window or vent to crawl through ... or that chandelier.

The elevator doors start to close, then spring open again. The creatures are solid enough to trigger elevator doors, not to mention claw, bite, and chomp. They are certainly solid enough to do a damsel-in-distress grab-and-dash.

You know, the usual.

With a hand on the grappling hook, I squint at the chandelier. Will it come crashing down on me mid-swing, effectively doing all the bone-crushing work for the dragons? Steam fills the elevator lobby area. The dragons won't risk a full blast and burn themselves out of their playground. But a stream of fire in my direction?

I don't wait to find out. I swing the grappling hook up and over the chandelier's arms. Light bulbs shatter. I tug. Cracks appear along the ceiling. Plaster dust floats down, fogging the air and coating the floor, the table, the dragon. Before I can swing, a great sucking comes from the elevator—a wind tunnel drawing me in. I grip the rope and brace my feet against the floor. Then the winds reverse.

The explosion of sound startles me. No heat. No fire. Just slime.

"Gesundheit," I say and swing up and over the sniffling dragon.

I land in the hallway, carpet soaking up the sound of my boots. Iridescent dragon snot speckles the textured wallpaper and coats the toes of my boots. I yank the rope one last time. The entire chandelier and half the ceiling crash to the floor. I sprint around the corner to avoid ricocheting debris. Even so, I choke on dust. My eyes water. I blink fast and hard, taste the grit against my lips. At the end of the hallway, a door flies open.

Luke sticks his head out. "What the hell?"

I give him a little finger wave and run.

ONLY UNDERWATER LAMPS light the pool area, bathing everything in a liquid blue. My boots squish against damp tile. Moist air clings to my face, turning the plaster dust into muck. With my back to the wall, I ease the lifesaving pole from its bracket. Since Luke's grappling hook is now part of the third-floor decor, I need *something*—a tool, a weapon. I test its weight against my palm. Light but strong. It will do.

Now that I'm here, I have the thankless job of luring both dragons to this spot. That shouldn't be too hard. After all, I'm a damsel in distress. Luring is what I do. I take mincing steps around the pool and coo stupid things like, "Oh, no, I might get my satin slippers all wet."

I've never met a creature yet who could tell the difference between satin slippers and steel-toed boots.

Minutes tick by with nothing but the gentle lap of water and my damp footfalls. This was the plan. We didn't have a backup plan in case the creatures didn't show. I'm a damsel in distress. They *always* show.

Except for now.

I kneel at the pool's edge and rinse the plaster from my face. Perhaps it's the water's chemical cocktail—too much bleach and chlorine—that convinces me, but nothing supernatural ever happens in this particular space.

But if the creatures didn't follow me (and they should have, they really should have—I should be trussed up now, tied to the diving board or cooking in the hot tub), then there's only one other spot they could be: their lair.

Which is where Luke was headed—without any backup plan of his own. Can I intercept him? I glance at my watch. Plenty of time before sunrise. Still enough time to—possibly—save Luke. Without another thought, I sprint past the heated towel rack and lounge chairs and crash into the glass doors separating the pool from the mezzanine.

I push. I pull. I rattle the handles so hard the glass shudders. Then I see a telltale glint on the other side of the doors. A dragon scale. I whirl and face the pool. What will it be? Damsel-in-Distress Stew? Or perhaps Luke is the main course, and I'm dessert.

Panic and chlorine clog my throat. Another way out—there must be one. I slip across damp tiles, careen into the changing room doors. These, too, are locked. I survey the space—the lounge chairs, discarded drink glasses with pink sludge and crushed paper umbrellas, a stack of rumpled towels—and discover a way out.

I find the service elevator behind a screen. Steam hisses and clouds roll through the room, as if the water in the pool is already boiling. I wonder if the dragons plan to serve me *al dente*. As soon as the doors screech open, I jump inside, press every button I can, and realize I'm still clutching the lifesaving pole only when the doors clang shut.

I LAND in the most obvious spot for a lair, down in the basement. The dank and dark, home to boilers and furnaces and the creatures most everyone else has forgotten. Only in this case, it seems the creatures have forgotten this space. Then again, these are dragons—by their very nature, quirky and particular. In this case, there's a pair. A couple, perhaps?

Oh. A couple. Of course. I push the up button on the elevator. There's no time for stairs. I can only hope I'm right and don't end up as a char-broiled snack. When the doors open, I step inside and select the modern equivalent of the high tower: the penthouse suite.

You'd think, as a damsel in distress, I'd be well acquainted with pent-house suites. Sadly, my luck runs toward trolls and ogres. On the rare occasions I'm captured, I end up in landfills or junkyards or, for the occa-sional eco-conscious goblins, recycling centers.

The doors open on the penthouse level. Smoke fills the elevator compartment. The acrid scent tickles the back of my throat, and I choke on a cough. I step out and crunch something beneath the sole of my boot. The remains shine in rainbow patterns the way only a dragon scale can.

I take a cautious look around. The glimmer is in full force here. Despite the smoke, I can taste the magic that lets the dragons lie dormant during the day and come out to play at night. They haven't taken over the entire floor, not yet, but the lair is well established.

I creep forward, pole outstretched like a spear, eyes cast downward. The last thing I want is to track through a pile of ash. That can mean only one thing. The tracker community may be combative, but the death of one of our own weighs heavy. My stomach squeezes tight. I clutch the pole harder. I want to close my eyes, because I don't want to see that pile of ash. I keep them open out of fear and respect.

At the end of the hall, I brush fingertips over the penthouse door then press my palm against the paneled wood. Warm, but not searing hot. That's something. Now for a distraction. I need something loud and sure, something these dragons won't miss.

I lean against the wall, and that something thumps against my chest. Luke's whistle. I grip it between my teeth and blow with all my might. Then I sprint down the corridor and launch myself behind a settee. The hiding place is flimsy. But once dragons get up a good gallop, they have a difficult time stopping, never mind turning around.

The penthouse door flies open. Claws scrape against the Italian marble floor, leaving wide grooves in its surface. The dragons galumph straight for the elevator, bypassing the settee. I crawl from beneath it, scrabble to gain purchase, then race for the penthouse.

I slam the door. It doesn't matter if the dragons hear. They're too clever to stay fooled for long anyway. Still, I throw the deadbolt for the slight delay it will give me. For good measure, I jam the lifesaving pole behind the handle.

"Luke?" I call out.

A grunt comes from the bedroom. Among satin sheets, rose petals, and candlelight, I find him, all trussed up, bound ankle and wrist, damsel-in-distress style. He grunts again, words muffled by a pink bandana—*my* bandana—gagging his mouth. So much for luck.

I can't help it; I know it's cruel. I laugh.

"You wouldn't happen to have a knife, would you?" he says when I undo the gag, a frown fighting the relief on his face.

"Swiss Army." I slice through the ropes around his wrists and set to work on his ankles.

A crash reverberates through the entire penthouse. My hands shake and the blade skitters up and over the rope, but it only catches on Luke's jeans. A whoosh fills the air, followed by the cheerful crackle of burning wood.

"We have all of three seconds," Luke says.

In those three seconds, I hack away the last of the rope. Luke smashes the window with a chair. He secures a grappling hook (one covered with plaster dust) and swings us—me clutched in one arm—out the window, past jagged glass, and over the ledge.

We land one story below, breezing through an already-opened window. When our feet touch ground, Luke releases me. I tumble into yet another canary yellow chair, knocking it over. I suck in air free of smoke, grateful for the hard floor that has just bruised my hip bones. As landings go, this one wasn't half-bad. I catch Luke's eye and point to the window.

"I like to go in with a back-up plan," he says.

An admirable quality for a knight in shining armor.

"You're pretty handy with a knife," he adds.

"You're not bad with ropes."

The building trembles. Plaster rains down, dusting my skin—again. The elevator doors pop open and shut.

"We should leave," I say. "They'll destroy everything just to get to us."

Even their own playground. Threat to their treasure brings out the nasty side of shadow creatures.

To my surprise, Luke takes my hand to help me up. He keeps a grip on it during our entire flight down the stairs. Even outside, with the first rays of sun banishing the night, he doesn't let go. He pulls us forward, intent on getting us away, while I scan the structure.

"All clear?" he asks.

"Looks that way. For now."

Four blocks from the hotel, we slow our steps. I keep the vigil, always tossing a quick glance behind. With the rising sun, the glimmer loosens its hold. The dragons will return to mist and shadows. The hotel will right itself before any of the regular guests can notice anything amiss. Already, glass in the smashed windows has repaired itself.

"I never thought to look in the penthouse until you came along," Luke says.

I inspire thoughts of the penthouse? Is this a good thing?

"The living room was the treasure trove, but I decided to check the bedroom before leaving," he continues. "I walked in on them while they were ... I mean, he was—"

"Entertaining a special lady friend?" I supply.

A flush washes across his cheekbones—a hint of pink to match the sunrise. It's kind of adorable.

"Yeah." He clears his throat. "That."

Luke pulls a small velvet sack from his shirt. "By our contract." He tips the bag and coins flow into his palm. "Fifty-fifty split. You earned it."

"So did you."

"It wasn't all bad," he says, "working with you."

Is that a compliment? I peer at him, intrigued. "Well, you *are* good with ropes," I say. "And I don't loathe you like I do most knights in shining armor."

He tosses the coins in the air and catches them neatly again. "When was the last time you earned a haul like this?"

Almost never. Damsels in distress always get the short end of things, even when we're the ones who make things happen. I can't count the number of times my fellow trackers have left me bound, wrist and ankle, and made off with the treasure. Even though my boots are singed and snot covered, my hair a plaster-streaked mess, this time, the prize was worth it. This time, I had a worthy partner.

"There's a lot more where this came from." Luke stares hard just past my shoulder, like the only way he can say this is to not look at me. "We could spend days, weeks, and still not find it all."

We? "So you're not reporting me as a claim jumper?"

His lips twitch. "Well, you know, I can't seem to flush them on my own."

"That's my specialty."

"We'd need a contract."

I nod toward a diner at the end of the block. They serve a huge breakfast special—eggs over easy, sizzling bacon, pancakes drenched in maple syrup—the perfect meal after a night of successful tracking.

"Everyone knows a contract written on the back of a paper placemat is totally binding," I say. "We could talk about it. Maybe over some coffee?"

The sun crests the hotel, casting the street in a glow to rival the canary yellow furniture, banishing the creatures to shadow for another day. We turn toward the diner. Luke tosses the coins and lets them fall into his hand one last time.

"Maybe we should," he says.

Knight at the Royal Arms was first published in Pulp Literature Summer 2017: Issue 15.

STRAYING FROM THE PATH

FAIRY TALE RETELLING

It was a wolf, rather than an ailing grandmother, that tempted Red into the woods. All day his cries echoed, small, plaintive-sounding things that filled the forest. By the time she found him, night had fallen and the blood on the snow looked black.

By moonlight, she pried his paw from the rusted jaws of the trap. He ran from her. And why wouldn't he? It was her kind that set the trap to begin with. The wolf limped through the underbrush, tail between his legs. Later, if you asked her at what point she fell in love, she would've said that night. At the time, all she knew was how his injured gait made her heart lurch.

Later that night, Red spied his yellow eyes from well beyond the woodpile at the edge of the forest. The next evening, she left a meat pie on the lowest stack of wood. By morning, the tin had been licked clean.

And so went the winter. As the days grew colder and her supplies dwindled, she cut back on her own portion of meat. She could go without, but the wolf was still healing. Now when she walked in the forest, she never feared brigands or the overly-friendly woodcutters. When men called on her, they found the howl of a single male wolf so unnerving that they left their teacups half full, crumb cake uneaten.

When at last the snow melted, and the sun heated the earth, Red took to bathing in the stream behind the house. No one dared disturb her. Every night, she set out a meat pie. Every morning, she collected the empty tin.

Except for the morning she didn't. Flies buzzed around the soggy crust, the filling, chewed and pilfered by tiny mouths and claws. She threw on her cape and ventured into the forest—alone.

The trail was easy enough to follow. Drops of blood, tufts of gray fur. The farther into the forest she walked, the slower her steps. What was done was done. All she could do was delay her own knowledge of it, spend a few more minutes free of a world where, every time she closed her eyes, all she saw was matted fur and severed paws—far too many to count.

That night, for the first time in months, she did not bake a meat pie.

The scratching came when the coals in the fireplace were mere embers. There, at the door, sat her wolf, bloodied but no weaker for his fight. He cocked his head as if to say: *Where's my meat pie?*

She threw her arms around him, buried her face against his neck, and cried until the dirt in his fur became streams of mud.

When the townsfolk came, bearing axes and ropes, she threw open the door for them.

Why *no*, she hadn't seen any wolves at all lately. In fact, she'd stopped her treks through the forest for fear of them. Instead, she now cared for her grandmother here, in her very own cottage.

The men tiptoed from the room, not wishing to wake the old lady. The women rubbed their chins, hoping old age would not bring such a crop of whiskers.

After that, suitors stopped visiting. Although Red always sent them on their way with a meat pie, they found her grandmother's beady eyes unsettling.

People forgot about Red, her grandmother who, while always ailing, never departed this world for the next. But on moonlit nights, townsfolk stumbling from the tavern swore they heard a woman's laughter mixed in with the howls echoing in the night air.

Straying from the Path was first published in Flash Fiction Online and subsequently in Cicada and in audio at The Centropic Oracle.

LIKE BREAD LOVES SALT

FANTASY

A knock on the door wakes me from dreams of salt. I rub the grit from my mouth before pressing the tip of my tongue to my fingers. I do this gingerly, as if my dreams can poison me.

Salt.

A breeze rustles the leaves of the oak that shades my room, the sound like a whisper. In that whisper, I hear words.

Like bread loves salt.

The sound is too soft, too hollow for me to grab onto and shake into recognition. But I know—or at least, think I know—who speaks those words. With a second knock, I forget everything except the taste of salt on my lips.

Few people knock on my door these days. The chances I want to speak to the person on the other side are so dismal that, at first, my hand refuses to unlatch the deadbolt. But I do. I always do. There, standing on the threshold, is the wound for my salt.

"Anna," I say.

Salt has visited her as well, or at least, it colors her hair. Her skin is fine and powdery, more like sugar. Anna is many things; sweet has never been one of them.

"You stole him." Her voice is even, as if she's simply informing me that my morning paper has been delivered. And oh, look; it has. I prefer newsprint to television and the internet, the dry feel of it against my skin, the residue of ink, words peppered on the salt of the page.

I scoot past her to scoop up the paper. "Look." I point to a headline. It's a poor attempt to change the subject, but I try nevertheless. "They're saying this heat will break."

"You stole him." This time, her voice holds an edge. Any louder and the neighbors will peek through their curtains. Any louder and the bead of sweat rolling down my spine will become a torrent.

"Anna, I don't know what—"

"Roger! You stole Roger!" She grips the handrail, her fingers tight, knuckles thick, like knobs.

"Roger's dead," I say, in that voice reserved for small children, dogs, and the aged. I dread the day I will hear it spoken at me, although by then, God willing, I won't notice. "Remember? We buried him in April."

It's July now. I don't think Anna's forgotten, or that this is the onset of dementia. Maybe it's the heat. Maybe it's a stage of grief.

"I dream of you two, *together*." She pokes a finger in my chest. "I see you. I see you with him, see what you do, what you've always done, for all those years behind my back."

"Roger and I were never together," I tell her. "He loved you." This is the truth. And yet, the salt on my lips tastes like a lie.

"But I see you." And now her words are a whimper.

I urge her inside. She slumps at the kitchen table. I brew tea. I hit the speed-dial on my cell phone. When Renee arrives, still pajama-clad, the salt is the flavor of guilt. But it's Renee who apologizes.

"Oh, Aunt Jane, I'm so sorry." She shakes a headful of curls that bear only the slightest trace of salt. "She's been having these crazy dreams about ... Dad. We've been going to a therapist. It's been good for us, but ..." Renee trails off, swipes her fingers over her lips as if she, too, can taste the salt in the air.

At the door, before they leave, Anna turns and says:

"You stole him."

Now it sounds like a death sentence.

That night, I taste the salt in my sleep. I hear the whispered words.

Like bread loves salt.

It's true. I always have. Bread only needs a pinch of salt to sustain her.

But that love is three months gone. Oh, we were so careful. How can a love confined to dreams hurt anyone but the dreamers? Fifty years of nights. Fifty years of dreams. Fifty years of stealing salt.

And now, that residue of salt is all I have left.

*Like Bread Loves Salt was inspired by the many **love like salt** folktales.*

THE WAY HOME

FAIRY TALE RETELLING

The braid went slack in his hands, and the prince knew.

He'd been deceived.

In the moment before he fell, when he hung suspended in the air, the prince confronted the thorns that would steal his sight.

He refused to blink.

The pain was an exquisite brightness, the blood hot and wet. He clambered to his feet, drew his sword, and swung blindly.

The cackle of the witch's laughter echoed in the air.

The prince stumbled across the countryside, sword unsheathed. He whirled in panic at the cries of birds and rustles in the underbrush. And always, as he walked, the faint whisper of the witch's laughter followed him.

At last, his feet found a crossroads. The earth was smooth here, and his boots met nothing other than small stones and gentle ruts. He paused and sniffed.

A ripe, earthy scent rose up, warmed by the sun, the air filled with promise.

The marsh beckoned. The prince turned and left the road behind.

He was days into his trek when the cries of an infant accompanied his walk. His legs were weak with fever, and so too, the prince reasoned, was his head. Whatever promise had led him into this marsh eluded him.

The prince sank into the muck only to hear a startled cry moments later.

"My love? Is it really you?"

His lips were so dry that he couldn't utter her name. Rapunzel knelt beside him, her tears bathing his face, easing the pain in his eyes. He raised a hand to stroke her cheek and missed.

He saw nothing but brightness and shadows. Of all the sights the thorns had stolen, he would miss the intelligence in Rapunzel's gaze the most.

"Come," she said, "come with me now."

"I can't—"

"Can't what, my prince?"

"I can't rescue you."

"Can you walk?"

With her words, his legs found their strength. "I can walk."

"Then come meet your son ... and your daughter."

With time, the prince's feet learned which paths to take in and out of the marsh. His fingers became adept at finding and patching holes in the thatched roof of their little cottage. His children grew, and although he couldn't see them, his son smelled of lilacs and morning dew, his daughter like wild roses and rain.

Each day, he ventured farther from the cottage, all in hopes of finding the crossroads once again, of finding rescue, and what that might mean. A true marriage. Proper schooling for the little prince and princess. He could resume his place in the kingdom.

It was the king's own counselor who found him, standing in the center of the crossroads one hot, summer day. Despite his blindness, the prince recognized the king's most trusted advisor, and the man rejoiced to have found the long, lost prince.

His feet knew the marsh so well that the prince raced to the little cottage without care. He found Rapunzel and swung her around, then hoisted the children to his shoulders.

"We are saved!" he cried. "We can go home."

"Home?" the children echoed.

"To the palace, where we will live the way we were meant to."

Rapunzel remained strangely silent.

"My dear," he said. "Are you not happy? Haven't you only ever wanted to escape?"

"Yes. Escape." Her words were soft and hollow, and the prince barely heard them over the clatter of the carriages arriving to bear them to the palace.

Was it the noise that struck first, or the stench? Both swirled around him like a thick, damp cloud. So many voices, and all of them demanding something of him. So many smells. Waves of perfume. The dank scent of mildew. The hint of refuse that never left the air no matter where he ventured in the palace.

Nursemaids commandeered his children. Ladies-in-waiting swept Rapunzel away. The king prattled about diplomacy and trade routes and political alliances.

At their welcome home feast, in the clatter of dishes and hearty toasts ringing out, the echo of the witch's cackle rose thin and high, a taunt meant for his ears only.

The prince knew.

This time, he'd deceived himself.

That night, he ran his hands over every inch of his chambers. His thoughts fractured each time the witch's cackle sounded in his ears. Even if he could escape, how would he rescue Rapunzel and the children?

What caught his attention first? The scrape of leather on stone? The delicate gasp of exertion? He knew the moment Rapunzel burst through the window, landing with a soft thud on the stone floor.

"Come," she said. "Your children are waiting below."

"How is it you—?"

She silenced his question with a gentle finger to his lips. "Your children have stolen all the silk sheets from the royal beds."

If he could not see the glint of intelligence in her gaze, he caught it in her tone.

"My father's included?"

"And I have braided them into a ladder, your father's included. Do you remember, my prince, how to scale a tower wall on a braided ladder?"

Indeed, he did.

"Come," she said.

He let Rapunzel take his hand. At the window's ledge, he cupped her cheek.

"I have been so blind."

In answer, she merely kissed him.

And yes, his hands did remember how to grip a braided ladder.

Together, they raced through the palace grounds, into the forest, until—at last—they reached the crossroads.

The prince stood there with his little family, the warmth of the sunrise touching his face. Something earthy and ripe rose in the air. He turned toward its source.

The marsh beckoned.

The Way Home was first published at Long and Short Reviews (and yes, Rapunzel is one of my favorite fairy tales to retell).

JULY

For July, I serialized *In a Manner of Speaking*, which was first published in *Selfies from the End of the World: Historical Accounts of the Apocalypse* and in audio at Escape Pod.

IN A MANNER OF SPEAKING

POST-APOCALYPTIC

I use the last of the good candles to build the radio. I still have light. The fire burns, and there is a never-ending supply of the cheap, waxy candles in the storeroom. I will—eventually—burn through all of those. My fire will die. The cold will invade this space.

But today I have a radio. Today I will speak to the world—or what's left of it. I compare my radio to the picture in the instructions. It looks the same, but not all the steps had illustrations. This troubles me. My radio may not work.

I crank the handle to charge the battery. This feels good. This warms my arms, and I must take deep breaths to keep going. I shake out my hand and crank some more. When buzz and static fill my ears, I nearly jump. That, too, sounds warm. I am so used to the cold. The creak and groan of ice, the howl of the wind. These cold sounds are their own kind of silence. They hold nothing warm or wet or alive.

I decide on a frequency for no other reason than I like the number. I press the button on the mouthpiece. This, according to the instructions, will let the world hear me.

"Hello?" My voice warbles and I leap back, as if something might spring from the speakers.

Nothing does, of course. In fact, nothing happens at all. It takes more than one try to reach the world.

"Hello? Hello? Is anyone there? Can you hear me? I would like to talk to you."

Perhaps I should try another frequency—or try a little patience. If someone is out there with a radio, might they right now be cranking a handle to charge a battery, or sleeping, or adding wood to their fire? This last is something I must do and soon. The embers grow a bright orange, but the chill has invaded the edges of the room.

That means venturing outside. Of all the chores, I like this one the least. The trek to the shed is short, but nothing lights my way. The dark is just that: dark. While the cold is fierce, I know nothing can lurk outside my shelter, waiting to pounce. And yet, every time I collect wood, it's as if a predator stalks me. I anticipate claws digging into my shoulder, sharp teeth at my neck, my spine cracked in half.

But the only thing outside my shelter is the cold. But it is the cold that will take me in the end. So in a sense, I am its prey and it is stalking me.

With my parka buttoned tight, I clip myself to the rope between my shelter and the shed. Wind tears at me, and I plod to the shed. I pat the pile of wood, reassured that yes, it is substantial. For now. With my arms full, I push against the wind and spill into the shelter.

It's then I hear something. At first, I don't recognize it because it's been so long since I've heard that sound. Then the notion of it lights my mind. I fly across the room, wood spilling from my arms, the wind banging the door behind me.

It's a voice.

I grab the mouthpiece, my thumb clumsy through wool mittens.

"Hello! Hello! Are you there? Can you hear me? Hello?"

The wind screams at my back. The door slams against the wall, the noise like a death knell.

"Please. Talk to me."

My small space is chaos. Whirling snow, slamming door, biting wind, and scattered wood. It is too loud and too cold for anyone to hear me over the radio, and I have foolishly let the heat escape. It will take hours to warm the air to the point where I can sit without my body convulsing with shivers.

I have been so very foolish.

I fight the wind to shut the door. With it latched, I turn to inspect the mess. Stoke the fire first. Perhaps by the time I stack the wood and sweep the debris, the flames will throw enough heat that I can sit, crank the radio, and try again.

After I clean, after I heat my insides with broth, I crank the handle and try the radio again. I send my voice into the endless night, into the world, maybe even the universe. My voice could go on forever, long after I am gone. But that doesn't seem to matter.

No one answers.

WHEN I WAKE, my nose is chilled, but only slightly. The air holds enough warmth that I can move and think. The fire is hungry, I can tell, but content to give me heat for the moment. Last night's folly has not ruined anything. My gaze lands on the radio, and I wonder. Is it more of a curse than a possible blessing?

I will try again today. It will not hurt to try. It will keep me warm and keep me busy. As long as I don't hope too much, it cannot hurt me, either.

After I eat a can of peaches for breakfast, I set to the task of cranking the handle and giving the battery a full charge. I debate switching frequencies. I wonder if that voice I heard was merely wishful thinking. These thoughts do not stop my thumb from pressing the button.

"Hello? Are you there? I think I heard you last night. Well, it's always night here. I mean, before. I heard you before."

Even now, without the sun, I still think in night and day, breakfast and dinner. I could have broth for breakfast, but I never do. I could reconstitute eggs and eat them for dinner, but again, I never do. I am a creature of habits. Now, these habits are all I have left.

"Is there anyone there?" I speak slowly, in case these words must fight the static to reach whoever is on the other side. "Should I change frequencies?"

This seems to be a silly question. If no one has answered my other calls, I'm not certain why this would compel them to. My fingers touch the dial. I'm about to spin it when something crackles over the speaker.

"No."

I stare at the space in front of the radio as if it's possible to see the owner of this voice.

"No?" My reply is a tiny thing.

"Don't ... don't change the frequency ... there's a good girl. Hold tight, I'm having some technical difficulties, but I'm here."

"I don't understand. You can hear me?"

"I can hear you."

"You have a radio too?"

"In a manner of speaking. I have a way to talk to your radio, at least."

Again, I stare at the space in front of the radio. I even wave a hand in the air. The voice is so rich and deep and clear. Yes, there is no static on my frequency. I wonder if that is something this other voice has done.

"Are you a man?" I ask.

"In a manner of speaking."

I laugh. The button on the mouthpiece is still depressed, so this voice, this man, hears my laughter. His own in response is as rich as his voice.

"I don't know what that means," I say.

"I don't either, except that I was a man, once—or male, at least. If that makes sense," he says, his reply filled with both humor and sadness. "Now I am, perhaps, less than that."

I still don't understand, but I'm not certain it matters. Not when there's a voice on the other side of this endless night, not when that voice wants to talk to me.

"I'm Soshi," I say, a strange, unaccountable shyness invading my voice and heating my cheeks.

"It's a pleasure to meet you, Soshi. I am Jatar."

I like the way his name feels in my mouth, and I say it out loud. "Jatar." Yes, it is delicious. Speaking is delicious. I touch my cheeks. The skin burns hot, but my fingers are like ice. The fire. Too late, I realize I've let it die down far too much.

"Oh, no," I murmur. "I forgot about the fire."

"Go, go. Tend to your fire. Then fix yourself something to eat, and come back and charge your battery. I will be here, on this frequency."

"Always? When I call, you will be there?"

"In these times, Soshi, there aren't many things I can promise. But I will promise you this. I will always be on this frequency, and I will always hear your call."

~

JATAR WON'T TALK to me until I've assured him that I've fed myself, tended to the fire, and the other chores. How he knows I need to do these things puzzles me. Of course, I did fling my words into the darkness before we found each other. So I ask him.

"Yes," he says. "I did hear you. I have trouble on my end. Your radio is nothing like the device I use."

"You still have trouble?"

"Had. I mean, I had trouble. But you can hear me now, yes?"

"Yes." Sometimes I want to nod or smile, but I know he can't see these things. We have nothing but voices to guide us—their tone, their thickness or thinness. How a smile makes the throat warm and disapproval has an edge.

"You are not on earth," I say, "are you?"

The frequency carries his sigh to me, and the sound holds reluctance. "No, I am not."

"You are lucky then."

"I don't know about that."

"Where are you?"

"I don't know about that, either." By the way he says this, I know he wants me to laugh.

I do, but I also want to know the answer. "Where are you?"

"I'm not certain *where* matters all that much, not anymore."

"But you must be somewhere."

"Must I, dear girl? Must I really?"

I don't know how to answer that. I crank the handle to charge the battery, just so I don't lose the connection. I hate that, every morning—or what I call morning—charging the battery, sprouting sweat, and praying that Jatar's voice will come over the speaker and fill my little room with warmth.

"Maybe you are in my radio," I say now.

This time, he laughs. "What I wouldn't give to be there, living inside your radio."

"You would have to be very small," I say. "Smaller than a mouse."

"You wouldn't need to feed me very much."

No, I wouldn't. A thought seizes me. I think of small things, tiny things, mouse-sized things. I think of their absence.

"I killed them," I say. The confession both lifts me up and weighs on me. I know its truth.

Our frequency is clear of buzz and static. So when there's silence, it stretches long and empty.

"Who do you think you've killed," Jatar says at last, his words quiet and low.

"The mice. When I first ... found this place, there were droppings everywhere. The food is in metal containers and on metal shelves. But I stopped leaving crumbs. No more crumbs, no more mice."

"And it's you, not the lack of sun or heat that's responsible."

"I don't need to eat every last crumb."

A few nights ago, I left a bit of cracker on the floor, deliberately. I placed it well away from my sleeping pallet. My first nights in this space, I was consumed with the fear of mice, of rats, crawling over me in my sleep. I jerked awake so many times, breathing hard, cold sweat washing across my skin that I almost gave up on sleeping. But this time, when I woke, the crumb remained, untouched.

"Oh, dear girl, you did not kill the mice. They no doubt went elsewhere. They are resourceful creatures. Besides, they carry diseases. They could contaminate your food, your water..."

Jatar's voice fades, either from the buzzing in my head or failing battery power. I remember standing over that crumb, then falling on my knees next to it. For how long I stared, I don't know. Here's what I do know:

I picked it up and ate it.

"I can't talk now, Jatar," I say into the mouthpiece.

"Soshi, please. Listen to me, you did not kill the mice." Jatar's voice fills the air. He does not stop talking, not even when I refuse to respond. "You'll lose me soon if you don't crank the handle." He knows the life of the battery—or at least how to gauge it. "Crank the handle, at least. Tell me you're still with me."

But I don't. I sit, curled by the fire, chin on my knees. I could've captured a mouse, tempted it with some crumbs, built a home for it, close enough to the fire so it would always be warm. We would dine together, morning and night. I could spare what it would need to survive. I would have given it a good mouse name.

But I don't have a mouse. Something about that makes me clutch my legs to my chest. Salt from tears irritates my cheeks, but it's only later, when the tracks have dried, that I scrub my face with my palms. I've forgotten to eat, and the fire is low, but it's the radio that I reach for. My chest heaves as I crank the handle.

"Jatar," I say when there's enough power to carry my voice. "I want a mouse."

"I know you do, dear girl. I know you do."

He is there; he is always there. Maybe he does live in my radio. Maybe Jatar is my mouse.

"I know you do," he says one last time. His sigh carries so much weight I'm surprised the air isn't thick with the sound. "Your fire," he prompts.

"I should stoke it."

"Dinner?"

"Not yet."

"Tend to your chores. I'll be here when you're done."

"You will?"

"Where else would I go?"

⌇

I HAVE FOUND A RUBBER BAND, one that feels stretchy and fresh in my fingers. Its edges have not rotted away. It is strong, and when I wrap it around the mouthpiece, the button remains depressed. I love my radio, but now I am no longer tethered to it. I can use both hands while talking to Jatar.

Not that he can see my hands. But I can stoke the fire, feed myself, and crank the handle. I can fall silent, and he will not worry—too much. He can hear the rustle of my boots against the floor, the whisper of the broom, the crack and sizzle when I stoke the fire.

"Have you gathered wood recently?" he asks now.

"Last night ... yesterday. It's stacked high. I don't dare bring anymore in for a while."

The air is too dry; sparks from the fire have too great a range. The thing that keeps me alive can also kill me. At least then I'd be warm, I tell myself. I don't speak these words to Jatar, but my laugh gives me away.

"That sounds morbid."

"It is," I admit. "I was thinking about the fire, how it might kill me before the cold does."

"I wish you wouldn't—"

"It's like that poem about the world ending in fire and ice. And I think it could be both, couldn't it?"

"I suppose it could, and suppose we change the subject?"

I agree, but don't know what to say at first. Jatar does not talk much about himself, although I wish he would. That doesn't stop me from trying.

"Can you see the stars where you are?" I ask.

"On occasion, yes, I can."

"Ours left. Actually, that's not right. I'm guessing they're still in the sky."

"Your guess would be correct."

"We blotted them out, all the stars, our sun, and now we have nothing. You know, when I first found this place, you could still see the stars from here. I thought: *oh, I am so lucky*. There used to be a stream. It even had fish, although they swam funny, so I never ate them."

"That seems like a wise decision."

His words have a teasing quality that makes me want to talk more so I can hear the humor and approval in his tone.

"It must have been a beautiful spot, with the mountains and the woods. I wonder why no one else ever came up after I did. Was it just too late?"

"Perhaps they weren't as smart as you."

"I don't think that's it. I think something happened, but I just don't know what that something is."

"Hm." Jatar sounds as if he's giving this much thought. "It's possible that the only thing to happen was self-inflicted, especially with the cities, as crowded as they were. Disease, fighting. It's hard to say."

"The cities *were* crowded. It's why we left." I nod before stopping myself, since Jatar can't see me. I may be the only witness to these things, and yet, I might as well be blind for all I've seen. Self-inflicted. The phrase makes me think of something else I found along the stream, something else I witnessed, and yet didn't.

"I'm wearing a dead woman's boots," I say.

I must shock Jatar with this confession. Silence greets me, and I wonder if I need to crank the handle again. At long last, he coughs.

"Dear girl, Soshi ... I don't know what you mean by that."

"When there was still some sunlight, when I could walk along the stream, I found a body, a skeleton, really. Small, like me, so I'm guessing it was a woman. She was mostly bones, but the gun was still in her hand, and for some reason, nothing had chewed away the boots on her feet. Thick leather. They're heavy, but they are very good boots."

"The boots on her feet." Jatar says these words slowly. "Your boots?"

"I had to shake her bones from them, but yes. I took her boots."

"Did you leave her gun?"

"By that time, there was nothing left to shoot. I didn't see the point, even though I was still scared. I didn't think anyone would climb up this high in the mountains, not if they hadn't already."

"So you left the gun." Jatar's voice is tight as if this is something he absolutely must know.

"I left the gun," I say. "What would I shoot at? The wind? What would that do? Maybe cause an avalanche?"

"Yes, I suppose it could." He clears his throat. "I don't like this subject either."

"Then you tell me something about you."

"I am not that interesting."

"Are you a scientist?"

Jatar is intelligent; I can tell he holds back in saying things, perhaps so I don't feel bad for not being all that smart myself.

"A scientist?" he says. "Is that what you think I am?"

"You are very smart."

"I don't know about that, but you could call me a scientist, in a manner of speaking."

I sigh. The radio carries the sound to wherever Jatar is, and he laughs.

"What do you study? Planets? Stars? Solar systems?"

"Yes, you could say that. I ... take the temperature of things. Some of those things include stars and planets."

"Earth?"

There's the slightest hitch in our frequency, the slightest bit of hesitation in his voice. "No, actually, Earth wasn't something I monitored."

"But you are now?"

"On my own time."

"You must have a lot of time."

Here, he laughs, the sound so clear and hearty, I can't help but laugh as well.

"Oh, yes, I do," he says. "I have time to spare."

"I wish I knew what day it was," I say.

I am trying to draw Jatar out, get him to respond. Today he has been so very quiet.

"I always know what day it is," he says.

"Somehow, I don't think it's the same as mine."

"It is, and it isn't."

"Because if I knew what day it was, we could have a party."

"What kind of party?"

"Well, that depends on the day. See? It's important."

His laugh filters through the speakers.

"It could even be my birthday."

"Oh, dear girl, it certainly could. You deserve lots of birthday parties."

"Would you get me a present?"

"As many as I could carry to you."

"Like what?"

"How about a mouse?"

"I would very much like a mouse. I would name it Jatar."

A harrumph comes from the speakers, one so strong the radio seems to vibrate with it.

"I think," Jatar says, his words slow, "that I should be offended."

Before I can explain that having a mouse named after you is an honor, the floorboards shake beneath my feet. I give a little cry, no more than a yelp from the back of my throat, but Jatar hears.

"What is it?" he demands.

"I don't know. The house is ..."

I can't find words to describe the tremors that run through it. It's like my house has suddenly caught a fever and is shaking with chills. Then there's an awful groan.

"Oh, dear girl," Jatar says, and now his voice is low, but taut, as if it were nothing more than a rubber band stretched to its limits. "Stay by me—I mean, the radio. Stay by the radio. Do not open the door. Do not go outside. Stay as still and as quiet as you can."

I retreat to the radio, grip the mouthpiece, although I don't need to. Another groan sounds. It is like nothing I've heard, not even in the days when we fought to leave the city, and certainly my mountain has never made such noises.

"What is it?" I whisper, my lips only a breath away from the mouthpiece.

"I have heard this sound before."

"Will it eat me?"

"No." This word is not quite as tight as all his others. It almost sounds like he wants to laugh. "It won't eat you, dear girl."

The roar comes next, so loud it steals my breath. It reminds me of the few trains that still ran, back when we were walking, back before I was alone. We'd follow the tracks, and the roar would sneak up on you. Someone always kept watch.

Or did. Because, of course, the trains stopped running after a while. We still followed the tracks. They would lead us somewhere important, somewhere safe. I'm not sure how true that was, because they didn't lead me here, to my mountain, where I've been safe.

Until now.

The floorboards jump beneath my feet. The force knocks me into the wall and knocks embers from the fireplace. I claw my way across the floor. Before I can cup the glowing ember in my hands, I jerk back. I glance around, but the world shakes too hard, and my feet are too unsteady. Already smoke rises from the wood slats. I bite my lip and sacrifice the back of my left hand and shove the ember into the hearth.

I must scream. My throat aches as if I have. Jatar's voice pours from the speaker in response. He must fight to be heard over the roar and rumble and chaos that have swallowed my house.

Then, everything is quiet. The world. Jatar. So quiet I can hear the fire sputter. My gaze goes there first. Build the fire back up, make it safe. My left hand is nearly useless. If pain could scream, it would fill this space, this mountain, this world. I worry that I have done more damage than I can repair.

First things first. The fire. I build it up. I don't know if it's the stoked fire or if my hand makes me feel as if I'm on fire, but the air is warm, warmer than before. I glance about, knowing I must dig out some first aid supplies, perhaps scoop up some snow or ice from outside.

"Jatar?" I say, hoping to hear his voice.

Nothing.

Panic seizes me before I remember: the battery. It's an awkward thing, cranking the handle with my right hand, bracing the radio with my left elbow, but I manage it.

"Jatar?" I say, before I even have a full charge.

"Soshi? Dear girl, are you okay?"

"I burnt myself, but that's better than the house burning down. I'm going to get the first aid kit."

Actually, in the storeroom, I have many first aid kits, more than I could ever use.

"And maybe some snow," I add, making my way across the room. My legs wobble, and I take unsteady and erratic steps.

Behind me, Jatar is saying something, but he sounds so very far away. Shock, I think. How do I cure myself of that? Hand first, then the shock. I open the door to the outside. All I want to do is grope around, grab a handful of that sharp, crystalized mix of icy snow, and cool the fire of my skin.

At first, I don't understand what I see. I can only open the door part way. Something solid, cold, and white blocks its progress. The rope lifeline that leads to the woodshed is gone. That is no matter. Because my woodshed is also gone. Either that, or it's buried beneath a mountain's worth of snow.

Why the avalanche spared my little house, I do not know. But it has. And yet, it hardly feels benevolent. I do not feel grateful.

For a very long time, I do nothing but stare at the snow. Then I shut the door. I throw the deadbolt.

I will never open it again.

❧

I USE the last of the dying embers to light a cheap candle. The flame throws little light and even less heat. A couple of them on the hearth chase away the worst of the dark—if not the cold. Jatar is speaking to me now, urging me forward. Before the cold can steal all my rational thoughts, I scrawl *Crank the handle* on any surface I might chance to look at—the floor, the walls, the plastic tub that once held the blankets and clothes I stumble around in.

My fingers are black from the burnt bit of wood that was my makeshift pen. I use as little water as possible to wash, although this is from habit. I will run out before the water does.

"The storeroom," Jatar says. "You can navigate in the dark. I'll help you. Don't take a candle."

"All right." I push to standing.

"Go straight back and then to your left."

"My left." I don't say it as a question, but that's what it is.

"That's the hand with the burn." He never scolds, even when my words come out stupid.

"On the shelf, above your head, there will be another bin of blankets and things to keep you warm."

Halfway inside the storeroom, my mind blanks. Everything is dark, but Jatar's voice echoes behind me.

"A few more steps, dear girl. Just a few."

How he knows what I need to do, I can't say. Perhaps, before the avalanche, I spoke of these things. Yes. I nod to myself. I did. I told him where everything was and now he's telling me. I lug the bin from the shelf and emerge into the dim light of the main room.

My movement causes one of my candles to sputter. It gutters and dies. Maybe it's the cheap wax, but it sounds like someone drowning.

"Soshi? Are you there?"

"Yes, I'm here."

"That noise?"

"One of my candles," I say. "The flame went out."

"It sounded horrific."

"It sounded like someone's throat being slit."

Jatar's voice fills the speakers, but I don't understand him. His voice has a musical quality to it, as if he uses notes rather than words. But I recognize the tone.

He is scolding me.

At last he comes to himself, the notes fading into lyrics I understand.

"Soshi, please."

He doesn't call me *dear girl*, and I think that hurts more than anything else. That makes me rush to explain before the cold steals this piece of me as well.

"I said that because I know what it sounds like. I've heard it before. It's why I left the group. They weren't collecting children because they were kind. They were collecting children because they were hungry."

Jatar is silent.

"I ran away," I continue. "I'd rather die alone than be someone's dinner. I left the group, stopped following the train tracks, and found my mountain."

"I had no idea, dear girl, no idea. You've never ... I mean, I didn't know."

"I don't like to think about it."

"Then we won't speak of it ever again. Go on, open the bin. There are warm things inside."

I pull the items out, one by one. They are heavy in my hands, thick wool coats that might weigh more than I do at this point. There are light things as well, down-filled jackets and sleeping bags that sprout tiny feathers when I squeeze them. At the very bottom, there is something furry and soft. I don't recognize it, and it isn't something you wear. It almost looks like...

"Jatar! I have a mouse!"

"Do you now?" He sounds amused.

"Yes! Did you ... did you find a way to send me a mouse?"

"I did, dear girl, I did."

"Is it my birthday?"

"I think it might be."

"I should have a can of peaches then."

"You should have two."

"Oh, I don't know if I could eat two whole cans." I am not as hungry as I used to be. Sometimes Jatar must bully me into eating.

"Try," he says now. "Pretend I'm there, and the second can is for me."

In the end, I manage to eat one and a half cans. This gives me energy to make tea. The drink heats my throat, my stomach, and for a few moments, I can pretend I feel warm.

"You know what you should do, now that you have a mouse?" he asks.

"What?" I am amazed that there's something I can do, so he has my full attention.

"Build a nest, one you can share with it. You can keep each other warm."

I do as he says, piling the heavy coats along the floor and against the wall near the hearth. I move the radio within arm's reach. I can keep the candles lit from here. I curl into the blankets and pull the mouse to me.

"Would you mind," I ask, "if I called him Jatar?"

"I would be honored."

CRANK THE HANDLE.

I know the words mean something, something important. I know there's something I must do, but can't remember. When the last of the candles dies and the dark erases the words, it's almost a relief.

I pull my mouse to me, cuddle him against my neck. He is so soft.

"Don't be scared," I whisper.

Because he is scared, of the dark, of the cold so sharp it feels like a knife's blade. I dig us further into our nest.

"Close your eyes, Jatar. Go to sleep."

I shut my eyes. The sound of a voice pricks my ears, but I think this voice is in my head, not in my house. It is a rich voice, amused and musical. When I try, I can make this voice laugh.

And in that laughter, there is warmth.

IT'S the silence in the end that's the worst, when Soshi's voice no longer fills my shuttlecraft, when I know she's alone, in the dark. She has her mouse, I tell myself; she has her version of Jatar. She is not alone. This thought offers nothing, not even a cold sort of comfort.

Earth was never in my sector of responsibility. Before Soshi, I knew very little of it, just that it was another small, life-bearing planet. Enough small, life-bearing planets implode on our watch that one more hardly makes a difference.

Except, of course, when it does.

As always, the jolt takes me unaware, throws me into the control panel. Pain shoots along my extremities. The grind of metal on metal follows and what sounds like a ripping. I brace against the floor, the craft shuddering beneath me. I count to three.

And then it ends. Everything is solid around me. Everything is as it should be. Everything is the same.

"Hello?"

Including Soshi.

"Hello? Hello? Is anyone there? Can you hear me? I would like to talk to you."

Why my communications system picks up her transmission, I don't know. It hasn't failed to yet, just as the crash never fails to surprise me, never fails to injure. I push to stand, then fall back. I strain and stretch, managed to press a button, call out a few words, although they are rough. My memories are intact, but each time, I must relearn her language. In those precious moments, it is easy to lose her.

"Hello! Hello! Are you there? Can you hear me? Hello?"

I can't find the will to move. I'm not certain I have it in me to live through this again—I've lost track of the number of times.

"Please. Talk to me."

If I lie here and soak in my own juices, what good will that do? But if I claw to stand, lock onto her frequency, what good will *that* do?

Every time is different. Every time ... breaks me a little more. My sigh comes across the frequency, changes her thought or her footfall or something, and I open up another vista into her soul. Just when I thought I knew all of Soshi's trials, she tells me of shaking bones from a dead woman's boots and those who collect children in order to eat them.

I spend this time between her first call and that last, desperate one deciding. Earlier, I researched. While Earth never was in my sector, our information is complete, and what's stored on the shuttlecraft is more than I'll ever need. Quite against my will, I've become the foremost expert on hypothermia in humans.

When the end is near, I coax her into burrowing, better that than paradoxical undressing. I know when the avalanche will strike and her best chance to survive it. Once she stepped outside and it took her. I listened to icy silence until the battery on the radio finally died.

I have a complete mental inventory of her storeroom. What she finds in the bottom of that bin, I'm never certain. A child's toy? A fur-lined glove? A hat meant for an infant, perhaps, with whimsical ears.

"Hello? Are you there? I think I heard you last night. Well, it's always night here. I mean, before. I heard you before."

My strength returns, but so does my resolve not to answer. Does it matter, one way or another, if I'm there for her? Must I bear witness? She dies. She always dies. Once, I'd like that not to happen.

"Is there anyone there?" Her words are slow, deliberate, plaintive. "Should I change frequencies?"

Her question holds humor, as if she recognizes that it's a somewhat ridiculous thing to ask. The first time I heard it, I launched myself to my feet, smashed into the control panel, and opened a communications channel. Now, I hesitate, but thoughts cloud my mind. She will not find her mouse without me. She will step into that avalanche.

She will die alone.

I propel myself off the floor. I land with a crack against the control panel. I still ooze, and I coat the surface with what can only be described as slime, at least in human terms.

"No." It's more of a cough than a word, but it crosses space and time and opens her up to me.

"No?"

Her voice is filled with so much hope, choking out a reply is almost impossible. The panel is such a mess that establishing a permanent link is, also, almost impossible.

"Don't ... don't change the frequency ... there's a good girl. Hold tight, I'm having some technical difficulties, but I'm here."

I'm always here.

In a manner of speaking.

AUGUST

For August, it was stories about battles, real and imagined, and which ones are worth fighting.

LAND OF THE FREE (HAIRCUTS)

STORY IN FREE VERSE

The place to find the cheapest haircuts in the Khobar Towers
is the fourth floor apartment of Tower D.
I should know because Paul wields the scissors, and his haircuts
are always free.

Soldiers try to give me their place in line.
I wave away their offers, not wanting
to sandwich time with Paul
between two privates.

The line snakes. Paul's platoon sergeant smirks.
He thinks it's ridiculous that Paul and I
pretend not to be married. He rolls his eyes, mutters,
Officers, and shakes out an unfiltered Camel from the pack he carries
in his ammo pouch.

The sun slants low in the sky, and when my turn
finally comes, afternoon light fills the apartment,
floods the balcony, turning clouds of cigarette smoke
a tarnished gold.

Paul sees me and the scissors snip shut.
He holds himself to impossible standards
while in uniform.
No PDA goes without saying,
but if he can run his hands over every single
scalp in Echo Company, there's no reason why
he can't touch mine.

Still, the price of this haircut may be more
than I am willing to pay.
But I sit in the folding chair.
I shut my eyes.
I hold my breath.
Beth, he says, *Really?*
I nod, tugging my bangs to my nose, hiding
behind my excuse. I only wanted to see him.
But I can't tell him that, not in so many words.

He pulls a strand of hair, then another.
It's like cutting spun gold. And his voice is softer
than the smoke on the balcony.

Two stories above, someone stabs the buttons
of a boom box, and the first notes mingle
with the smoke.
Paul's scissors snap closed.

That song. The unofficial anthem of everyone
in the Khobar Towers,
although I'm sure I've never heard it
before coming to Dhahran.

But you can't walk a block without cheap speakers
distorting Lee Greenwood's voice, or someone belting out,
God Bless the USA!

I'd pull on a gasmask, Paul says, *but I'd still be able to hear it.*

Paul's patriotism has never been sentimental, and I'm glad to see
my soldier cynic hasn't lost his touch with either words or scissors.

But by the time the song fades, and the Islamic call to prayer
takes its place, the evening sun can barely crest the balcony rail.
A single shaft of light slants through the balcony doors
and illuminates the bits of gold scattered
around the folding chair. And I find myself wondering
how much more of us will be left behind.

*Land of the Free Haircuts first appeared in Proud to Be: Writing by American
Warriors, Volume 2 and also made an appearance in my young adult novel The
Fine Art of Holding Your Breath.*

MIDNIGHT AT THE HADES
UNDERGROUND

FANTASY

*D*uring all the millennia of his existence, Hades had found contentment in so few things. One of those was in the simple act of tending bar.

Granted, it was his own bar, in his own club, far below the sunbaked asphalt and concrete above. A city, and a large one, filled with the clamor and detritus of humanity. Where, exactly? Well, where didn't matter. The Hades Underground was everywhere.

The Hades Underground never closed.

Zeus leaned back against the bar, a cut-crystal glass in one hand, filled with Glenlivet and ambrosia—a deity-only concoction. Hades mixed drinks for the rare mortal. Although when he did, it was always their last.

"Brother," Zeus said now. "You have outdone yourself with this." He raised his glass, indicating the dance floor that pulsated with flashes of blue and yellow, high back booths in midnight velvet, the hallways that led deeper into the bowels of the club. Some mortals wandered down those halls never to return.

Hades liked to think of this last as a feature rather than a bug. He surveyed his club with satisfaction.

Yes, I really have.

"Even she seems to appreciate it," Zeus added, a certain slyness in his tone.

Hades refused the bait. Persephone haunted the periphery of his vision, of his whole being. There, in the middle of the dance floor—the riot of blues and yellows and greens like springtime—she danced. A group of loyal nymphs created a tight circle around her, with mortal hangers-on forming a wider one.

No one dared approach.

"There are others, you know," Zeus said.

"We don't need to have this conversation again."

Zeus and his matchmaking? No. No, thank you.

"Oh, I think we do." Zeus pulled out his phone. How he loved that gadget. The constant stream of images and sounds. The entire world in the palm of his hand. Never had the King of the Olympians been so sated.

Who was he at this moment in time? Some tech billionaire, Zeke or Zucker-something-or-other. Hades had long ago stopped keeping track of Zeus's personas.

"Look," his brother commanded.

Pictures of women flashed across the screen, one after the other after the other, in a never-ending parade. Hades didn't bother to count.

"And that's just tonight," Zeus added.

Yes, of course. Zeus invariably swiped right.

"Thank you, Brother, for your counsel," Hades said. "I'll take it under consideration."

Zeus laughed, a booming sound that sliced through the chatter, the thump of the bass, and for the barest instant, brought the club to a standstill. Even Persephone halted mid-twirl to see what her father found so amusing.

He slapped Hades on the back, the impact like a thunderbolt. "You could, at least, tend to your little shadow." Zeus nodded toward the end of the bar. "She's been there all night."

All week, actually. Hades cast her a glance, barely a whisper of a look. Most patrons found his full attention distressing, at best. He didn't wish to inflict that on her.

"She's an old soul," is all he said. "It gives her comfort to sit here."

"She's more than that." Zeus stood, swallowed the last of his drink, and then crushed the glass between his fingers. When he unclenched his fist, the shards rose into the air and filled the club with starlight. "And she's looking for more than just comfort."

He sauntered off, one of Persephone's mortal hangers-on in his sights, his first conquest of the evening.

~

HADES IGNORED HER—THAT little shadow, as Zeus called her. For a solid hour, Hades wiped down the bar of gleaming ebony, polished glasses with a cloth the color of lilies, took delight in the weight of the lead crystal against his palm.

There were so few visceral pleasures left to him. He let himself revel in this one.

But Zeus was right, at least in one respect. He should do something about her. It wasn't her time; she wasn't the type to fritter her lifespan away—no matter how long or short—sitting in his club.

She was a fighter, and always had been, more an acolyte of Ares than death's handmaiden.

He approached, shrouding his gaze. She stared at him straight on. Hades suspected that he could lift the veil and she wouldn't glance away. That was like her. No matter the end, she always met it well.

He signaled one of his mortal bartenders to pour her another drink. The concoction was startling sweet and free of alcohol.

"I don't merit one of yours?" she asked when he slid the glass in front of her.

"It's not your time."

"Isn't it?"

"Wouldn't I know?"

"You might lie."

"I might." He nodded to concede the point. "But I seldom do."

She carried with her the scent of harsh wind and dust, cordite and flames, of slick and quicksilver blood. Afghanistan, then. Her eyes held that look, but then they had for centuries now. Once earned, a thousand-yard stare seldom faded. He wondered: Did such ancient eyes in the face of an infant ever startle her mothers?

"Are you tired, my child?" Perhaps it *was* her time. He'd been wrong before. His gaze darted toward the dance floor. Yes. So very wrong.

She countered with a question of her own. "Why won't you let me thank you?"

He raised a palm skyward. "Have I done something to deserve gratitude?"

"It was you." She ran her fingertips around the circumference of the glass, full circle, a trip from birth to death. "Actually, it's always you. At first, I thought it was Ares who came for me in the end. But war isn't like that."

"My nephew is many things. Compassionate isn't one of them."

"I'm sorry." She gave her head a slight shake. "I don't remember all the times."

"Truly? I have no wish for you to."

"And I don't remember any before the year 1431."

Even an old soul such as this one could comprehend dying only so many times. He'd erase every instance if he could. But some mortals were more aware than others, and that made it hard for them to forget.

And when the world decided you were a saint? Even harder.

"Humans live their lives as if they have an unlimited number of them," he said.

"But most only have the one."

"Yes. That's the irony."

"Are there others like me?" she asked.

"A few," he acknowledged. "Fewer still who comprehend what they are."

"They made me a saint, you know." She laughed, not Zeus's booming guffaw. This sound had a subtle, insidious sorrow. Those in nearby booths tilted their heads to catch the whisper of it. Those on the dance floor stumbled, mid-step.

Even Persephone.

"Yes. I know." And his own words were heavy with sorrow.

"I never want to be a saint again." Her gaze returned not to him, but the surface of the bar, as if she could peer into its depths. "It wasn't the stake or the fire, but all those people pinning their hopes on me. It was a relief when you came. You didn't need to offer your hand."

"You didn't need to take it."

"Where does the pain go? Do you absorb it?"

"Mortal pain can't touch me."

"Do you wish that it could?"

Hades paused in the task of polishing yet another glass. The crystal crumbled in his hands, although if he were to release these shards, they'd fill the club with all manner of winged creatures, bats and ravens, and things not seen outside of Tartarus.

For the briefest moment, he unveiled his gaze.

She withstood it.

Yes, of course, she did. His little saint. His Joan. She would've withstood the flames as well had he not taken them from her.

"You never answered my question," he said. "Are you tired?"

"He won't stop whispering to me. He makes it sound so very simple, so very easy, so very right."

"War is never those things."

"I know." She peered up at him as if daring him to unveil his gaze a second time. "But what is left for me?"

"The Elysian Fields?"

"So, heaven."

"In a manner of speaking. Anything you might want, might be, might desire is yours for the asking."

"That sounds ... boring."

Now he laughed, the echo of it reverberating through the floors of the club. The music hiccupped, and the speakers screeched in protest. A hush fell. Even the gaggle of nymphs ceased their giggling.

"Perfection often is," he said.

Her gaze darted toward the dance floor. "Is it really?"

Before he could answer, a presence burst into the club. A man, although with a mere glance, it was difficult to tell. Most patrons only dared furtive looks. Some shrank back, into booths or against the walls, hearts pounding frantic prayers. Others preened and swooned, bloodlust thick in the air.

Yes, his nephew liked to make an entrance.

Was Ares here for this little saint? Was the mention of the Elysian Fields too much? *Can't lose a single soldier in the waging of war, can we now?*

Ares swooped in, slipping onto the stool next to her. "I've missed you, my sweet. Indeed, I thought you'd gone AWOL." He brought her hand to his lips and caressed the palm, the tender underside of her wrist.

"Really?" She raised an eyebrow, her expression filled with doubt, playfulness, and the assurance of a beloved favorite. "You thought that?"

"Feared it." Ares released her hand and struck a fist against his chest, over the spot where a mortal's heart would beat. "We still have much to do together, you and me."

Hades anchored a hand on his nephew's shoulder. "She needs rest. Don't use her like this."

"While you have so much to offer?" His nephew regarded him through half-lidded eyes. "This is quaint, Uncle. But really, Hades Underground? Where else would it be?"

She laughed then, and the sound cut Hades like nothing he'd felt in ages. In it was his loneliness, that great expanse of nothing that greeted him every moment of his existence.

He was Hades Underground, and Hades Underground was him. Dark, endless, and ultimately empty.

And now it was midnight. The glitter ball over the dance floor threw beams of sunlight throughout the space. The processional began, Persephone at its center, flanked by nymphs and mortals, all clad in dresses that swayed like petals and cascaded like sea foam.

Hades retreated, left Ares to the spoils of this little scrimmage. Who was this mortal girl to him, anyway?

Besides, he had drinks to mix.

Crystal sang out as he poured and stirred—ambrosia, nectar, and a splash of vodka for the nymphs. They weren't particular, so he always used an off-brand variety.

Then he mixed the club's signature drink—and clever patrons knew to order a Persephone instead of a pomegranate cosmopolitan. Hades stirred in a dash of ambrosia.

And, of course, actual pomegranate seeds. Six, to be precise.

They gathered around the bar, Persephone, the nymphs, and her mortal followers alike, squeezing out the other patrons. Her entourage wasn't especially polite, but as a group, they awed. Others in the club stepped aside, swallowed their complaints, or basked in the glow of spring incarnate.

Slender fingers grasped for equally slender stems of glasses, like plucking flowers from a field. Midnight at the Hades Underground brought sunlight and spring and the taste of nectar against your tongue.

No one—mortal or god—ever left before midnight.

Except, perhaps, his little saint. He didn't need to glance toward the end of the bar to discern the empty stool.

Persephone had yet to sip her drink. It went that way some nights—most nights, actually. Perhaps if her feet were sore, or if she'd grown weary of her current entourage, she'd deign a mouthful.

Most nights, she threw the drink in his face.

To say he didn't deserve that would be a lie.

But tonight she halted, drink mere inches from her lips. Something jostled the group of nymphs. They stumbled aside, the force like a scythe slicing through wheat. The commotion caught Persephone's attention, and she set the glass on the bar.

At the center of the commotion—and its cause—stood his little saint, staring down his goddess.

Gods don't breathe, not the way mortals do, but just then, everything went still inside him.

On the bar, the drink glowed an arterial red.

Certainly, mortals weren't faster than gods, but his little saint snatched the glass with the power of Ares behind her. With the practiced ease of a soldier, she swallowed. What she lacked in finesse she made up for in ferocity.

She drank it—vodka, ambrosia, pomegranate seeds, and all.

She slammed the glass onto the bar. The crystal shattered, the sound a gunshot. Sparks erupted throughout the club, like tracer rounds and flares in a night sky.

Hades braced for a fight. Surely this was the first volley in a coming war. Any moment, he expected Ares to roar back in, rile up the mortals, and force Persephone and her entourage from the club.

He expected blood.

Instead, his little saint turned to him.

"May I?" she asked, her hand extended in the manner he'd always offered his. "I know we both have our relationship baggage." She rolled her eyes, a move that was both goddess-like and purely mortal. "But I think you could use the rest."

"As could you?"

"As could I."

Persephone stamped her foot.

Hades turned to her, surprised she was—at last—a mere afterthought. "Go."

Her eyes—those impossibly blue eyes, the color of the spring sky—widened.

"Or stay," he amended. After all, he'd fashioned the Hades Underground for her. "It"—he waved a hand—"runs itself."

"But—"

"My dear, you have never wanted to be Queen of the Underworld."

"But—"

"It was my mistake to force you. And for that?" He inclined his head. "I apologize."

He then turned to his Joan, his saint.

His ... savior?

He offered his arm. Only when she took it did the emptiness relinquish its hold.

"Is that 'no' to the Elysian Fields then?" he asked.

"There are other options, right?"

"None of them very pleasant."

"Truly?" She tapped her forehead. "Isn't it all up here?"

"What do you think?"

He led her down one of the endless hallways, the path worn smooth by the soles of so many souls.

"We make our own hell," she said. When he didn't respond, she prompted, "Am I right?"

"Hm? I can't really say. Trade secret and all."

"You can't? Or you won't?" Her words were full of skepticism and humor. She knew. Of course, she knew. Then her voice softened, and she added, "What's your hell then?"

He nearly glanced behind him, at the renewed frenzy on the dance floor, the golds and the blues and the greens. But no one knew the cost of looking back better than Hades did. So he focused on the images that consumed his little saint, the ones that formed the walls of her own personal hell.

He expected cordite and flames, but they only seasoned the anguish.

No, it was the expanse, the emptiness, the loneliness—of backs turned, hands never offered, promises never kept.

"It won't be like that," was all he said.

"How long do I have?" she asked.

"An eternity, if you wish it."

Their footfalls echoed behind them, obliterating sounds that haunted them both—the thump of the bass, the clink of crystal, the rapport of weapons, the thunder of artillery.

"But only if you wish it."

Midnight at the Hades Underground was an exclusive story for The (Love) Stories for 2020 project.

THE SAINT OF BRIGHT RED THINGS

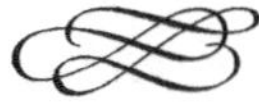

HISTORICAL, WWII

The sharpness that stabbed her lungs each time she pulled a breath did not scare Mari. The spike of pain in her temple was of little consequence. No, it was the clean sheets against her skin, the pillow that cradled her head, and the soft prayers of the Sisters that frightened her the most.

The last thing she remembered was the screech of the train. The last thing she saw was a spider web of cracked window glass splattered with brilliant red. After that, blue sky, crushed grass beneath her, stones stabbing her spine. Her purse, the straps looped through one arm. The tug when she refused to give it up. The last thing she heard were those orders barked in German.

The last thing she said?

Oh, God, not in English. Please, not in English. The panic sliced through the fog clouding her mind, but the clarity didn't last. A new bank rolled in, doubt married to fear—and pain. The spike of it radiated across her skull, down her neck.

Even so, sounds penetrated. A rattling cart. Consoling murmurs. The gentle whisk of fabric against the floor.

With deep reluctance, Mari cracked open her eyes. The light assaulted her, the stab of it like something solid, something she could swallow, something that would choke her. She took quick, shallow breaths, and spread her arms until her fingertips reached each side of the bed, searching, searching. Her forearm felt naked without the purse's straps. She came away with nothing but the clean edge of the sheets. Under, then? Or on a side table? Check everywhere. Oh, but that meant moving.

"You're awake." The nun wasn't much older than she was, with hazel eyes and freckles far too frivolous for the somber wimple. "Would you like some water?"

The sister helped her sit. It was all Mari could do not to cry out when the water flooded her mouth, soothed her throat. Had she screamed when the train jumped the tracks? Her throat was raw enough for it.

"Better?" the nun asked.

Again, she nodded.

"Where am I?" The words came rough as if she hadn't spoken for days.

"You're in hospital." The nun murmured the name of the town—somewhere between Paris and Blois.

"What happened?"

"You should ask..." The nun glanced toward the entrance to the ward. She didn't elaborate. She didn't need to.

There, in shadows, stood a man. Even from this distance he was obviously German, and from his bearing, obviously an officer. Mari licked her lips, swallowed back the bile in her throat, and reached once again for the water.

The man's footfalls echoed against the floor. A hush fell over the space, as if they all held their breaths for the length of his stroll down the center of the ward. The sister turned and busied herself with the cart of medication, the wings of her wimple hiding her face.

He halted at the foot of the bed with a single click of his heels and an almost gracious bow. "Fraulein."

She nodded, squinted against the light, his form blurry.

"I am Major Messner," he said.

She blinked. Was he the local commander, then? That would account for the hush, that collective intake of breath. Still, was he better or worse than the Gestapo? Better, certainly, although much depended upon what sort of man Major Messner was.

"I was hoping you could assist us."

One who spoke passable French, at least.

"You were in a train wreck. The tracks were sabotaged," he continued. "We are hoping those passengers riding on the west side might be able to ... provide us with information."

Images came flooding back. That spider web in red. Her purse clutched tight, even when the jolt threw her into the window. Had she been traveling north or south? This, she couldn't remember. The uncertainty of that simmered in her belly like slow-acting poison.

"Do you remember anything, Fraulein?" the Major prompted. "Anything at all? Perhaps you were glancing out the window and saw something ... someone?"

"I remember very little," she said. This, blessedly, was true. Her words, however, betrayed the state of her throat. She reached a hand for the water glass only to find him plucking it from the side table and bringing it to her lips.

"*Merci*," she managed.

"Let's start with something easier, shall we? Where were you headed?"

The uncertainty returned, panic gripping her mind, rendering her mute. North or South? Which was it? Sweat bloomed along her limbs, the thin blanket and cool sheets suddenly stifling. Where she was headed depended so much on who she was. The name on her papers would tell her, and those would be in her purse.

She was ... who then? Marguerite, the dancer? (Bless her mother's insistence on ballet lessons.) No. Too flashy. Marguerite would never leave Paris for ... she eyed the small ward ... wherever here was. Too provincial. Françoise, the shop girl? Yes! She was little Françoise, almost certainly.

Mari hadn't been herself, hadn't been Marigold Jenkins since her mother planted a perfumed kiss on her cheek and fled Paris for the endless blue skies and palm trees of Hollywood, her father in tow. And then, of course, the Nazis came.

"I was returning to Paris after visiting my mother in the countryside," she said, as if her mother would ever live in the countryside in any nation. "She's ... not well."

"Returning?" The major cocked an eyebrow. A single word filled with doubt. A single gesture a death sentence.

But she was Françoise, a silly bit of fluff. Despite the ache, Mari tilted her head, trained her eyes on him, and in all innocence asked, "Was I going, Major?"

His jaw twitched. It was enough of a lifeline for her to continue.

"Truthfully, Major, I think only my throat remembers what happened." She let her fingertips light on her neck.

"Understandable."

Was it? And would this German officer understand when she provided no information, real or fabricated?

"I will return when you're able to talk."

Before he turned to leave, Mari called out, "Major Messner?"

He inclined his head, unfailingly polite. He was, she realized, not as young as she first assumed, his hair shined silver rather than gold, and the lines around his eyes and mouth spoke of a man who had seen a certain share of life before the war.

"My purse. I don't suppose." She glanced away, down at her hands folded demurely on the blanket. "It's a ... never mind."

To her surprise, he took a knee at her bedside. "Go on."

"It's only." And here, she peered up from beneath her lashes. "My lipstick, and compact." Mari touched her cheek. "I only wanted ... but it's not important."

Major Messner laughed, the sound indulgent. "You shall have your purse, Fraulein. I shall see to it personally."

"*Merci.*" *And thank you, Françoise, you silly, vain cow.*

His footsteps echoed again on his walk up the ward. When he cleared the door, it was if everyone took their first breath in fifteen minutes. Mari's heart thudded. Was her request bold or merely reckless? How closely would they inspect her purse before turning it over to her?

The nun returned with a pitcher of water. Under the cover of refilling Mari's glass, she spoke.

"I should tell you, Mademoiselle, that Major Messner likes to ... cultivate pretty brunettes."

Mari raised her chin. Her hair, although tangled, looked nearly black against the white of her pillow.

"Despite this." The nun's fingers lighted on Mari's temple. "And this." They moved to her cheek. "You are very pretty indeed."

"Is that a warning, Sister?"

"No." The woman turned from her. "But it may be your salvation."

~

MAJOR MESSNER WAS a man who kept his promises, or at least ones made to pretty brunettes. The next morning, the purse was resting on the side table, its red crocodile skin far too brash for the hushed atmosphere of the ward.

Henri hated the purse, always said it called too much attention to her. What he meant was Nazi attention, in particular the sort of Nazi officer who cultivated pretty girls.

"We must fade into the background, one of a thousand Parisians made drab by the war. We do not want their attention." Henri said this with the authority of a father figure and then continued with the persuasiveness of a lover. "*You* do not want their attention. You do not want to be thought a collaborator."

"But I am frivolous," Mari had argued, "either as Marguerite or Françoise. It marks me as a fool, not a collaborator."

The purse was like a broadcast signal. It told the world, or at least, those here in France, that she was not a threat. She was silly and thoughtless and spent money she didn't have for things she didn't need. After last month's successful run, even Henri had agreed. Mari was their best courier.

Now she reached a hand for her purse, her salvation. Inside, she encountered her papers. The air pent up in her lungs seeped out. No whoosh of breath. No obvious relief. But yes, she was Françoise.

She rummaged until her fingers encountered her compact and lipstick tube. The little brush was missing. No matter. She could dab some on, lightly, with her ring finger. To have him fetch her makeup and then not use it would invite folly, indeed. What she didn't use on her lips, she could smear on her cheeks, give herself a schoolgirl blush.

Something told her that Major Messner would like that.

Mari ran her fingertips around the compact. Aside from her mother, only she knew of the false bottom. Not even Henri knew. She eased it open just enough to slip her pinky inside, to check to see if the contents were there.

They were. The slip of paper. With codes. Always a dangerous thing.

Possibly the most dangerous thing of all. But necessary. And in this case, small. She could chew up the evidence and wash it down with the half glass of water that sat on the table.

Mari felt herself sink into the bed, her pillow soft beneath her head. She was safe. They all were safe. All she needed to do was slip the paper from the compact and send it down her throat. Her fingers inched toward the paper when a single thought froze her.

A trap.

What if the Major had found the list? What if her purse, delivered so promptly, was bait? What if they were waiting to see what she would do, whether she was working for the resistance or was merely an empty-headed shop girl?

Leave the list in place or slip it out?

She eased the false bottom closed—for now—and opened the compact. A tiny yelp emerged from her throat. Oh, she wouldn't need any additional color from the lipstick—she had far too much of it already, in ugly purples blooming across her cheek. Both eyes looked bruised. Her lips were uncommonly red, and she couldn't account for it. Applying makeup to a face in such condition seemed nearly as foolish as keeping that slip of paper hidden.

She closed the compact without making a sound. Then she clutched it and the lipstick against her chest. It was like keeping a vigil.

Hold very still. Be very quiet. Act the part of the shop girl, so happy to have her things back. Stay alert. Do not sleep. Above all, do not sleep.

Only when the footsteps taken with military precision stopped at the end of her bed did she realize that she had succumbed to sleep, lipstick and compact loose in her grip.

Her hand convulsed around the compact. It was an instinctive move that Mari hoped the Major didn't see. His gaze darted to her clenched hand and then met her eyes. This man missed very little.

"I didn't mean to startle you, Fraulein."

"No, I ... I merely dozed off."

"The sisters said your head injury might make you sleepy."

Did they? She supposed they had. Certainly that wasn't a lie. And yet.

The information, or perhaps the way it was phrased felt ... dishonest. How many patients escaped interrogation due to sleepiness? Perhaps the sisters added something to the soup served earlier. Had it tasted odd? Mari blinked, trying to bring Major Messner into focus.

"I also made the mistake of looking into the mirror," she said, for it sounded like something Françoise might confess.

"The bruises will heal." He turned then, nodded at the nun attending the ward.

She rushed over with a straight-back chair and placed it next to Mari's bed.

"Thank you, Sister." He gave the perfunctory bow. So polite. So civilized. So deceptive. How could a nation of so unerringly correct individuals be so brutal as well?

The Major sat, arms resting on his thighs, hands clasped. He leaned forward. "The bruises will heal," he said, again, this time his voice softer, as if the words he used might heal her face. "There won't be any lasting damage, except, perhaps to your memory."

"My memory, Major?"

"Of the accident. The doctor mentioned that head trauma can cause memory lapses, especially of the event itself."

"I remember blood—I think it was blood. It was red." Mari fingered the lipstick. "But then, so is my lipstick. And I remember hearing German, but that must have been after."

Yes, after," he echoed. "Those are ... good details, good things to remember."

Were they? What was this man about and what did he want from her, other than—to quote the sister—cultivate her?

"Your compact is quite intricate," he said.

"It was my mother's." A truth among all the lies. Also something a shop girl like Françoise might not own. Or she might. With the war, one never knew, did they?

"I'm afraid my lipstick won't last, at least not until..."

Until what, Mari, you fool? The end of the war? Yes, the perfect topic of conversation when speaking to a German officer.

"May I?" He held out his hand.

Mari unclenched her fingers, a slow unfurling that she hoped looked more like pain than reluctance. She passed him the tube—a precious commodity, that. He inspected it with clinical detachment.

"It should last," he said. "If you're frugal."

"How frugal will I have to be, Major?"

"That depends," he said. "I am not the only official interested in the train accident." His gaze flickered toward the door and the presence that shadowed the entrance. Plain clothes, not military. Gestapo then?

"You might want to use your compact, freshen up before they speak with you." He stood and turned his back as if to give her privacy for the task.

A trap or her salvation? And if she took that salvation, what was the cost? The shadows at the threshold stirred. She slipped the list from the false bottom, tore it once, twice, then shoved the pieces into her mouth. The paper was thin, like onionskin, but stuck everywhere—her molars, the roof of her mouth, against her tongue.

The sound that emerged from her throat was muted, barely a cough, but the Major handed her a glass of water. She washed away the list of codes, and he took the glass from her hand with one last bit of advice.

"Remember those good details, Fraulein."

~

It wasn't the first time silly Françoise had attracted the attention of the Gestapo. It was, however, the first time they asked her about one of their own.

"How well do you know Major Messner, Fraulein?"

"How ... well?" Mari scrunched up her forehead, as if terminally confused by the man's question. His gaunt face reminded her of a cadaver. The war had not been kind to him. She guessed that peace, when it arrived, would be less kind.

Her whole body trembled. But then, she reasoned, little Françoise would also tremble if confronted by the Gestapo.

"He ... asked me about the train accident, what I remembered. Then he brought me my purse." She displayed the compact and the lipstick in outstretched hands almost like making an offering.

"Yes," the man said. He cast the items a disdainful look, but—opinion aside—swept them up and passed them to his partner. "We need them for our own investigation. This as well." He caught up her purse and passed that along as well.

"So you've never met the Major before?"

"I don't meet many Germans, only those that come into the shop, and then only Monsieur Reime deals with them because..." She glanced away, eyes downcast.

"Because why, Fraulein?"

She shook her head. "I'm not supposed to know."

The man leaned forward. "Indeed. And why is that?"

Mari bit her lip. She cast a look at the nun who stood several feet away. In a flash of inspiration, she crossed herself. She pushed forward, and if on cue, the Gestapo agent leaned ever closer.

"*Préservatifs.*" She hid her face in her hands, peering at the men through a v in her fingers. Yes, silly Françoise barely knew what a condom was, never mind having cause to use one. "They ... trade in *Préservatifs.*"

The man's lips twitched, ever so slightly. His partner looked away, and she had the distinct impression he was laughing.

"Of course, Fraulein," the man said. "You ... shouldn't know of such things."

She regurgitated her good details. *I remember seeing red—like my lipstick. It's red, too. And hearing German. But that was after. You must have brought everyone here, to the hospital. That was kind of you.*

"Yes, Fraulein, we brought everyone here," the man said. He stood. "I will still need to take your things."

She nodded.

"But you have been most helpful."

She saw the look he gave his partner, a barely contained roll of the eyes for the silly French cow who had nothing on her mind but her bright red purse and lipstick.

Only when they cleared the door did she dare exhale and shut her eyes. And only when the lights were dimmed for the night did she allow herself to cry.

~

HE WAS WAITING for her when she left the hospital.

Mari walked the cobblestone path with care, oddly out of balance without her purse. Yes, the Gestapo had kept that, and her mother's compact, and the bright red lipstick. They were no doubt in the hands of some other silly French cow or perhaps a German one. What a prize all three items would make.

The spoils of war.

Major Messner clicked his heels and gave her that slight bow. "You look well, Fraulein. Your bruises are healing."

She touched her cheek. "Yes. They are."

"I have something for you."

What could that be? When he didn't move, she knew it was her job, as the civilian, the lesser in this relationship, to step closer. So she did. Honestly, hadn't she taken that step already, back in the hospital?

"Your hand," he said.

She held it out. A moment later, the tube of bright red lipstick fell into her palm.

"I couldn't retrieve your purse or the compact. Beautiful item. Lovely craftsmanship. Was it really your mother's?"

"It was," she admitted.

"For that, I am sorry."

She let her fingers curl around the lipstick tube.

"I made the convincing case that I wanted to embark on my own little affair." He spoke these words not to her, but just past her shoulder, as if absorbed in the sight of the road behind her. Mari nearly turned to see what had captured his attention, but knew she'd discern nothing.

"You might say my ... proclivities are well known." Now he looked at her. "Returning your lipstick would *clinch the deal*, as you Americans might say."

Her heart lurched. Her vision tunneled to a single bright point. She stumbled, an ankle twisting beneath her weight. He caught her arm, steadied her.

"It's all right," he whispered.

Was it? How could it be? Her mouth dry, she stared up at him, his eyes shaded by the brim of his uniform hat.

"What gave me away?" she whispered.

"Nothing you need worry about."

She exhaled a jagged rasp.

"Well, truthfully, your accent."

She'd spoken French as a toddler. Henri always said she had a charming way with words. As Marguerite, she could croon, smoky and seductive.

"You sound like her, a distinct American twang."

Had that one summer at her grandmother's—roasting beneath the relentless Savannah sun—betrayed her?

"As I said," he continued, "nothing you should worry about. I might be the only man in the Reich who might recognize such a thing."

"Her?" she ventured.

He pressed his lips together, something like a sigh escaping him. "Her name was Rachel. Her father was an American, from Texas, I believe."

That would account for the twang.

"Her mother was French." He paused, considered the road behind Mari again. "And a Jew. And Rachel?" He shut his eyes for an instant. "She was stubborn. Even so, I could have saved her."

Mari nodded, the love affair playing out before her eyes. A young German officer and a Jewess? Yes, that was destined to end badly.

"I chose not to."

"Would she see it that way?"

His laugh was short and bitter. "I suspect that, if she could, she would ask me that very same thing."

"What do you want from me?"

It was a bold question, here under the linden trees. Their leaves rattled as if they disapproved of that boldness, of the thought that had entered her head. Would she let this man, this German, this Nazi cultivate her?

Yes. Yes, she would.

"Do you pray, Fraulein?"

"Pray?"

He nodded toward the church at the end of the street. Her mother had worshiped at the altar of Diaghilev and the Ballet Russe, and then later, vodka. Her father paid homage to simile and metaphor, not that Hollywood appreciated either. Mari herself had no faith, unless it was the belief her lipstick would last until the end of the war.

"Do you want me to pray for you, Major Messner?"

"I want you to pray for a quick end to this war."

"What will you do then?"

He stared past her again, his eyes ever alert. Slight movement caught her attention. His hand. His sidearm.

"Then I will pray for your soul," she said

"Don't waste your prayers on things that don't exist."

The rumble of an automobile caught her up short. The momentary flicker of panic in his eyes shot fear through her. A Citroën rumbled past, sleek and black, its pace slowing to a crawl, the sun glinting off the double chevrons of its grill. The Major leaned in, clutched her chin with a finger and thumb.

"You are so very much like her that I am nearly tempted," he said a moment before he kissed her.

The car sped up.

In the quiet, he released her. He nodded once, bowed, and Mari took uncertain steps down the lane and toward the church. Her heels clicked, the leaves rattled, and the far off sound of a car backfiring—or of a gunshot—echoed.

The church was cool and dark. Mari covered her head, crossed herself, and collapsed into a pew. She stayed for hours. She thought he might come for her.

He didn't.

The weight of something, his soul perhaps, drove her to her knees. She knelt, forehead on clasped hands, and prayed to the saint of bright red things—of lipstick and handbags and filigrees of blood in cracked windows. It was far easier than praying for those things that didn't exist —a French shop girl named Françoise, a Jewess named Rachel, a German officer named Major Messner.

And a lone American named Marigold Jenkins.

The Saint of Bright Red Things was first published in The Binge-Watching Cure.

LETTERS OF SMOKE AND ASH

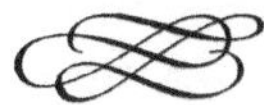

PARANORMAL

Madam,
I have no idea how your missives have found their way among my papers. And yet, here they are, scrawled notes filled with rambling angst more suited to a twelve-year-old than a grown woman. (I'm assuming that you are both grown and a woman; there's no need to correct me if I'm in error.)

Whatever sorcery this is, I ask you: <u>please cease</u>. I have actual correspondence to attend to.
Alistair Payne

P.S. After reading your missives, I encourage you, for the love of all that's holy, to find some sort of therapy.

Sir,
I have no idea who you are or how you're reading my private words. Or, for that matter, after realizing that, yes, they are private, that you continue to do so.

There is no such thing as sorcery, and this prank isn't funny. <u>You're</u> not funny. You're cruel.

Not that it's any of your business, but my "missives" as you call them are part of my therapy. I'm supposed to burn them, but I can't stand the smell of smoke, so I tuck them away into this box. I don't read them. No one else should either.
Lacey Grant

Ms. Grant,
I assure you, there is such a thing as sorcery. Those of us who practice the craft are always on the lookout for those who wield it as well.

I suspected you as one of those. Indeed, I still do, since—yet again—several missives, along with your note, have found their way into my correspondence box. This annoys and vexes me. I only wish to know why, every time I lift the lid, I find yet another scrap from you.

Perhaps if you stopped writing, things would right themselves.
Alistair Payne

Mr. Payne,
You are aptly named. But you know what? I'm not going to stop writing my "missives" or using this box simply because it inconveniences you.

I don't care where my journal entries go or what you do with them. Crumple them up or take pleasure in burning them. Toss them in the recycling. It's a relief to open the lid and not see them in here.
Lacey Grant

Ms. Grant,
I take no pleasure in burning.

Mr. Payne,
Then we have that in common.

❧

Dear Ms. Grant,
It's been a few weeks now, and I wonder if you've found a new way to …

deal with your journal entries. At first, I was relieved not to see them among my correspondence each and every time I lifted the lid.

Then I started to worry. It's evident that you're hurting. It's also apparent that you have a keen and vibrant mind.
To be honest, I miss them. There's a good deal of sass among all that pain.

If you wish to continue your therapy, by all means, do so. I won't even respond if you don't wish me to. Nor will I read what you have written. I'll simply tuck the "missives" to one side and let them be.

Regards,
Alistair Payne

Dear Mr. Payne,
Did you just call me sassy?
Lacey Grant

Dear Ms. Grant,
I believe I referred to your words and thoughts as "having sass," but I suspect the adjective applies to the writer as well. I don't mean that in a trivial sense.

You're confronting your pain, and that's no small feat. Take it from a man who has had many decades of practice in avoiding his own.

Regards,
Alistair

Dear Mr. Payne,
You could write missives of your own, you know, if you were looking to get rid of that pain.
Lacey

Dear Ms. Grant,
And relinquish my name? I think not.

Alistair

Dear Alistair,
For the first time in a very long time, I laughed. <u>You</u> made me laugh.

Thank you,
Lacey

Dear Lacey,
I wish I'd been there to hear your laughter. I'm certain it's filled with a certain amount of—dare I say it—sass.

I've noticed a lack of journal entries. If that part of your therapy is over and you've moved on, then I congratulate you. If you're avoiding it for any other reason, please continue. I meant what I said. I won't read them.

Your private words will remain that way. You have my promise.

Regards,
Alistair

Dear Alistair,
No, I'm still supposed to write my journal entries. I haven't been because I don't want to put them in the box. I don't want to burden you with them. These thin sheets of paper feel so heavy to me.

Most of all, I'd rather see your notes. I would rather keep writing to you. I'm tired of my journal entries. I'm tired of all the things that end up in them. I'm tired of writing to an uncaring universe. I'd rather write to a person.

I'd rather write to you.

But I doubt you want that.
Lacey

My dear Lacey,
I am a man who owns a box whose sole purpose is to hold correspondence. What makes you think I don't want to receive your letters?

You're right in one respect: the universe does not care. This isn't to say it's deliberately cruel. When you're as vast as the universe is, you can't play favorites. You set things in motion and then let them be.

Sometimes that is for the best; often, it is not.

You could continue your therapy in our letters if you so choose. I understand that you served in the military. To be frank, I've not kept up with the recent wars. I've seen too many and fought in several that few have heard of, never mind remember.

I understand the wasteland of the aftermath, how something can be vast and empty and claustrophobic all at once. I know what it's like to burn and be burned. I've surveyed that wasteland and have been left wondering what it was all for.

Certainly, we had a reason for our destruction. In the end, it's sometimes impossible to find that reason.

But we do not need to talk about such matters. We can do those mundane but delightful things correspondents do, such as provide advice and swap recipes. For instance, as of late, I have come into a surplus of figs. Regretfully, I have no idea what to do with them.

Yours truly,
Alistair

Oh, Alistair,
How many wars have you fought in? Honestly, I'm not sure I understand who—or what—you are. You mentioned sorcery. Are you a wizard? Are you very old? I would feel foolish asking you these questions except that some sort of magic must be involved. There's no other way that my notes find you and yours reach me.

I remember many things about my time in the military, about the war, but none of them make sense. I can't form them into a narrative, either in my head or on paper. This is why part of my therapy is writing things down. Things are trapped, locked away in my mind. If I can coax them out, expose them to sunlight, perhaps they will ... not go away. None of this will ever go away.

Perhaps I won't feel so fractured. Perhaps, with time, I can stitch the pieces of myself back together again.

But I'd rather ponder your fig dilemma. I'm including a recipe for a chocolate and fig tart. I've never tried it, but I found it on the internet, and it sounds delicious.

Yours truly,
Lacey

Dear Lacey,
Ah, I must get myself an internet one of these days. At one time, in what seems like an eon ago, I was what they refer to as a lead adopter (I believe that's the term).

I am more of a Luddite these days, although I have no desire to destroy machinery. Neither do I eschew technology. I fancy myself a bit of a kitchen witch, and the gadgets these days have made prep time a joy rather than a chore.

So, there, I've answered one of your questions. I am a witch. Women and men can be witches, and where, when, and how this wizard distinction came about, I can't say. (I imagine that's one of the many things an internet might tell me.)

In mortal terms, I am ancient. In witch terms, I am in my prime, such as it is. Witches have a lifespan that can stretch across the ages.

I have lost so many friends already. Mortals burst into one's life, bright as a flame, only to be doused just as quickly. You all live such short, hard, beautiful lives, but after a while, the pain of saying goodbye becomes too much. Perhaps this was why I was a bit brusque with you in our initial exchanges.

Witches turn to other things, hobbyhorses, and perfecting the art of the curmudgeon. They bake twenty chocolate and fig tarts for the elementary school silent auction and then slip away before anyone can thank them. Because they know that they'll outlive every single kindergartener who wanders past their table.

It's why they ... I ... enjoy exchanging letters and notes. Words remain even when the friends do not.

I suspect some sort of sorcery connects my correspondence box with yours. Perhaps they were fashioned from the heart of the same tree. Two halves of a whole, if you will.

Yours,
Alistair

Oh, my dear Alistair,
Yes, I think I understand. It's easier to push people away. It was always easier to keep new arrivals in our unit at a distance. Not to be mean or cruel, but as a way to protect yourself.

Because when we went out, there was a chance—a good chance—we wouldn't all come back. There was a chance some of us would come back in pieces, physically, emotionally. When you've been broken, I'm not sure it matters which pieces are flesh and blood and which ones are merely in your head.

I know so many people who think they want to live forever. Isn't that the goal? Immortality? I can't imagine what it would be like to lose everyone you love again, and again, and then again.

I think you might end up shattered. I hope you're not shattered, dear Alistair.
Lacey

My dearest Lacey,
You are too kind, and I should not burden you with such things as my longevity. I assure you, witches come equip with coping mechanisms. I've mentioned my fondness for kitchen witchery. Truly, I have stepped into my kitchen at Thanksgiving and not emerged until the spring equinox.

Some spells and concoctions take time and patience. I can put something to simmer over the fire and then settle into the rocking chair I keep next to the hearth. I read and, of course, write to my heart's content—for days or even weeks.

We have companionship in the form of familiars. These souls come back to us time and time again as different creatures: a cat one decade, an owl the next, and so on. It's delightful to discover an old friend in a new physique.

Truly, if a witch is wise, he or she realizes that it's not the quantity of friendship, but the quality.

Your friend,
Alistair

Dear Alistair,
I think I would like that sort of life, one where I could put a pot on to simmer and then curl up and maybe read or write or knit.

I'm learning how to knit, although I'm not very good at it. All I can make are square potholders. Honestly, not a single one has come out as an actual square. Can I make you one? You'll have to tell me where to send it. I'm not sure it's something a correspondence box can deliver.

Does it bother you to sit by the fire, since it burns? Last week, my veterans' support group went on a hayride that ended in a bonfire. The hay made me sneeze, but I didn't mind too much. The fire was beautiful and awful.

I found I couldn't get close to it. I knew it couldn't hurt me. Well, I knew that in my head. My body had other ideas. The fire, the burning—it's what I remember most about the attack where I was injured. I never went back. After my wounds healed, I was discharged from the Army. I've been ... had been ... a soldier since I was eighteen. Some days, I don't know how to be anything else.

I stared and stared and stared until the fire died down, and a couple of the farmworkers doused the flames with water.

In the smoke and ashes, I swear I saw something. It sounds crazy, but it looked like figures, people rising into the air and then coming apart. And yes, I know detecting patterns is something humans do—seeing the Virgin Mary in a piece of toast and all that.

Still, I would swear these figures were real.

Even crazier, I stayed because I thought those people needed someone to watch them go.

I shouldn't even place this letter into the box except that witnessing those things made me feel ... not better, but helpful, perhaps, purposeful. That maybe there's something else I can do in this world besides soldiering.

Between that and writing to you, I feel more like myself.

Your friend,
Lacey

Oh, my dearest Lacey,
Indeed, there must be a bit of magic about you, a power that goes

beyond our twin correspondence boxes. I can't say for certain what you saw. Depending on where you were, the possibilities are endless.

Undoubtedly, the souls of the trees burning were among the figures you saw. Invariably, they appear old and wise (most trees are, but some are simply stubborn and foolhardy).
As for the rest, well, the ground on where the fire burned determines that. What you saw was likely the aftereffects of past events, an echo of something that occurred. Those souls wanted a witness. You honored them by giving them that.

I, too, have a complicated relationship with fire. I still maintain a fire in my hearth. Some spells demand flame and cast iron and will not abide ceramic-coated cookware and the electric stove. In the winter, a fire is lovely and warm.

And yet.

I hesitate to tell you this, as I do not wish to cause you any additional pain. It is all in the past for me.

I have thrice been burned at the stake.

In theory, anyway.

In practice? Witches don't burn; mortals do. So often—too often—a friend of mine had been caught up in the same net that snagged me. Or, far more likely, snagged because of me.

I can change my form in such cases as this, appear as nothing more than smoke and ash.
I can—and could—do nothing to save my mortal friends.
Perhaps it is this that makes me so reluctant to make new ones.

Fire is such a necessary, destructive thing, but there are times when I wish I could simply do without it.
Alistair

P.S. A kitchen witch is always on the lookout for new potholders. No, I don't think the correspondence box works that way, but give it a try. Who knows what sort of magic it wields.

Dear Lacey,
I'm not certain what has happened. I'm not certain this letter will reach you. Today when I opened my correspondence box, a thin stream of smoke rose from the interior. Instead of a note, ash greeted me, fine as silt, smelling charred and damp.

I don't know what to make of this. Was it our talk of fire and smoke? Certainly, a hand-knitted potholder couldn't wreak such damage.

Did something terrible happen? I worry that our exchanges took a turn toward darker thoughts and feelings. Perhaps that was not for the best. Perhaps I'm at fault here.

If you can, please respond and let me know how you are.

Your friend,
Alistair

Oh, my dear Lacey,
I have done it this time, haven't I? Nothing remains of our correspondence except my last (presumably) unread letter to you. I was tempted to break the promise I made to not read your journal entries. But those, too, have turned to ash.

If this is of your own doing, if you wish to break off our correspondence, I will honor that. I beg of you, however, to jot a single line to that effect. Let me know you're alive, that you've moved on.

I will wish you well and shower you with all my blessings.
Alistair

Dear Lacey,
A wise man once told me:

This is how the world burns, my friend. Not all at once, but one human heart at a time.

He meant it as a warning, I believe. I had—and perhaps still do have—the propensity to rush into things, in witch terms at least. Friendships, relationships, new-fangled kitchen gadgets. Once, so very long ago, I even had a mortal family of my own.

Today I feel my heart burn. I miss you, dear friend.
Alistair

Dear Lacey,
Today I ventured from my cottage and took a trip to the library. There, I asked a reference librarian for assistance in using the internet they have for patrons.

Awkwardness ensued. I simply cannot keep up with human fashions. I have a few spells that maintain the clothes I do own in pristine condition. I purchase a new coat once every hundred years or so. I might upgrade if something catches my eyes. (Of late, I must admit, nothing has.)

Given all that, even on my best days, I appear eccentric. I dressed up today, thinking it would help my case. I suspect that this, too, was a miscalculation.

The conversation with the young gentleman went something like this:

Librarian: What else can you tell me about your friend?
Me: She was in the military.
Librarian: That's a start. How old is she?
Me: I haven't the foggiest.
Librarian: Where does she live?
Me: If I knew that, I wouldn't be here, requesting your help, would I?

Librarian: You said you were pen pals.

Well, yes, I had said that. It seemed reasonable enough at the time.

Me: She's in the military and recently moved.

Yes, a lie, and not a very good one. Honestly, I'm in such a state, and I didn't think any of this through.

Librarian: In that case, maybe it's better if you let her get in touch with you.

Wariness and pity warred across his face. His voice? The sort you'd use when trying to appease a willful child or someone slightly disreputable.

The obvious struck me then. I admit that I often miss the obvious. I think of myself as a witch first, and as a man second, or even third. Yet, there I was, an oddly dressed older man seeking out someone who is most likely a young woman.

I left right as he signaled his supervisor, a woman with hair the color of steel and a demeanor to match.

Perhaps the next step is getting an internet of my own. Perhaps I should venture from my cottage more often. I take the local paper, but I don't know where you live. If you are halfway across the country or the world, I might never know what's become of you.

Or perhaps I will take that young man's advice.

Maybe it's better if I let you get in touch with me if you can, if you still want to.

I will place this letter in my correspondence box and then wander into my kitchen to conjure up a spell of blessing for you.

It's been an honor and a pleasure knowing you.

Be well, my friend.
Alistair

～

Dear Alistair,
I emailed the link to the article about your tarts. Click on it, and when it appears in your browser, click the little star. That will make it a favorite, and you can return to the article any time you want.

Thank you again for the lovely new correspondence box. I still have no idea how you conjured one so quickly (and yes, I suspect you actually did conjure it).

I know my apartment house won't burn down again. Two fires are enough for any lifetime. Then I remember how you've been burned three times already. Maybe fire doesn't keep count. From now on, I will store my correspondence box next to my bed in case of an emergency. There's not much else I would want to save.

A wise man once told me:

Words remain even when the friends do not.

I'm going to put this note in the box now. I'm still not convinced it will work.

Your friend,
Lacey

My dear, dear Lacey,
Of course, it worked. I recall mentioning that you had a bit of magic about you. And oh, look! Here is your note, and now, my response.

Thank you for helping me obtain an internet of my own. I imagine I was a poor and exasperating student. Your patience knows no bounds.

Yes, I have read the article numerous times. And yes, I am that vain, but mostly I'm flabbergasted.

Mysterious benefactor's tarts save art and music programs.

Between you and me? I may have woven in a spell (or two). As you can imagine, chocolate makes an excellent conduit for magic. Still, I had no idea the spell was potent enough to start a bidding war.

I'm also a bit flabbergasted that this article led you to me. I swear, I would've recognized you anyway, but arriving on my door stoop with a potholder was a nice touch, sassy even.

I won't say fire is sentient or that it latches onto individuals. Still, in my experience, it tends to favor those it has touched before. I will continue my blessing spell. Now that I've met you IRL, as the kids say (the kids do say that, don't they?), it will be all the more powerful.

Thank you again for being clever and sassy and for finding me.
Alistair

Dear Alistair,
Thank you for helping me find me.
Your friend,
Lacey

P.S. Yes, in some respects, you are still aptly named.

Letters of Smoke and Ash was an exclusive story for The (Love) Stories for 2020 project.

SEPTEMBER

September was filled with stories of dragons and trolls.

FIRE AND IVY

FANTASY

*I*vy Bremer stood at the edge of Merryside Township, shotgun in hand. Behind her, flags from the Fourth of July celebration fluttered. Pollen hung in the air, casting everything in a yellow glow.

Her arms ached from gripping the shotgun, her hip protesting the weight of the revolver strapped there. Both weapons were heirlooms, handed down from generation to generation until they sat in the town museum, displayed in shadow boxes, their purpose forgotten. That morning, Ivy had smashed the glass and freed them both.

Mayor was a thankless job—interim mayor even more so. It served her right for skipping that last city council meeting. Or maybe not. Maybe it was because she'd been standing in this very spot twelve months earlier. She'd seen him first. Either way, she was here now.

He was coming. The breeze shifted, lifting sticky strands of hair from her neck. A buzzing filled the morning, the sound like the drone of a prop airplane. Each approaching footfall shook the earth, a reverberation that traveled up her legs, captured her limbs and wrapped around her heart.

Ivy glanced behind her, at the town too quiet to be a real town, and caught the menacing shadow of the catapult. Silver pails glinted, and hoses coiled like snakes, strategically placed for the fire brigade.

As if that could stop the burning.

When had she known? Certainly not that first day, when she'd nearly drowned in the depths of those amber eyes, his gaze alight with the heat of flame behind it. Amber eyes! Why hadn't she thought to question that?

The breeze picked up. The footfalls remained ever steady, and the buzzing seemed to penetrate her eardrums. In the fields bordering the road, cornstalks quaked. To Ivy, it looked as though they trembled with fear.

When had she known? Not at that first city council meeting, when they unanimously voted him mayor. She'd only felt hopeful. Not when he'd taken her under his wing—how apt—a month later. She'd only felt protected. Not when he proposed. She'd only felt cherished.

Was it the record profits for every business in Merryside? The flood of scholarships for their graduating seniors, the grants to improve the schools, the roads, the infrastructure?

They'd basked in the bounty, never thinking of what it might cost.

So, when had she known?

After the warmest January on record?

Perhaps.

After surveying the charred remains of the winter wheat?

Definitely.

Now she stood at the edge of town, the only one who never took coin, the only one who gave, the only one who could stand there. She widened her stance. The shotgun, heavy as it was, reassured her. The revolver at her hip felt right, like she was born to wear it.

He would not pass.

A thin column of smoke rose from the horizon. His footfalls shook the ground so much that her knees buckled—certainly, that wasn't from fear. At first, all she saw was his head and the misty smoke issuing from his nostrils. The tip of his tail flicked into view. Had he been a dog—which, of course, he wasn't—Ivy would've said he was happy to see her.

Then all of him came into view. His bulk cast a shadow along the road, shading her from the sun long before he took his final step.

"Ivy." Her name from his mouth was both sulfurous and sensual. "Did the cowards send you to stop me?"

"I came on my own accord. I'm the mayor now."

A laugh burst forth, one filled with brimstone. "A thankless job, is it not?"

His scales glinted in the summer sun, throwing rainbows across her vision. His talons sunk into the ground rhythmically, as if he were a cat kneading its owner's lap. The claws churned up asphalt and dirt. Despite herself, Ivy calculated the repair costs and weighed them against the town's diminishing budget.

But his eyes. Those amber eyes. Those were the same. She recognized herself in their reflection.

"Do you bar me entrance?" he asked, the question issuing with a stream of smoke.

She hesitated for a mere fraction of a second. "I do."

He bowed his head as if in defeat. "Do you love me?"

This time, she spoke without the hint of a delay, her heart answering for her. "I do."

Something crackled then, like a fire coming to life. Behind her came a whisper of sand and the sound of bows being pulled taut. She held up a hand, and both sounds ceased.

"Then grant me entrance," he said, voice low, melodious, almost human. "Let me collect what's mine."

With deliberation, Ivy set the shotgun on the ground. She unbuckled the holster from around her waist and placed that next to the shotgun. She felt suddenly lighter without the weight of either, like she might step off into the air and float away.

Instead, she took a single step forward. Waves of heat washed over her skin. Her lungs struggled for oxygen, and sweat coursed down her spine.

"This is what's yours." She placed her hands on either side of his muzzle and kissed him.

The earth trembled. Ivy squeezed her eyes shut, but that didn't stop the single tear from slipping down her cheek. In an instant, the dry heat stole it away.

The sizzling started near his tail. It traveled along his spine, the scales falling away in ones and twos, and then faster, their clatter like rain on a tin roof. Then her world imploded in a cloud of acrid smoke.

The wind picked up again, chasing away the clouds of smoke and revealing a man crumpled on the road in front of her. There he was, that same dark-haired stranger who had strolled into town a year ago.

Ivy crouched next to him, eased her thigh beneath his head, cradled his face with her hands.

His eyes locked onto hers. "Why?"

"They would've harnessed you, used you—or killed you in the attempt."

"Or I, them. That's the way it is, the way it's always been."

"Not now. Not anymore." A tear wove a track through the grime on her cheek. "I had to stop this ... them, and I'm ... sorry."

He shut his eyes, bliss washing across his face. He had the look of a man finally free. "I'm not."

Another teardrop slipped from her cheek and hissed against his skin. His eyes—those amber eyes—flew open. He brought his fingertips to his mouth and then pressed them against her lips in a dry and dusty kiss.

"Goodbye, Ivy." He smiled at her. In it, she caught the feral glint of teeth and tender mouth that had so willingly kissed her own. "And thank you."

The fire that consumed him burned cold. The smoke was thick but sweet. One moment, his weight was solid against her thigh. The next, it was as light as the pollen in the air.

Then, he was gone.

All that remained was dust and ash. Something shimmered there among the specks of gray and black—a single scale. Ivy held it between her finger and thumb, turning it this way and that. Its surface shattered the light, threw a rainbow of color so bright it might blind. She let it rest in her palm before tucking the scale into her pocket.

Ivy stood. She didn't bother to strap on the holster. She simply pulled the revolver from it. A single shot incapacitated the catapult mechanism, its net hanging loose and now useless. With the shotgun on her shoulder, she marched into town.

No one said a word as she returned the weapons to the museum. They were heirlooms, certainly, with their own sort of magic. Ivy licked the dust from her lips and regarded the relics, locked away in their shadow boxes once again. With luck, that was where they'd stay.

After that, all she had to do was point. Without a word, children collected the buckets. The volunteer fire brigade rolled up the hoses.

Members of the city council dismantled the catapult, destroyed the arrows, filled in the trap.

Ivy surveyed the work. Behind her, the cornstalks whispered in the wind. On the breeze, she heard the echo of his promise.

I give you one year and one year only.

Everyone had wanted more, her heart included. She pulled the scale from her pocket, and it glinted in the sun. She held it aloft and let it cast a rainbow across the entire town of Merryside.

Everyone froze in place, like they had that first day a year ago. For a moment, her heart leaped; something that felt like hope filled her chest. Ivy glanced behind her, willing him to step into view.

What she saw instead, through that prism of light, was what could be—if they let it. That was its own sort of hope.

Ivy pocketed the scale. Decision made, she walked toward the town hall and the mayor's office. The breeze dried the last remaining tear on her cheek.

Yes, she thought.

She'd give it a year.

Fire and Ivy is another story exclusive to The (Love) Stories for 2020 project.

THE TROLL IN IT

PARANORMAL

I lean across the guard desk as the glimmer settles in the lobby. The whisper of it raises hairs on the back of my neck. The guards' faces relax in the muted glow.

All is quiet—except for some gentle snoring.

I stretch and switch off the cameras covering the loading dock and the ones in the stairwell. Then I catch a glimpse of myself at the guard desk. Yes, of course, it will be *my* face the police will scrutinize tomorrow morning.

Decorative plants cast shadows in the dim light, their leaves wavering in the breeze from the ventilation system. Chin lifted, I gauge the air. Now that the glimmer has fallen completely, I can taste the shadow creature that lives here. The space is full of that anticipation before a hunt and the promise of treasure at the end.

But is it a troll? I'm not convinced. I'm a damsel in distress, after all. I *know* trolls.

The sound of boots thudding pulls my attention to the large double doors that lead to the loading dock. One door creaks open as if the person on the other side doesn't trust that I've cut the feed to the cameras.

Granted, all four of them are shadow trackers, like I am. The five of us together?

Well, we have trust issues.

In the center of the lobby, I stand, hands on hips. The rest of the team emerges with painfully slow steps. I resist the urge to roll my eyes. The glimmer only lasts for so long. We don't have all night. Or rather, that's *all* we have.

This office building houses not only a software company but also a law firm and a yoga studio on the mezzanine. The moment the sun crests the horizon, and the glimmer lifts, someone is bursting through the front doors. I don't want to be around for that.

I tap a foot clad in a steel-toe boot and wait.

"All clear, Trombelle?" comes a voice from those double doors.

"Of course, it is." My sigh echoes in the quiet of the lobby.

The leader of this little expedition is Parker Pankhurst. He's a pain to deal with and has the bad habit of grabbing his share of the treasure and running. According to him, he's turned over a new leaf. These days, he specializes in ridding places of malignant shadow creatures (trolls would be among those) for both a fee and any treasure found in their lair.

As business models go, it's not a bad one.

"We don't have to bring you along," he says to me now.

That's the thing. They do. Nothing happens without a damsel in distress to lure a shadow creature from its lair. True, we often end up bound, ankles and wrists, eyebrows singed. But if a creature has no reason to leave its lair, it won't.

No unguarded lair? No treasure. It's that simple.

Trust me, nothing's venturing out for the likes of Parker Pankhurst.

"Stop being such a knave, Pankhurst." A new voice joins the conversation, this of Luke Milner.

In truth, the criticism is a bit harsh. Parker Pankhurst *is* a knave; he can't help his DNA the same way I can't.

The same way Luke Milner, knight in shining armor, can't.

It's who we are and why we're able to track the shadow creatures to begin with.

Pankhurst casts Luke a dour look before nodding to the stairwell. "Let's go," is all he says.

The IT department is on the third floor. Even so, I feel the climb in my thighs. I'm glad we're not trekking all the way up to the executive suites. Although maybe we should. I'm still not convinced there's a troll here.

On the other hand, a crafty sort of shadow creature—say, a dragon— would make its home on the top floor, where it would have a spectacular view, not to mention the run of the executive washrooms.

On the third floor, we emerge to a forest of cubicles. Pankhurst leads us through the rows, each turn taking us deeper into the maze. When we reach what looks like a collaboration area, he holds up a hand, and the rest of us halt.

"Here," he says. "Here's where we set the trap."

Yes, and I'm the bait.

"Do you sense a troll?" I whisper to Luke. Maybe my instincts are off, and I'm simply not detecting it.

"Not at all," he says.

"Then—?"

He shrugs. Luke is all angles and planes, chiseled good looks. Shrugging just makes him appear elegant.

"We should at least be able to smell it," he adds.

"Trombelle, over here." Pankhurst barks the order. Next to me, Luke bristles.

I comply since it puts me front and center, and I can make my case. Pankhurst takes me by the wrists and tugs me toward a whiteboard on wheels. He secures me to one of the supports before locking each wheel in place with a solid click.

"Do any of you smell a troll?" I say. "Because I don't smell a troll."

The other two in our party—a blacksmith and her apprentice— exchange glances.

"Trust me," Pankhurst says. "It's here."

"We should be able to smell it," I insist. "This place should reek."

And reek so badly that even when the sunrise banishes the glimmer, the stench would linger. Just how badly? Take a pair of old sneakers, simmer them in dog pee, and toss in a couple of rotten eggs for good measure. Inhale deeply and multiply that by a thousand.

That's a troll.

"I'll level with you." Pankhurst turns, addressing us all. "I got a tip from a reliable source. There's a troll. It's making its home back in the server rooms. That's where the rest of us are headed."

I'm less than reassured. Luke's mouth is a grim line. The blacksmith blinks a couple of times, shakes her head, and then secures her long black hair into a ponytail. Her apprentice looks bedraggled. They could probably use their portion of the treasure.

"You okay with this, Posey?" Luke's at my side, a hand on my bound wrists.

"I guess I have to be," I say. "It's what I do, right?"

He's wearing a pink bandana tied around his upper arm, my token from our first outing together. Since then, we've partnered a couple of times. Typically, knights in shining armor are all too little, too late.

Not Luke. If anything, he's *too* scrupulous.

"If things get ... bad, I'll double back and get you."

I nod, and as much as I want to trust Luke, I've heard this promise from other knights far too many times before.

"But just in case." He slips something cool and metallic into my hands and leaves me with a wink.

I'll grant you that winking is in the knight in shining armor skill set. Still, I'm pretty sure Luke must practice endlessly in front of a mirror.

They head off, through the maze of cubicles. I wonder if rather than a troll, there's a Minotaur hiding among all those twists and turns.

If so, we may all end up as a midnight snack.

ONLY WHEN THE scuffling of boots on carpet fades do I investigate the object in my hands. My thumbnail finds a metallic groove. There's just enough give in the ropes around my wrists that I can spring open the pocketknife.

The barest hints of the workaday world hang in the air—burnt microwave popcorn and room-temperature lattes all mixed with starch and sweat. At least this isn't *my* world. Sometimes it *is* better being a damsel in distress, the occasional singed eyebrows notwithstanding.

I get to work sawing my way through the rope. I don't dare cut all the way through. The troll—or whatever shadow creature is here—will know. Never mind that they can't tell steel-toed boots from dainty satin slippers or practical canvas pants from flowing gowns. They'll know the second I've cut the last thread of rope.

And if they know, they won't venture from their lair to investigate. Never mind no treasure, Luke and the others could end up as that midnight snack.

I can only imagine Parker Pankhurst's wrath if I botch this hunt—and what it might do to my standing in the tracker community, and Luke's as well. Not that I'd mention his part in this. Still, knaves have a way of finding things out.

So I saw at the rope and wait, saw and wait, holding my breath each time the knife slips in my fingers. When I notice the shift in the air, I can't say. The glimmer glows brighter, enough to make the whiteboard shimmer behind me. A clattering comes from several rows away. It's a light tap-tap-tap of a noise, almost joyful.

It's certainly not the sound of a troll dragging its knuckles across industrial-grade carpet.

My heart kicks up a notch. I scan the workstations, but nothing looks out of place—just endless rows of chairs and monitors. There's a rustling and then a decided chomp. All at once, something leaps from one cube to the next, clearing the five-foot-high wall with ease.

Then the creature—or whatever this thing is—bleats.

It sounds like it's laughing, or more precisely, laughing at me.

This is no troll.

I don't bother with the pocketknife. Instead, I yank my wrists apart and break the last threads of rope. I rub the tender, red marks around my wrists and consider my next move.

The bleating echoes down one of the many cubicle aisles.

I decide to follow.

THE TWISTS and turns are endless; truly, there can't be so many employees in this company. I suspect a combination of the glimmer and the shadow creature itself. This is an illusion meant to throw me off its tracks.

I creep past cube after cube, taking each opening with caution because there's always the chance that this creature is leading me into a trap.

In fact, I'd bet my share of the treasure that it is. Even so, I trail after it. Luke would advocate caution. I know he would. Again, blame my DNA. I'd rather run after a creature, get myself into a tight fix, take the chance that this time it won't end in a damsel-in-distress grab and dash.

I reach the end of a row and halt. The space in front of me is so dark and vast that it resembles the opening of a cave.

The creature slips inside with a playful kick of its hind legs. There's that clattering again, like the sound of something hard striking stone. Then nothing but a gentle thud, thud, thud.

I pause outside the entrance. Dark shapes loom from either side. The scent of burnt popcorn is stronger here, as is the aroma of charred coffee. Blinking lights come from one corner, and it's then I know where I am.

It's the kitchen break area for this floor, lit by the numbers on the microwave ovens.

The thump, thump, thump continues. The sound is headache-inducing. I wince and rub my temples.

The creature pauses in its relentless battering to let out a plaintive bleat.

Trap, I tell myself. This is just the sort of trap someone—or something—might set for a damsel in distress. But the crying is too real, the creature's distress palpable.

I decide to take it by surprise. I leap into the kitchen area, pocketknife at the ready. I slap my free hand against the light switch and confront the creature.

There, by the garbage, a microwave popcorn bag in its mouth, is the world's most adorable baby goat.

THE BABY GOAT drops the popcorn bag and lets out a tremendous bleat. I stash the pocketknife and then drop to my knees so we're on the same level.

"I'm not going to hurt you," I say, my voice as soft as I can make it.

It stops bleating, but eyes me, the look in those strange, rectangular pupils wary and full of stranger danger.

"You know I'm not going to hurt you."

It must, simply because, at the moment, my DNA is kicking in but hard. I want to give it a bath, tie a ribbon around its neck (although it would probably eat that), and give it lots of hugs and kisses. Or maybe pose it for some cute Instagram photos.

I'm a damsel in distress, after all.

It bleats again and bumps its head against the side of a cabinet.

"Do you need help?"

Now it jumps about, its little hooves clattering against the linoleum tile.

It has already amassed what amounts to a goatly treasure. The microwave popcorn bags, of course, but also a stack of paper to-go cups, a bag of Jolly Ranchers with only the grape ones left, and five greasy pizza boxes.

The cabinet it keeps bumping its head against?

The mother lode, also known as the kitchen garbage can.

The cabinet is one of those new models. The slightest pressure of your hand opens the door. As long as you press in the right spot—and not endlessly knock your head against its center.

I pull out first one and then another sack, both brimming with apple cores and grease-soaked paper towels. The plastic is translucent, and the baby goat dances with glee at the sight of Lean Cuisine packages and giant filters filled with soggy coffee grounds.

I knot the sacks so they won't disgorge their contents all over the floor.

"Where to?" I ask the baby goat.

With a wag of its tail, it tippity-taps toward the entrance.

I swallow back a pang of guilt along with stale air and a hint of rancid butter. I'm not tricking it, not really. If there ever was a troll in IT, it's long gone—as is its treasure.

Still, I'd like to know what this little fellow is up to.

Also? I really want to tie a bow around its neck.

WE ARE deep in the bowels of the server room. My skin puckers from the chill, and my breath emerges in great clouds of fog. The baby goat leads the way, its hooves a light tapping on the elevated floor. I follow, the slosh and scrape of the garbage bags in my wake.

The glimmer is thicker here, like stardust. The air sparkles, but it's a cold beauty. In all my years of tracking, I've never encountered a glimmer quite this strong.

A prickly sensation crawls up my spine. I glance over my shoulder, but if something's spying on us, I can't see it. I also can't see my way back out of this forest of servers. It's icy and dark, and the sort of spooky that makes me think of goblins, orcs, and especially trolls.

Not for the first time, I wonder who is playing the trick here.

If you were a goat and had a troll problem (as goats so often do), you might lure a damsel in distress into its lair as a way to appease it. Yes, this baby goat is adorable. That doesn't mean it isn't a crafty little bastard.

And yes, I know. I didn't just walk into this.

I volunteered.

Worse, I left Luke behind. He doesn't know where I am. Then again, I have no idea where he and the rest of the group have gotten themselves to. The IT department isn't as vast as all that, not normally anyway.

With the strength of this glimmer? That's another matter. The glimmer can bend to a shadow creature's will and create a world for it, one free of annoying trackers like Parker Pankhurst. There's a good chance Luke, Pankhurst, and the others are wandering through the maze of cubicles no closer to the creature's lair than when they first started.

The goat leads me around a final corner, and there, standing in the center of the space, a club raised in one meaty hand, stands a troll.

The garbage sacks slip from my grip and land with a splat on the floor. I choke back a scream on the off chance the troll hasn't seen me yet. I'm about to dash back the way we came. There might be no end to the server room, but this particular spot is definitely a dead end.

I don't move.

Neither does the troll.

We stand like that, both of us like stone until I realize that there's a good chance one of us actually *is* stone.

The air is a bit ripe—all coffee grounds and barnyard—but not troll-level ripe. Nothing emerges from its mouth. No roar or howl or the truly strange obscenities trolls favor. I inch forward, the baby goat dancing about me, and swipe a finger along one bulging arm.

Stone—from its hairy toes all the way to its bald, wart-infested head.

"How did you do that?" I ask.

The goat springs and kicks its hind legs. It bleats what must be a tremendously funny story judging by the tone.

"So, there really *was* a troll in IT."

"Indeed, there was."

The voice freezes me in place. The baby goat halts its scampering and ducks its head as if it's been caught skipping school.

A ponderous clacking sounds against the floor. The steps are serious, and I resist the urge to straighten my shirt and retie my bootlaces. From one of the rows of servers, a second goat emerges.

It's wearing a pair of rimless glasses and a black turtleneck sweater. The goat gives me a brief once over before taking a knee and inclining its head.

"William Gruff the Third, at your service," he says.

I bob a curtsey. "Posey Trombelle."

"Posey?"

"Short for Poinsettia. I was—"

"A Christmas baby, no doubt."

I raise an eyebrow. Usually, I have to explain my name. This is one clever goat.

William Gruff turns a disapproving eye on the baby goat at my side. "And you led her here?"

The baby goat bleats and stamps its hooves. Then it scampers around the overflowing sacks of garbage, both bags threatening to burst.

"It seems," William Gruff says, turning back to me, "that in all our precautions, we overlooked damsels in distress."

"Everybody always does."

It's all *sorry about the goblins* or *what do you mean, you didn't get your cut of the treasure.*

"Now that you're here, why don't I show you around?" William Gruff nods toward a room shrouded by a glimmer so thick it looks like a curtain of golden beads.

Without recourse, I heft the garbage sacks and follow both goats inside.

~

"Here's where the magic happens," William Gruff announces.

And yes, he means that quite literally.

The space hums, not so much with industry, but the activity of a single goat working on a desktop computer. I'm not sure how, exactly, its hooves hit all the right keys, or any keys for that matter. Again, magic.

The baby goat bites open one of the garbage sacks and scurries to bring its compatriot a series of treats: an oily bag of microwave popcorn, the Jolly Ranchers, and a dripping filter filled with coffee grounds.

William Gruff chews a to-go cup contemplatively. "We need to keep our programmer happy after all."

I count the goats once, twice, and a third time. Yes. There are only three of them. Of course there are. And they're doing what, exactly?

"Are you running a ... startup?"

William Gruff plucks a business card from nowhere and shoves it along the floor with a hoof.

Gruff Cyber Security
Industry Leader in Eradicating Trolls

Because of course they are.

Again, I peer at William Gruff, at the turtleneck, the glasses, the distinct tuft on his chin that could best be described as Jobsian.

"How—?" I begin.

"You've met our angel investor, I believe."

The troll in IT. I can't help it. I laugh. The baby goat bleats its approval. Even the second goat lifts its head in acknowledgment.

Then all hell breaks loose.

~

The claxon is zombie-movie loud and obnoxious. The glimmer around us shudders. William Gruff charges forward and crashes into me.

"Who did you lead in here?" he demands. "Who? Who? Is it Pankhurst?"

"Pankhurst?" I stumble backward under the onslaught. "Oh, no."

William Gruff pauses, but I suspect that's only to gather steam for another attack. "Yes or no? Is it Pankhurst?"

"Yes, it's Pankhurst." I raise my hands, hoping to ward off another jab from those mean-looking horns. "But I didn't bring him here, not on purpose."

But maybe he used me. Oh, no maybe about it. I'm the overlooked precaution, after all. And Parker Pankhurst—that knave—knew that all along.

"Didn't you?" William Gruff swipes one hoof and then the other across the floor, gearing up for a colossal attack.

"He tied me up and left me for troll bait." I hold out my hands and point to the faint red marks around each wrist.

William Gruff turns to the baby goat. "Is that true?"

The baby goat scampers about, bleating and stamping hooves in what sounds like a drawn-out explanation. Then it comes to stand by me. *Oh, I love it so much.* When this is over, I plan to bathe it, brush out its hair, and dress it in little outfits—with its consent, of course.

Pankhurst bursts through the glimmer. "Get them! Get all of them." He whirls and points at me. "Get her! She's conspiring with them."

The blacksmith leaps onto a desk, but stops when her gaze lands first on the goat and then on me. Luke skids to a halt. The apprentice, wisely, chooses to hang back.

"Posey?" Luke's brow clouds with confusion and what might be hurt. "What are you doing here?"

"There's no troll, not anymore. There's no treasure." I want to explain about the startup and cyber security, but I can't put it into words because I don't have the whole story.

"They stole my treasure." Pankhurst jabs a finger at William Gruff.

"You left us for dead." William Gruff takes a ponderous step forward. "You tethered this little one in a conference room, left him with no chance of escape. We were nothing but bait to you."

Pankhurst's entire face turns red. "You lie."

"And then you ran." William Gruff looks serene, but there's a terrible glint in those rectangular pupils. "We cleaned up your mess. We reaped the rewards."

"You'd believe them." Pankhurst gestures, a dismissive flick of his wrist toward the goats. "Over a human."

No one speaks. The glimmer vibrates a warning. Daybreak is imminent. We're all in trouble if we're still here when the sun rises.

I glance down at the little goat at my feet. Its expression is both soulful and hopeful.

"Yes," I say. "I would."

Parker Pankhurst whirls then and charges not at William Gruff, but at me.

The baby goat leaps, one of those feats that can take him over those five-foot-high cubicle walls. But he's so tiny and no match for the combined muscle and beer-gut girth of Parker Pankhurst.

Frantic, I race forward. I'm not fast enough; I'm not strong enough. The second before the collision, the baby goat is plucked from the air and cradled in the capable arms of Luke Milner, knight in shining armor.

He tucks, rolls, and deposits the baby goat safely beneath a desk. He springs to his feet, ready to take all comers. Instead of charging again, Parker Pankhurst shrugs, palms skywards, and shoots us all a slimy smile.

Then the bastard turns and runs.

It's then I notice the blacksmith and her apprentice have already vanished. It's then I notice the glimmer fading into nothing. The sun must be up, and that means we have no way out.

"Hurry, both of you."

The order comes from William Gruff. The baby goat darts from beneath the desk and butts the back of my legs, urging me farther into their room. With a solid kick of a hind leg, it shuts the door.

"Spend the day with us," William Gruff says.

"But—" I scan the room. I can't see the glimmer, but it whispers against the back of my neck, caresses my cheeks in a ghostly kiss. "How—?"

Luke looks as perplexed as I feel. He reaches out a hand as if he might touch the glimmer that isn't actually there.

"You've heard of artificial intelligence, haven't you?" William Gruff says.

"Of course," I say, "but this isn't—"

"Possible?" He forages around in a garbage sack and plucks out another to-go cup. He gives it three thoughtful chews. "Are you certain?"

A computer-generated glimmer? Really? No wonder Parker

Pankhurst was so interested. Access to the glimmer, day or night? You could do anything with that.

Like launch your own tech startup.

"So this room." I turn in a slow circle, taking it all in. "It's protected by the glimmer."

William Gruff gives a nod.

"And we're safe?"

"As long as you don't stray from here. Once the sun sets and the glimmer returns to the rest of the building, you may leave. I'll grant you safe passage through the server room."

"My face is all over the security footage," I say.

William Gruff nods at the second goat, who clatters the keyboard with its hooves. "Not anymore, it isn't."

Luke and I exchange glances. He gives me another of those elegant little shrugs. I pluck at the bandana tied to his arm.

"Mind if I borrow this?"

He gives me a tired smile. I don't know if that's from this long night or me in general. I suspect the latter.

"Not at all," he says, and that smile turns indulgent.

I tug the bandana free and, in a matter of minutes, have it fashioned into the cutest bow. I hold it out for the baby goat's approval. He doesn't eat it, which is good enough for me.

From the depths of my cargo pants, I pull out my phone and hand it to Luke.

"Take our picture?"

When you're a shadow tracker, most nights end without any treasure. This isn't one of those nights—or days, as the case may be. Both Luke and I leave with shares in Gruff Cyber Security.

I join the yoga studio. Since goat yoga is a thing, no one questions me when I show up with an actual baby goat.

My #goatsofinstagram posts keep racking up views, and I have hundreds of new followers.

Sure, somewhere out there, Parker Pankhurst has a poisoned arrow with my name on it.

But I have something he doesn't.
A knight in shining armor and three devoted attack goats.

The Troll in IT was an exclusive story for The (Love) Stories for 2020 project.

THE MILLER'S DAUGHTER

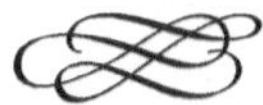

FAIRY TALE RETELLING

The part at the end, when I tear myself in half, is the worst. But it's dramatic, and everyone seems to like it. Besides, I've perfected the move.

Mind you, I don't actually tear myself in half. That would hurt. When I stomp my foot, much like a toddler, it opens a passageway to another forest, another miller's daughter, another king intent on fortune.

I'm not sure why I slip through this passageway, only that I do. I'm not sure how it happens, only that it does. I leave one life for another, each familiar, but distinct. I've done this for so many years that I've forgotten what it's like to have a life of my own.

The forest around me is still. I breathe in dry leaves. My limbs feel sluggish, my head even more so. When the sky stops spinning, I'll need to bolt. I might already be too late. Right now, the hangman may be tightening the noose around the neck of the miller's daughter. That's happened more times than I care to count.

It's hard to save someone mid-execution.

I inhale a steadying breath and push from the forest floor only to careen into the first oak I see. Its bark scrapes my cheek, but the thick trunk stops my fall. My head spins. I clutch the tree like a lovesick girl and wait.

When I merely see double, I head for the village.

From a farmer's clothesline, I procure a shirt with flapping tails and a tattered overcoat. I jam an abandoned straw hat on my head. The oversized clothes make me appear old, shrunken.

As I leave, a billy goat bleats a reprimand at me.

Stalls line the village square with everything from rosy apples to funnel cakes sizzling in oil. Baskets bump my hips and arms as people hurry past. I can't move. I am a hollow thing, starved, not just for food, but a real meal, a real bed, a real home.

A real life.

When did it all change? When did *I* change? A curse, perhaps. Or I bargained with the wrong crone. Or perhaps I did nothing, and it's simply my fate to watch life from the outside.

I shake myself—the miller's daughter. I must find her.

The tavern. I always start my search there. Nine times out of ten, that's where I'll find her worthless father.

Sometimes he's weeping, it's true. Sometimes he isn't even at the tavern, but at home, wringing his hands and concocting foolish rescue plans. Most of the time?

He's drinking, on credit.

That's where he is today, surrounded by ne'er-do-wells, a barmaid on his knee. But if he's here, if he's drinking, it means his daughter is confronting a room full of straw.

I must wait until dark. Even then, obstacles line my path: palace guards, winding corridors, and any number of locked doors.

But people are creatures of habit and convenience. I've crept inside countless castles, pried open dozens of locks, procured keys hanging from the same hook, in the same spot, in nearly identical guardrooms a hundred times over. Tonight is no exception, and I tie the keys to a bit of rope that I loop around my waist.

On the other hand, the miller's daughter is unpredictable. Sometimes she's crying. Sometimes she's resigned or angry. Sometimes she's both and refuses my help.

It's better now that I obscure my face, hide my true form. Those first times? My appearance was so shocking that no amount of reasoning could calm her down. Guards poured into the room, followed by the king himself. And I found myself slipping through that passageway far earlier than I had planned.

So it's with caution that I ease open the door. The miller's daughter stands in the center of the room, eyes dry, gaze contemplating the truly mammoth pile of straw. This king must be extraordinarily greedy. When she catches sight of me, she nods as if she's been expecting her supernatural helper—and I'm late.

"The king wants me to spin this straw into gold." She casts an almost regal hand toward the towering pile.

"That's quite a task," I reply. "One I'm well suited for. I could help you."

She raises an eyebrow. "For a price?"

I execute a low bow. "But of course."

She tugs a ring from her finger. "Will this do?"

I barely glance at it, because, yes, of course, it will. People are wary of getting something for nothing. I don't need the ring, can't take it with me when I travel to yet another miller's daughter and her predicament, but it always makes this part go easier.

"Rest, my child," I say, indicating a wool blanket in one corner. "You will wake to find this room filled with gold."

The miller's daughter lifts the hem of her skirt and retreats, settling in, her back to the room. She is unusually compliant. I pause, taste the air, breathe in the dry, scratchy scent of hay. The room is as it always is, and yet, I hesitate. But only for a moment. There's no time to waste.

I return to the farm and lead the billy goat and several of his companions into the room filled with straw. No one ever questions an old peasant herding goats, not even in the middle of the night. I set them to work, and they'll gladly eat their fill.

It's not like I can spin straw into gold. That's ridiculous.

The keys to the kingdom jangle at my side—quite literally—including those that unlock the royal coffers. Rarely do I find them empty.

The greedier the king, the more gold he already has.

This king's treasure room glows. I pick my way through a maze of coins and jewels, of gold buried beneath more gold, a vast amount to last a hundred lifetimes. I unearth the ancient treasures, the acquisitions long forgotten.

It takes all night to lug enough gold to replace the straw. It always does. By morning, I'm covered in the ancestral greed and grime of this current king. As recompense, before I leave, I slip enough coins into my overcoat pocket to see me through the inevitable wedding and birth of the first child.

Predictably, I receive the necklace for my second night's efforts, and by the third night, I'm floating with relief. It was so easy this time. All I need to do is extract the promise of her first-born, fill the room with gold, and take a well-deserved rest before my final performance.

I bound into the room, but skid to a stop at her outstretched hand.

"You're not needed here," she says.

"But..." I survey the mountain of straw that towers over us—bale upon bale stacked precariously until I'm certain the entire mound will tip over and crush us both.

"If I spin this straw into gold, the king says he'll marry me, and if I don't, he will kill me."

"He'll keep his word," At least, he always has—so far. "He'll marry you."

"I would marry a man who has thrice threaten to execute me simply because I cannot perform the impossible?"

She shakes her head so hard, her glossy black braid comes undone. Her hair tumbles free. On reflex, I clutch the hat closer to my scalp.

"No, I don't wish to marry such a man, not even to save my life." She leans forward as if to peer at me. I shrink further into my coat. "You've been more than kind, but your services are no longer needed."

Stunned, I open my mouth, but no words come out. I grope in my pockets and offer up the ring and the necklace.

"Those are yours," she says. "They belong to you."

I try all night long, but she won't budge. With the first rays of dawn, I leave the room, my eyes prickly and raw from hay and sorrow.

I attend the execution. I owe her that. Upon the scaffold, in the village square, the hangman is shrouded; she is not. Her black braid glows in the morning light, and she surveys the gathering crowd with what looks like pity rather than fear, her eyes sharp and alert.

She scans each newcomer. At first, I think she's searching for her father. When her gaze touches mine, the miller's daughter smiles, and I realize she's been looking for me. My stomach clenches, and I can't glance away.

The hangman places the noose around her neck.

With her gaze still locked on mine, the miller's daughter winks.

The hangman releases the trap door. The crowd gasps.

But she doesn't hang. Her neck doesn't snap. Beneath her, the cobblestones shimmer. The rope unravels, and she slips through an all too familiar passageway.

I'm not sure how it happens, only that it does.

The village square erupts in chaos, crying and wailing and shouts of *witchcraft*. My heart pounds so hard it fills my throat. I am frozen in place, hollowed out.

I remain there long after the crowd disperses, and the guards dismantle the scaffold. I stay for so long that the bustle returns, and the stalls reopen. Warm spice and the scent of ale dull the edges of my earlier terror.

It's only then I pull the hat from my head. My braid tumbles to my shoulder, glossy and black, a mirror image of the miller's daughter. I stare up at the space where the scaffolding stood.

Did she know from the start?

I brush my foot against the cobblestone. If I stamp hard enough, will I, too, vanish, leave as she did, as I've always done in the past?

I decide not to try.

Instead, I pull the ring and necklace from my pocket.

Those are yours. They belong to you.

It's been ages since I felt the weight of the chain around my neck, but I secure it now and slip on the ring.

I am the miller's daughter. I cast a glance over my shoulder toward the tavern but decide not to bother with this world's version of my father.

After all, I have a pocketful of coin. The possibilities of what that might buy loom large: a real meal, a real bed, a real home.

A life.

I turn toward the stall, the one with the funnel cakes sizzling in oil, and decide to start there.

Rumpelstiltskin is another one of those fairy tales that I think deserve a retelling (or two).

FANTASY

The knock on my door comes before sunrise. Three quick raps that sound sharp and official. When I answer and see Mayor Simos on my stoop, the words *sharp* and *official* sear my thoughts.

"It's time," she says.

Her face is creased from sleep and the weight of her office. A breeze rustles loose strands of her hair, wisps escaping the coronet braids.

I want to ask *time for what*, but her expression is cold and foreboding. I know I don't want the answer.

"Bring your tools," she adds, and then, almost as an afterthought, "and the book."

Ah, yes. The book. A simple word that answers all my questions.

I know where it is, of course, locked in the trunk at the foot of my bed. The key, heavy cast iron, weighs down the cord looped around my neck. The cast iron flashes cold, then hot, against my skin.

I'm not certain I remember how to insert the key into the lock, not certain I can lift the lid. I haven't done so since my grandmother passed the book to me before she passed on herself.

"Miri," the mayor prompts, and she is all sharp edges with a razor-like gaze.

"Yes, sorry. Just a minute."

I don't invite her in. Instead, I shut the door against the protest that's forming on her lips. I sag against the wood. There are few privileges to being me, but this is one of them.

The trunk at the foot of my bed is ancient and solid. The wood is reinforced with iron bands, the lock larger than both my fists. The key slips into the lock easier than I think it should. The tumblers click with far more assurance than I feel.

When I lift the lid, a fine layer of dust bursts into the air, filling my mouth, grit stinging my eyes. My nose twitches, but I hold in the sneeze.

I stare at the inside of the trunk, at the items I thought I'd never need to use. The saw with its serrated edge. The plane and the awl. The long, elegant pick with the hook at its tip. I pack these into a canvas bag. Next comes the book.

No one has touched it since my grandmother wrapped it in linen and placed it here. The trunk itself hasn't moved in decades. I now sleep in the bed she slept in, the bed she died in.

The second my fingertips brush the linen, I'm afraid the soft material will crumble in my hands. The book must remain wrapped, at least for the trip to the caves. After that? Well, after that, I guess we'll see what's inside.

I open the door on Mayor Simos, her fist poised to knock. The reprimand is sharp in her eyes until her gaze lands on the bundle in my arms.

Even Mayor Simos respects the book.

The sun casts a glow on the horizon. There's enough light to paint the sky indigo. And enough that I can see the playground where the village children gallop and run with the hatchlings, the earth bare and packed from feet, claws, and the swish and thump of tails.

When I was younger, I sat far back from the playground, up in the tree that shades the house my grandmother—and now I—live in. With my belly flush against a thick branch, my arms wrapped tight, I'd watch, envy fizzing inside me.

I wanted a hatchling of my own. I wanted to be chosen.

I am, of course. Chosen, that is. The book in my arms is proof of that. But I would never choose this path for myself. I would never choose it for anyone else, either.

Mayor Simos leads the way. Her coat, trimmed with gold braid, sways as we trudge toward the foothills north of the village. Cottages give way to pastures until we reach the foothills. The sun crests the horizon. Its warmth touches the back of my neck, almost like it's urging me forward.

Tendrils of smoke issue from the caves. These caves, the ones closest to the village, are not our destination. This is where the hatchlings sleep. Their gentle snoring makes me think of puppies dozing by the fire. Somewhere, deep down, that envy fizzes once again.

Mayor Simos casts a glare over her shoulder as if my longing is both tangible and unseemly. I will my expression to remain placid, and we continue our trek up the mountain.

The snoring grows deeper, more sonorous the farther up we go. The cave openings are larger. If you were to wander inside, you might be lost for days—or forever. It would all depend on the humor of the occupant.

At last, we reach the final cave on this branch of the path. Dragon's End, we call it. Nothing but blackness pours from the entrance. Worse is the silence. I strain my ears, hoping for a muted snore, but hear nothing.

"How long?" I ask.

"Five days, we think," Mayor Simos says. "It's hard to tell. They don't need much in their retirement, so the shepherds seldom visit more than once a week."

I nod as if this is vital information I can use. It isn't. I have no idea what will greet me when I enter the cave.

We stand at the entrance for so long it becomes clear that Mayor Simos is waiting on something. Profound words? A dismissal? I don't know. But there is one thing I'm sure of.

I go in alone.

I turn to do just that, but the mayor takes my arm.

"Miri, I'm sorry."

"Sorry?"

"It may have been more than five days."

"Has no one come around to check?"

I see the answer in her gaze. No, no one has, perhaps not for a very long time.

Instead of envy, anger bursts to life inside me. How could no one check? You could send a child of five up the slope. It isn't dangerous. They care for our own in the way we do their hatchlings. They would never harm a child.

I clutch the book to my chest, the linen rustling in my hands.

"I'm sorry," Mayor Simos says again. "I should've sent someone around. I simply didn't think..."

I shake my head and shake away her apology. Maybe it's her fault. Maybe it isn't. I'm not sure it matters. No one in living memory has performed this task. Even my grandmother was a small girl when her own grandmother told her of the last dragon tended to in this manner. That tale has been lost over time. No one knows, for certain, what happened.

This is not supposed to be happening. I was never meant to take this trek up the path. I was supposed to live my quiet life. At some point, I'd give birth to a girl, who in time, would birth one of her own. I would pass the tools and the book onto my granddaughter. This undertaking is one that skips a generation.

Dragons live for such a long time. Chances of any of them needing our services are inestimably small. None of us ever thinks we'll be the one to journey up the mountain, enter a dark and foreboding cave, crack open the book, and read the words inside.

After that? Here's where the oral instructions become vague. My grandmother wouldn't—or perhaps *couldn't*—tell me.

I go in alone. Without Mayor Simos. Without any counsel. Without any hope of coming out again.

I draw in a breath. The sun has touched the valley below us. If I listen hard, the delicate snoring of the hatchlings fills my ears. I step forward, the cool air of the cave washing over me. Before I can dive in, before I can fully commit, Mayor Simos touches my arm.

"The book," she says.

Ah, yes. The book. I consider it now, still clutched against my chest.

"In a week," I say. "Send someone in for it. A child would be best."

Her grip on my arm tightens.

"They would never harm a child," I add. No matter what mess is left in my wake, this mountain possesses enough residual enchantment for a child to navigate into and back out of the cave. "A hatchling, perhaps, could go with them."

Her grasp lessens, but I still feel her fingers against my skin. I don't know what else she can tell me, but I want to enter the cave before she delivers any additional bad news.

So I wrench free, my arm and then sleeve slipping from her hold. I dive into the cave, committing fully. This is one rule I know, the one rule my grandmother insisted I follow.

Once past the threshold, do not hesitate.

~

BUT I DO. I halt several steps inside the cave. Behind me, the entrance is barely a flicker of light. Before me? The cave splits in two, no four, no six directions.

"Which do I choose?" I say these words aloud as if there's something else in the cave with me, something sentient and far cleverer than I am.

Nothing answers my plea except for the echo of my own voice, tiny and forlorn. I peer down each tunnel, but nothing distinguishes one from the other. Perhaps they all lead to where I need to go. Perhaps that's why there's no need to hesitate.

I pick the fourth tunnel, simply because I like the number four, and stride forward. The moment I do, a rumbling sounds behind me.

Rocks tumble and slide down the sides of the cave. I dash forward, pebbles and stones chasing after me. The walls of the cave shake. The earthen floor trembles, my feet skidding on the unstable surface. At last, a final boulder fills the path and blocks the entrance completely.

Yes. Of course. Do not hesitate.

I take quick, shallow breaths in the dust-laden air. The taste of earth fills my mouth. My heart thunders, much like the rocks and stones did. I wait until the dust and my breathing settle.

I peer toward the entrance. "How will they retrieve the book now?" I'm not sure who—or what—I'm asking. The rocks that block the path? Whatever force sent them tumbling in the first place?

As if in answer, a hint of sulfur rides the air.

"I guess that's their problem, not mine."

A rumble reaches me. I want to say it sounds like a laugh or, at the very least, a snort. More likely, the rocks are merely settling.

It's not dark. At least, not as dark as it should be. A thin sliver of light emanates from the depths of the mountain. I've already hesitated enough.

I follow the only path open to me.

~

THE STRAP of my canvas sack bites into the flesh of my shoulder. My arms ache from clutching the book. My fingers cramp from where I've gripped the sides. I can feel the hours I've trekked in my legs. My mouth is parched.

The muted light guides me. It's barely there, this sliver of illumination. I don't question it. To question it is to lose it, and I can ill afford to lose this one small advantage.

I have no provisions, didn't think to bring any. Slowly, over the past hours, my anger at the shepherds has simmered into sympathy. How do you care for something can't find?

And if I can't find the dragon? What then?

The thought makes me stumble. I reach out a hand, my aim the cave wall, or really anything to keep me from falling, breaking an arm—or worse, a leg. The moment my fingers brush against the cave's surface, a golden glow fills the space.

I remain there, palm flush with the cave wall, the stone cool beneath my touch. The glow around me, however? That looks warm and inviting. My eyes adjust, and I step closer to inspect the source.

Embedded in the walls, the ceiling, and even the floor are coins, layer after layer of them. Gold and silver shine forth. The coin of our realm, yes, that's expected, but it's more than that. I trace my fingers along the bumps and edges, trying to discern the languages written there. They are either from places too far away or too long ago for me to recognize.

I continue forward.

Other hues join the gold and silver of the coins, the walls now studded with gems—rubies and sapphires and emeralds. Some fall as I pass, as if the slight breeze from my movements is enough to dislodge them from their perch in the cave wall.

I wonder at this. Did the shepherds never wander this deep into the cave? A single gem could keep a family fed for generations. Certainly, the dragons allow this sort of barter—a small token in exchange for care.

A wave of dizziness strikes me. The air is, perhaps, a bit thin back here. Still, it would be worth the journey, even without the lure of riches. I don't understand why no one has ventured this far into the cave. I would gladly tend to a dragon, were I to have one.

Gladly.

The dizziness crashes over me again, forcing me to my knees. Before me, the path is pristine. Behind me, my footsteps are sharp outlines in the dust. No one has been this way for ages. My chest tightens until pain radiates along my breastbone. I'm not truly dizzy. I'm not deprived of air. This is something else, something that's simmered and fizzed for a long time.

All I ever wanted was a hatchling of my own.

What I have now is someone's loyal and neglected companion, a creature who, while not dead, is not that far away from death.

Dragons can be killed, certainly. In battle. With the sharp edge of a sword angled just so or with boulders flung with catapults. But they can't die naturally, not as humans do. As part of our alliance, we offer them this one, final service.

It falls to one family, generation after generation. This family is forbidden any other contact with dragons, from hatchlings to elders. It's said to contaminate the pact. Often we're never called upon to complete this final task.

Until we are.

Like today.

I FIND MY BREATH. A few moments later, I muster the strength to stand and for the journey still ahead of me. The cave glows blood-red now from the gemstones in the walls. Perhaps this is intentional, meant as a warning, and my pulse beats in my throat.

I round a bend in the cave. And there, just like that—blocking my way forward—is a dragon. Its girth at midsection blocks my view of its tail and the cave beyond. I can only assume there's a cave beyond, at any rate. Perhaps the cave ends here, and the dragon, grown so vast in old age, can no longer crawl free.

The claws on its forelimbs shine like mother of pearl. Its eyes are closed, mouth as well. If the creature breathes, I cannot detect it. Perhaps someone—a shepherd, maybe—has already done my job.

But there is no stench of death, of decay. The cave is dry, the air scented with a strange mix of brimstone and pine. It is not unpleasant.

I ease the canvas sack from my shoulder. The tools jangle, and I freeze, afraid the noise will wake the dragon.

It doesn't move.

I place the book, still in its linen wrap, on the floor as well.

I don't know what to do. It occurs to me that the answers are in the book. That's why it's been passed down from generation to generation, cared for, but never read. I've never even been tempted before. I only ever wanted a dragon, never to kill one.

With careful fingers, I unwrap the linen. The leather cover is worn, the gold embossed title barely legible. I turn to the first page and find ...

Nothing.

I flip to another page, and then another. I tear through the book, unconcerned with its age or condition. Nothing but yellowed parchment greets me. No words, not even barely legible ones in faded ink. All the pages are blank. At last, I stand and shake the book, hoping for a loose page or a note or something to flutter to the cave floor.

"I don't understand."

I whisper the words. They swirl in the space around me, their echo soft yet insistent before the sensation of being scrutinized washes over me.

I glance up and find myself staring into the golden eye of an ancient dragon.

EVERYTHING I THOUGHT I knew about my task has vanished. I'm to take my tools, the book. I am to perform what amounts to last rites for an ancient dragon. It will be in such a deep sleep that the steps I must perform to end its life won't disturb it. This, my grandmother assured me.

Now that ancient dragon is gazing at me. A stream of smoke rises from its nostrils. Again, that odor of brimstone and pine surrounds me. I can taste the smoke against my tongue. The book slips from my fingers and crashes to the cave floor.

"I see they've sent me a child."

The voice is deep and sonorous. It rolls through the space and shakes my bones.

"I'm no child." My voice quavers, but the words come stronger than I expect. I lift my chin. "I live on my own," I insist, as if this is proof of my maturation.

The dragon snorts a spurt of smoke. "Little more than a hatchling."

"What am I to do?" I point to the book. "It doesn't say."

"Doesn't it? Are you quite certain?"

Oh, spare me mind games with an ancient dragon. I'm ill-equipped for this sort of sparring. Besides, it must know even if I don't. But it will no doubt make me work for that knowledge.

"Am I to kill you?" I see no reason not to be blunt.

"Are you? That seems rather rude. We've only just met, after all."

"Then am I your...?" I trail off, a wholly different thought occurring to me.

"Sacrificial lamb, the morsel meant to appease me?" It tilts its head so both glowing yellow eyes can survey me, from the top of my head to the tips of my dusty boots. "You're rather small for that."

"Then, what am I?"

Its claws retract and then rake the earthen floor in front of me. "What you are, my child, is very much stuck."

I VERY MUCH AM. Stuck, that is. Had the shepherds performed their assigned tasks, there would be provisions in here, a cistern of water at least.

"Why am I here?"

"Have you consulted your book?"

I spear it with a glare. Without water, I won't live out the week. So I will be fierce in my dealings with the dragon.

The creature snorts another laugh. "Humans, always so inquisitive, and yet, so oddly obedient. Did it never occur to you to have a peek inside? Gird your loins for your one task in life?"

Well, no, it hadn't. I spent my time gazing at the hatchlings. "I never wanted this."

"Well, it seems to me you have it." A sigh rumbles in its throat, dual streams of smoke rising from its nostrils. "A child, and an incurious one at that. What a disappointment."

"At least it's mutual."

"Oh, perhaps this child has some fire, after all."

The dragon looks not at me, but past me with so much concentration, I must resist the urge to glance over my shoulder. That's what it wants, of course. But no one shares this space with us.

"We seem to have reached an impasse," the dragon says. "You have no idea how to complete your task—"

"Do you?"

The dragon regards me with narrowed eyes before continuing. "It's any guess who will succumb first. I will be reduced to some nether-slumber while you." Once again, it surveys me from head to foot. "Will eventually shrivel up. Will I be conscious long enough to blow the dust of your bones from this spot? Who's to say? Shall we place bets? Winner take all?"

My heart thuds heavily in my chest, a slow, painful sort of beat. Perhaps this is why elder dragons are banished to the upper caves. All I ever wanted was a hatchling, a dragon of my own. But this one? It's an old, bitter, cruel thing, and I want nothing to do with it.

There's no escaping its girth, but I find an outcropping of rocks on the side farthest from the dragon. I take my tools and the book.

Yes, even the book. The leather is soft enough, and so are the pages. It will make an adequate pillow. Perhaps that's all it was ever meant to be.

"Ah, yes, and now the poor thing pouts." Its words are a mere whisper, although clearly, it wants me to hear them. "I abhor tears," the dragon adds, louder now. "So, if at all possible, refrain from crying."

This last is the only thing we agree upon.

I comply.

IN MY DREAM, I am a warrior, a dragon as my mount. In my dream, we soar through the air, dodging arrows alight with flame. In my dream, the roar of battle shakes my bones.

My eyes fly open. The roar continues even as my dream fades. The world is dark, my bed like stone, nothing but the scent of brimstone and pine.

Then I remember.

The roaring grows ever louder. In the middle of the cave, the dragon thrashes its head. Its eyes are shut tight. It must be dreaming. The same sort of dream? Of battlefields and fire? Or is this something more, something worse?

It thrashes again. The agony in its cry races up my legs, my spine, settles at the base of my skull. I don't think. I do not hesitate.

I rush forward, dodging its swinging head, nearly eclipsed by its jaw. I've never touched a dragon before. But from my perch in the tree, I've watched the village children do this so many times.

I leap and wrap my arms around the dragon's neck. I hold on with all my strength even as my legs swing beneath me. One foot connects with the dragon's chest, although I doubt it feels the impact.

"Shh." I keep my voice low and soothing. There's a trick to this, to the hushing of dragons. To say I have no training is true. But I listened; I practiced using that same tree branch. "Shh."

Its head continues to swing, but slower now. My arms ache, but I clutch its neck, my feet scraping the cave floor.

"Evelynne ... Evelynne."

The cry rips through me. I've been so consumed with wanting a dragon of my own that I never considered what happens when the human a hatchling first bonds with is killed or dies.

How many humans does a dragon lose during its lifespan?

It could make you bitter. It could make you cruel. Perhaps this is why, at a dragon's end, they are banished to the upper caves.

"Evelynne."

The dragon's swaying comes to an abrupt halt. I dangle from its neck. I cannot see its face, but I suspect those great golden eyes are now open.

I let go and drop to the cave floor.

It takes one look at me and then collapses as if its head is too heavy for its neck.

I am a bitter disappointment. The yellow gaze the dragon casts tells me that. I remain immobile on the cave floor, palms against the dusty surface.

"You should not know how to do that," it says.

No, I shouldn't.

"Lace your hands," it commands.

So I do. True, it took years to learn the correct placement, of which finger goes where. Incorrect placement of fingers, of hands against a dragon's neck will enrage rather than soothe. It's a skill even those with hatchlings find difficult to perfect. Indeed, I had no idea if I was performing it correctly at all.

Until now.

"How do you come by this knowledge, child?" A fiery edge laces the dragon's words, and its displeasure tastes like sulfur.

"My house overlooks the village playground." My voice comes out steady and dull. "I would watch the hatchlings and the children. I would practice on a tree branch."

"There's more to it than that." The dragon shakes its enormous head, its jaw whooshing mere feet above me. "There's the bonding, the spell-casting. You should not ... we should not."

Because it's forbidden, this contact. No thrill of fear courses through me, no regret. I would gladly calm this creature once again, given half a chance. I would gladly do it even if it meant my death. To prove it, I push to stand and anchor my hands on my hips.

Those great amber eyes blink, a shuttering of its gaze. When the dragon opens its eyes once again, something has shifted in its expression.

"What have they done to you, child?"

I shake my head, uncertain what it means.

"Why sequester the most talented humans like that?" The dragon murmurs the words, the question meant for its own pondering rather than for me.

Despite that, I decide on my own question. "Why do they banish the old ones to the caves?"

The dragon swings its head around so quickly that I'm nearly flattened against the floor. It regards me for a moment before speaking again.

"Forgive me, child."

"Whatever for?"

"My temper, my rash judgment. Undoubtedly I've lived long enough not to give in to either."

"Or maybe it's because you have lived so long you gave into both."

Something sparks in that golden gaze. Its lip curls, revealing sharp and gleaming teeth. "Yes. Precisely. Do you suppose they count on that?"

Do they? I glance back at the way I came. Even if I had strength and time on my side, digging through the debris would be impossible. I peer into the darkness behind the dragon's girth.

"What is at the other end?" I ask.

"Other than my tail?"

"Yes." I laugh because its tone is sly and full of humor. "Other than that."

"A dead end, appropriately enough."

I turn my gaze upward and follow the trajectory of the smoke that rises from the dragon's nostrils.

"That is merely a thin layer of rock," I say.

"Oh, my child, I am old."

"So old as that? Truly?"

"My wings. I—"

The walls around us groan, and the dragon trembles with the effort to spread its wings.

"You see," it adds. "I have tried."

"But, they have given me tools." I race to the alcove and weigh each tool in my palm, judging the merits of each. I return with the awl.

I hold it up so the dragon can see.

"Indeed," it intones. "That was their mistake."

The dragon lowers its head. A thousand times, I have seen the children and their hatchlings perform this maneuver. I step carefully, only lighting a foot on its forehead before settling between its horns.

Something washes over me, that scent of pine and brimstone again, along with something more—the feeling that I belong here.

The dragon raises its head, so my own nearly brushes the cave's ceiling.

"Close your eyes," I whisper.

With my first strike, dust rains down, followed by a stream of sunlight. It touches my cheeks and makes the dragon's scales glow a fiery red. Its power, its strength, rushes through me.

This is why they confine the ancient ones to Dragon's End. Or perhaps it's why we're both here. Together, we are something more, something powerful.

With a final chip at the thin crust, the earth that blocks the way out tumbles down.

"You're free," I say.

"No, my child, *we* are." A stream of smoke rises from its nostrils, and this dragon reminds me of an old man with a pipe, contemplating a riddle. "I don't suppose you've had a flying lesson, have you?"

"I don't suppose I have."

"But you've seen how it's done."

"A thousand times."

"Then you should be adequate. But first things first. Go get the book."

The book? I peer to where it still remains on the floor, leather cracked from where my cheek rested against the cover.

"Don't you need to return it?"

The slyness in the dragon's voice has me sliding down its neck, scooping up the book, and then returning to that spot of honor.

"I have no saddle," it says, "and no reins. You'll have to hold on."

"I have years of practice."

The dragon's wings tremble and shake. Its hind legs quiver. With a mighty leap, it clears the edge of the cave and unfurls its wings.

"What is your name, child?" The question reaches not my ears, but my mind. Its thoughts touch mine, and the sensation is as intimate as a kiss.

"Miri."

"I am Mercurial."

"Of course you are."

The dragon snorts a laugh and sends sparks into the air. "It is also my name."

Mercurial swoops toward the village, wings shadowing the earth below. We are close enough now that I can see the chaos erupt on the playground. At the sight of Mercurial, a dozen hatchlings scamper and fling themselves in the air, wings beating furiously until they tumble and land once again. Their children race after them, laughing and crying out.

Work at the mill halts. The village elders emerge from what must have been a meeting, Mayor Simos among them.

"Now, my dear."

I toss the book into the air. When it's halfway to the ground, Mercurial shoots a stream of fire at it. The book lands at the mayor's feet, flames chewing through the parchment.

"What a shame," I say.

"Yes. All that knowledge, forever lost." Mercurial circles the village a final time. "Where to, my sweet?"

"The farthest I've ever been from home is Dragon's End."

"Then hang on. We have the entire world before us."

So I do. I entwine my arms around Mercurial's neck. I don't look back.

Not even once.

Dragon's End was written specifically for The (Love) Stories for 2020 project.

OCTOBER

For October it was tales of ghosts and witches and things that go bump in the night.

GHOST IN THE COFFEE MACHINE

PARANORMAL

When it comes to ghosts, my grandmother has one solution: brew a pot of coffee. Like today, in Sadie Lancaster's kitchen.

Sadie clutches her hands beneath her chin and stares at our percolator, her eyes huge. The thing gurgles and hisses as if it resents being pressed into service. My own reflection in its side is distorted. When I was younger, I thought this was how ghosts see our world.

In places with bad infestations, they swirl around the percolator. I can reach out, touch hot moist air with one hand and the icy patch of dry with the other. One time, a ghost slipped inside. It rattled around until the percolator sprang from the table and hit the floor, splashing scalding water everywhere.

I still wear the scars of that across my shins.

But Sadie's ghosts are barely ghosts at all. I'd call them sprites. They might annoy you on the way to the bathroom at three a.m., but little more. They also, as my grandmother points out, help pay the bills. So I remain silent while she pours the coffee: three cups black, three cups with sugar, three cups with cream, and three cups extra light and extra sweet. Twelve cups. Always. If anyone complains, my grandmother snorts and says, "As if no one has a preference once they've died."

Don't get her started on instant coffee, either. Since I was five, my job involves carrying the cups throughout the house, up and down stairs, into bedrooms, dining alcoves, walk-in closets. We never skip the bathroom, no matter what.

"The last place you'd want a ghost," my grandmother says to Sadie. "Lecherous little beasts."

I walk past the two women, my steps slow and steady. I still burn myself, make no mistake. My hands wear the scars of multiple scaldings. We keep a burn kit in the truck. But as I place the last cup on the edge of the sink, I smile. At least I won't need that today. I rush back to the kitchen for the Tupperware.

Some ghost catchers use glass jars, but ghosts confined to small spaces can manifest images—grotesque or obscene or both. Ghosts, generally speaking, are pissed off and rude, which is why you don't want one in your toilet. We buy the containers with the opaque sides, since what you can't see won't offend you. I use several at Sadie's that afternoon, although truthfully, I only snag three little sprites in the den.

"She's imagining things," I whisper to my grandmother.

"Yes." Her hand steadies my shoulder. "But how many repeat customers do we get?"

She has a point. We're good. When we're really in the zone—the right type of coffee beans, perfect brewing temperature, clean catches—a house might stay ghost-free for decades. If we're not careful, there won't be any ghosts left to catch.

With the sprites in the back of our pickup, we rumble down the county road that leads out of town and into endless fields of corn and soybean. Ten miles out, there's a windbreak with a little creek. This is where we'll set the sprites free. They'll be, if not happy, content at least, and in no hurry to find other humans to haunt. I'm setting the sprites free—legs braced, container at arm's length—when my grandmother speaks.

"When I'm gone, Katy-girl, I'll come back and show you how to rid them once and for all."

I sigh. I've heard this before. "But then I'd be getting rid of you."

"You wouldn't like me as a ghost. Besides, they don't belong on this plane. This has been my life's work." She touches three fingers to her heart. "I don't see why it shouldn't be my afterlife's work as well."

She always says this. I always tell her she'll live a good long time. Then we drive home, empty containers rattling against the flatbed, percolator perched between us, belted in, our third—and quite possibly most important—passenger.

~

THAT WAS THREE MONTHS AGO. If my grandmother raged against the dying of the light, it didn't show in her expression the following morning when I found her. She left me her house, the family business, and of course, the dented, silver percolator. I have yet to see a hint of my grandmother's ghost. I'm not sure I want to.

The house is quiet without her in it. Even the ghosts have stayed away. I shake the canister of roasted beans, give it a sniff, certain I'll need to dump it and buy fresh within a matter of days.

Sadie Lancaster calls as the first cascade of beans hits the garbage sack. I decide on those fresh beans now, and instead of running next door, I jump into my truck and head for the Coffee Depot.

Ten minutes later, I pull up in front of Sadie's house, but I don't find her cowering on the porch (her usual position pre-eradication). Percolator under one arm, I ring the bell.

"Oh, Katy," she says, urging me inside. She beams like she has a secret. "There's someone I want you to meet."

This is it. My grandmother has chosen Sadie's house as the spot for her grand reappearance and that's why Sadie isn't scared. My steps quicken, heart fluttering something crazy. Do I want to see my grandmother like this? I've never been afraid of ghosts, but this is different.

The aroma hits me first—rich, aromatic, turmeric, saffron, and a hint of rose petal. Sun glints off the sides of a samovar squatting in the center of the kitchen table, in the very place I always set the percolator. I clutch the thing to my chest as if that can protect us from its flashy usurper on the table. The samovar is gold-plated brass—I squint at it—in the Persian style instead of Russian.

"Katy," Sadie says, throwing her arms wide, "I want you to meet Malcolm Armand. He catches ghosts with tea the way you do with coffee." Her fingers twitch as if she's urging us closer together. I stand my ground. "You two have so much in common," she adds.

Malcolm runs a hand over smooth, dark hair. His white dress shirt gleams in the sunlight streaming through the kitchen windows. I'm in torn jeans and a T-shirt. Why anyone would attempt ghost catching in something so fancy is beyond me. Even so? I can't help but feel grubby in comparison.

"It's nice to meet you," he says, extending that same hand, one without a single blemish or scar.

I fight the urge to whip my own hands behind my back, out of sight. I gulp a breath and shake his hand, breaking contact the second it's polite (okay, maybe a couple of seconds before it's polite). I try not to stare too hard at Malcolm, so I let my gaze travel the kitchen, the dining alcove. No ghosts here. I'd be surprised to find even the weakest sprite. And certainly, my grandmother isn't in residence.

That leaves me alone with Malcolm—and the tea-scented suspicion about where all my business is going.

When I walk into Springside Long-term Care, the first thing I see is Malcolm standing in the center of the common area, enchanting all the residents, the gold-plated samovar glowing on a side table next to him. I freeze, so every time the automatic doors try to close, they bounce back open again. This draws attention. I sigh, give up my plan to sneak out, and step forward to meet the facility manager.

"Oh, Katy," she says, a flush rising up her neck, "I meant to call, so you wouldn't make the trip out here." She waves a hand at Malcolm. "He offered a "try before you buy" and well ... the residents just love him."

Or at least most of the female ones do. They gather around Malcolm and his shiny, shiny samovar, their *oohs* and *ahhs* mixing with the scented steam.

I don't point out that Springside is—and always has been—a gratis account. Older people, my grandmother always said, are haunted by many things. It's only right that we chase some of their ghosts away.

I'm backing toward the door, willing myself not to inhale a hint of rose petal and saffron, when a bony hand grips my wrist. The percolator crashes to the floor, adding one more dent to its history.

"Katy-girl, are you going to let him get away with that?" Mr. Carlotta nearly growls the words. He may hold the world's record for longest unrequited crush, in his case, on my grandmother. Even now, sorrow lines his eyes. His fingers tremble against my wrist.

"What can I do?" I wave my free hand toward Malcolm. "He's so flashy."

"More like a flash in the pan. Mark my words."

A part of me grabs onto what Mr. Carlotta says. Be patient. Business will pick up the second it's clear you can't catch ghosts with tea. Because honestly, who ever heard of that? My practical side—the side that pays the property taxes and utility bills—wonders if the local coffee shop is hiring.

I TRACE the scars on the backs of my hands while waiting for the Coffee Depot's assistant manager. My qualifications are thin. I know ghost hunting and how to brew a damn good cup of coffee. But customer service? Well, when you ghost hunt, people don't mind if you shove them out of the way, not if you trap the otherworldly thing shaking their house to the foundation.

At the Coffee Depot? They probably frown on customer shoving. Still, the converted train station is quaint and life as a barista can't be that bad, can it?

The assistant manager plops down across from me. He wipes fake sweat from his brow and gives me a grin.

"So," he says. "Tell me a bit about yourself."

"I make the best damn coffee you've ever tasted." I declare this because I've read online that you should be confident in your interview.

He chuckles but doesn't sound amused. "I'm sure you do. But tell me," and now, the amusement is back, "what about frothing milk?"

I like cappuccino, even if frothing milk is something I've never done. Likewise, I'm sure there are many fine answers to his question. I do not choose any of them.

Instead, I say, "Why would you want to do that?" It's like I'm possessed by the spirit of my grandmother, since in that moment, I sound just like her.

"Right," he says. He clears his throat, then gives me a long look. "I'll take that challenge. Go make me the best damn cup of coffee I've ever tasted."

So I do. I stand, and with his nod, round the counter so I'm on the other side. My fingers barely brush the silver, industrial sized coffee machine when it starts to tremble. The thing wheezes. The tile beneath my feet shudders, sending a shockwave that resonates from toes to jaw. Next to me, the barista's teeth clack together, and she pitches toward the cash register, clinging to it. Then, the machine erupts, spewing water and coffee grounds with so much force, they coat the ceiling, the walls, and all of the tables.

I OFFER TO CLEAN UP. I offer to rid their machine of its ghost—for free. Everyone is damp, but since the water was only lukewarm, no one was scalded. This is why the assistant manager pushes me out of the store instead of calling the police.

As the door closes, his voice echoes behind me. "Yes, do you have the number for Malcolm Armand ...?"

Something won't let me leave the sidewalk in front of the shop. My feet remain rooted there, next to the planters with the sugar maples. I stand there so long it's a wonder I don't sprout leaves. But since I do stand there so long, I'm treated to the view of Malcolm Armand double parking and springing from his two-seater. In the passenger seat, belted in like a trophy girlfriend, sits the samovar.

"That's not very practical," I say.

He halts in his trek up the walk, samovar held away from me. "What?"

"Where do you put the ghosts? I mean, once you capture them." I point at the convertible. "There's no room."

He eyes me, my coffee-soaked shirt, stained slacks, and all. He sniffs, nose wrinkling, and tromps into the shop without another look in my direction. I turn, uproot my feet, and inch toward the front window.

Inside is the mess I made, but I ignore that. What I want to see is how Malcolm works, what he does, how he entices the ghosts. I stare so long, the sun dries the back of my shirt. I study the inside of the shop, the placement of the samovar, and track Malcolm's every move until the assistant manager jerks a cord and Venetian blinds block my view.

Whatever grips me about the shop—the ghost or Malcolm—loosens its hold. Dismissed, I trudge home, leaving a set of coffee-colored footprints in my wake.

"K-k-aty? Are you there?"

The call comes at nine in the morning, on a day so sunny and bright, only the most dedicated pessimist could remain that way. Since I have all my overdue bills spread out on the dining room table, I'm well on my way to joining their ranks.

"Sadie?" It sounds like her, but I've never heard her voice so shaky.

"Please hurry."

"What's going on? Where are you?"

"My porch. They won't let me inside."

"Who won't?"

"The ghosts."

"Why don't you call Malcolm?" The question comes out sharp, laced with acid and jealousy.

"He's t-trapped inside."

"Trapped?"

"Dead?" Sadie's voice hitches.

"Ghosts don't ..." *Kill.* No, normally ghosts don't. But they can. "I'll be right over."

The second I pull the half and half from the fridge and give it a good whiff, I realize *right over* isn't happening. I toss the reeking carton into the garbage and head to the canister with the beans. A few lone ones rattle in the bottom. I haven't been back to the Coffee Depot since my disastrous interview, but it looks like I'll be stopping there today.

With the percolator strapped in its seat, a four-pound bag of sugar snug against it, and several containers of half and half on the truck's floor, I run two red lights on my way to the Coffee Depot. By the time the little bell above the door stops jingling, the assistant manager is rounding the counter. He stalks forward, arms loaded down with bags of coffee beans. He skids to a halt and shoves the beans at me.

"But—" I begin.

He holds up a cell phone. On the screen, a message reads:

Malcolm: Give her anything she wants.

Still uncertain, I blink at the words. In my arms, I hold everything I want, or at least need. For now. I head for the door.

"Call or text if you need a resupply," the assistant manager shouts after me. "I'll have someone run it over."

The door whooshes closed before I can say thanks.

I TEST out the front door, the garage, even the window to the bathroom. Every surface I touch ices my fingertips. Sadie Lancaster's house is in full-on ghost infestation. Usually something like this takes years to build up, or a sudden invasion of strong ghosts—a group of them. True, I haven't cleared the sprites in a month or so, but that can't be the cause of this.

My gaze travels the structure, from chimney to foundation. All the windows are black, the cheery blue paint molting into a dead gray. I need to get inside. I need to do that now. So I do the most logical thing. I march up the porch steps, press my palm against the doorbell, and let it ring for an entire minute. Then I cross my arms over my chest and tap my foot.

"Nobody's getting any coffee if someone doesn't open up this door." I sound bossy, just like my grandmother. I kind of like it.

A moment later, the door creaks on its hinges. I scoop up the percolator and my bag of supplies and race for the kitchen.

"Malcolm?" I call out. "Are you okay?"

Is he even here? Maybe he went out the back once the ghosts released their hold on the doors. I plug in the percolator and take a few deep breaths so I don't rush the preparations. Ghosts this strong will need the best coffee I can brew.

I survey the beans the assistant manager shoved at me. One hundred percent Kona? Really? Shame to waste that on ghosts. But the air prickles the skin on my arms. It must be fifty degrees in here and getting colder. One hundred percent Kona might not do the trick if I don't hurry.

"Katy?" A voice rasps.

For a second, I mistake it for a ghost.

"Katy?"

No. Too deep, too human for that.

"Malcolm?"

"In the dining room."

I set the percolator to brew and run. On the threshold, I trip over something bulky and sail through the air. I land hard, but manage to tuck and roll. When I stop, the blown out end of a gold-plated samovar fills my view, the brass twisted into vicious curlicues.

A groan comes from the threshold. Malcolm props himself up on one elbow, his cell phone clutched in one hand, his shirt, torn and tea-stained.

"What happened?" I say.

"It just ... blew. I was adding in a sprite when—"

"Wait. You've been storing all the ghosts." I heft the samovar, careful of the edges. "In here?"

He nods.

"You don't release them?"

"Never have." He shakes his head, eyes downcast. "Honestly? I don't know how."

This sad, honest confession tugs at me. We don't have time, however, to go over the finer points of ghost hunting.

"Can you stand?" I ask. "Walk?"

"I think so."

"Then you can help."

In the kitchen, I pour the twelve cups. Malcolm adds the half and half and sugar. His hands are steady, and he stirs each cup without spilling a single drop. My grandmother would approve.

From there, we divide and conquer, carrying the cups to various spots in the house.

"Be sure to put one in the master bath," I call from the living room. "There's bound to be one in there."

"It won't let me in," he says a moment later.

Oh, really? Nasty little bugger. Ghosts and their toilet humor.

At the door to the bathroom, I ease the cup of coffee from Malcolm's hands then kick on the door. It flies open with all the strength of the supernatural behind it.

Malcolm places a hand on my arm. "I don't think—"

"It'll be okay." I hear it for the lie it is, and so must Malcolm, but he lets me go.

I close the door and place the coffee on the vanity. That icy patch of air flutters past, swirls into the steam, and revels in it. Oh, it is having the best time—at everyone's expense, too. Before I can trap it beneath some Tupperware, that same feeling from the coffee shop washes over me. This is the ghost in the coffee machine. This is ... my grandmother.

The realization makes me drop the container. Malcolm pounds on the door, but I ignore him.

"Grandma?"

Now, the ghost swoops around me, a frigid caress against my cheek.

"What are you doing? I thought—"

Something that sounds like *hush* fills the air. Whatever her mission, it's not for me to question.

"I love you," I say. "And I miss you."

I pick up the container and my grandmother flows inside, compliantly. I secure the lid and hug the Tupperware to my chest. During her life, my grandmother was right about most everything. But here's where she was wrong:

I do like her as a ghost.

WE DRIVE out to the nature preserve, a good thirty miles from town. In a deserted campsite, I demonstrate how to open containers and set ghosts free. I even let Malcolm release a few. (Only the sprites, but you have to start somewhere.)

"Will they come back?" he asks.

"The strong ones can, but most choose to stay here, or find an old barn to haunt. Something's got to scare all those Scouts on camping trips, right?"

Malcolm studies the backs of his hands. The beautiful olive skin is pink from scalding.

"You should put something on that," I say. "Before it scars."

"A little scarring never hurt anyone. I'm sorry for a lot of things." He raises his hands. "But not for this."

I nod and he gives me a piercing look that I swear could scar—if I let it.

"You know something," he says, "I think this will work."

"What will?"

"You and me. I'm all sizzle, and you're the steak."

"I'm a vegetarian."

He throws his head back and laughs. And while I have no clue what he means, I can't help but like the sound of his laughter.

I LET my fingers trace the gold lettering on the window—for the tenth time in as many minutes. I can't help it, can hardly believe the words are real.

K&M Ghost Eradication Specialists

In the store window, the gold-plated brass samovar sits, backside hidden in midnight velvet. Somehow, Malcolm talked the bank manager into a small business loan. Somehow, we're on retainer with the only law office and investment firm in town. Somehow, my worry about bills and property taxes has evaporated.

Malcolm still wears the scars from what we call the day of the ghosts. He boasts a few fresh ones as well. So do I. We take a new, electric samovar with us when we go out on a call. Because even I must admit: some ghosts prefer tea. Sometimes I feel that particular presence and an icy caress along my cheek. Sometimes I say things that make Malcolm throw his head back and laugh.

What I don't tell Malcolm: I do it on purpose.

What I don't tell my grandmother: I know what her afterlife's mission really is.

And I love her for it.

Ghost in the Coffee Machine was first published in Coffee: 14 Caffeinated Tales of the Fantastic. This story also kicked off what might be the world's most niche series.

WITH HAIR OF TEETH AND CLAW

FAIRY TALE RETELLING

She caught the thief with his hand wrapped around the stem of a flower, its spike of golden flocked petals sprouting from his fist. The brim of his hat shrouded his features, and the overcast night made it impossible to identify him. Even so, the witch knew a desperate husband when she encountered one.

"Let go of the lion's tail," she said, her words crisp as the air, with just enough bite to get her point across, but not so much that she didn't appear neighborly. She'd always been a good neighbor.

"My wife, Mistress Witch." The man sunk to his knees. "She is with child."

"Yes. I know."

In truth, the entire village knew every time the babe kicked or the woman's back ached or her ankles swelled. Never had so many prayed for a timely birth.

"She craves all things fresh, all things green, all the things that grow in your garden. Please, Mistress. I will work, split logs, do whatever you ask, but let me take some of your bounty home to her, so our babe might grow strong."

A first love, a first child, it was enough to make anyone a fool—or a thief. The witch spread her arms wide. "Take, neighbor, take all that your wife craves." She grabbed hold of his hand. "Except for this."

Beneath her grip, he unclenched his fist. The plant he held—lion's tail, as the locals called it—dropped to the ground, stem broken, bright petals crushed.

"Leave the lion's tail," the witch said. "She should not eat it while with child, and I cannot be responsible for what happens if she does."

The man bowed, his movements jerky and frantic. The witch helped him pluck the best greens and place them in a basket. She saw him to the edge of her property, and when he hesitated, she urged him forward.

"Go," she said, voice gentle. "Take the greens and return to your wife."

When the man had left, the witch bent and plucked the lion's tail from the ground. She stroked the petals and wondered if his wife had already tasted of the plant.

That could be very bad indeed.

THE BABE WAS BORN STRONG, with a lusty cry and deep blue eyes that peered out at the world around her. Within a week, the entire village predicted she'd be a beauty. Within a month, her golden hair fell to her chin, the strands thick and wild. By nearly a year, the strands fought all attempts to comb them.

It was then that cries emerged from the cottage, by day and night, until the babe's mother ran from the house. Neighbors peered from their windows and did nothing, but the noise brought the witch from her garden.

The woman trembled, skirts in tatters, arms scratched. Blood oozed from wounds. In her hands, she clutched a pair of shears. She pointed the tip at the house and the infant inside.

"That is not my child. That cannot be my child."

She stood like that, her arm shaking, the shears more weapon than tool.

The witch examined the woman, gave a curt nod, then proceeded inside the cottage. Scattered strands of gold littered the floorboards from hearth to door. Other than a soft whimper, the room was quiet. She crouched to approach the babe.

"Shh ... there you go. You are not in danger, and I will not hurt you." She gathered the child to her and stroked the remaining tufts of hair.

"See? I'm a friend. Let's find your mother."

The child cried out, fists clenched, but the witch hummed a lullaby, one with the power to sedate a charging troll. The babe blinked and then stared at the witch with curious blue eyes. The sight of them transfixed her, and the old witch's heart caught for a moment before resuming its natural beat. They stepped into the sunlight and into the crowd that now surrounded the cottage.

"She's the one!" the mother said, jabbing her shears toward the witch. "She poisoned me with the plants from her garden."

"Your husband stole from my garden to satisfy your cravings."

The woman's hand shook, the tip of the shears bobbing. "That cannot be my child. She looks nothing like me."

Laughter rippled through the crowd. True, the woman was no beauty, and her husband no prince. The woman turned her wrath on the closest bystanders, silver shears glinting in the sunlight. The crowd eased back, catching laughter into cupped hands.

"Oh, then perhaps the child is mine?" the witch asked.

This time, no one held back their laughter.

"So you think I wasn't a beauty in my day?" The witch scanned the crowd, the babe still secured in one arm. "Master Tailor, I believe you know different."

The old man shuffled and stammered, a ruddy cast to his weathered cheeks. The witch turned back to the babe's mother.

"You do not want your child?" she said to the woman.

"That is not my child."

"Then who will care for her?" The witch held the child aloft for the village to see. "No one, then?"

She considered the quiet bundle in her arms. A beauty, it was true, but those deep blue eyes were uncanny, knowing. No wonder this simple woman trembled at the sight of her own child.

The witch cast a look toward her own cottage and the garden with its walls—ones that kept her tender plants safe from hooves and teeth. They kept the variety of weeds she cultivated from invading her neighbors' gardens. Walls were handy but not foolproof. Her gaze met the babe's, and once again, her heart caught.

In this case, perhaps she was the fool.

"I will care for her," the witch declared. "Please, before I take her with me, tell me her name."

The woman blinked as if waking from a dream. "She has no name."

"You have not named your child?" No wonder the babe lashed out. Even now, at the sound of the woman's voice, those short tufts of hair bristled, and the child cried out again.

"Oh, my poor child," the witch murmured, "fate has been cruel."

No one stopped the witch from taking the child. No one uttered a word of protest. When the witch passed the mother, so she might say goodbye, the woman only turned her back on both the witch and her own child.

To the witch's surprise, the husband followed her home, weighed down by the cradle, a wee table, and a chair.

"Please, Mistress Witch, take these things for the child."

The witch nodded, held open the door to her cottage so the man might bring the items inside.

"Would you like to say goodbye before you leave?" she asked.

He had none of his wife's hesitation. His hand cupped the babe's cheek. The tufts of hair wavered as if blown by a soft breeze, and the babe's eyes were luminous.

"Goodbye, sweet girl. Goodbye, my Rapunzel."

"Is that the child's name?" the witch asked.

"It is what I wanted to name her," he said, his voice wistful.

"Then Rapunzel she'll be."

WITH RAPUNZEL still in the crook of her arm, the witch gazed about her cottage. Oh, it was a poor place to raise a child. Too many dried herbs that, consumed incorrectly, might injure or kill. Too many sharp objects. She inspected the child's head. Scars from the shears crisscrossed her raw scalp. Clearly Rapunzel was no stranger to those.

She would need to find a grate for the hearth, a cow or goat for milking, soft cloth for diapers, and something other than the stained gown Rapunzel was wearing.

"It's been many years since I've even held a child," she said to the babe. "And I've never had any of my own."

At the thought, her heart caught once again. Had she ever intended to raise a child? Did she regret the time spent in the pursuit of her potions and spells? No. The village was a healthier, happier place for her efforts, even when its citizens didn't fully comprehend them.

"We can make do for now." The witch placed Rapunzel in her cradle. "I can soften bread in weak tea and stew some apples. Does that meet with your approval?"

Rapunzel sat up in her cradle, that unnerving blue-eyed stare never leaving the witch's face. Then the child clapped her hands together and gurgled.

"Well, I see that it does. Tomorrow we will explore the village, get you some proper things. But tonight? Let's get to know one another."

It was late when Rapunzel fell asleep in the witch's arms. She eased her into the cradle only to be caught short by the babe's cries moments later.

She knelt at the cradle's side, cupped a hand against the child's soft cheek. "We both must get some rest."

The babe quieted immediately, but the moment the witch withdrew her hand, the cries started anew, stronger, more strident than before.

"Oh, very well, it has been a rough day."

She scooped the babe up and carried her to the large bed behind a curtained wall.

"I imagine you could use the comfort."

But when the witch extinguished the lamp and felt the babe curled at her side, tiny fingers clutching her thumb, she wondered which one of them truly needed the comfort.

IT WAS NOT the sudden acquisition of a child that shocked the witch. No, she'd come to terms with that during the darkest hours of the night. It was not the surprise of a cow tethered to the cottage gate. This, she suspected, was a gift from Master Tailor.

It was the way Rapunzel's hair had grown overnight. The strands curled and swirled. They felt like silk flowing through the witch's fingers, their length already to the child's chin.

The witch pulled ancient volumes from a shelf and thumbed through them, searching for something, anything that might tell her what manner of sorcery this was. She thought back to the man in her garden all those months ago. What had she given him?

She peered at the child who sat at her wee table. "Was it a combination of plants your mother ate?"

Rapunzel slapped the wood of the table, blue eyes stormy, hair undulating. It bristled, strands on end like that of a thistle.

"She is still your mother," the witch said, her voice soft but no nonsense.

Another slap.

"Do you wish to be my daughter?"

Ah, the gurgle again. The hair calmed itself. Rapunzel peered at the witch, her blue eyes dark and serene.

"You shall be the daughter of my heart. Does that suit you?"

Rapunzel stood and toddled over to the witch. She clutched at her skirts with tiny fists.

"I see that it does." The witch bent down and clutched the child close. When she had Rapunzel nestled against her chest, the witch found herself stroking strands of that hair, much like she'd done all those months ago with the petals of the lion's tail. The locks slipped through her fingers as if they had a mind of their own.

"Inquisitive little beasts," she murmured.

And then froze. *The lion's tail.*

What manner of sorcery indeed.

"We have all been very, very foolish, I'm afraid," she whispered into the child's hair, "and you will be the one to pay for our folly."

THE WITCH TOOK Rapunzel with her everywhere. Aside from the father, there was no one she could trust in the village to watch the child and not gossip. And gossip they would. Already rumors flew about the miraculous growth of the child's hair.

Every morning, the witch worked to contain the strands before leaving the house. In a bonnet. Secured with bows. The strands had a life of their own, flowing through her fingers, curling into points, flicking back and forth, very much like a tail.

"Until we reach the woods, child," the witch would say. "Contain them until we reach the woods."

Rapunzel blinked, a frown marring her little brow as if she were trying hard to comply.

Even with the babe in a sling, the witch felt lighter on her treks into the forest. With her age, she knew the senselessness of rushing. Leave that to the young. She'd complete her tasks all in good time. This morning was no different.

In a clearing, she set Rapunzel on a blanket, handed her a crust of bread to gnaw on, and began her work.

"I will teach you this," she said, flicking a glance and her words over one shoulder. "I will teach you which plants to consume and which ones to avoid. I'll show you when to cut, how to cut, and when neither of those things matters."

The witch inched her way around the clearing, always darting a look toward its center, toward Rapunzel. The child seemed content to chew her bread, clap her hands, and track the witch's progress. Not for the first time, her thoughts drifted to Rapunzel's mother. How could she abandon such a child? So compliant. So calm.

"We will see how long that lasts, won't we?" the witch said with a wink.

Perhaps it was that steely gaze or the miracle of the hair that now hid the scars on Rapunzel's scalp, but the witch swore the child understood more than she ought.

"Which makes me feel less foolish when I talk to myself," she added.

Rapunzel gurgled.

The witch was near the old willow tree when a cry sounded behind her. Her throat tightened, and she was certain some harm had come to Rapunzel. Or perhaps the mother had a change of heart, followed them this morning, and was intent on stealing the child away.

Instead, when she turned, the witch came nose to nose with a river rat. The thing was large and hairy, its gray fur matted and stinking of stagnant water. This was not the sort of creature that kept the barn cats fat. This was the sort of creature that took whiskers and tails as trophies.

Where there was one rat, there would be another; they hunted in pairs. She'd survive a bite, although the infection would linger, and nastily so. Rapunzel? The daughter of her heart? A child barely bigger than a cat?

The cry went up again. The witch started forward, taking an inventory of the arsenal she had on hand. A pair of shears. Some twine. A handful of willow branches that she might fashion into a switch.

Rapunzel still sat in the center of the clearing. Despite the tears that washed her cheeks and tiny hands clenched into fists, she was unharmed. It was the sight of the child's hair that froze the witch in place.

The strands had grown, not by inches, but whole yards. They flowed across the clearing as if exploring new territory. They curled and lashed out, the ends sharpening into points. Like teeth. Like claws.

Several locks had already trapped the second rat, bound it neck to tail, so all the witch could see of it was its grubby nose and crooked whiskers. Now several locks worked in tandem, approaching the first rat from two sides and from behind. The creature hissed—at the witch, at its predicament. A predator such as this always knew when it had met its match.

It made one desperate lunge, an attempt to inflict injury before succumbing itself. Claws extended, teeth bared, it launched itself from the branch, its target the witch's face.

The golden strands of Rapunzel's hair caught the beast midair. A slashing. A slicing. The carcass tumbled to the ground and landed with a soft thud.

Only for a moment did the witch hesitate. Only for a moment did she consider what the villagers might make of this child. Cries of monster echoed in the back of her mind. But then she rushed to the center of the clearing. The golden strands parted, let the witch through to her child, and she clutched Rapunzel to her.

With that tender embrace and her quiet words, the hair relaxed its guard. The strands softened their points, retracted until their length was a touch longer than earlier that day.

The witch cupped Rapunzel's face. "Do you know what it is you can do, child?"

Rapunzel stared, unblinking.

"Is it even you who is doing this, or is it your wonderfully monstrous hair?"

At the words, the strands extended, a lock wrapping around the witch's wrist, none too gently.

"Cut that out," she said to the golden rope around her wrist. "It takes offense far too quickly. We will have to work on that."

The hair tightened its grasp, while a separate lock flicked back and forth, once again an angry tail.

"If you are to live in this world, you will need to learn to control your hair."

Rapunzel stared back, steely-eyed as ever. Then she clapped her hands together and gurgled.

The hair relaxed its grip and flowed into golden ringlets.

The witch released a sigh. Yes, to live in this world. That would not be an easy thing.

RAPUNZEL SOON OUTGREW her cradle and wee table and chair. Her hair evaded all attempts to tame or trim it, and the strands quickly traveled down her back to her knees, until it swept the ground. Every morning, the witch would braid the strands, and Rapunzel would loop the plaits around her arms or her waist. She grew into her beauty and her strength, for she did everything under the weight of her hair.

The witch became deft at avoiding the majority of the villagers who might cause problems. The father was kind and no worry. He left Rapunzel all manner of carvings and trinkets. Master Tailor kept them in cow's milk, although the witch made a point to avoid his wife.

Once, on a walk to the forest, they encountered Rapunzel's mother. The woman herded two children—twins—in front of her. The girls danced along the lane, skinny arms freckled, red hair thin but flowing down their backs—free of all of the constraints the witch placed on Rapunzel's hair.

The daughter of her heart halted, her spine impossibly straight beneath the weight of all her hair. She locked her gaze on the trio, strands of hair straining against their braids.

Then one lock escaped, slithered down the lane after the mother and two girls. A few strands wrapped themselves around the woman's ankle. It was then the witch pulled the shears from her apron pocket and snipped the lock.

The strands released their grip, twitched much like a dying snake, and at last ceased all movement. The woman walked on, oblivious.

"She cannot hurt you, child," the witch said.

Rapunzel glared, a non-answer if there ever was one. She was at that age—no longer a true child, not yet a woman. And the witch knew she'd spoken a lie.

Of course the mother still had the power to hurt. All mothers did. Try as she might, the witch couldn't banish the image of the quivering strands of hair, lying dusty along the lane. Try as she might, she couldn't muster the courage to ask for forgiveness.

But that night, Rapunzel crept into the witch's bed, curled next to her, and clutched her thumb with long, slender fingers.

~

ONE MORNING, in Rapunzel's sixteenth year, they awoke to an odd humming that came from outside the cottage. Rapunzel peered through the shutters, her hands poised to open them to the morning sunshine, her fingers unmoving.

"Child, please, let in the fresh air," the witch said.

Rapunzel's hands remained still. "There are many strange men outside our door."

On the way to the door, the witch secured a broom. She sprang across the threshold, broom handle connecting with a jaw here, a temple there.

"Go, go! All of you. She is too young to marry."

True, Rapunzel had fully grown into her beauty, and when tame, her hair was a sight to behold, glimmering without the benefit of light. The witch had not anticipated this, however. Not so soon, and not so many suitors.

In retrospect, perhaps she should have.

Rapunzel's father took to guarding the path to the cottage, but this only worked for so long. Men came daily, hourly, knocks on the door, the windows. More than one man tried the chimney only to find his breeches smoldering from a stoked fire.

After a night of off-key serenading that had left them both bleary-eyed, the witch decided.

"We must leave the village."

The daughter of her heart peered through the shutters, the tips of her braids twitching. "Why do they want me? They do not even know me."

"They want your beauty."

"But my beauty isn't me. If that is all they want, then surely I will disappoint them."

"That is something none of them understand."

Rapunzel's gaze darted toward the door. Already a fresh crop of men lined the path, their murmurs rising in the morning air.

"But how?" she asked. "How will we leave?"

"Do they make you angry?"

"Oh, they do."

"Remember that when you step outside, and all will be well."

Rapunzel's father packed the wagon and hitched the horses. For the first time since the day he gave his daughter away, he ventured inside the witch's cottage, cupped her cheek, and told her goodbye forever.

The witch stepped from her cottage for the last time, cries and calls of the men thickening the air around her.

"Going somewhere, Mistress Witch?"

"Can we follow?"

"Is there room in your wagon for me?"

Men lined the path three deep. The witch traveled its center until she reached the wagon. There, she climbed into the driver's seat and took the reins from Rapunzel's father. She gave him a reassuring nod before speaking to the men who had chased her from her home.

"Gentlemen," she said, "if I were you, I'd step back."

No one heeded her warning.

When Rapunzel emerged, the cries grew louder still. Jeering and whistles and bids for attention. One man and then another blocked her path. Two grabbed her wrists. A third—the tallest and fairest, the only one dressed in nobleman's attire—pushed the others aside in his quest for her.

But when the last of her unencumbered hair cleared the doorway, a gasp filled the air. The strands whipped and whirled, the ends sharpening into teeth, into claws. The men released her. Some ran, the nobleman among them. Others froze in place. Rapunzel walked, expression serene, hands folded in front of her, while her hair dispatched the men.

The slate walkway ran with blood. Bits of flesh speckled the walls of the witch's garden. The cries went from jeering to unearthly, the agony sharp in the air.

No one followed them from the village.

THEY RODE FOR DAYS, stopping only to sleep. The first night, when Rapunzel wished to keep them dry from the rain, her hair wove itself into a shelter.

"Oh, it can shield as well," Rapunzel said, her fingers investigating the crosshatch of strands above their heads, her eyes curious once again.

"Indeed it can, my child. Indeed it can."

At last they came to the borderlands, to a stone watchtower long abandoned. The space around it was vast and empty—only hill after hill that stretched into the horizon. No sign of a village, a farm, or even a hunter's cabin. Desolate and barren and the perfect spot for the two of them.

"Here," the witch said. "We can make this our home."

And yet, as she said these words, the ground shook with the force of approaching horses. In the distance, the standard of the war prince fluttered above a line of soldiers on horseback.

"Quick, Rapunzel, hide. In the wagon. Pull in all your hair."

The wagon creaked with the weight of Rapunzel and all her hair. The horses whinnied as if they wished to cover the sound. They were good beasts, the witch thought, and they loved Rapunzel almost as much as she did.

When the war prince arrived, the witch bowed low.

"Mistress Witch, may I ask what you're about?" the prince asked.

He was a powerful man, large and dark, a mask partially shrouding his features. His eyes, black and inquisitive, took in everything. They surveyed the tower, the horses, the wagon, all before returning to the witch.

"But of course, Your Highness," the witch said. "I plan to use this tower for my home. It is no longer in your use, is that right?"

"That's true, but the borderlands are dangerous, and my army is small in number." He waved a hand at the group behind him. They were a motley crew, large and small, green-skinned or not, pockmarked or masked for reasons the witch decided not to contemplate.

"I cannot guarantee your protection," he added.

"And I do not ask for it. All I ask for is quiet to practice my craft."

"And if a troll happens by while you're practicing your craft?" Now those dark eyes were lit with humor.

"Oh, Your Highness, I have lived long enough to know exactly what to do with a troll if one happens by."

The prince laughed. "I believe you do, Mistress Witch. But be warned, this is a lonely stretch of land. Men seldom travel it."

"That's what makes it perfect, Your Highness."

He laughed again, as if he took her meaning. He bid her farewell and rode away, his soldiers following, their horses kicking up dust that floated on the humid air. The witch tasted that air and licked her lips.

"It shall rain soon," she declared. "Let's get settled."

The watchtower had a single entrance that the witch sealed over once their belongings were inside. It was cozy here, space enough to work and live, and the window let in sunlight and fresh air but would shield them from rain.

"But how shall we leave?" Rapunzel asked.

"I shall climb down the face of the tower," the witch said. "There are hand and footholds that should not crumble beneath my weight. Or perhaps your clever hair might weave itself into a ladder."

At the suggestion, the golden strands did just that, the construction so quick it produced a breeze within the circular room.

"But I cannot climb down a ladder of my own hair," Rapunzel began, then clamped her mouth shut. "Oh, I see. This is to be my prison."

"Not a prison, child, but a sanctuary." The witch laid her palm against Rapunzel's cheek. "If your hair were not so fierce, so untamable, you might seek a quiet life in some faraway village. But when we left, your hair felled two dozen strong men."

"And no one wants to live near a monster."

The witch tugged her close, wrapping her bony arms around the daughter of her heart. "You are no monster—"

"But my hair—"

"Seeks out injustice. It always has. Why would it attack the woman who gave you life, but not your father? Why does it lash out at men whose only interest is your beauty?"

"The world doesn't want that sort of justice, does it?"

"I'm afraid it does not."

"I will stay, then." Rapunzel gathered handfuls of her hair. It flowed and swayed and cascaded to the floor in waves. "We shall stay. Perhaps I can teach it to behave."

The witch spent her days in the forest, gathering herbs and berries. Every fortnight, she ventured to the nearest village for supplies. She traded with merchants there, weaving her deception. Just an old crone brewing potions and remedies. That spring, the lion's tail grew thick in the woods. Every time the witch caught sight of it, she flinched, only to confront yet another clump a few feet away.

Rapunzel practiced remedies and potions along with the witch. Together they cultivated containers of herbs and small plants so Rapunzel might feel the soil beneath her fingers without leaving the tower. Beneath her touch, the plants flourished. She coaxed all manner of exotic flowers from the soil, even those the witch had never managed to on her own. Their petals brightened the little room and perfumed the air.

At night, she studied history and took a particular interest in the battles once waged in the borderlands and the ghosts said to walk and howl, searching for their old regiments or gutted homes.

"I do not hear these howls," Rapunzel said one evening. She lifted the heavy locks beneath her hands. "Perhaps my hair is too thick against my ears."

"Perhaps people search for excuses not to inhabit these lands," the witch said.

"Perhaps." Rapunzel remained at the window for a long time, her gaze exploring the borderlands, the very tips of her hair twitching like that of a penned beast.

For eight months, they lived in quiet in their watchtower. The war prince had been right. Few strayed this close to the border. Once, the prince himself rode by on patrol, a small group of soldiers at his side.

"I see you live well, Mistress Witch," he called out.

The witch leaned from the tower's window and called back, "Very well and very alone, Your Highness. However, I see you have added to your party."

The witch inclined her head as the prince's younger brother rode forward. He was light where the war prince was dark, unmasked and unscarred. Even from a distance, the witch felt those legendary gray eyes taking in everything. In this, he was very much like his brother.

With a hand, she shielded her own eyes and hid her frown. There was something about him that unsettled her. True, she never paid much heed to palace gossip. Even so, she knew that the younger prince preferred the boudoir to the battlefield for his conquests.

With as much stealth as possible, she gestured at Rapunzel, urging the child to conceal herself further, to constrain every last strand of golden hair. Rapunzel merely covered her mouth with a hand so as to not to laugh out loud, her hair rippling across the floor with repressed mirth.

"Perhaps this stretch of land is not so lonely for you now, Your Highness," the witch said, her voice rougher than she liked.

The war prince cast his brother a look. "Perhaps not."

As the party rode off, the witch considered that perhaps she and the war prince also had something in common.

They were both liars.

LATER, the witch would admit that she'd grown complacent. Life with the daughter of her heart was more than she had ever hoped for. Her trips to the village grew more frequent. Perhaps those gave her away. Perhaps she called too loudly for Rapunzel to lower her ladder of hair. Perhaps someone followed her, spied on them, although who would be curious about an old crone living alone, the witch couldn't say.

But when she returned from her most recent trip to the village and saw not the golden ladder of hair but one of wood propped against the tower, the witch knew she'd betrayed Rapunzel in some fashion. She dropped the reins and leaped from the wagon. The horse, so gentle and loving, simply continued forward to meet its sister. The witch scampered up the ladder, her hands catching on the rough grain so much she had to claw her way to the window.

There, in the center of the room, Rapunzel stood. Around her, strands of her hair whipped and whirled, the ends sharp and deadly. Like teeth. Like claws. A monster of a thing. On the floor? A man.

A dead man—a dead nobleman from the looks of his clothes—one who had suffered the death of a thousand cuts, a thousand bites. One whose breeches were around his ankles. One whose hand had torn away the bodice of Rapunzel's dress.

"He surprised me. I never heard him until he cleared the window." Rapunzel stared straight ahead, her gaze on the window, not on the man, and not on the witch, a hollow look haunting her blue eyes. "And then ... and then ... Mother, I'm ... I'm ..."

"No!" While flight had never been one of the witch's skills, she flew across the room, cradled Rapunzel to her. "You are not sorry. This is not your fault."

"But—"

"He is dead. A lone nobleman, venturing out on his own, in the borderlands? This will surprise no one."

"Turn him," Rapunzel said, her voice devoid of emotion, a dead thing.

Panic gripped the witch, had her by the throat. With a foot, she complied, heaving the dead man onto his back. Fair hair. Royal crest.

The war prince's brother.

"He will come searching, won't he?" Rapunzel said. This was no question. "The war prince will search for his brother."

"Perhaps. The borderlands are vast. It may be months before we see him again. And by then?" The witch surveyed the man, the window, and considered how they might accomplish this next task.

"If your hair can lower him to the ground, I shall bury him in the woods. I feel winter in my bones. An early snowfall will be welcome."

Rapunzel nodded. "I shall scrub his blood from our floor."

Without another word, Rapunzel's hair wrapped the man from head to foot and lowered him through the tower's window. When the witch reached the ground, she was surprised to find the longest strands of hair in a dense copse behind the tower, the claws already digging a grave.

By the time the witch found a shovel, the man was deep in the ground. So she took up an ax and splintered the ladder into kindling. And by the time she finished that chore, those beastly strands of hair had scattered dry leaves across the grave, the fresh-turned soil all but hidden.

She eased a hand beneath a lock of that hair. "Thank you," she said. "Thank you for protecting her, thank you for being so fierce."

The strands wrapped and unwrapped themselves around her wrist before caressing her cheek.

DESPITE HER OWN WORDS, the witch knew. A dead prince was still a dead prince, and justice would be served. A week later, when the war prince rode up with a contingent of his soldiers, she was ready to face that justice.

"Good day to you, Mistress Witch."

The witch stood at the base of the tower. "And to you, Your Highness." She bowed low. She liked this dark and masked prince, even though today he would, no doubt, declare her death sentence.

"I wonder if you can help me."

"I will try, Your Highness."

"My brother has gone missing. You met him on our last patrol through these parts. Did you happen to see him or even converse with him?"

Behind the prince, one of his soldiers unleashed a dog. Oh, yes, the witch thought, he knew the answer already. A moment later, so did everyone else. The hound let out a howl before digging at the fresh grave.

"Tell me, Mistress Witch, how did he come to die?"

She drew herself up tall, raised her chin. "I killed him, Your Highness."

To her surprise, the prince laughed—a dark, somber laugh to be sure, but a laugh, nevertheless. "I doubt that."

"Doubt what you will, Your Highness, but do you see anyone else here?"

"You have just admitted to murder, and of one of the royal family. Do you wish for death?"

"I am but an old crone, and death does not scare me."

"I suspect you might scare death itself," the prince murmured. "But you leave me no choice." With a sigh, he addressed the soldier next to him. "Arrest her." He returned his attention to the witch. "Unless you can give me a compelling reason not to."

"I can give you that reason."

The voice came from above, and it rang high and clear and unimpeded over the borderlands. The witch whirled, her chest constricting. No. Not Rapunzel. *No.* She shook her head, but the daughter of her heart paid her no heed.

Without another word, Rapunzel stepped onto the window's ledge. She jumped, her hair fanning out behind her before rushing to the ground to cushion her fall. She landed on her feet, knee-deep in golden locks.

"Your Highness, no," the witch began. "Please listen. She—"

The prince held up a hand, silencing her. "Let her speak."

"I killed him, Your Highness," Rapunzel said.

"Did you now? And you are?"

"Rapunzel."

"Rapunzel? With hair of teeth and claw?"

"I ... is that what they call me?"

"You are but a legend, a whispered story. I—" He broke off, his gaze drawn to the woods where the younger prince was buried. "My brother spoke of you."

"I am very real, Your Highness, and I have killed your brother."

"You confess to murder, then?"

"In self-defense, but yes, I do."

The prince fell silent. The soldiers behind him shifted in their saddles. The one who managed the dog corralled and leashed the beast. Then with a single, deliberate motion, the prince removed the black leather mask to reveal a face crisscrossed with scars.

"Look upon this face, Rapunzel," he commanded.

And she did.

"I have lost my only brother."

"I am sorry for your loss, Your Highness."

"You must understand that yes, he was my brother, and I confess to loving the boy he once was, but not the man he became." The prince contemplated Rapunzel as he spoke, as if taking in her full measure, as if sizing up an opponent. "That, perhaps, was unfair of me, unfair to him."

The prince drew his sword, the metal blade singing out. He aimed the blow directly at Rapunzel. A cry lodged in the witch's throat, and it took all her strength not to sink to her knees.

Rapunzel's hair whipped and whirled. When the frenzy subsided, she and the prince stood mere feet from each other, the tip of his sword poised at the hollow of her collarbone, the claws of her hair wrapped around his neck.

His soldiers sprang forward, weapons drawn.

"Stand down!" the prince called. When no one moved, he sheathed his own sword and said, "Stand down. She doesn't intend to injure me."

"True. I don't." With Rapunzel's words, her hair unraveled from around the prince's neck.

"And why is that?" He rubbed the skin of his throat, the move born of curiosity rather than pain.

"You did not intend to hurt me."

"And your hair." He gestured to the locks undulating along her back and on the ground. "It knew that."

"Yes, Your Highness."

A smile lit the prince's scarred face, then a laugh made it almost handsome. "Then I am lucky, for that was only my guess." This time when he contemplated Rapunzel, his gaze was lit with interest. "And now I face another sort of dilemma, for I not only lost my brother but my best fighter."

The witch's heart caught. The tips of her fingers grew cold, her legs numb. "Your Highness, you can't possibly mean—"

Once again, the prince silenced the witch's protest with the barest flick of his wrist.

"I mean everything I say, Mistress Witch." He directed his gaze toward Rapunzel once again. "Will you join my company and replace the man you have killed?"

Murmurs rose from the assembled soldiers. One stepped forward, probed a lock of hair with the toe of his boot. The strands curled around his ankle, and the man landed on the ground.

"She is but a girl!" another called out.

"I am strong," Rapunzel said. She hefted her hair in both her hands. "I have been carrying the weight of this all my life."

"A burden for certain," the prince said.

"How will she ride?" someone else asked. "We have no cart for all that hair. We travel light."

Before the soldier even stopped speaking, her hair swirled. It wove complicated patterns, fitted itself to her body until she was covered in what looked like golden chainmail.

"It seems I won't need any armor," Rapunzel said. "Or a cart."

"Any more dissent? Perhaps you'd like to confer with my brother." The prince gestured at the grave. "I'm certain he has an opinion on the matter."

With the prince's words, the witch knew: the matter was settled. Strength returned to her limbs, and a strange, detached determination filled her. She saddled a horse, and the sisters whinnied their goodbyes, tails swishing. She secured a bag of provisions and one of potions and remedies. If she could, the witch would have packed her heart as well, for it was too swollen and sore in her own chest.

"Goodbye, daughter of my heart." The witch presented the reins to Rapunzel.

"Mother?" Rapunzel's eyes grew large, as if only now she realized the consequences of her choice. "I don't want—"

The witch hushed her. "Of course you do. It is right and good for children to leave home, to have adventures. This prince is a good man," she added. "He will not lead you astray."

"I can't promise you comfort," the prince added. "Or even safety. But adventure? That I can promise."

Rapunzel's gaze went once again to the horizon, her eyes lit with the promise of the adventure that it held.

"Go with him, child. Go be free."

Rapunzel hugged the witch, mounted her horse, and joined the prince's company. They rode off, and the witch tracked them until Rapunzel blended into the horizon. Even then, the witch stood at the base of the tower. At last she turned and confronted its surface.

"I'm not sure I know the spell to conjure up another entrance, or a staircase, for that matter." She said these words to the horse, who snuffled and snorted a reply. "I'm not sure these old bones can stand the climb."

Before the witch could even try, a golden ladder tumbled from the window. She grasped the silky strands, hardly daring to breathe, and climbed up to the ledge. Once she stood inside, the strands returned to the tower. They flowed through the window and into one of Rapunzel's containers of exotic flowers, where they burrowed beneath the soil.

Then, in a moment that was no more than a blink of an eye, a stem pushed up and through, and the bloom of a lion's tail unfurled.

With Hair of Teeth and Claw was first published in The Shapeshifter Chronicles.

ABANDONMENT ISSUES

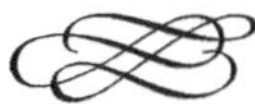

PARANORMAL

here are places you don't want to wake up.

Flat on your back in a plowed-under field, clumps of earth stabbing your spine.

That's one of them.

A CEO's office, your own drool defacing the mahogany desk, the room dark, the only sounds the hum of a custodian's vacuum and your own thudding heart.

That's another.

Aberdeen Proving Grounds, in the Joint Personal Effects Depot, surrounded by containers that hold so little and yet, so, so much.

That's a third.

Today, when I wake up, my joints ache with cold. I'm on my back as if I've been dropped from one reality into another. Around me, metal ticks and groans. It's the sound of abandonment. No footfalls. No hint of breathing except my own. Empty places feel empty. This, I've learned.

I consider when to sit up. Too soon, too quickly, and I'll vomit. This, too, I've learned—the hard way.

From my vantage point on the floor, I study the space. It looks industrial, with row upon row of control panels with dials and gauges. The layer of grime on the floor might act as insulation—if it weren't so disgusting.

Despite all this, there's nothing specific to grasp. No signs with words, no distinct sounds except the rasp of my own breath. No clue as to where I might be.

I press a palm against the cold tile, but before I can sit, I do hear something new.

Slow, deliberate footsteps punctuate the air around me. I bolt upright, scramble to my feet, only to pitch forward into a control console. My head swims. My vision tunnels. A second later, I coat a series of dials and buttons with a spray of vomit.

"Weak," a voice behind me says. "Always so weak."

I spin and then regret it as another wave of nausea hits me. I grope the panel behind me, fingers reaching for a dry, solid spot.

"Tell me, at least, that you've figured it out."

The man before me must be at least seven feet tall. He wears a long black coat. The scent of damp wool clogs the space between us while a swirl of smoke rises in the air. His face looks as though someone has carved it in alabaster, all sharp edges and angles—and familiar. I've seen him before. I blink. Yes, certainly.

But where?

"You've made the connection, haven't you?" he says.

Stray thoughts fill my mind, the barest tendril of an idea. I consider the trips I've taken and the places I've landed.

The field, for instance, with its old farmhouse. In the root cellar, I found a lockbox. Inside that, a deed with my grandfather's name. Evidence of bounty lost in the Great Depression. Moments after my fingers touched the yellowed paper, something whisked me back to my actual life.

The man's lips curl into a hint of a smile. No, *someone* whisked me back.

In that CEO's office, I found a birth certificate, listing my name, my mother's, and a third—the one embossed in gold on the door. Again, I could only hold the paper for seconds before that particular place vanished as well.

This is why, when I found myself in the Personal Effects Depot, I held my breath. My fingers inched their way through Gabe's container until I found the one thing I couldn't bear to leave behind. I gripped the chain of his dog tags so tightly that the tiny ball bearings left welts on my skin. But I had them. They traveled back with me.

I have them now.

But how does this place, with its soot and oil and years of grime, relate? Cold, impersonal, insubstantial. Even this man of smoke and oil could evaporate in an instant.

Assuming he doesn't kill me first.

My confusion must show on my face because the man shakes his head and makes a tsking sound.

"Weak and slow. I can't imagine how you've made it this far."

While I don't know what he means, I can only agree.

He takes a step forward. And I, still clutching the console, take three skittering steps to the side. My mind races. Dog tags and deeds and birth certificates. What does it all mean?

"Of course, you are pretty," the man says. "The pretty ones are never very bright."

I stop taking those skittering, hesitant steps. With all my will, I hope he closes those last few feet between us. I have a roundhouse kick I'd like him to meet. Behind me, something drips, the steady plink of a dam about to break.

"Nothing?" the man asks.

My mouth is dry. I long to tip my head back and catch a few drops of that water. Even if I could, it wouldn't loosen any words.

"Ah, well," he says. "At least you are pretty. There's consolation in that." He grins, and something sparks in his eyes. "For me, at least."

I grip the console tighter. The man steps forward, raises a hand as if to caress my cheek. I don't let him. That last step leaves him open. Perhaps it's meant to intimidate, this stance, to show off his height or that he doesn't find me a threat.

What it does is give me a target.

My foot ricochets off him three times—knee, groin, jaw. A crack. A thud. A howl. I should finish him off, but perhaps he is right: I am too weak. Instead, I shake out my leg, push from the console, and run.

A CADENCE POUNDS in my head along with my footfalls. *Dog tags* and *deeds* and *birth certificates*, and then, *Oklahoma, Chicago, Afghanistan.* If I run fast enough, maybe I can catch the connection that eludes me.

Everything is cold and damp and empty. An occasional drip lands on my nose or the back of my neck and sends shivers skittering across my skin.

My footsteps are too loud, my breathing too heavy. It's all I hear in my frantic charge down this passageway. If someone chases me, I won't know until too late. With that thought, I spin, search the dimly lit corridor behind me—no impossibly tall man with alabaster skin. I wheel around and continue my headlong dash forward.

The object I crash into is solid and warm. It says, "Oomph," when it strikes the floor. So do I. The landing jars my wrists, paralyzes my arms. I can't move them, not to fight, not to defend myself. I kick away from the figure opposite me, legs struggling, hands useless. Then the figure—a man—lunges.

He grabs my feet and nothing more.

"Hang ..." His head droops with the effort to breathe, to speak. "On. Won't hurt you."

Gradually, I inch into a sitting position, still braced to run. When he lifts his head, I peer into the dark eyes of not the man I dispatched with a roundhouse kick, but those of my brother, Gabe.

Gabe. Who died in Afghanistan. All I can do is mouth his name. No sound emerges from my throat except for one, plaintive croak.

"Yeah," he says. "I know."

"I ... how?" My voice is rough, but the words, at last, are there.

He shakes his head.

The implication—the connection—hits me, sends me reeling backward so I might collapse on the floor again. My arms, still weak, tremble beneath me. I scan the space around me, this *here* that really isn't.

"Am I dead?" My question is quiet, and it sinks in the cold air around us.

"I don't know," Gabe says.

"Why are we here?"

He shakes his head. "I keep traveling—flashing, really—to different places, then back to Afghanistan. Always Afghanistan."

"The Army sent someone to the house. They knocked on the door..."

I break off, not wanting to narrate Gabe's death, not now, not here, not ever.

How I knew, even before opening the door, the shadow of a uniform through the etched glass, like smoke and oil blotting out the sun. He doesn't need to know these things.

"I keep going back to Afghanistan," he says. "Hell, I wish I wouldn't. Anywhere else must be better." His gaze surveys the dark, damp space around us. "Well, almost anywhere." He climbs to his feet and then offers me his hand.

Despite the cold, metallic air, his skin is so warm.

Even with Gabe at my side, this place is strange and hollow. Abandoned, like that field in Oklahoma, that daughter in Chicago, the soldier in Afghanistan. And yet, different.

It's missing life or some essential component of life. After all, a plowed-under field has its uses. A birth certificate can list a father who might not live in your life, but at least he lives. The personal effects of a soldier represent a life that once was.

But this place has none of that. It's too empty, too impersonal to be hell.

"Do you think this might be purgatory?" I ask Gabe.

Before he can answer, sharp, slow applause echoes. It's a brutal sound that infects the air with cruelty.

"Brava, Miss Malloy." It's the impossibly tall man again, all alabaster white and yet shrouded in smoke and oil. "You're not as slow as I first suspected and certainly not as dimwitted as your ... what is he, exactly? Your half-brother?" He casts a look at Gabe. "Honestly, it's as if you enjoy dying in Afghanistan."

Behind me, Gabe shifts, his hand resting on the small of my back, a posture that means he plans to take the fight over flight option—and wants me to do the opposite. But I'm pretty good with a roundhouse kick —thanks to Gabe—so all I do is tense in reply.

"Yes." The man rubs his jaw. "You are fairly competent."

"Am I also dead?"

"Are you?" And now his voice is laced with that smoke and oil, the sound deep and seductive. It's enough to make you flutter your eyelids shut, if only for a moment. When I do, I see him, the harbinger of death, standing on my doorstep, wearing—of all things—an Army uniform with chaplain insignia.

"It's up to me, then?" I say.

"Is it?" His tone matches the single, arched eyebrow.

I officially loathe the man in front of us. An oily smile spreads across his face. He revels in my hate, soaks it in.

"It's so pure," he says, "undiluted. Absolute. You don't often hate, which makes it all the more delicious."

Gabe bristles and steps in front of me.

"Oh, go on, big brother. Protect her, if you can, and if I don't dispatch you back to Afghanistan."

"Run," Gabe says, the word a growl. "Run and don't look back."

"I tried that," I say. "It didn't work." *I could run forever.*

"And I will always catch you," the man says.

"Run!" This time, Gabe's voice cracks.

I see what the man of smoke and oil plans to do. If he can read my thoughts, then perhaps I can sense his intentions. Static fills the air. I smell dry heat. Grit fills my mouth. I work to blink sand from my eyes. I land somewhere real this time.

Afghanistan.

A battle wages, but in this pocket of craggy hills and rock, the three of us stand as if we're the only people in the world.

The man of smoke and oil raises a hand.

I throw myself in front of Gabe and catch the full blast meant for him, pieces of it like shrapnel. They pierce my chest, my legs, my heart. I think I must be torn to ribbons. The impact throws me into Gabe.

Twin cries of "No!" echo around me.

Gabe gathers me in his arms. "Marta, what have you done?" He looks up, his fierce gaze locked on the alabaster man. "Don't do this, not to her. Don't let it happen."

"It ... can't," I say, even though my lungs seer with each word. "I never died in Afghanistan."

I pull the set of dog tags from beneath my shirt. The blast has fused them together. Smoke rises from the charred aluminum. And yet, the chain is cool to the touch.

"Yours." I drop the chain around Gabe's neck.

With a single howl, the man of smoke and oil evaporates, leaving behind only acrid air and soot. I breathe in both, and then everything vanishes.

❧

I JOLT AWAKE, and everything is white. For an instant, panic seizes me. But death doesn't smell like antiseptic, and I doubt the soundtrack for the afterlife contains soft clicks and beeps. I sit up, blink, and stare at Gabe.

His hospital gown is askew, exposing a bandaged shoulder. My fingers itch to adjust the gown, but my hands are clenched in his. Together we hold the dog tags as if they are a string of prayer beads.

At one time, I would have said that a hospital is a place where you didn't want to wake up. Now I know that isn't true.

Something teases my peripheral vision. I jerk my head, certain I've seen the man of smoke and oil, caught a glimpse of his alabaster face. And while a man does stand in the doorway, he only holds a pitcher of water.

"Sorry," he says. "I thought you might like something to drink.

I nod my thanks, my heart too high in my throat for words.

"He's done so much better since you arrived," the man adds.

I nod again.

"I doubt my sister would fly all the way to Germany for me." With that, he sets the pitcher on the tray table and leaves the room.

Gabe cracks open his eyes. "I bet his sister wouldn't throw herself in front of some psycho demon's death ray, either."

"You didn't die in Afghanistan."

"Doesn't look like it."

"Why?"

Gabe unfurls his fingers and studies the mangled dog tags. "You changed things when you refused to abandon me, even when I told you to run, even." He rattles the tags. "Even after I died."

I nod but remain silent. A glimpse of oily smoke catches my attention. There, in the corner of the room, but the inky tendrils scatter so quickly, I'm not sure they were there at all.

"Here." Gabe raises the chain. Compliantly, I lower my head so he won't have to strain. "You wear these from now on." He pauses, and I wonder if he can see the oily smoke or just senses it. "They'll keep you safe."

I clutch the dog tags tight in my palm and know this one thing: They will.

Abandonment Issues may be the closest thing to horror that I've written (clearly, I scare easily).

THE GHOST MUST GO ON

PARANORMAL

Locker thirty-five in Springside High School has always been haunted.

At least, as far as I know.

I press a hand against the cool metal, searching out the sensation that tells me an otherworldly presence is nearby. My business partner, Malcolm Armand, places his hand above mine. He stands so close that the pocket of air between us warms with the scent of nutmeg and Ivory Soap.

"Do you sense anything?" I ask, keeping my voice hushed in the long-emptied hallway.

It's like we're violating some rule, milling about the corridors long after everyone has left for the day. No teachers. No kids. Some places feel off when completely empty. A high school is one of them.

"There it is," Malcolm says. "Do you feel that?"

Something stirs beneath my palm. It feels like a yawn. "I think we woke it up."

"Man, I've met some lazy ghosts, but this one barely registers. I'm not sure it's an actual ghost, never mind our culprit."

"It's not," I say. "I only wanted to make sure."

Truthfully, part of me wanted to check on an old friend. The ghost of locker thirty-five might not possess a sparkling personality, but it is consistent. I'm not sure there is a culprit, not in this case, and we're in for a long night of walking the halls and checking bathrooms for a ghost that doesn't exist.

"Does it ever do anything?" he asks.

"Only on pep rally days, then it"—I wave a hand at the locker—"expels everything onto the floor. It gets excited. I think."

During my four years at Springside High, I never had locker thirty-five, although I've stepped over the mess its occupant made plenty of times.

"Performance anxiety?" Malcolm suggests. "I used to throw up before every cross country meet."

I turn to him. The hallway is dark enough that reading the expression in his eyes is difficult, but this surprises me. Malcolm is always so confident, so self-assured. I've only known him a few months, but if you asked me, I'd say he had one of those charmed high school experiences.

"Really?" I say.

"Yeah. Really." He takes my hand. "Come on. Let's tell Gregory he doesn't have a ghost problem."

His skin is so warm against mine. Technically, we're working, which means, technically, we shouldn't be holding hands. But the lines blur after five in the afternoon. Malcolm, my business partner, becomes Malcolm, my boyfriend. We have rules around this because, as co-owners of K&M Ghost Eradication Specialists, we work so well together.

We don't want K&M the couple ruining that.

But rules have exceptions. I think holding hands with Malcolm while walking the halls of my old high school happens to be one of those.

"What do we tell Gregory instead?" Malcolm asks.

"That it's most likely kids playing a practical joke on him? I mean, I'm sure they've all seen the Ghost B Gone webcasts. They're still up on YouTube."

Before Gregory took on a substitute-teaching job and volunteered to direct the school play, he was Gregory B Gone of Ghost B Gone, a web show that did weekly ghost evictions.

Granted, the most dangerous thing they ever "evicted" was a sprite— well, almost. There was that encounter with an evil entity, but that never ended up on video. It's not something any of us like to talk about.

"He wants more than anything to see a real ghost," Malcolm says.

Oh, he does. He really does. That Gregory built an entire career and life around something he couldn't see, never mind sense, still puzzles me.

"This plays right into that," Malcolm adds.

I'm sure this is something the entire cast and crew of *You Can't Take It with You* have figured out. So when we arrive at the auditorium doors to find Gregory out front, expression lit with anticipation, I take the easy way out.

"You tell him," I whisper to Malcolm.

Unfortunately, Gregory hears.

"Tell me what? You found something, didn't you? I was right this time! Tell me I was right."

Malcolm skewers me with a look. "Coward," he mouths.

Why, yes. Yes, I am. Besides, of the two of us, Malcolm is the one who can work a room, talk to anyone, convince the only law firm in town that they need us on retainer. (You'd be surprised how many divorce lawyers end up haunted.) He can handle Gregory.

Me? Well, I make the coffee.

Malcolm shakes his head. It's a slow, consoling sort of gesture. "You know, Katy and I were talking, and we think it's probably a practical joke your students are playing on you."

"We open in less than a week." Gregory throws an arm toward the auditorium's double doors. "Why would they do that?"

"Because they can. Because they're high school kids." Malcolm shrugs. "Maybe they want to see Ghost B Gone in action."

Gregory strokes his beard. It's closer to a goatee now, more award-winning director than rugged ghost hunter.

"So the flickering lights with no one in the booth?" he asks.

"A timer," Malcolm says. "That's pretty easy to rig up. I can even show you how."

"What about all the thumps and bumps?"

"Special effects?" I say. "I mean, you guys *are* in a theater. You have that sort of thing, right?"

"The malfunctioning curtain?" Gregory tries again. "That couldn't be caused by a student, could it? The whole thing came crashing down.

Someone could've been hurt, and the kids were shook. I let them go early."

And that was when he called us. I want to suggest that the kids took things too far, so of course, they were scared. I cast a glance at Malcolm and see the same conclusion reflected in his eyes.

"And nothing since, right?" Malcolm says. "Things don't happen when you're here alone."

"I feel like I'm being watched." Gregory rubs a hand across the back of his neck and shudders. "It's kind of creepy, actually."

I decline to point out the overabundance of security cameras in the school.

Gregory pushes open the auditorium door and secures it with a stopper. He waves toward the stage and the curtain pooled at its edge. "So all of this? Just a practical joke?"

We head down the aisle to where we've left our field kit. I open my mouth to speak, to frame my response in the nicest way possible when an otherworldly presence invades the space. It's insidious at first, like a fine mist you don't notice until your clothes cling to your limbs and your hair is plastered to your scalp.

Gregory remains despondent, arms crossed, expression dour. His sense of the supernatural is nearly nonexistent. But Malcolm's isn't. I reach for his hand and find him doing the same. We lace fingers just as a jolt runs through me, cold, wild, and wholly unpredictable.

Then an unearthly howl fills the entire auditorium, one that we all hear—even Gregory.

BEHIND US, the auditorium doors slam shut. The lights flicker. An icy surge of air flows up the aisle, bathing us in goosebumps. The presence swirls around us, pushing us into one of the rows.

"Coffee?" Malcolm asks.

"Down front, in the field kit."

"We're about to go into a full-on ghost infestation here," he says, his voice taking on an edge.

I know, and the cold that comes with that will render the coffee we do have useless. We'll have to backtrack, get the camp stove, or figure out a way to brew on the premises. Assuming this thing will let us leave. The way it's shoving us into our seats makes that unlikely.

The ghost pushes again. I'm braced against Malcolm. He holds me steady, but his arms tremble with the effort. Gregory, on the other hand, lands hard in one of the seats. When he tries to stand, he's shoved back down again.

All ghosts want something, are driven by one overriding desire. Often this is nothing more than to feel human again, which is why coffee works so well to catch them. But some ghosts have an agenda. This one has enough strength that I'm not certain a cup of coffee will distract it long enough so we can trap it.

Assuming, of course, we can reach the field kit and the set of precision-made German thermoses filled with Kona blend.

With us pinned in the theater's prime viewing spots, the ghost retreats to the stage. It flows over the fallen curtain, the material undulating, and lets out another howl. The lights flicker again until a single spotlight shines on center stage.

"Katy?" Malcolm stares straight ahead. His voice is low, perfectly measured. "Do you think this ghost wants to star in a play?"

"A ghost could want that?" Gregory asks.

A ghost could. Not so long ago, Malcolm and I caught a ghost that wanted nothing more than constant attention and praise. Why shouldn't a ghost want to star in a show?

"You're brilliant," I whisper to Malcolm.

"Eh, not really."

But I catch a hint of a smile.

I clutch the seat in front of me and pull myself to standing. An icy cold finger shoves me backward, but Malcolm steadies me with a hand on the small of my back.

"I don't have a program," I declare. "I want to know who the star of the show is."

The neat stacks of programs by the door shoot upward. The space erupts in a flurry of paper. I duck, hands covering my head, but the sting of paper slicing skin is sharp. Malcolm swears. The cyclone of torn scraps tightens until it has swallowed up every last program. Then, like a cloudburst, the whole thing explodes, and bits of paper rain down on us.

Next to me, Gregory turns ashen. He stares, mouth slack, and then he buries his head in his hands.

"Those were the programs for opening night."

"Sorry?" I say, but it comes out small, pathetic, and useless.

Malcolm leans down to pluck a wayward program from the floor. He flattens the paper against his thigh. I read the list of names and realize my mistake.

Of course. The program is filled with student names, the actual performers in the play. No ghost included.

But then, neither are we. Well, Gregory is, as director. With that thought, an idea takes shape. I'm still standing—barely, but I straighten and call out.

"Malcolm, haven't you always wanted to work in the light booth, but no one would let you?"

Gregory casts me a look like I've lost my mind. To Malcolm's credit, he merely grins, those dark eyes of his taking on a gleam. He almost always knows what I'm thinking—and trusts me even when he doesn't.

"Yeah," he says, "there was this clique at school, the theater group. I never got the chance."

"Well, I've always wanted to be a stagehand." My voice doesn't ring quite as false now. There's something about talking nonsense to ghosts— and especially talking nonsense to ghosts with Malcolm—that inspires confidence. Besides, as a stagehand, I can approach the stage.

And then, I can grab the field kit and start pouring coffee.

"We have our director," I say, easing past Gregory.

He peers at me through the v made by his fingers. The look is both accusatory and curious. "We have our tech crew." I nod at Malcolm, who starts creeping along the row in the opposite direction.

I throw my arms wide. "And we have our star!"

The stage shimmers with the ghostly presence. Then the image contracts into an almost humanlike form. I squint, trying to detect something familiar about its shape, something that might give us a clue to what this ghost wants. Its outline is blurry, but I get the impression of an otherworldly sword in a scabbard at its side.

There must be thousands of plays that involve swords, but my mind goes blank. I can't think of a single one.

I approach cautiously, each step deliberate. I inch forward, crouching lower and lower with each step. By the time I reach the first row, I'm hunkered down, next to the floor. I loop the canvas straps around one arm and hurry toward the stairs to my left.

Center stage, there's a table already set up. It's the perfect spot to place the cups and start pouring the coffee. For a ghost this strong, we'll need all twelve cups: three black, three with half and half, three with sugar, and three extra sweet and extra light.

Always twelve, always the same combination. My grandmother, who taught me everything about ghost hunting, was adamant about this.

"As if ghosts don't have a preference," she'd always say.

I'm halfway there when I need to shield my eyes from the glare of the spotlight.

"Hang on," Malcolm says. His voice echoes in the quiet auditorium, and it's odd to have him sound so close without having him by my side.

I miss his sturdy warmth, his conviction. He either knows what to do or believes I know what I'm doing. In most cases, I'm running on instinct —this time included.

The brightness fades to something softer, an evening sort of glow. I blink, scan the stage, and locate the ghost. It's wavering as if it can't decide whether it likes me interfering with its show.

"Katy," Gregory calls out in a stage whisper. "There's a scene in *You Can't Take It with You* where Alice and her father have an emotional moment. It's just the two characters on stage. Maybe that's what this thing wants, to act out a scene."

I shake my head, not because he's wrong, but because he's so very right. And I know what comes next. My heart takes up residence in my throat. I can barely swallow and must force the protest from my mouth. "I don't know the play."

Gregory rummages in his messenger bag and pulls out a script. "I'll feed you the lines."

I meant to be a stagehand, to pour some coffee, ready a Tupperware container, and pounce on the ghost once it drank its fill. I have no intention of starring in a play, not with a ghost as a leading man, not even if the audience is only Malcolm and Gregory. Heat floods my cheeks, the sensation prickling. Even in the soft glow of the stage lighting, my blush must be apparent.

So must my discomfort, my awkwardness. Suddenly, I don't know what to do with my limbs.

"Just repeat the lines and pour the coffee," Malcolm says, his voice low, encouraging. "I bet that's all it takes."

So I do. Gregory feeds me each line. I stumble through the words. My hands shake, and I slosh coffee over the rim of three cups. I'm never this sloppy, haven't been this sloppy since I was eight.

At the scene's end, I'm supposed to embrace my father—or rather, my character is supposed to embrace her father. The ghost continues to waver by my side. Once or twice, it surged forward, swooped around the coffee cups, and then retreated.

The coffee's starting the cool. It won't tempt ghosts—or humans—for much longer. The ghost makes a final pass. As I'm reaching for the Tupperware, it settles next to the cup with extra cream and sugar.

"Yes." Malcolm's whisper fills the auditorium.

I'm poised to make the catch when the ghost slips beneath the table. All at once, the table leaves the floor, shooting upward. Cups scatter everywhere, and coffee splatters across the stage, onto the curtain, and—of course—onto me.

~

"KATY!"

Malcolm's voice is so loud that the speakers screech a protest. I slam my hands over my ears, not that it helps.

"Katy," he says, quieter now. "Are you okay? Did you get scalded?"

Scalding is an occupational hazard. I pluck damp sleeves from my arms, blow on the back of my hands. A few spots sting, but nothing requires immediate attention or the burn kit we keep in my truck.

"I'm okay. The coffee was already cool."

Well, cool-ish, anyway.

"You're sure?" Doubt laces Malcolm's voice. Yes, he knows I might lie about something like this.

"I'm sure. Really."

I peer into the rows below me. Gregory is standing, arms slack, script dangling from his fingers. He mouths something that might be a curse or a prayer.

"Maybe it doesn't like comedies?" I say.

To be honest, part of me is relieved. I don't want to stumble through more lines or playact on stage. I want to catch this ghost, go home, and wash the sticky, coffee-soaked sugar from my skin. I have the feeling that won't be happening any time soon.

Despite the spotlight's glare, I see the moment Gregory's eyes widen. His mouth opens, but it's Malcolm's voice I hear.

"Katy! Watch out! To your left ... right. Just—"

The creak of wheels against wooden floorboards has me jerking around. Barreling toward me is a structure that appears positively medieval—a battering ram or some elaborate device for scaling castle walls.

I leap back as the thing zooms past. It stops, abruptly, a few feet from where I now stand. Dust mingles with the scent of coffee, and I feel grit in my eyes and against my lips.

I sneeze.

"Oh," Gregory says, almost conversationally. "It's the balcony."

"Balcony?" I squeak.

"From last fall's *Romeo and Juliet*."

Of course.

From nowhere, a script lands at my feet with a thump. I pick it up before the puddles of coffee can do too much damage. I'm not surprised by the playwright's name.

William Shakespeare.

"Maybe it wants to do the balcony scene from *Romeo and Juliet*," Gregory suggests.

The ghost whirls around, its joy tangible. It fills the air with sparks; the underlying menace, the threat of a full-on ghost infestation lessens —slightly.

The ghost flies upward and smashes itself against the glass of the sound booth. Malcolm yelps, and his cry reverberates through the theater.

"Mood lighting, tech crew," Gregory says, sounding every inch the put-upon director. "We can't keep our star waiting."

The ghost returns to the stage the moment the lights dim, and Malcolm paints the area around me a deep indigo. Tiny fragments of light speckle the floor beneath my feet, the backdrop behind me, and I want to ask him how he figured out how to create starlight.

"Uh, Katy?" Gregory says.

I turn to face him, arms crossed over my chest.

"The scene needs a Juliet," he says. When I don't respond, he adds, "That's you."

He's right. The way this ghost swirls about, bumping against the back of my knees, I can already sense what it wants—me, on the balcony, waiting for my Romeo.

"I don't suppose you'd want to do a role reversal?" I say to it.

The whirling doubles, flavoring the air with anger—and more dust.

"Yeah," I mutter, "I didn't think so."

The balcony is oversized, cumbersome. Its shadow stretches across the stage, and I feel tiny in comparison.

"Secure the wheels," Gregory calls out. "We don't want you rolling off the stage."

No, no, we don't.

With the toe of my sneaker, I lock each wheel into place. Then I grip the rails that will help me navigate the set of stairs to the top. The climb takes longer than I expect, and my thighs protest each steep step I take.

Once I'm at the top, I grip the balcony's edge and peer out over the auditorium. Even though I'm fully dressed—if coffee-soaked—even though it's only Malcolm and Gregory witnessing this debacle, I feel exposed. I feel ... alone.

I feel like I'm back in high school, back when I was the girl who caught ghosts with her grandmother, the girl who made numerous trips into the boys' locker room to do just that.

The girl who was always the odd one out.

"You're Juliet. Look ... pensive," Gregory commands, still in director mode. He's scrolling frantically through something on his phone. He eyes me, and then his phone's screen. "I'll read Romeo."

He clears his throat, and when he speaks again, his full, modulated tone startles me so much that I nearly tip off the balcony.

"But, soft! what light through yonder window breaks? It is the east, and Juliet is the sun."

"*Damn*," comes Malcolm's whisper through the speakers. "I need to learn to do that."

The ghost surges upward as if it's Romeo, and I'm truly its Juliet.

Gregory continues to speak, low and sonorous, things like: *O, it is my love!* and *O, that I were a glove upon that hand, That I might touch that cheek!*

Malcolm coughs, once, twice, the third time coming out as a growl. Gregory casts him a quick look over his shoulder. Whatever passes between them is lost on me.

I'm still leaning forward as if I'm hanging onto every one of my ghost Romeo's words. The planks beneath my feet creak. I tap the wood, not certain the construction is all that sturdy. I grip the rail of the balcony even tighter.

I'm so distracted by this that when Gregory clears his throat, for what must be at least the third time, I start.

"What?" I say.

"Not what, *wherefore.*"

Wherefore? Oh. *Wherefore art thou.* Of course.

"Romeo," I begin, and my voice is a thin, reedy thing. "Romeo, wherefore art thou, Romeo?"

At least I know these lines, but then, I think everyone knows these lines. I'm poised to continue, to utter the next couple of sentences, at least. The next line is there on my tongue, so strong I can almost taste it: *Deny thy father and refuse thy name, for if thou wilt not but be sworn my love, and I'll no longer be a Capulet.*

Before I can, the planks beneath my feet groan again. The sound is ominous and fills the auditorium.

"Katy," Malcolm begins, his voice hushed and worried. "Maybe you should—"

I never hear what Malcolm thinks I should do. I plummet through the balcony floor, the only thing keeping me from falling to my death— or at least grave injury—is my grip on the balcony's rail.

I think I scream. At least, my throat aches in the aftermath of my plunge. One plank hits the stage with a thud, the other swings next to me, barely tethered to the structure by a couple of nails. At least, I think they're nails. I'm mostly concentrating on my tenuous hold on the rail, not to mention the long drop below.

And the fact I don't have too many options.

Gregory starts for the stage, but before he can clear the row he's been standing in, Malcolm tears down the aisle. He doesn't bother with the stairs but launches himself up and onto the stage.

And then he is there, standing beneath me, arms outstretched.

"Cross country?" I manage.

"And track in the spring."

"Varsity?"

He gives me a sheepish look. "Co-captain my senior year."

Around us, the scene is still set. The light is soft, like twilight. Malcolm looks every inch a knight in shining armor—or at least one in loafers and a pressed dress shirt. He looks like a boy I might have crushed on in high school, the one who might have never acknowledge my existence.

That isn't Malcolm. If I have any doubts about that, they vanish the moment he gives me one of his sweet, dark-roast smiles.

"Let go," is all he says.

"But—"

"Let go."

"Won't I hurt you?"

"You could never hurt me."

Sweat builds beneath my grip. My arms ache from fingertips to shoulders. Another minute and this won't be a choice. I'll slip.

"And I won't drop you, Katy."

So I shut my eyes, and with one deliberate movement, I commit.

I let go.

The fall lasts forever and is over in a second. Malcolm catches me. He teeters for a moment, then we both crumple to the stage. We remain there, panting, gasping, and when I catch his eye, I don't even need to ask.

He's okay.

So am I.

"Uh, guys," Gregory says. "You should probably do something about that."

We struggle to stand, Malcolm tugging me up with a hand, and confront the thing that Gregory is pointing at.

Center stage, one of my Tupperware containers sits. It's one of the larger ones, and it's missing its lid. That, in itself, isn't so remarkable. What's remarkable is what happens to be inside the container.

Our ghost.

Malcolm laces his fingers with mine, and we approach, steps soft and controlled. But I'm not sure the effort matters. When we reach the ghost, it floats contently inside the Tupperware. Something that sounds like a ghostly sigh fills the space around us, and in it, I think I hear an apology.

I kneel next to the container and ease on the lid.

"Now what?" Malcolm's hand rests on my shoulder. "Nature preserve?"

That's our standard procedure for releasing a ghost once we've caught it. For the really nasty ones, we drive further out. Once, we went all the way to Wisconsin.

I hold up the container and peer at the ghost inside. "Actually, I have another idea."

WE HOLD hands all the way to locker thirty-five. The fact that it's dark and the halls are empty doesn't bother me on this trip. We stand in front of the locker, Tupperware positioned at the vents. My fingers are on the lid, although I haven't cracked it.

"You sure about this?" Malcolm asks.

"Not totally," I admit. "But I think this one just wants to belong ... somewhere. Maybe that somewhere is here?"

"Sounds good to me."

"We can always come back." I rap the side of the Tupperware with my knuckles. "If this one doesn't behave."

Inside the container, the ghost swirls its agreement. At least, I think it agrees with me. With ghosts, you never can tell. I crack the lid.

The ghost streams through the vent. I place my palm against the locker, and Malcolm adds his above mine.

"Verdict?" he asks.

There's a bit of nudging, some jockeying for space, but then nothing but warmth.

"I think it belongs here," I say.

"I think you're right."

Malcolm takes my hand again. When we reach the doors to the school, his arm wraps around my waist.

And I think: *Yes.*
I belong here.

The Ghost Must Go On is a standalone Coffee and Ghosts short story.

THE MAD SCIENTIST NEXT DOOR

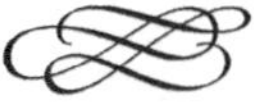

PARANORMAL

To: Emilia Brandenburg
From: Alistair Payne
Subject: That infernal racket

Madam,

I don't know what possesses you to conduct your experiments at three o'clock in the morning, but on behalf of all our neighbors, I'm begging you to stop immediately.

The solar panels, unsightly as they are, at least provide a function. I concede that the Rube Goldberg machine is educational.

This latest contraption of yours? What, pray tell, is its purpose? Other than to shake my house to its very foundation, I see no reason for its existence. I can't begin to fathom what you're doing or what your electricity bill must be.

For the sake of the neighborhood, I implore you to cease at once.

Alistair Payne

To: Alistair Payne
From: Emilia Brandenburg
Subject: Re: That infernal racket

Sir,

What possesses you to be skulking around after dark? I nearly dialed 911 the other night, thinking a prowler was about.

If you must know, I conduct my experiments in the wee hours as a courtesy to the neighborhood, as to not cause a brownout during the summer months. Besides, the Rileys have never complained.

Doctor Emilia Brandenburg

P.S. My electricity bill is none of your business.

To: Members of the Hemlock Homeowners Association
From: H.H.A. Board of Directors
Subject: Meet your new president!

It's with great pleasure that I announce the results of last week's election. Wanda Waverly will serve as the Hemlock Homeowners Association's president effective immediately.

Although a new resident, as owner/manager of the Pick-n-Quick chain of convenience stores, Wanda brings her business acumen to the position of president. We are pleased she has decided to not only call our little community home but has stepped up to serve as well.

Daniel Brown, Esq.

To: Emilia Brandenburg
From: Alistair Payne
Subject: Re: That infernal racket

Doctor Brandenburg,

The Rileys are far too polite to lodge any sort of complaint. I shall take this to the board and the new president. See if I don't.

Alistair Payne

To: Emilia Brandenburg
From: Alistair Payne
Subject: That ghastly eyesore

Really, Doctor? A *fence*?

To: Alistair Payne
From: Emilia Brandenburg
Subject: Re: That ghastly eyesore

Sir,

My cedar fence is lovely, board-approved, and offers adequate privacy for both parties. Of course, this assumes that one party does not skulk about during the witching hour with his ear pressed against the slats.

Speaking of eyesores, tell me, please, how long that cauldron has been moldering on your front lawn. A few flakes found their way into my yard, and I conducted several tests. My estimate is at least fifty years.

To: Members of the Hemlock Homeowners Association
From: Wanda Waverly
Subject: Bylaws

To clarify some points brought up in last night's association meeting:

- All structures, temporary or permanent, must not exceed the dimensions outlined in appendix D of the H.H.A. bylaws.
- Lawn ornaments are limited to three, must be no taller than two feet, and considered generally tasteful.

Wanda Waverly

President, Hemlock Homeowners Association

To: Alistair Payne
From: Emilia Brandenburg
Subject: You win

Sir,

I cannot believe you are so petty as to lodge a complaint against my fence. If I didn't know better, I'd suspect you of some sort of witchcraft. I measured the boards myself, and I know they were in compliance with the bylaws.

But down it goes until next spring.

E. Brandenburg

To: Emilia Brandenburg
From: Alistair Payne
Subject: Good riddance

Dear Doctor,

It is hardly my fault if you cannot competently wield a ruler.

A.P.

To: Alistair Payne
From: Emilia Brandenburg
Subject: Good fences

Sir,

I always thought Frost was being ironic when he wrote *good fences make good neighbors*.

Now I know better.

E. Brandenburg

P.S. Your animosity toward me is one thing, but the Riley's play structure as well? Shame, sir. Shame on you.

P.P.S. Don't bother to respond. I've blocked your email, and any additional missives from you will go straight to spam.

To: Members of the Hemlock Homeowners Association
From: Wanda Waverly
Subject: Halloween

To clarify some *additional* points from the previous association meeting:

- Due to safety concerns, the annual Halloween parade has been suspended indefinitely.
- Any structure erected for a holiday event needs approval, *in writing*, from the H.H.A. board ninety days in advance.
- All items handed out for trick-or-treat must be wrapped and sealed. The Pick-n-Quick outside the main gate is offering H.H.A. members a 5% discount on all candy.

Wanda Waverly
President, Hemlock Homeowners Association

To: Alistair Payne
From: Emilia Brandenburg
Subject: Wrapped treats

Mr. Payne,

I left some cellophane wrappers on your front porch. I constructed them based on the treats you distributed after last year's Halloween parade. I think you will find that they will provide adequate coverage and pass muster with the board.

Yours,

Emilia Brandenburg

P.S. The eldest Riley child, Alyssa, works as my apprentice, as you may already know. She's informed me that contrary to my earlier accusation, you have toiled to … modify the Riley's play structure so it conforms to the bylaws.

I'm not sure how you accomplished this. My own tools are finely calibrated, and certainly, the inspector for the H.H.A. possesses adequate ones. No need to tell me. The squeals and laughter from the Riley's backyard are all I need to hear.

To: Emilia Brandenburg
From: Alistair Payne
Subject: Re: Wrapped treats

Doctor Brandenburg,

Let me extend my gratitude for the wrappers. While they caused a few raised eyebrows (I thought our esteemed president's would vanish into her hairline), my treats were—undeniably—wrapped and sealed.

And thus, Halloween—along with the Riley's play structure—was salvaged, at least somewhat.

Yours,
Alistair Payne

P.S. I could explain how the glamour on the play structure works, but that would defeat its purpose.

P.S.S I sorely missed your yearly light show.

To: Alistair Payne
From: Emilia Brandenburg
Subject: Halloween

Mr. Payne,

Well, yes, everyone loves a Tesla coil—or nearly everyone. I find myself nostalgic for previous Halloweens—the parade, the costumes, the children's cries of delight when you unveil the gingerbread house. I don't see the point in denying them all that.

I must confess that this year simply didn't feel like Halloween.

True, my sugar skeletons always pale in comparison to your gingerbread people. I suspect the adults only take my treatises out of pity (and no one thinks "trick or treatise" as amusing as I do). Of course, everyone leaves before the anatomy lecture.

And yet, I've come to rely on Halloween, along with the Hemlock block party, as a way to interact with my neighbors. This year's curtailed celebration has hit me harder than I care to admit.

Yours,
Emilia Brandenburg

To: Emilia Brandenburg
From: Alistair Payne
Subject: Re: Halloween

My dear Doctor,

I wish to assuage your melancholy. Trust that I have lived enough years to see more than my fair share of petty tyrants. I predict this Wanda Waverly will move on in due course to terrorize yet another homeowners association.

In the meantime, I will spend the winter working with the beautification committee and planning next spring's gardens. They will be spectacular.

Yours,
Alistair Payne

P.S. Trick or treatise is beyond charming. If I promise no tricks, may I read one of your treatises?

To: Alistair Payne
From: Emilia Brandenburg
Subject: the gardens

Dear Mr. Payne,

Botany has never been my forte, but I eagerly await the coming spring's glory that is your garden. How you outdo yourself every year, I simply cannot fathom. The Hemlock Community entryway is the envy of all.

I do, however, have some thoughts on streamlining the irrigation system. Please refer to the schematics in the attached PDF.

Yours truly,
Emilia

To: Members of the Hemlock Homeowners Association
From: Wanda Waverly
Subject: Spring has sprung!

Can you believe winter is finally over? Whew! That was a long one.

In anticipation of spring and all it brings, I would like to announce the following changes, effective immediately:

The beautification committee has been disbanded. Instead, H.H.A. has hired a landscaping company that will take over the planting and care of the foliage around the community's entryway and main gate.

Regarding the main gate, H.H.A. has contracted with a security company for the front entrance. The gate will be locked at midnight every evening and unlocked at six in the morning.

Happy spring, everyone!

Wanda Waverly
President, Hemlock Homeowners Association

To: Members of the Hemlock Homeowners Association
From: Wanda Waverly
Subject: The Main Gate

It has come to the board's attention that locking the main gate between the hours of midnight and six a.m. has put undue hardship on some residents of Hemlock Community.

Rest assured, we only had your safety in mind when we implemented these rules. Our aim was to keep out any undesirables that might threaten the residents.

That being said, this is no excuse for deliberate sabotage! When the perpetrator is found, justice will be swift.

The board can (and will!) revoke membership in the H.H.A. Without membership, the perpetrator can no longer live in Hemlock Community. Further, the board can (and will!) foreclose on the perpetrator's house and subsequently evict him or her. See paragraph four, sub-paragraph three in the bylaws.

In the meantime, to pay for a security upgrade to the main gate, including keycards for all residents, we will use the funds earmarked for the annual block party.

Wanda Waverly
President, Hemlock Homeowners Association

To: Alistair Payne
From: Emilia Brandenburg
Subject: last night's meeting

Alistair,

I thought my heart would burst from my chest during last night's meeting.

Would they have poor Mrs. Riley wait outside the gate for hours on end? I simply let her inside the development. That's hardly a crime. And yet, I'm certain this Waverly woman suspects it was me.

Granted, everyone who's about during the later hours knows that Mrs. Riley and I often share conversation over a cup of tea when she returns from her shift.

Although, really, even with the upgrade, this new security system is laughable. It's not keeping anyone out, although I suspect it's keeping many of us in.

Of course, with a little rewiring ... nothing a child of five couldn't do ... except for rigging the system to play *The Imperial March* whenever Wanda Waverly drives through the main gate.

Now, in the light of day, I concede that may have been taking things too far.

And yet, I find that I can't regret it, either.

Yours,
Em

P.S. *The Imperial March* is from a movie called *Star Wars*. I've included a link to an article about it on Wikipedia.

To: Emilia Brandenburg
From: Alistair Payne
Subject: Re: last night's meeting

Emilia,

Taking things too far? Not nearly far enough. I've been offering the landscaping company my expertise, gratis of course. Not that they've taken any of my advice. The poor hydrangeas; they may never recover.

Ah, but they're a loquacious crew, and I've unearthed an interesting fact. The owner of this company is Wanda Waverly's daughter.

What a strange, petty nepotism this is.

Alistair

P.S. You have me pegged. My ignorance of current cultural phenomena provides the Riley children with endless hours of amusement. I no doubt will provide this same service to their grandchildren.

I do, however, have a passing familiarity with *Star Wars*. The franchise appears to have a number of vocal and passionate devotees.

To: Emilia Brandenburg
From: Alistair Payne
Subject: That hideous sign in your front yard

Emilia,

I could not believe the sight that greeted my eyes upon waking this morning.

A *For Sale* sign? I'm not certain what's worse—the garish design or how the support appears to impale your front yard.

Tell me all that's the matter. Certainly, things aren't so dire as this?

Alistair

To: Alistair Payne
From: Emilia Brandenburg
Subject: Re: That hideous sign in your front yard

Alistair,

Indeed things are that dire. Every time I step off my front porch, there she is, that Waverly woman, clipboard in hand.

In the last two weeks, I've received five citations. One more, and I forfeit my home. If I can't find a buyer, the association can (and will!) foreclose on my house.

Beyond that, I suspect she, or the board, or someone is throttling the power supply into my house. I was conducting a *delicate* experiment in my third-floor laboratory the other night, one that needed a constant stream of electricity.

Suffice to say that I did not achieve that constant stream of electricity. Suffice to say I no longer have a functional third-floor laboratory—or eyebrows.

Worst of all? I was accosted last night. As you know, it's my habit to stroll through the development in between experiments. It clears my head and refreshes me. But last night, a security guard curtailed my walk. He said I wasn't allowed to stroll after midnight.

When did the development start employing roving security guards? Did I miss that announcement? Although he was, to use your own term, rather loquacious. Did you know that the owner of the security company is Wanda Waverly's nephew?

In distress,
Em

To: Emilia Brandenburg
From: Alistair Payne
Subject: The gloves come off

My dearest Emilia,

As I've mentioned, I've weathered my fair share of petty tyrants. Remind me to tell you how I thrice defeated eminent domain claims on this particular plot of land. The Payne residence remains, as it has for … let's say, decades.

I cannot abide by this treatment of my friends and neighbors. I'm uncertain of what I shall do, but trust me, dear Doctor, I will do something.

Alistair

P.S. Your estimate about the cauldron is correct, or nearly so. It's been there for a good sixty years. It's a stubborn thing, and I cannot convince it to move. That it just barely meets the prescribed dimensions for lawn ornamentation no doubt vexes Wanda Waverly greatly.

To: Alistair Payne
From: Emilia Brandenburg
Subject: Re: The gloves come off

My dear Alistair,

So which am I? A friend or merely a neighbor?

Em

To: Emilia Brandenburg
From: Alistair Payne
Subject: Re: The gloves come off

You, my dear Doctor, have the rare distinction of being both.

To: Alistair Payne
From: Emilia Brandenburg
Subject: Worried

My dear Alistair,

I do not like the look of that strange mist that surrounds your house. It feels malevolent to me. As unscientific as that sounds, I stand by that assessment.

I do not pretend to understand your craft. However, I know that any work created in the throes of anger will not have the desired outcome.

Yes, I know you witnessed this morning's sixth citation. The entire neighborhood was privileged to witness that event. If you truly want to help, perhaps you could make my third-floor laboratory vanish. I'll never find a buyer at this rate.

Please, my dear friend, I beg of you. Don't do anything you may regret.

Em

To: Emilia Brandenburg
From: Alistair Payne
Subject: The Emperor's New Clothes

Dearest Em,

Have you read that fairy tale? I wouldn't say our current association president is wandering around naked (certainly there's a stipulation against that in the bylaws, but I digress). She does, however, have a few transparency issues.

I have an idea, one that does not involve my craft or your discipline. Are you willing to hear me out? I'll meet you at our adjoining property line at the witching hour.

Yours,
Alistair

To: Alistair Payne
From: Emilia Brandenburg
Subject: Re: The Emperor's New Clothes

Dearest Alistair,

I am still completely flabbergasted, even after sleeping on the idea.

Do you really think it will work? I cannot possibly be the best choice. After all, you've lived here longer than I have. You would hold more sway, would you not?

Em

To: Emilia Brandenburg
From: Alistair Payne
Subject: Re: The Emperor's New Clothes

Dearest Em,

I have lived *everywhere* longer than you have. I am set in my ways, set in my craft. If you were to flip open one of those illustrated dictionaries, you would find my portrait next to the entry for curmudgeon. Were I not to get my way, I'd be tempted to conjure a few special apples or perhaps an unsightly pox.

You, on the other hand? With your keen mind and willingness to take in data, experiment, adjust your hypothesis based on new information? How you eagerly gather input and listen to those around you?

Why, yes, you are obviously the best choice for this endeavor.

I have every confidence in you.

Alistair

To: Alistair Payne
From: Emilia Brandenburg
Subject: Curmudgeon

This, from the man who handcrafts a life-size gingerbread house for the neighborhood children each Halloween? And then sends them home with pocketfuls of treats?

Oh, yes, you are *quite* the curmudgeon.

Em

To: Alistair Payne
From: Emilia Brandenburg
Subject: Last night

Oh, my dearest Alistair, please tell me you did not employ your craft to sway last night's outcome.

I can hardly believe it's true. But if it is, I want it to be an honest prize.

Em

To: Emilia Brandenburg
From: Alistair Payne
Subject: Re: Last Night

My dear Doctor, you wound me. Do you think I would employ enchantment to obtain what I want?

Yes, yes, I *might*. Certainly, in the past, I have. In this case? Other than canvassing on your behalf and ensuring there was no subterfuge from any quarter, I performed no other tasks.

Alistair

P.S. Besides, I can hardly cook up an enchantment with my cauldron on my front lawn, can I now.

To: Members of the Hemlock Homeowners Association
From: H.H.A. Board of Directors
Subject: Meet your new president!

It's with great pleasure that I announce the results of last week's election. Dr. Emilia Brandenburg will serve as the Hemlock Homeowners Association's president effective immediately.

Emilia has made Hemlock her home for the past five years and has—quite literally—brightened the entire development. We look forward to her fresh ideas and vast experience in her new role as president.

Daniel Brown, Esq.

To: Members of the Hemlock Homeowners Association
From: Emilia Brandenburg
Subject: Bylaws and Halloween

Effective immediately:

- The annual Halloween parade will take place starting at 6:30 p.m. on the 31st. Everyone is invited to participate.
- The beautification committee will reform under the auspices of Mr. Alistair Payne in time to decorate the entryway and parade route. All volunteers are welcome.
- A belated block party and impromptu association meeting will take place in front of the gingerbread house at the end of the Halloween parade.

Emilia Brandenburg
President, Hemlock Homeowners Association

To: Emilia Brandenburg
From: Alistair Payne
Subject: Halloween

My dearest Em,

To assuage any doubt you might be feeling this morning: You were simply splendid in your new role, as I knew you would be.

You will make a fine president.

With all my admiration,
Alistair

P.S. Your Tesla coil was magnificent.

This is the second outing for my curmudgeon witch Alistair Payne. If he keeps this up, he may find himself in a novel.

NOVEMBER

For November, it was stories of saying goodbye, letting things go, and
endings that bring about new beginnings.

ALEAG THE GREAT

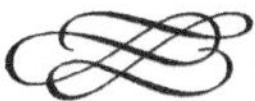

FANTASY

The hue and cry of the villagers woke Aleag from a sound sleep. Dreams of ice and granite shattered, leaving him with the scent of spring in his nostrils—the elusive and tantalizing hint of violet, the heavy perfume of lily of the valley. He stretched, dug his claws into the earth, and peered down the mountain.

The villagers clambered up the mountainside, pitchforks and hand-crafted spears clutched in their fists—as if such things could pierce his scales.

Did they need to do this every spring? At best, it was tedious. At worst?

At worse, something—or more likely someone—would knock the delicate balance between human and dragon off-kilter. Aleag was growing weary of the whole charade. He wouldn't be responsible for the resulting destruction.

At the center of the crowd, a young woman stumbled. Her wrists were bound, her feet bare and oddly pink. Her gown fluttered around her ankles like sea foam. Every few steps, she glanced over her shoulder as if the threat was behind her instead of straight ahead.

Curious, Aleag emerged from his cave, tail casting a graceful arc once free of its confines. Sun glinted off his scales, its heat warming his blood and clearing the last of the icy dreams from his head.

He could taste his next meal in the air.

The villagers approached, scrambling over the last rocks and boulders to reach the outcropping that held his cave. The lord mayor took the lead. The man's blood trembled in his veins. Aleag could feel it from where he waited.

Interesting how some men conquered fear with the threat of shame.

Then again, when you were offering up such a tasty morsel, courage had little to do with it.

Aleag deigned to meet them at the stake, the location where—year after year—they secured their sacrificial lamb, where—year after year—they would barter.

Aleag always bartered.

After all, he saw no reason to make this easy for them.

SOMEONE YANKED THE ROPE. Lily stumbled forward, more a dog on a leash than a human being. That someone jerked again. Not Peter. No, never Peter, not in his new role as village lord mayor. Peter wouldn't soil his hands in all this.

The rope passed from villager to villager—her friends, her neighbors, her patients—until, at last, it was Jack who had the unlucky chore of tying her to the stake.

"I'm sorry, Lily," he whispered, an anxious glance in Peter's direction.

"No more than I am."

She'd known from the start that if it ever came to something like this, Jack would choose Peter over her. He always had, always did, and always with an apology.

At least tethered to the stake, she could see her little cottage in the valley below. Still intact. Still safe. Someday, it might prove useful again, if not to her, then someone very much like her.

The dragon approached, footfalls shaking the ground, pebbles scattering down the slope. A few bounced and came to rest against her bare feet, the feeling of them cool against her skin, like a balm. For the first time in a week, her feet stopped their ceaseless ache.

The dragon snuffled and sniffed, the force of his exhales ruffling her hair.

"And you are?" His voice was impossibly low, a quiet murmur meant for her ears only.

"Lily." She managed that single word with her own quiet power, surprising herself, if not him.

"Of the valley?"

"If that's what you wish."

He snuffled again. "I thought I'd detected spring in the air, but I doubt my wishes have anything to do with this proceeding."

"Then we have that in common."

He surveyed her with his large yellow eyes, her startled reflection staring back at her from the dark pupil. It was an astonishing thing to be seen so completely. At that moment, Lily felt her entire being exposed—the secrets she kept in the cottage, the ones buried deep in her heart.

"And you are?" She knew his name; all the villagers did. Every spring, they scaled the mountain. Or rather, most of them did. Lily always remained in her cottage out of protest.

Until this spring, anyway.

Still, it only seemed polite to ask.

The dragon inclined his head. "Aleag."

Peter stepped onto a nearby boulder, out of grasping range, Lily noted. He wore a sky blue sash of silk about his waist, indicating his rank as lord mayor. He puffed up his chest and began to speak.

"Aleag the Great! As is our tradition, we bring you an offering of spring!"

"Are you really?" Lily asked under her breath.

A hint of steam rose from the dragon's nostrils, almost in question. "Am I what?"

"Great."

The dragon snorted a stream of fire that sent the villagers scampering down the incline. Even Peter tripped and fell backward, Jack's outstretched arms breaking his fall.

"It would seem," Aleag said, humor and heat in his words, "that I'm at least adequate."

When one was staring down certain death, one generally didn't laugh. And yet. Lily found herself biting back the smile. "What would you need to do to be great?"

"Oh, the usual, I suppose. Crush a few villages beneath my claws, lay waste to the harvest, incinerate a couple of forests." A sigh rumbled in his chest, the sensation shaking the earth beneath her feet. "I find I lack the enthusiasm for such things."

Below, the villagers scrabbled back up the mountain, slower this time, their footfalls wary. Peter glared at Lily as if she were the one responsible for his undignified tumble.

Perhaps he had a point.

Lily turned to Aleag. Oh, but he was a fine creature. If not for her untimely end, she could admire him. Indeed, a creature such as this should be worshiped.

"What's going to happen?" she asked.

Aleag swiveled his head and stared at her with the force of both eyes. Even without the stake and rope, Lily would've been trapped by his gaze alone—prey to his predator.

"My child," he said. "Have you no idea?"

PETER CLAWED his way up the boulder a second time. Sweat had sprouted along his spine the moment they'd left the village. Now it coursed, a river overflowing its banks. The back of his tunic was drenched, the stain spreading into the sash's heavy silk.

Leave it to Lily to make the creature laugh. Laugh! Of all things.

He brushed his hands against his thighs. His wrists ached from the fall, and the tender flesh of his palms—it had been several seasons since he'd worked the harvest—stung. He pulled himself up straight. He was the lord mayor, after all. As such, he was due a certain amount of respect.

"Aleag the Great!" Peter tried for the second time. "As is our tradition, we bring you an offering of spring!"

The dragon scrutinized him, from the top of his head to the bottom of his leather-clad feet. The gaze was unrelenting. Tingling erupted along Peter's skin, a shower of needles, the sensation both sharp and tantalizing.

This is what these creatures did, of course. They made you crave the pain and welcome your own demise. Peter shook his head, blew out a breath, and cleared his thoughts.

Or tried to.

"An offering." The words rumbled as if the dragon were bored. "What if I don't find it ... adequate?"

Before Peter could answer, Lily and this ... this ... this *creature* exchanged glances. It was as if they both found the situation humorous.

Heat rose in his cheeks. "She is our most treasured asset, our village healer. We do this to honor you."

"Your healer?" The dragon swiveled his head, that remorseless gaze sweeping over Peter before the creature set its sights on Lily. "Pray tell, why would you sacrifice your healer?"

"To honor you." Peter puffed out his chest again. He knew, of course, how dragons were, how they wouldn't accept a sacrifice without some bartering, without knowing what it cost the village. The last lord mayor had told him such. That the most difficult part of the job was selecting a maiden each spring.

Truth be told? This year, it hadn't been that hard.

"So, when the blacksmith blisters his hand," Aleag intoned, "the carpenter tumbles from a cottage roof, countless women labor to birth children, are you telling me your healer won't be missed?"

"There are other healers in this land."

"Perhaps there are, and perhaps seeing how cavalierly you treat your own, they will decide not to make your village their home."

"Perhaps, but our village is filled with a number of wise women. We will do without."

His words sounded tinny, their echo doubling back on him. Behind him, the disgruntled murmur of a dozen of those wise women made his ears burn. Doubt churned in his stomach. He pressed a hand against his belly to steady himself.

Truly, Lily wasn't that skilled. Truly! Any old fool could coax women through labor and set a broken bone. Yes, Lily had the touch. The mere brush of her fingertips could cool a fever or soothe a colicky infant.

She had brought him back from the brink, certainly. Peter exhaled as if the thickness in his lungs remained. Yes, she'd brought him back; for that, he'd always be grateful. But he could not abide—

"I refused his offer."

Lily's words rang clear, loud enough—he swore—to be heard in the valley below.

"Hm?" Aleag's murmur emerged with a puff of smoke. "What was that, my dear?"

"He proposed," Lily said. "I refused. Then he threatened me, and I refused again."

"And now, you're here." Aleag swung his head around, that penetrating gaze finding Peter once again. "How interesting."

~

AND HERE ALEAG thought this proceeding was going to be a bore. He peered into the crowd. The lord mayor looked, in turns, a putrid, sickly green and flushed to the point of violence. Yes, shame made a man do many things he might later regret.

"We were friends, always had been, since we were children." Lily twisted, her gaze going from the lord mayor and then to Aleag. "But I had no wish to marry him. I have no wish to marry at all."

Aleag snorted another stream of smoke. "You are wise beyond your years, my dear."

Laughter rippled through the crowd. Women near the back bent their heads together, their whispers low and conspiratorial.

"Perhaps," Aleag began, and now he addressed those beyond the lord mayor and the few men who remained at his side with pitchforks and spears. "Perhaps you should rethink your sacrifice. It seems to me that a man who could be so vindictive is perhaps not the man you want as lord mayor."

Oh, and now the lord mayor turned a delightful shade of gray. He wobbled in his stance. Shame. Ambition. These things were never good for the soul.

"Stop it."

Aleag blinked. Lily's voice halted the soliloquy he'd been brewing in the back of his mind. Indeed, there was so much to work with. The defiant damsel, the spurned lover, the innocuous and yet sly third who hovered in the background. A fierce column of women who looked on the verge of toppling the lord mayor. The men, slowly but certainly slinking down the slope.

"Excuse me, my dear?"

"I said, stop it. Stop toying with us. It's deliberately cruel, and you know it."

He stared at her, his gaze unflinching. To her credit, she withstood it. "What is it, then, do you suggest I do?"

She tilted her chin in his direction and held up her bound wrists. "Take your sacrifice."

~

SILENCE SETTLED on the crowd before a ghastly cry went up. The sound was filled with despair and remorse, and so much shame that it shook Lily to her core.

Peter leaped forward, hands scrambling on the smooth surface of the incline. He pawed his way forward, boots skidding against the rock.

"No!" he cried. "No!"

Lily spun away from him, her whole being intent on the dragon. "Do it. Do it now."

Aleag gave her a slow blink as if he didn't need to move, as if time wasn't of the essence.

"Because it will serve him right?" he asked.

"Because every other outcome is worse."

Worse for Jack, for Peter, certainly for the village. Even if they couldn't see it.

"Let me be the last sacrifice this village needs to make."

Something sparked in Aleag's expression, a glint in those yellow eyes. His lip curled, revealing the teeth that would soon be the end of her.

And yet, Lily felt ... nothing.

No, that was hardly true. Her heartbeat thrummed in her throat, the roar of blood in her ears. She stole one last glance at her little cottage below. It had been a good home. Certainly, until a week ago, it had been a good life as well.

"This is what you want?" the dragon asked.

"It is."

"Very well, then. I'm more than happy to oblige. You are the smaller morsel, but dare I say, bound to be the tastier one."

"He with the most teeth gets to say what he wants."

Aleag snorted yet another stream of smoke. "You have a sharp wit, my dear. Pity I have to eat you."

"I don't think you're capable of pity."

Those were Lily's last words. For a moment, she saw the world around her in all its colors—the glorious blue sky, the sun painting clouds on the horizon pink, the green and red-roofed cottages in the village below.

And then everything was black.

PETER FELL TO HIS KNEES. He was late, much too late. The sweat that coursed down his spine washed across his entire body, his skin flashing cold, then hot, and cold yet again. He mouthed words, senseless things, the only coherent syllable that of an ending chant.

"No, no, no, no."

The men holding pitchforks let them clatter to the ground. They crept away with barely a glance backward.

The women of the village cast him looks so caustic that certainly his skin would erupt in blisters. They, too, departed down the mountainside, in groups of twos and threes, their murmurs rising upward, taunting him.

Murderer ... coward.
Fool.

It was this last that rankled most, although Peter couldn't say why.

Then, only the three of them remained on the mountaintop: Peter, Jack, and of course, the dragon.

"Was ... was she really the last?" Where he found the courage to ask, Peter couldn't say. His words came out thick and phlegmy. He sounded like a child with a cold, not the lord mayor of a thriving village.

"Indeed. In all the years I have bargained with your village, it's a wonder no one else ever thought to ask."

Peter pushed to his feet. He wobbled, only to have Jack steady him by the elbows. He shook off his friend and stumbled forward.

"Are you telling me that all we had to do was *ask*?"

"Why not? It seems like a reasonable request, does it not? *Please stop eating our maidens, if you would, dragon, sir.*" Aleag said this last in a singsong, the taunt grating at Peter's insides.

Peter glanced around, wondering if he might pick up a pitchfork and run this damnable creature through the heart.

"I wouldn't try if I were you," Aleag said as if reading his thoughts. "The request would still have required a sacrifice. The previous lord mayor knew as much."

Peter's mouth fell open. The air in his lungs grew thin, and his breath came in gasps like he'd never inhale fully and completely again.

"Go," the dragon ordered. "Leave now. Take this knowledge and become a better leader of your village than he was."

The creature retreated to his cave. A mist covered the cavern's opening and settled on Peter's face like morning dew.

He continued to stand there for a very long time.

At last, Jack plucked his elbow. "She's gone."

Peter nodded, his gaze fixed on the cave. He took one long, last shuddering breath and let Jack lead him down the mountainside.

THE AFTERMATH WAS Aleag's favorite part. On this side of the mountain, nothing impeded his view—no village, no smoke, no pitchforks—nothing but the endless valley and the river below. He'd take a season—spend time counting the wildflowers in all the nooks and crannies—before deciding where to settle next.

He let his chin rest on his crossed forepaws and waited.

It would be a while before the damsel in distress woke from her slumber.

WHAT LILY NOTICED FIRST, she couldn't say. The sun warming her limbs? The cool stone beneath her back? Or was it the elusive, tantalizing scent of violets washed with fresh pine?

When she opened her eyes, nothing but the dragon filled her view.

Sunlight glinted off his scales, and she squinted, raised a hand to her brow until her eyes adjusted.

She was … alive?

"How did you sleep, my dear?" Aleag lifted his head just enough to look at her full on and then settled back down, almost like a hound at the hearth.

She raised herself on one elbow. "What did you do?"

"How did you sleep?" he asked again, not impatient, but certainly implacable.

Lily pushed strands of hair from her cheeks. She sat up and considered how she felt. Refreshed. Renewed. "Very well, actually."

"I thought as much. A good sign, that."

"Is it?"

"Indeed. The maidens who sleep the best find the most success on the other side."

Lily glanced about. Yes, she recognized this side of the mountain. Often she'd trek here, searching out herbs and rare mushrooms, gathering up the profusion of wildflowers that grew in the valleys. "Wait … other maidens?"

"My dear, you don't think I actually eat any of you, do you?" A shudder ran through his form, scales rippling like water. "Credit me with a bit of taste."

"Then what do you do with them?"

"Chat for a bit and then send them on their way."

"On their way … then the sacrifice?"

"Is never returning to the village, never letting anyone know they're alive. Most agree that's a small price, considering the alternative."

"So each spring, they simply walk away?"

"As you will do, as well."

Lily wrapped her arms around her legs and let her chin rest on her knees. "You agreed never to take another."

"The time had come. I was growing bored with the whole charade."

"What will you do?"

"Find a new spot to settle, another mountain. I assure you, the world is filled with mountains, with any number of well-appointed caves."

Lily stood, stretched. Excitement thrummed in her veins. No, she couldn't return to her cottage—that was clear—but perhaps she could begin a new life elsewhere. She glanced down at her feet, the skin still aglow with pink from their scalding. Before she went anywhere, she'd need to find some shoes.

"My dear, are you willing to make another exchange?" Aleag nodded at her feet.

"I might be," she said.

"In that case, do you see that clump of violets over there, in the outcropping?"

They were a lovely bunch, lavender and cream-colored, their scent subtle and sweet. Lily nodded.

"Bring them to me?" The dragon kneaded the ground with his claws. "I don't possess the dexterity for such matters."

She gathered the bunch and then continued from there until her arms overflowed with blossoms. She returned to the outcropping and placed them gently in front of Aleag.

He plucked one and then another with tongue and lips, movements precise and dainty. He shut his eyes, and a sigh escaped him, the sound of it pure contentment.

"Thank you, my dear." He caught her in his gaze and nodded at her feet. "How did you come by such a burn?"

"When I ... refused Peter—"

"The lord mayor?"

"Yes, when I refused him, he got upset, knocked my cauldron from the hearth. The stew soaked my shoes." Lily stepped close and raised the hem of her dress. "I'm lucky it was only a bad scalding."

Aleag blew a stream of smoke across her skin. It was cool like spring, and fresh. It stole the last of the heat from the burn, the pink fading, the scars healing. Now she shut her eyes in pure contentment.

"Thank you."

"It was my pleasure. I don't often partake in such a feast." Aleag flexed his claws. "I can't pick them myself, after all."

The sound of scrabbling caught Lily up short. The noise came from behind her. She spun in time to see Jack scale the lip of the outcropping.

Jack took a few stumbling steps forward and halted. He unslung a knapsack from his shoulders and placed it at Lily's feet.

"It's not much," he said, "but there's some clothes, good boots, and a few of your books. I hope I chose the right ones, and, of course, your stash of coins from beneath the loose floorboard."

Lily shook her head. "I ... don't understand."

"Usually, my grandmother is the one who does this." Jack peered around her to address Aleag. "I hope you don't mind, sir."

"Under the circumstances? Quite understandable."

"The women in the village? They *know*?" Really? Then why hadn't she known?

"Only a few, and I only found out ... after everything with Peter."

Lily took the knapsack and ducked behind a boulder. She emerged dressed and ready for travel.

"Will you come with me?" she asked Jack.

"As far as the crossroads."

So like Jack, choosing Peter over her. He always had, always did, always would.

"He needs me," Jack said. "You don't."

Yes, perhaps that had always been true.

Lily approached Aleag and placed a kiss against his scaly snout. "You're a bastard, you know that?"

"Most dragons are, my dear."

"But thank you."

"Again, the pleasure was all mine."

Jack walked with Lily as far as the crossroads. She memorized the feel of his sturdiness next to her, his calloused palm next to her own. She'd miss him.

Even after everything.

THE VILLAGE PROSPERED under Peter's reign. The harvest never failed. The forests provided a never-ending supply of game. Every spring, violets covered the mountainside in a blanket of lavender and cream.

The sight always made him think of Lily.

As the years passed into decades, Peter became known as Dragon's Bane. He never confirmed the rumors—that he had singlehandedly dispatched a dragon from their village.

He never denied them either.

After his third wife died, Peter relinquished his role as lord mayor. He and Jack found a cottage on the outskirts of the village where they tended a few acres of land and spent long evenings in front of the hearth.

It was only then that Jack told Peter the rest of the story.

Aleag the Great is another dragon story written for the (Love) Stories for 2020 project.

VALENTINA

HISTORICAL, WWI

*V*alentina pressed her back against the trench wall and waited. Eight hundred feet away, the Germans waited in another set of trenches. Earlier, she'd peered over the top, watched men move up and down the front line.

She wondered if any of them peered back, detected something different in the Russian soldiers along this part of the line. Could they tell? Would they know? Would their lips curl in disgust at her shorn hair? An equal number of cheers and jeers still rang in her ears—from the parade through Petrograd, at the train station when they disembarked.

But now, as she waited, chest tight with anticipation, Valentina never thought the world could be so quiet, that a *war* could be so quiet. She waited for the whistle, lips pursed as if she were the one who would give the command.

Up and over the top. Across churned up earth and muck and barbed wire to the other side, to the Germans.

The Germans.

Her mother had taken a German lover once, years ago. He'd been not a beer-soaked lout, but prim, proper, face defined by round spectacles and a neat beard. Every time he encountered Valentina, he'd inclined his head like she were already a person worthy of respect, not a small child, not the illegitimate spawn of an opera singer.

Were there men like that waiting for her on the other side? She clutched her rifle and hoped not.

At dawn, the signal came. It rippled up and down the line. The first rays of sun touched the trench, and Valentina crawled to its top, pulled herself up and over.

No man's land. Certainly. No *woman's* land. That too. The sun warmed the back of her neck. Odd that, out of everything, she noticed its touch. Whizzing filled the air, the sound reverberating in her ears. Her vision tunneled, so if there was anything to her left or her right, she couldn't see it.

Maybe it was better that way.

A few yards from the trench, something grabbed her foot, threatened to pull the boot clean off. She pitched forward, her body smacking the mud. A moment later, something crumpled on top of her.

Something warm and heavy that forced the air from her lungs. Hot liquid soaked through the back of her uniform. Earth filled her mouth, metallic and rank. If war had a taste, then perhaps it was this. Valentina struggled to suck in a full breath, arms straining against her own weight and that of someone else.

With a heave, she pushed her comrade up and off and into the dirt.

Masha. A neat bullet wound through the center of her chest. The girl —her friend—stared blankly at the sky, unblinking. Valentina crawled forward, yanking her foot from the barbed wire that had caught it. She placed her hand on Masha's chest. She prayed, although, in truth, she hadn't been to Mass in years.

She wanted to shut her eyes; she wanted to cross herself. Instead, she inched forward through the dirt and eased Masha's eyes closed.

Ahead of her, members of her unit were already clearing the way, nearing that first trench. She scrambled to her feet and, crouching low, ran to catch up.

A cry went up when they took the first trench. And then the second. They were doing it! They were soldiers, *true soldiers*, not props, not propaganda, not objects to shame men into fighting. Who needed men when the women of Russia could fight?

Valentina plowed forward, intent on that third trench. They had the

Germans on the run! She leaped. She jumped. When that third line of trenches came into view, she thought nothing of plunging into one.

The trench held two men. With the shooting and the shouting, the occasional rounds of artillery, neither noticed the rattled and crash of her entrance. They were locked in their own dance. An officer, tall, lithe, Russian. A German soldier, rifle pointed at the officer's chest.

Valentina didn't think. She plunged again, bayonet at the ready. For a moment, she hovered, her entire weight balancing on the tip of her blade. Only then did the German notice her, his eyes wide with shock. She saw the moment her gender registered. Surprise. Shame.

Then she fell forward, the sharp edge of her bayonet sinking all the way through.

Her head buzzed. He mouthed a few words, a prayer, perhaps, and she watched the German die. She owed him that.

A hand on her shoulder jerked her from what felt like a trance. She spun, faced the man she'd saved.

"Are you all right?" he asked. "I think for now we're—" He broke off, his eyes widening almost as much as the German's had. "God in heaven, you're a woman! Not even. A mere girl."

Valentina brought her heels together and raised her chin. "I'm a sergeant in the 1st Russian Women's Battalion of Death."

The officer sank against the trench wall. His features were indistinct, but she'd viewed enough men from up on stage, from behind a curtain that she could discern their type, no matter how dimly lit they were.

This one? Part of the aristocracy, the sort that secured box seats, the sort that could pass through the throng backstage, knock on a dressing room door, be granted entrance.

What the hell was he doing in this trench?

"We are doomed." He directed these words not to her but toward the sky above. "Clearly, we're doomed if they mean for us to fight the Germans with schoolgirls at our side."

And although the words weren't meant for her and weren't even in Russian, Valentina responded.

"*Je parle français.*"

"Of course you do," he said. "German as well? That might prove useful."

"And Italian." They'd spent a glorious year in Italy—well, glorious up until the end. Her mother's voice had never rung so clear than it did in Milan.

"English?" the officer ventured.

She shook her head. Her mother had never taken a British lover, although she always told Valentina that the best way to learn another language was across the expanse of a pillow and between soft bed linens.

Or sequestered in a cocoon of blankets at the foot of the bed, which was where Valentina had spent so many of her nights.

The officer's gaze shifted. He scanned the sky above them again, placed a hand on the trench wall as if he could intuit the battle from the vibrations that shook the earth.

When his gaze returned to her, something had shifted. "First, thank you," he said. "And again, are you all right?"

She nodded.

"Have you ... I mean, I'm not certain how to..." He gestured toward the German crumpled at their feet. "Have you killed in battle before?"

"Not in battle."

Her answer widened his eyes again. "I see," he said, although there was no way he possibly could.

"My mother," she began.

He held up a hand. "Speak no more. I understand."

She doubted that but remained silent. Oh, the blood. So much blood. They had to flee Italy, of course, and Paris held only temporary safety. On their return to Russia, her mother adopted a new stage name, sang once again.

But her voice never rang as clear as it had before.

"He would've killed her," Valentina added, although whether she was speaking to him—or herself—she couldn't say.

"Of course." The officer raised his rifle. "It's what men do. And now the women are here, trying to clean up our mess. I'm afraid you're too late. This war is already lost."

She shook her head. "I don't believe that."

"I wish with all my heart I didn't either."

"Are you going to fight?" Would he flee? He didn't seem the type, but then she imagined that, once upon a time, the men who now wandered Petrograd in tattered uniforms hadn't been the type either.

But this man could run anywhere. The world was open to him. He'd be safe in Paris, Italy too.

"The war may be lost," he said, "but I'm still fool enough to fight in it."

He surveyed her, from the top of her head down to her boots, his gaze critical. On its own accord, her spine stiffened. The trench wall shielded her completely even though she was standing at attention.

"Fight at my side, Sergeant?"

She nodded, once.

For the third time that day, Valentina crawled up and over a line of trenches. This time, she was not alone.

They moved forward quickly, coming up behind lines that Russian soldiers had already secured, past groups of captured Germans, past some of her own comrades. They ran hard into the setting sun. Her eyes watered beneath its glare. Her limbs ached from a day spent clawing up and down trench walls, sprinting and jumping, throwing herself onto the earth.

Where had the hours gone? Certainly, she'd only just speared that German through with her bayonet. And yet, here they stood, on the edge of a forest, the sun dipping below the horizon.

He'd held up his hand to stop her advance, but her own feet had halted along with his.

Her ear caught not the sounds of battle, but clinking glass, raucous cries. Something sharp stung her nose. Panic flooded her, and she reached for her gas mask.

The officer stayed her hand.

"That won't be necessary."

"I don't understand."

"I think I do." He nodded toward the copse of birches. "Come with me."

At the sound of shattering glass, they sped up. At the bunker, they froze again.

Women, armed and uniformed much as she was, used the stocks of their rifles to smash bottle after bottle. Men roared. Some shoved, grabbed at the rifles, only to be pushed back. Some men gave up the fight, fell to their knees, and rescued what vodka they could before it soaked into the earth.

The officer swore. "It won't be the communists, or the anarchists, or even the Provisional Government that will lose the war for us. It will be this." He pointed at the men desperately slurping at the ground. "And the Germans know that."

"They left it here then, for the men to find?" she ventured.

"Indeed they did."

The sound of a gunshot silenced everyone. A keening rose into the air, followed by shouts.

"She shot them! She shot them!"

Again, they ran, found the crowd gathered around a bunker.

At the entrance, Valentina's commander stood, tall and proud. She was fierce, had fought with the Cossacks before the government put her in charge of the Women's Battalion.

"Yes, I shot them both! Dereliction of duty. Does anyone here question that?"

There, on the ground, in a soup of blood and vodka, were a man and woman, both partially dressed, a bare leg here, an expanse of belly there, the embrace mangled but clear.

"Did you know her?" the officer whispered.

Valentina nodded. "Sophia. Her name is ... was Sophia."

"I believe our association may put you in harm's way." He stepped away from her and approached the commander from the opposite side of where they'd been standing.

He didn't outrank her commander, although Valentina wondered if that mattered. He was a man, an officer, and he'd been fighting in this war much longer than they had. But he offered up a salute and merely inclined his head when listening to the commander's response.

It was such a simple thing. Something told her that he'd see to it no one else was shot for any reason. Certainly, Sophia and this soldier were only making love. It looked ... mutual, at least. With all that blood, it was hard to tell.

So much blood.

No one expected the counterattack. No, that wasn't true, Valentina realized when the officer appeared at her side once again, grabbed her hand, and pulled her from the main thrust of the assault.

They ran deep into the forest, dodging tree limbs and branches. Pine needles raked her face, and their scent was thick in her mouth. They raced until the sounds of the battle faded, and the earth no longer shook beneath their feet. They ran until he stumbled, and they came to rest beneath a tree.

There they sat, his ragged breathing filling the night. In the quiet, Valentina heard the scampering of tiny feet, the rustle of leaves. She peered through the canopy above and spied the stars.

"Dmitri Sergeevich," he said. "My name," he added when she didn't respond. "I never introduced myself."

It was such a simple thing, this offering up of his name.

"Valentina Andreovna."

"Hm." Something in his tone suggested he approved—of what, she wasn't sure.

"What do we do now?" she asked.

"What all lost children do. We head into the forest."

"Will you fight again?"

"Will you?" He lumbered to his feet, bracing a hand against the trunk. "Ah, that's the question, isn't it, Valentina Andreovna."

He offered his hand, the one not clutching the bark. After a moment's hesitation, she took it. He craned his neck skyward and studied the stars.

"North, I think." He released her hand and pulled a flask from the inside of his uniform tunic. He took a long draw before passing it to her. "To fortify yourself for the walk."

She brought the flask to her mouth, the metal cold against her lips. The sharpness returned, vodka flooding her tongue, washing away the grit, the trace of pine, the residue of gunpowder. When she finished, nothing remained except for the taste of blood.

They walked north, their steps unhurried, unhindered as if they truly had left the war behind. Valentina tested her voice. The vodka had cleared the cobwebs from her throat. After a few bars, when Dmitri Sergeevich didn't shush her, she launched into song.

It was a lullaby her mother used to sing, one meant to soothe both her current lover and illegitimate child. And if Valentina didn't possess half the voice her mother did, she knew this.

That night, under the Russian sky, it had never rung so clear.

Valentina was inspired by the events surrounding the 1st Russian Women's Battalion of Death's participation in the Kerensky Offensive of July 1917.

342

THE MAZE

SCIENCE FICTION

O N THE TWELFTH DAY, Cadet Eppie Langtry found the cracks in the wall.

She'd stopped her trek through the maze and leaned against its smooth surface. Exhaustion from the first six hours washed through her, the force of it pushing her into the unforgiving wall. After a few quick breaths, she wiped a hand across her eyes and rolled her shoulder. It was nothing more than a simple push to get going. But beneath her, something shifted.

Eppie sprang back, gulping cold air. She inched closer and probed the crevice with her fingers. The unrelenting and unchanging wall of the past twelve days slid against her skin. She nudged the wall with her shoulder, the way you might a best friend, as if she and this impenetrable white slab had anything in common. The crevice deepened.

Eppie glanced upward. The walls and ceiling were bare, but so bright that some days, she wanted to crouch into a ball, bury her head in her arms, and simply rock the twelve hour shift away.

She never did. The stories of those who had halted for too long kept her trudging forward through the maze. With her shoulder molding new shapes in the wall, Eppie latched onto the first glimmer of ... *something*. Like everyone else in her class, she'd spent hours pounding the surface, scratching the walls, kicking as hard as she could. Not even blood from torn fingernails was a match for the bright, white glare. Worse, after that first day, everyone's boots went missing from their lockers, and they now navigated the icy maze in bare feet.

Her toes ached with the cold. Eppie sandwiched one foot on top of the other and inspected the dip in the wall her shoulder had made. She poked at the wall with her fingertips, and the pliant give became unrelenting again. It was as if the maze resented her earlier attempts of kicking and scratching.

Eppie blew out a breath. "I'd be resentful too," she said, her words barely reaching her ears. It was as if the walls absorbed both the sound of her voice and what she had to say.

She tried her shoulder again, rolling it around, gentle, persistent, but giving it a bit of rhythm, like a dance routine. If the cadre were filming this—and no doubt they were—she must look ridiculous. A giggle escaped her lips, and Eppie slapped a hand across her mouth. She hadn't laughed in how many days? Certainly not the last twelve.

Beneath her shoulder, the crevice grew into a valley. Since the wall seemed to like her shoulder, what about a hip? Now she *was* dancing. Hip, shoulder, step. Hip, shoulder, step. Hip, shoulder...

Something solid and warm blocked her progress. Eppie halted, drinking in the first hint of heat in more than six hours. Was this the key, then? Movement? Friction? The wall beneath her still glowed white. It looked deceptively cold, but its warmth was delicious. She turned her face toward the wall, tongue flicking across her lips. What if she leaned forward? What if she let her mouth graze the surface? What then?

She was a mere breath away when the wall beneath her skin coughed.

HANK

Cadet Hank Su stomped through the corridor. No matter how hard he tried, the bright white swallowed the sound of his footfalls until all that remained were small, pathetic steps against the frigid floor. No matter how hard he screamed, the walls absorbed it. By dinner, his throat was so raw, even water scraped on the way down. He crashed from side to side. He kicked until they took away his boots. He gathered up all his strength and bolted down the corridor.

Gentle curves morphed into straight, hard surfaces—almost on a whim—and he slammed into the wall, this time not on purpose. Hank experimented with speed, sprints and slow jogs, but always moving forward. After that first day, when his best friend Ryan didn't come back, Hank had known this was no ordinary training exercise. Every night, he confronted that empty bunk next to his. To stop seeing the image of the stripped mattress and empty footlocker, Hank bent his head forward and ran with all his strength, grateful for the crash at the end.

But today, day twelve, he walked the corridors, keeping his pace steady. When he stood still, the walls closed in. If he extended his arms, certainly he'd be able to touch both sides at once. Every time he tried? The walls exhaled. There was no other word for it. And they left him standing in the center of the hall, fingertips straining for the cold surface on either side of him.

An illusion. A trick. Something someone was recording. Would the cadre play it back, at the end of the exercise, so everyone could laugh at him? He shook his head, banishing that notion—and the thought that there was no end to this. That was why they punched the walls. That was why they kicked. Didn't the cadre understand that? Or maybe they did, and that was the point.

Hank inched closer to one wall, letting his fingers trail along its surface. So smooth. So cold. An ache bloomed beneath his fingertips. He moved closer still, resting his forehead against the wall. The shock of cold almost made him jerk back. But as unrelenting as the wall was, it soothed his brow, made his throat feel less parched. Hank inhaled, held the recycled air in his lungs, then blew out a long breath and pitched forward.

There, on the wall—like the indentation on a pillow—was the impression of his forehead. With hands and fingers, he probed the dent. Nothing. In frustration, he leaned his head in the same spot, and the wall gave way again.

This time, Hank stood still. The corridor remained quiet. The lights blared down, like they always had. A dry, stale taste had invaded his mouth a few hours back. But this? This was new. This held hope. He rolled his head from side to side, the motion so gentle, his eyelids grew heavy. It was like an icy lullaby, and after six hours of running the maze, a relief.

The going was slow, but the wall yielded beneath his head. He forgot about running, about screaming, about kicking. He forgot about feeling foolish. Who cared? At last he was getting somewhere.

The giggle stopped all his progress. Hank felt his eyes grow wide. Certainly his mouth hung open. A giggle. A girl's giggle. He stepped back and surveyed the wall.

"Hello?" His voice sounded rough, so he coughed to clear it.

Nothing. Right. Walls didn't giggle. That didn't stop him from trying again. "Hello?"

"Is someone there?" The voice sounded light, but steady, and even better, real. Not some computer-simulated thing—and Hank knew all about those. This was a real girl.

Or, at least, Hank hoped she was. Instead of jumping back, he surged forward and cracked his head against the wall.

"Ow." His voice sank into the walls around him, and it was almost like he hadn't spoken at all.

"Are you okay?"

"I head-butted the wall."

"You can't do that," the girl said. "You've got to go slow."

"I know that."

"And use body parts that haven't hit the wall, either."

"I know that too." Or, at least, he did now.

"Does your head still work?"

What kind of question was that? Hank stared at the wall so hard, the surface blurred red.

"I mean," she said, "since you hit the wall with it."

Oh. Of course. He was an idiot. "Let me try." He eased forward, resting his head against the wall. From one side to the other, he rolled his head, the cold dulling the pain from the bruise.

His feet remained in the same spot, but the wall felt pliant under his forehead. He brought up a hand, testing the surface not with fingertips that had scratched, but with the heel of his hand. The sensation didn't register at first, but a small circle beneath his palm radiated warmth.

"Do you feel that?" he asked. "The heat?"

"I do."

"What do you think it is?"

A moment passed, a single heartbeat of hesitation. "Us?"

Was it? The reflex to jerk away nearly had him on the opposite side of the corridor. Instead, he stretched his fingers and pressed them against the wall. Warmth ran along his skin, pooled in his palm. The girl. It had to be, standing like he was, her hand against his.

"What's your—?" he began.

The claxon alarm rang. The walls faded. The floor vanished beneath his feet. The plummet stole his breath, felt endless until the jolt of hitting the ground. He found himself in the assembly yard, like he had after every twelve-hour shift, along with all the others in his class. Lines formed for the dining hall. By rote, Hank joined one.

"Hey, Hank!" someone called.

He didn't answer. Instead, he traced patterns across his palm. If he closed his eyes, he could still feel her warmth. When he opened them, Hank realized one thing:

He didn't even know her name.

EPPIE

Eppie scanned the dining facility, gaze darting, hopeful and quick. Too many times, she'd spotted someone, someone like her, someone with a secret. Her heart would speed up. She'd open her mouth to call out, raise a hand to wave, only to have that someone turn away.

Could she find the boy? If so, what then? How would that help them tomorrow, when they both went back inside the maze? She took her seat and pushed her dinner around her plate. Eat, she told herself. Build up your strength. Tonight's stew was smooth, at least. And hot. The center of the spoonful burnt her tongue, and the heat of it seared the back of her throat.

Eppie clutched her water cup, brought the rim to her lips, and drowned the heat. When she set the cup down, the sharp gaze of a matron fell on her.

"What did you do?" her friend Chara asked.

Eppie shook her head. "I didn't do anything." Except make the maze move. Except talk to a boy, who was somewhere beyond the yellow dividing line that ran the entire length of the dining facility.

But what if the cadre had seen Eppie and the boy, heard them talk? Well, what of it? Eppie folded her arms across her chest. She raised her chin and stared back at the matron.

The woman glanced away.

"Eppie ...?" Chara said.

Eppie put a finger to her lips. "Not here."

She was scraping her plate clean when the bell sounded. Normally, they'd be released into the yard for a precious hour of social interaction, but not at this point in their training, not while they were all navigating the maze. Instead, they walked the lines to their separate dormitories, were pushed through showers, and watched the lights flicker above their bunks.

"Wakeup at zero four hundred, ladies," the matron said. "That comes awfully early."

"Actually, it comes at the same time every day," Chara whispered.

Eppie giggled. The feel of it in her throat made her think of dancing with the maze. The boy. His warmth.

"There's more to the maze," she whispered to Chara.

The matron's footfalls sounded in the aisle between the two rows of beds.

"I'm not sure it's a maze at all," she added.

The footsteps grew louder, then slowed, then stopped—right beside Eppie's bunk.

"Cadet Langtry?"

"Yes, Matron?"

"If I were you, I'd conserve my energy by not speaking."

Eppie stilled her breath even as her thoughts raced. "Yes, Matron."

So they knew? They must. If the cadre couldn't use the maze to observe them, then they had planted something in their uniforms, a tracking device, perhaps. A sudden, delicious thought of flinging off her uniform filled her head. Flinging it off and running through the maze naked. Flinging it off and finding that boy. He'd keep her warm.

Now *that* would be a dance worth doing.

HANK

Hank stood at the entry point to the maze. He was alone in his own little corridor. They all were. If he held still, he could hear the others, their breathing, an occasional shoulder slam against the wall. No one liked going in, but the sooner they did, the sooner the day would end.

Day thirteen.

When his door whooshed open, Hank took soft steps. He let his fingertips skim the wall, the gentlest of touches. He could hold a baby bird and not injure it. Still, the cold against the soles of his feet, and the idea of the girl, urged him forward, faster and faster.

Soft and fast, he chanted to himself. Soft and fast.

Could he find her? He'd thought of her—dreamed of her—all night. Was she thinking of him? Dreaming of him? Did she even want to find him?

In nearly two weeks, what they'd both discovered yesterday was the first thing that hadn't hurt. He wanted more of that, so after half an hour (by his guess), he decided to cozy up to the wall.

He veered right, simply because he was right-handed. Hank hesitated. Was that predictable? Or maybe no second-guessing? The maze probably hated that. After all, he did.

Hank froze, his palm against the wall's surface. When, exactly, had the maze started having opinions?

"But you do," he whispered. Was it sentient? Would it eat them? It hadn't bothered to in the past twelve days, so he didn't see why it should start now.

"Do you have a name?" he asked, his face close now to the bright white of the wall. "I was stupid," he added. "I didn't ask the girl what her name was. I'm worried I won't be able to find her."

He stood now, both hands against the wall, his face inches away, legs spread. "Can you help me?"

Beneath his palms, something shifted, as if a wave deep within the wall itself had rolled past.

"I'm sorry," he added, "I didn't know I could hurt you. I only thought they were trying to hurt us."

The wave surged past again, stronger this time, carrying him with it.

"Got it," he said, feet scurrying to catch up. "You want me to go that way."

Hank ran, faster than he could on his own. With that wave beneath his palm, he nearly flew. Cold air blasted him in the face. His eyes watered, and his mouth went dry. But he didn't care.

He was flying. He was going to find the girl.

EPPIE

Eppie kept her uniform on. Tempted as she was to chuck the whole thing, the air was too frigid. Plus, at the end of the shift, did she really want to end up in the assembly yard completely naked? No. No, she did not.

Today, when her fingertips met the wall, the surface gave, just a bit, beneath the pressure. Nothing too hard, nothing violent, but yet, when she pressed her whole hand—not just the palm—against the wall, she felt herself sink into it.

"Do you forgive me?" she asked. "We didn't know. They never said." And here she was, talking to the wall as if it were a real living thing. Was it? She pressed deeper into the surface and the wall swallowed her hand, up to her wrist.

"Oh!" It didn't hurt. In fact, it made her think of what it might be like to push your way into a marshmallow. During her first year at the Academy, they'd had those, complete with a campfire that threw sparks into the air, the sweet smell of burnt sugar filling her nose. Back when things had felt hopeful, the Academy a lucky break.

Eppie eased her other hand into the wall. "What went wrong? Was it always supposed to end this way?"

The surface moved under her touch, like it was melting, except it was still far too cold for that. "You are so cold," she said. "That doesn't seem right."

Could a living thing be so cold, even one from another planet or dimension, or wherever this thing was from? She let herself fall forward, arms spread wide as if for a giant hug. If the maze didn't catch her, she'd break her nose, maybe some bones. But she closed her eyes, let gravity take her, and fell head first into the marshmallow wall.

Three inches from the floor, the maze caught her.

"Thank you," she whispered. "I knew you would."

At that moment, something rolled over her. This was less of a marshmallow and more of a thick wave of frosting. With it came a whoop and a flash of heat. Heat. Warmth.

The boy.

"Hello!" Eppie clambered to her hands and knees. She was fully inside the wall now. She slogged forward. It felt like pushing through a meadow of velvet grass with stalks that grew taller than her head.

"Hello!" she called again, louder now. "Are you there?"

"Is that you?"

Of course it's me, Eppie wanted to say. But she knew what he meant. "From yesterday, right?"

"It is you!" he said. "And the maze, it somehow—"

"Brought us together." Even the ice cold interior couldn't cool the blush that flashed across her face. She didn't know what this boy looked like, didn't know his name. All she knew was that he liked to head-butt his way into things, that he was loud, that he was trying to find her.

And that made him oh so interesting.

"I'm over here," she said when he didn't respond.

"Yeah, that's just it. I don't know where 'here' is."

He laughed, and the maze around her shook. Gentle waves made the velvet insides quiver and sent her this way and that.

"The maze likes that," she said. "It likes to hear you laugh."

"How do you know?"

"I'm inside it, inside the walls."

"How on earth—?"

Eppie laughed. "Probably not."

"You're right about that," he said. "But how?"

"Remember the trust falls from first year?"

"I hated those."

"Same idea."

"Will you help me?"

"I don't know where you are." Eppie held her arms out, fingers investigating the velvet that surrounded her. His heat. She should search for his heat. But all that met her fingertips was more frigid air.

"Hey." His voice was soft. "Before I forget. What's your name?"

"Eppie Langtry."

"I'm Henry, Henry Su. But everyone calls me Hank."

"Can I call you Henry?"

"Uh, I guess. Sure."

"I don't want to be like everyone else."

HANK

He'd found her! He'd found the girl. Hank didn't even care that she wanted to call him Henry. No one ever did. In fact, Hank liked that he could be Henry, if just for this girl.

"I'm over here," he called.

"It's like you're everywhere." She laughed, and the sound flowed through the space, seemed to fill it.

"I think it likes it when *you* laugh," he said.

"So you think it's ... something, too."

"Yeah. But I don't know what."

"I almost want to say it's not here."

"Oh, it's here."

"I mean ..." She sighed, and that too, traveled through the walls. "It's from somewhere else, or another dimension, one that was rolled up small, but now is stretched thin." She paused, then added, "That's why it's cold. That's why it hurts."

"Who did the stretching?"

This time, Eppie's exhale filled his ears. They both knew the answer to his question. Whoever did the stretching also shoved them inside every morning.

"Why did it pick us?" Hank asked, his voice quiet. "I mean, you're special." Hank knew she was. The trust fall proved that. "But I'm nobody. Average grades, average test scores, average everything."

"I don't believe that."

"I can prove it. On the outside, at least."

"Maybe it's not what's on the outside that counts."

"So what do we do?" he asked. "How do we help it?"

"I don't know. The only thing I do know is that I want to feel your hand again."

Hank swallowed, hard. For a full ten seconds, he quite possibly forgot how to breathe. "Maybe." He coughed. "Maybe I should hold still, and you try to find me." He cleared his throat again and added, "It might be easier that way, since you're on the inside."

He let himself melt into the wall. The surface grew softer beneath him, more pliant. From somewhere deep inside the wall came a whooshing noise, a sloshing that sounded like someone pushing through knee-deep water.

"Have you ever seen a wheat field?" Eppie asked.

"Only in vids."

"This must be what it's like, walking through one, only the stalks are so soft."

A spot of heat brushed against his palms.

"Oh, I found you!" Eppie cried out before he could utter a word.

They stood like that, palm to palm. A circle of heat bloomed beneath their hands, spread into the wall itself.

"Do you feel that?" she asked.

Hank coughed again. "Yeah."

"I think it wants us closer together. You know, more points of contact."

"You okay with that?"

"Why wouldn't I be okay?" she said. "It's like dancing."

Well, he wasn't going to use that word, but yes, like dancing. They eased closer together. Was that her cheek against his lips?

"Why do you think it needs us?" he asked.

"I don't know."

"Do you think it's ... I don't know, using us? Not in a bad way. I mean, I barely know you, but I couldn't stop thinking of you last night. You know?"

"Yeah, I know."

"It feels ... right, and yet, nothing makes sense."

"Nothing about this last year makes sense. Weren't you excited to get into the Academy?"

He had been, just like his older brothers.

"I wasn't expecting it to be easy," Eppie continued. "But even the training that seemed stupid at the time had a point, and you kind of knew what that was, even if you didn't exactly."

Hank snorted. That was the Academy, all right. "Both my brothers graduated from here. Frederick never talks about the maze, and all Jon says is don't stop moving."

But they had stopped. And now?

"All that training," she said, "and then they put us in here, and it feels like … it feels like—"

"A mistake," he finished. "Someone's made a mistake, and they don't know how to fix it."

"Then why are they sending class after class through the maze?"

"Maybe they were hoping for the right combination?"

"Maybe they were hoping for us. Look."

Shadows played against the walls, the ceiling, and even the floor of the maze. Dark figures ran, punched walls, scratched and kicked. Hank wanted to scream. *Stop! You're not helping.*

"More than one dimension, then?" Eppie asked.

"I wasn't paying attention that day in class."

"I think this goes beyond anything they teach in class."

"That's probably part of the problem."

The claxon bell blared, echoing through the maze with enough force to rupture an eardrum. Hank felt it shake the walls. The surface beneath his hands trembled, like a wild creature racked with fear and pain. Before the bottom fell out—before the walls melted and his feet slid through nothing—he lunged forward.

Forget trust falls. This was a trust dive. He grabbed Eppie around the waist the same moment she clutched his shoulders. He wasn't losing her this time.

The second before they hit bottom, Eppie said:

"Don't let go."

EPPIE

Something about the assembly yard was different, and it wasn't simply because she was clutching the boy, Henry. They held onto each other, and Eppie took in the grass beneath her, the sky above, a twilight blue with a nearly full moon. And yet, when she stared hard, she saw the maze, or the outline of it, floating above their heads.

Others saw it too. Faces turned skyward. Necks, some long and slender, others thick and sturdy, were all she could see of her classmates. Another dimension? A being? Whatever it was, things were different.

Matrons and wardens converged on the yard, corralling boys and girls, not even caring that they mixed the groups.

"Find them!" someone shouted.

"Eppie!" Chara dashed up, breathless, hair streaming from its regulation bun. "They mean you."

For the first time, Eppie's gaze met Henry's. His soulful dark eyes looked worried. "Us?" he said.

He sprang to his feet and reached for her. Eppie grabbed on with one hand, pushing herself up with the other. Then, still clutching Henry, she ran. Their classmates parted for them, then filled the gap behind, forcing the wardens and matrons to shove, to pull out the tazons. Zaps, sizzles, and the cries of their classmates echoed behind them.

"What are they doing?" Eppie forced out between breaths.

"Something bad."

"What did we do?"

Henry glanced at her before sprinting harder. "Something bad?"

They raced past their classmates, intent on those last few steps to freedom. The protected forest around the Academy would shelter them. She knew enough, Eppie was sure, to survive for days in there, despite the lack of supplies. The two of them together? They'd make do.

At the very edge, where the scent of pine filled the air, and branches reached out as if to greet them, they slammed into a wall. Not like one from the maze. This wall was thick, electrified. It sent Eppie backward, through the air, her grip torn from Henry's.

Her hip crunched against the earth first, a sickening sound that made her think of broken bones. She rolled, hoping that would absorb the shock. She rolled and rolled, right into a pair of white, gleaming boots. She stared up into the glowing end of a tazon.

Eppie never raised her hands. Her mouth stayed closed. She held on, held her breath, and braced for what would happen next.

The jolt shot through her entire body, and then her world went black.

HANK

Hank had ended his day surrounded by black. Now, waking, it was all he saw. He reached out a hand, waved it, blinked, and waved it again. Nothing. Either the cell was lightproof, or the tazon had blinded him.

Or both. He'd heard about the cells. They all had. The cadre sent you there when you acted out. You were meant to reconsider your choices in this space, contemplate whether the rules were really that bad, whether the wardens and the matrons truly mistreated you.

Life choices. We all make them, the superintendent had intoned during first-year orientation.

Yeah. What a choice. All he'd done was what? Figure out the maze? Where was the reward for that? The accolades? He pushed himself up, tucked his legs beneath him, then reached a tentative hand above his head.

A meter, maybe a meter and a half. Not enough room to stand and barely enough to turn around. He inched his fingers along the walls, the floor, and the ceiling. The surface snagged callouses on his hands, the texture rough-hewn and unmoving. He scraped a knuckle and warm blood oozed between his fingers.

His head swam, an ache spreading across his skull. A panel slid back. Light flooded the space. He squinted, trying to peer out his cell, the panel, the door—or what he thought was the door—anything to give him more information.

"The prisoner is awake," someone said.

Prisoner?

"Ah, very good." A shadow crossed the open panel. "Comfortable, Cadet Su?" a smooth voice said. "I imagine fraternizing with female cadets is a great deal more fun than this."

What? He never ... well, sure, he thought about Eppie, but they'd just met—sort of. Plus, they'd been inside the maze. All rules were off.

Weren't they?

"Hungry?" the voice asked.

In response, Hank's stomach rumbled. Stupid, stupid. It made him look weak. Of course, getting thrown into a pitch-black cell didn't make him appear all that strong, or smart, either.

"Well then," the voice said, the solicitous tone chilling Hank's thoughts. "Why don't we have a little chat?"

EPPIE

The straight-back chair was unremarkable except for one thing: Eppie couldn't move. Her bare feet were flush against the floor. The surface flashed hot, then cold. She jerked against invisible bonds, unable to break contact. Sweat bathed her forehead, trickled down her spine.

"You're making it too hard on yourself," the matron said. "Simply tell us what happened. Then you can go back to the dorm, have a nice dinner, see your friends."

A false promise. She'd been trained—they all had—in resisting interrogation. Why did this matron think such simple offers would work now? The floor flashed again, a searing heat that forced a yelp from her throat.

That. It was one thing to read about torture, quite another for someone to cook the soles of your feet.

"You know," the matron said. "Cadet Su told us some interesting things."

The matron was all sly words and looks, playing mostly good cop. Eppie had braced for the inevitable switch—a new matron, or a warden, even. Pretending that Henry had said something might be standard procedure. In this case, it wasn't logical.

"He told us what you did."

What she did? Or what they'd done together? Neither of which amounted to much. Or perhaps, it amounted to so much that no one could understand what had happened. Eppie pictured the maze floating above the yard. The cadre wanted to control something they couldn't comprehend. And good luck with that.

"You can't hide anything from us," the woman said. "We have it all on vid, for playback, any time we like."

Then why bother asking? Eppie clamped her mouth shut. She'd stuck with the canned response, the one the cadre themselves taught. Name. Rank. Serial Number. You open your mouth, you give them an opening. Speak and you'll eventually say something you don't mean to—or can't take back.

"So, you don't mind that Cadet Su, that Hank, betrayed you?"

Perhaps someone named Cadet Su would betray her. And Hank? Well, how could you trust a Hank? Eppie shut her eyes and pictured Henry, his dark silky hair, his warm hands against her, around her waist, palm against palm as they ran. Maybe the Academy did have vids. But clearly their knowledge didn't add up to much if they didn't know the difference between Hank and Henry.

Eppie stared straight at the matron and laughed.

HANK

He knew the beating would come the moment laughter burst from his mouth. Cadet Langtry had betrayed him? Eppie? The few glimpses of the girl he'd had over the past two days told him how rock steady she was—much more than he was, that was for sure. How smart she was. After four years of training at the Academy, couldn't the cadre see that?

Maybe they did and figured he was the idiot in the equation. Well, that was partly true, because he had just laughed, loud and long, at their ludicrous suggestion. Another round with the tazon? Sure, why not? Tossed, bruised and battered, back into his pitch-black cell? Not surprising.

What surprised him were the questions—not the ones about Eppie, but the others. What was the maze made out of? How did they get inside the walls? (And really, only Eppie had, so why ask him?) The cadre controlled the entrance and exit, herded them through the maze day after day. Yet, they knew so little. Which made him, and Eppie, and their classmates what? Lab rats?

He pressed gentle fingers against his eyes. They were swelling shut, both of them, not that it mattered inside the cell. Still, it was so dark, he was afraid he'd forget whether his eyes were open or closed. He wondered if Eppie were doing the same, testing her own bruised eyes. He hated to think of her that way, hated that maybe it was all his fault. He pressed a hand against the wall, wishing for one intense moment that it was the maze again, that he'd detect her warmth, find her again.

"Henry?"

The soft voice made him bolt upright. He should have smacked the hell out of his forehead and given himself a second concussion. Instead, the rough stone gave way—like in the maze.

"Eppie?"

"I'm here."

"Where's here?"

"Inside the maze."

EPPIE

Eppie couldn't say when the floor beneath her bruised limbs cushioned rather than punished. Her hip stopped aching, then her ribs. She dozed, possibly, before her eyes went wide with amazement.

She was inside the maze again, but it was more than that now. Actually, when she considered it, the maze had always been more than that. It was something unto itself. And it wasn't tethered to this world any longer. It had broken free. They'd seen that in the yard. But it hadn't left. It had come back.

For her?

Yes, and not just for her.

"Let's find Henry," she told it.

And so they traveled. High above the Academy, Eppie breathed in the panic below. Hovercrafts for on-planet use, space transport, footlockers and bags scattered in the yard, and parents streaming through the halls in search of their children. Her stomach tightened. Her own parents? Had they been notified? Or was she not part of that world anymore?

The maze carried her through the long corridors of the Academy. She eavesdropped on hurried meetings, press conferences cut short. A scandal, with two cadets dead due to unauthorized experiments.

Dead?

"Please," she told the maze. "Where's Henry? Is he all right?"

So they floated lower, and lower, beneath the first floor, the basement, into the catacombs that fueled so many rumors among the cadets.

"All true?" she wondered out loud.

They passed her own cell. Her uniform, ghostly white, flat and listless, was crumpled on the floor. Perhaps the urge to lose her uniform had been right all along. She certainly didn't need it now.

A sob echoed through the dark hall and wrenched her heart, but she was powerless to console the mourner. The maze continued down the hall, down another level. Eppie held up her hand, like she had the first time she'd met Henry inside the maze.

"I'll know him," she said. "Just go slowly."

And so it did.

"There. There he is." That telltale warmth, the palm that fit against her own. Henry. "He's never been inside," she added. Not like she had. She knew the maze, and it knew her, but Henry? They hadn't gotten to that point.

"I think he'll trust you now. Will you try?"

And so the maze did.

"Eppie?"

"I'm here."

"Where's here?"

"Inside the maze."

He coughed, and his whole body shook with it. The maze trembled as if it too were in pain.

"Let go," she told Henry. "Just let go."

"How?"

"Take my hands."

Palm to palm, then laced fingers. She pulled him up, the now useless uniform empty and deflated on the floor.

"Where are we?" Henry asked.

"I'm not completely sure, but I think we're inside a baby universe," she said. "It was an experiment, here at the Academy, for years and years, and no one knew."

"Except for the cadets they ran through it."

"Exactly."

"So what is it now?"

"Now I think it's evolving." Her voice was hushed. "And I think it's evolving because of us, because we tried to find each other, because—"

"We knew there was something more."

They floated up, up, up, out of the catacombs, through the Academy, and hovered over the chaos of the yard. Then they went higher, into the stars.

"It'll need room to expand," Eppie said.

"Babies can't stay little forever."

Eppie laughed and shot forward, her form ethereal now. Henry caught her, and they twirled.

"Someday, we'll have to settle down," he said. "All three of us."

But for now they were simply a boy and a girl, with an entire universe between them.

I first published The Maze as part of a small compilation. It was also this small compilation that ended up getting me an invitation to submit a story to The Future Chronicles. This is my way of saying: put your work out there—you never know what might come of it.

HEART WHISPER

FANTASY

*I*sabelle Sterling pulled the pickup truck off the gravel road and bumped her way to the windbreak thirty feet in. With the engine off and the windows rolled all the way down, it was quiet—at last. A soft breeze whispered in the tall grasses and rattled cornstalks.

Isabelle jumped from the cab. The tallest stalks reached well beyond her waist. She peered down row after endless row, all black earth and rich green. The scent of soil was thick in the air, warm from the July sun.

Farming wasn't one of her skills. Marilyn wouldn't let her near the enclave's gardens—not even the potted herbs—for fear she might wilt them. Still, even Isabelle knew this was a good omen.

She headed for the passenger door and the precious cargo belted in the front seat—like a toddler. Her truck still wore the dust of Georgia, the black paint flecked with red, the deep rust the color of blood. She wore it too. Every time she licked her lips, she could taste the red clay earth.

Isabelle eased the wooden crate from the cooler in the front seat, kicked the door closed, and headed for the road.

The rest of the trip would be on foot. She wiggled her toes inside her combat boots. Since being discharged, she tugged them on once a year for this trek up the bluff.

They'd carried her through Afghanistan; they could carry her here as well.

At the crossroads, she inched forward, just enough to stand in the shade cast by the stop sign. Her truck waited patiently behind her.

Anyone traveling this road would disregard it, maybe figure a farmer was checking her crops. Or more likely, a farmer had abandoned it there in the windbreak, keys in the ignition, and left it and everything behind —a relic to relentless toil and debt. She'd seen three such pickups on her way to the bluffs.

Isabelle sighed. It wasn't the truck she was worried about.

This was her fifth year up the riverside bluff.

This was the year she wouldn't come back down.

She felt the rumble first through the soles of her boots. All the hairs on the back of her neck stood at attention. She spun, jumped back, heart pounding a cadence she couldn't control.

Breathe, breathe, *breathe*.

In the distance, a white pickup truck barreled forward, a cloud of dust blooming behind it—just a farmer, and nothing more.

Just a farmer.

She was, in the words of Marilyn, overreacting. Or hyper-reacting. After five years back on the soil of Black Earth, Minnesota, she knew better.

Or at least everyone thought she should.

The dust cloud grew larger, billowing like a sandstorm. Instead of slowing for the stop sign, the driver was gunning the engine and planning to run straight through.

She backed up, stumbled over the edge of the ditch.

It wasn't far enough.

The damn truck was coming straight for her.

Deliberately.

What. The. Hell.

The truck swerved, and she pitched backward into the ditch. A spray of pebbles pelted her bare arms. She lost her grip on the wooden crate. It fell to the ground with a crack, the sound like a gunshot. Its contents spilled among the rocks and weeds.

The truck flew through the stop sign. Then the driver jammed on the brakes, backed up, and came to a halt on the road right above her.

Isabelle blinked and braced her feet against the earth. The rumble of the engine competed with the roar of her pulse. Dust floated on the air, filled her mouth, scratched her eyes.

From inside the cab came the relentless hammering of death metal. The driver lowered the volume and then hung himself out the window, fingers drumming the flame decal on the side of the door.

"Sorry about that, honey. I didn't see you there."

Like hell he didn't. Isabelle gave him a stare, the one she'd perfected in boot camp, the one without a trace of emotion except for silent contempt.

"Need a ride?"

"Oh, I'm good." Her palms stung. Her tailbone ached. But what hurt the most were the remains of her cargo scattered all around her.

There was no salvaging that.

"You sure you don't need a hand?" The driver drummed the side of his truck even harder, a strange, staccato beat that made her heart pound a warning.

"Positive."

"A pretty girl like you, out here all alone? Someone might get the wrong idea."

"Someone might, but not you," she said, weaving magic into her voice. "You're smarter than that."

She could see the spell weave around the guy's head, tangling with sweaty strands of blond hair, clouding his blue eyes. And she saw the moment he shook it off, too.

Sadly, he wasn't smarter than that.

"Those peaches wouldn't be for me, would they, sweetheart?" His gaze went not to the scattered fruit but to her chest.

"No." This time, Isabelle dispensed with magic. Instead, she infused her words with all the Georgia sugar she could muster. "But these are."

With that, she raised both her middle fingers.

It was a dumb move, but after all the searching, the bartering, and thirty-six hours of driving, she didn't need to deal with some dude-bro joyriding around the area, scaring livestock and running over cats.

He wasn't local. Local boys (and girls) knew better than to get stupid around the river bluffs. They'd head into Mankato or even drive up to the Twin Cities.

This guy? If he didn't leave now, he might not leave at all. Not today of all days.

His fingers stopped their drumming. The knuckles of his hand went tight.

She needed to end this—quick.

Isabelle bared her teeth. The glamour was simple, barely a spell at all. She preferred fox or coyote. Today she wasn't taking chances.

She went with mountain lion.

During her first year in college, after her roommate's disastrous encounter at a frat party, Isabelle had taught her the trick—along with some hand-to-hand combat moves. Despite evidence to the contrary, the enclave insisted that there were those who could weave magic—and then everybody else.

Isabelle didn't believe it. Everyone had magic. Of some kind.

Except for maybe dude-bro here.

He blanched, blinked, and gaped, his mouth open like a fish left to flop around on the dock. Without taking his eyes off her, he put the truck in gear and inched respectfully up the road. At the stop sign, he took a right, the way leading to the interstate.

"There's a good boy," she said, her voice barely above a whisper. "And don't come back."

ISABELLE USED all but one bottle of water to give the peaches a bath. She cradled each one in her palm, the way a mother might hold an infant's head. She washed away the dirt, used a fingernail to pry pebbles from the tender flesh, and placed each one back into the crate as if tucking it in for a nap.

And she still had the three-mile walk ahead of her.

"Uphill, both ways," she said—ostensibly to the peaches—and laughed. Then she placed her palm against her heart and waited.

She wasn't sure what, exactly, she was waiting for. But the gesture calmed her, reassured her that her heart was still where it should be, that it still beat, that neither it nor she was completely broken.

A breeze chased strands of hair from her cheeks. The crossroads were quiet once again.

It was time.

She tucked the last bottle of water into a knapsack, hefted the crate to her hip, and started her trek up the river bluff.

~

THE BARTER HAD COME through at the last minute, as barters tended to do. Isabelle needed twelve perfect peaches. And no, she couldn't dash into a grocery store and toss a handful into a shopping basket.

Peaches, plucked by hand. And not just any hand, but that of enclave matriarch. And not just any peaches, but ones from Georgia.

Peaches were plentiful. What Isabelle lacked was something to offer in return. Then, she connected with an enclave courier in as desperate of straights as she was.

After that, it was nothing but the whisper of wheels against the inter-state and some truly terrible talk radio. At last, she reached the red clay of Georgia, where her counterpart, a woman named Denisha, met her at the southern enclave's peach orchard.

"Oh, snowdrop," Denisha said when Isabelle hopped out of her truck. "Let's get you out of this heat."

Isabelle laughed. She'd been to Georgia before—three weeks of airborne school in August, no less. But that had been a lifetime ago, and her blood was sluggish and thick from Minnesota winters.

She grabbed the cooler from the seat. The thing was icy, even after all that driving. A trace of its contents filtered into the thick Georgia air, at odds with her surroundings. A harsh, cold, fishy odor that—judging by Denisha's wrinkled nose—was overwhelming the sultry, sweet scent of peaches.

Inside the orchard's office, they headed for the kitchen area. Denisha poured them both some sweet tea. She was about Isabelle's age—late twenties or so, and she wore her hair in a coil of braids on top of her head. She looked like a queen capable of ruling her own enclave.

With the first sip, the sugar flowed through Isabelle's veins. Enclave brewed. It had to be. There was enough magic mixed with the sugar and caffeine to not only revive her but fuel her drive back home.

"So this is really a thing," Denisha said while Isabelle unpacked the cooler.

"It's a thing." Isabelle held up one of the packages. "Straight from the lutefisk capitol of the world."

The dried cod, soaked in water, then lye, and then water again—because who the hell eats lye—was a gelatinous, smelly, and baffling delicacy. She'd grown up in Minnesota and didn't understand it. She had no hope of explaining it to someone out of state.

"I thought she was joking with this request." Denisha shook her head. "I'm really hoping she doesn't ask me to share this year."

Isabelle's hand stilled on the package, the cold burning her fingertips. "She shares?"

"Sometimes. Depends on the request. Honestly, I think it's partly a test, you know—*will you do my bidding* and all that. But it's worth it, right? I wouldn't give up being a courier for anything."

Oh, how Isabelle wanted to ask. She wanted to ask *so badly*. Did Denisha see their enclave's patron? Speak with her? Share the yearly offering? What was that like? The thought of it made her heart drum against her ribcage and her palms sweat.

"Yeah," Isabelle said, heat prickling her cheeks, betraying her. "I wouldn't give it up either."

Denisha collected the packages of lutefisk. "So, I cook this ... how?"

"You can boil it, but it's probably better if you bake it. And if you have any bacon or pork drippings, you can serve that on the side."

"Everything's better with bacon."

"In this case, it might just save you."

Denisha laughed. "This is going to be an adventure." She packed the lutefisk into the refrigerator and then filled a thermos with sweet tea. "For your drive back."

"You don't—"

"Oh, yes, I do. You saved my ass. Those." Denisha pointed to where a crate of peaches sat, twelve perfect ones in a bed a straw. "Are for your patron. But these?" She hefted the thermos. "And those." Denisha gestured to a canvas sack overflowing with even more peaches. "Are for your drive back. Trust me, those things are magical. You'll eat the entire bag before you get home."

Denisha walked Isabelle to her truck and then gave her a hug so heartfelt it chased the air from her lungs.

"Text me if you need any help with the lutefisk."

"Count on it."

Isabelle drove off, opting for back roads rather than fight Atlanta's rush hour traffic. She felt as if she were leaving behind a friend, although really, she'd only known Denisha through messages on the courier group chat.

What did couriers do before the internet? In the Black Earth town hall, there was a photograph of a woman—a Sterling woman, one of Isabelle's ancestors—carrying a basket of something dear cradled in her arms.

The woman's feet were bare, her dress faded and frayed. The entire town looked as though it'd been coated in dust. In the background, an ancient Model T sat, discarded, forgotten, or most likely, both.

Isabelle thought about that woman on her drive back to Minnesota, wishing she could ask whether being a courier had been worth it.

HALFWAY UP THE BLUFF, the urge to pluck a peach from the crate and take a giant bite nearly overwhelmed Isabelle.

Denisha had been right. If not for her own bag of peaches, Isabelle would've eaten the offering. After that, driving past Black Earth and heading straight for the boundary waters—and paddling into Canada— would've been her only option.

It was one thing to scramble for an offering at the last minute, quite another to deliberately sabotage yourself.

Oh, but the peaches were tempting. They honeyed the air. The phantom sensation of juice running down her chin, sticky and tart, had her swiping at her skin. She'd eaten the entire bag within hours, amazed they hadn't sent her racing for a rest stop bathroom.

But these were enclave peaches, picked by a matriarch. Overindulging wasn't a danger; it was mandatory.

From this point on the river bluff path, she spied the cave opening, but only because she knew where to look. It was the darkness between pine needles and leaves. It was the cool that chased away some of the day's heat, sending a wash of goose bumps across her bare arms and legs.

She reached the spot where the mosquitoes stopped nattering in her ears and biting the back of her neck. The spot where most people turned around, their legs suddenly and oddly tired, their sunburn fierce despite thick layers of sunscreen, their water bottles mysteriously empty.

Isabelle kept going.

The path turned rocky. During her first run as a courier, she'd pulled on the combat boots on a whim, more from nostalgia rather than practicality.

Turned out to be a wise decision.

Her heart pounded again. Isabelle paused, shifted the crate on her hip so she could hold it with one hand, and pressed her free palm against her chest, waiting once again.

Her heart thrummed with a steady thump, thump, thump. During her last Army physical—one for yet another deployment requiring yet another round of shots—the doctor had paused, stethoscope pressed against Isabelle's chest.

"Has anyone ever told you that you have a heart murmur?"

Isabelle's breath caught in her throat. She gave her head one slow shake.

The doctor listened, the crease between her eyebrows deepening. "Strange no one has ever ... huh, this is weird. I'm going to order some tests."

The words froze Isabelle in place. She knew, even without the tests. It was the enclave.

She was being called home.

Even now, when her heart pounded or skipped a beat, when the air felt odd in her lungs, she'd hold herself still, listen with all her might, as if somehow she could hear the defects of her own heart.

She continued the trek, the climb registering in her thighs now. This last stretch always made her doubt. Was she on the right path? Would she walk in circles, searching for the cave and never finding it?

Then the entrance loomed, dark and foreboding, a place for bears or wolves or definitely something that might swallow you in a single gulp.

And well, yes, their patron could do that. But she—like all patrons— had a particular palate. Human flesh wasn't on the menu. Isabelle adjusted the crate in her grip.

Apparently peaches were.

She stepped across the boundary where the path ended and the flat, smooth surface of the cave entrance began. Cool air washed over her, chasing the sweat from her skin. A burst of color filled her eyes. Gemstones glinted in the sun—blood reds to dazzle, blues the color of midnight, and greens that made her think of those endless fields of corn.

The gems looked ripe, like they were their own kind of fruit. You could reach out and pluck one from the wall—if you were foolish enough to try, that is.

In the center of the entrance stood a small altar made of marble, its surface only a few inches larger than the crate she carried. The first time Isabelle had placed an offering there, relief filled the breathlessness in her lungs. Certainly she'd never be asked for something she couldn't carry.

In all five years, she hadn't. Perhaps that was enough of a reward.

She crouched and brushed the marble surface and then exhaled to chase away any errant grit or dust. The altar was clean; it always was. But it felt right to do this, to make this final gesture before she left.

Assuming she would leave this year.

As always, if her patron lingered inside the cave, Isabelle couldn't detect her. No sigh filled with smoke. No tail scraping the cave floor. Nothing but the gemstones glinting playfully and the altar waiting for her offering.

She eased the crate onto the surface and stood—one step back and then another.

Nothing.

Perhaps she'd been wrong about the five years. But no, when she'd returned from the Army, Marilyn had specifically said the previous courier—Isabelle's second cousin—had "finished" with her duties.

Her matriarch hadn't elaborated on what "finished" meant, exactly, only that the woman was nowhere to be found. And that it was Isabelle's turn.

And ten years ago, before she'd enlisted in the Army, there'd been another such turnover. Indeed, it was one of the reasons she did enlist. Out of sight, out of mind.

Now, here she was. Another Sterling woman after five years of service to a patron she'd never seen, never mind spoken to.

She'd tried, of course, that first year. She called out, peered into the cave, even dared to take a few steps inside. The hollow space swallowed her voice. The light from the gemstones faded a few feet inside the void.

No scent of brimstone or smoke, only that of clean, dry earth. If her patron lingered somewhere beyond, shrouded by the dark, Isabelle couldn't tell.

If not for the vanishing offering—last year's had been Mozart Kugeln from Vienna—she'd say nothing inhabited the cave at all.

So that was it: five years and nothing. Perhaps Marilyn would meet her at the crossroads where she'd left her truck and relieve her of her duties. Maybe this was like the Army. She'd done her time, served as best she could, but lacked the ... *heart* for anything else.

But it had been a good five years. She'd gotten her degree and traveled the world—this time to places where people weren't shooting at her.

That was worth something.

"Thank you," she said into the stillness. "It's been an honor to be your courier."

Isabelle was at the boundary, toes of her combat boots flirting with the edge, when a sonorous voice sounded behind her.

"Oh, my child, that sounds like a goodbye."

It was only after her discharge from the Army that Isabelle found herself freezing at the oddest provocations. She couldn't account for it.

After all, she'd stood in the open door of a C-130, the pines of Georgia thick beneath her as the plane banked for another run at the drop zone. She was out the door the second the light turned green, no hesitation. She could work in the sand, the mud, the rain. She knew when to be still and when to move.

But here in the civilian world? Here with her patron?

She froze.

"It's all right, my dear." The words were low, infused with brimstone and heat, mist and flowers.

It was such a strange, enticing combination that Isabelle found herself turning around. She froze once again, this time in awe. Her patron was a shimmering green that changed with the light—from one angle, the icy green of new growth, from another, the deep somber skin of a ripe avocado. Flecks of red raced along the surface of the scales. The forked tongue was red as well.

But the eyes were a glowing amber. And it was those serious eyes that surveyed her now.

"Are you really a dragon?" It was an impertinent sort of question, and Isabelle almost wished she could bite it back.

"Some people call me that. I prefer to think of myself as myself."

"Me, too."

"Indeed. It's a Sterling trait, one I've always admired."

Isabelle glanced about the cave. She knew that she wasn't some sort of damsel-in-distress sacrifice. *Why now* and *what next* both hovered on the tip of her tongue. At last, she went with:

"I don't understand."

"The enclave still needs you, my dear, they have always needed you and the Sterlings before you."

"To do what?"

"The hard work of making ends meet, I'm afraid."

"But, the gardens, and the farm, and the—"

"Etsy shop?" The dragon's voice rose, more amused than sardonic. "Not enough to survive on, never mind thrive. We have always sent the Sterlings into the world. They've always been the most capable of handling the vagaries of life."

Like making a thirty-six-hour roundtrip for a crate of peaches or dealing with dude-bros in their pickup trucks.

"Yes, exactly that." The dragon grinned.

At least, Isabelle assumed that's what all those teeth meant. She recalled the glamour she'd used on dude-bro. Forget fox, coyote, or even mountain lion.

Maybe she'd been a dragon all along.

"Indeed," her patron said. "You've also been a soldier and a scholar. For five years, you have catered to my ... whims. You're ready to strike out on your own."

"I'm to leave the enclave?"

"Not permanently, but for the time being, yes."

"Will the enclave call me home again?"

Wisps of smoke rose from the dragon's nostrils. She shook her head as if startled by Isabelle's question.

"My child, didn't you know? That was me."

Isabelle touched fingers to the left side of her chest. "But—"

"I had to break one small part of you so that you could come home to us." The dragon paused, and it was as if she spoke the next word with great reluctance. "Intact."

The meaning of that word—*intact*—sank in immediately. Isabelle had kept herself from watching the news, from keeping up with her old unit, searching the internet for details. Somehow, she knew. She knew exactly how that last deployment had ended.

The dragon blew out a smoke ring. It broke against Isabelle's chest, soothing but not healing her heart.

"It's not all bad, a whispering heart," her patron said. "If you listen closely, it can tell you what you want."

"I'm afraid I can't hear it."

"You will. With time." The dragon inclined her head toward the peaches, still on the altar. "Now, will you stay and join me for this repast?"

Isabelle took two steps forward and knelt at the altar. "I will."

A FULL MOON helped Isabelle navigate the path down the river bluff. Once in her truck, she rested her arms on the steering wheel and gazed through the windshield. Above her, through the fringe of cottonwood leaves, a field of stars littered the night sky.

She was going to miss this view.

Her phone, which she'd locked in the glove compartment, buzzed. She fumbled with the latch and pulled it out in time to see a text message flash across the screen.

Denisha: I never did ask. Were you on your fifth year too?
Isabelle: Get your walking papers?
Denisha: Sure did. I could use a brainstorming buddy if you're available.
Isabelle: I'll start driving south.
Denisha: I'll head north.
Isabelle: Meet you in the middle?
Denisha: Meet you in the middle.

When Isabelle returned to Black Earth, she found Marilyn on the town hall steps, haloed by lamplight. Two duffle bags, a suitcase, and three boxes—all of Isabelle's worldly possessions—surrounded her. In her hands, Marilyn held a small package wrapped in brown paper and tied with twine.

Without a word, she handed it to Isabelle. Inside was the picture of the barefoot woman, cradling the basket, chin tilted resolutely for that journey up the river bluff. Now, when Isabelle studied the photograph, she noticed something new.

The woman wore the barest trace of a smile as well.

"Her fifth year," Isabelle said.

"Yes, indeed." Marilyn hugged her then, arms thin but capable. "We will miss you, but you are ready."

"And when it's time to come home?"

Marilyn raised her gaze to the river bluff. "You'll know, one way or the other."

On her way out of Black Earth, Isabelle passed a truck pulled over on the side of the road, a white pickup with flame decals. It sat there, discarded, forgotten, or most likely, both. A relic to something, although she wasn't quite sure what.

She drove into the night, listening to the whisper of wheels against the interstate and for the quiet murmur of her own heart.

Heart Whisper is (yet another!) dragon story written for The (Love) Stories for 2020 Project.

DECEMBER

For December, it was stories about helpers, magical and otherwise.

SIMON THE COLD

FANTASY

I first met Simon the Cold outside the library on a night so icy it stole all the moisture from my breath. My feet crunched through the slushy mix of sand and snow. I walked with my head bowed, the air sharp against my cheeks. That was why I nearly crashed into the man bent over the garbage bin, its latticework gleaming with frost.

The glow from the man's headlamp illuminated the inside of the bin like a spotlight—not a single sliver of light was wasted. I stood for a moment, regaining my balance, my jeans stiff with cold, and watched the man pull treasures from the dark depths.

He glanced up and said to me, "You'd be surprised what people throw away."

When I didn't respond, he added, "Or maybe you wouldn't."

I forgot about the books I had on reserve. Instead, I raced to the second-floor cafe and bought the largest coffee on the menu board—the Caffeinator. With my pockets crammed with sugar packets and little containers of half and half, I ventured back outside. My boots skidded on the ice. A drop of coffee landed on my wrist, the scent warming the stale winter air, but I hardly felt it against my skin. My heart started pounding the second I spotted the man, still at the garbage bin. Heat flashed across my cheeks. I studied the cup in my hands. What was I doing? Was this in any way sensible?

Then I thought: *How can I not do this.*

So I marched forward, boots crunching, coffee sloshing, until the man raised his head and the headlamp shined its spotlight on me.

"I can't take that from you," he said.

I stood in the circle of his light, clutching the coffee, completely without words to convince him.

"And no tricks," he added. "You look like the tricky sort to me."

Perhaps it was nerves, or the cold, or the fact, I'm the least tricky person ever born, but I burst out laughing. "I'm not tricky at all," I said. "In fact, I'm pretty transparent."

"Ah, that you're not, girly. That you're not."

Normally, someone calling me girly—of all things—would crawl beneath my collar and chew away at my restraint. But this man meant it, if not with kindness, then as an acknowledgment.

I see you there, young person, and what you're trying to do. I've survived without you for this long and will continue to long after you've forgotten me.

That was why I took a step forward. He'd returned to sort his treasures, leaving me in the cold and the dark. He didn't glance up. He didn't stop his sorting. His fingers twitched ever so slightly. They were pale and stiff. Items slipped from their grasp, rattling the contents of the garbage bin.

I took another step forward.

"Old Simon hasn't had a shower, girly, for quite a while. Just take that as fair warning."

Nothing, I decided, could smell worse than this stale winter air. I took one last step and set the coffee on the edge of the garbage bin. From my pockets, I pulled the sugar packets and half and half.

"It's funny," I said, placing them next to the to-go cup. "You'd be surprised what some people throw away."

When he didn't respond, I added, "Or maybe you wouldn't."

I walked toward the parking lot and threaded through the cars until I reached my own. I didn't look back. That, I sensed, was part of the deal. So I left the lot by the back exit and drove the long way home.

~

IT WAS ONLY THAT NIGHT, in my dreams, that I saw with clarity the strange paleness of the man's skin. The color, the texture, was like wax poured over real skin, the hue still there, but hidden deep beneath the surface. In my dream, I worried about frostbite—his and mine. When I woke, the comforter was crumpled at the foot of the bed. My skin felt waxy and prickly. I ran the shower hot until steam filled the bathroom and I had melted all the wax away.

Outside was that brilliant, breakable cold. Snow cracked, ice shattered and popped. Everything painted in bright colors—white, blue, yellow—the only colors in the world, it seemed, or at least the only ones worth noticing.

Maybe that was why I didn't see the delivery truck. Maybe that was why I didn't hear the horn. Maybe that was why, at the last moment, I felt myself jerked backward by the hood of my coat. My arms flailed, and my boots skidded against the ice-slicked sidewalk. I tumbled into the alleyway behind me and fell into the arms of the person who'd grabbed me.

It was him, the man from the library, the one in my dreams. Old Simon, he'd called himself, but I couldn't remember if that was something he'd told me or part of my dream.

"You shouldn't have done that, girly," he said now. I didn't know if he meant stepping into traffic or buying him coffee the night before.

"Old Simon's got enough to do." He heaved me to my feet with surprising strength. "Don't need to add looking after you to my list."

"You don't look that old," I said.

When he laughed, all I could see was a young man beneath all that wax, rich dark skin hidden beneath the layers of what looked to be oh, so cold. Only his eyes weren't pale—or young-looking. This was a pair of eyes that had seen their share of winters and pedestrians trampled by horses, clipped by trolley cars, and bounced off windshields.

"I am old," he said. "I have much to do and no time for rescuing you." He brushed off his jeans and tugged his camouflage jacket into place by the epaulets.

"I can see that."

At the entrance to the alley, he paused but didn't turn around. "You can?"

"It's in your eyes. At least, most of it is."

"And the rest?"

"You're looking for something."

"That I am, girly."

"I'm Halley," I said, wanting to be clear on one thing if nothing else. No more *girly*. "Like the comet."

"Returned to give me some grief?"

"Maybe I'm here to help."

At that moment, I doubted my sanity. My pulse went thready. With a hand, I braced myself against the alley wall, my fingertips scraping icy mortar. I was a woman who lived on library books and television reruns of *Doctor Who*. I was young enough to still be called girly and not really mind. I was young enough to believe that someone like Simon the Cold had a mission and that I could help.

I was young enough to simply believe.

He hadn't moved from the alley's entrance—a good sign. He was listening, his head cocked back to catch all the telltale sounds of the alley. In front of him, cars churned up slush. Boots trampled sand and salt. But Simon's attention? All on me.

"We could start with another cup of coffee." I dropped my hand from the wall and walked toward the light.

"That we could, girly," he said when I reached him. "That we could."

I WENT with the ceramic mugs, despite the odd look from the barista. I picked up the solid black container of half and half and plunked it on the table, despite the odd looks from everyone else. Simon added cream and sugar like I thought he would. Patrons stared at me, at my cup, and the one opposite it. Their gazes flowed through Simon.

"People don't see you," I said.

"People generally don't see the homeless."

"But this is different."

"I'm still homeless, girly." He brought the mug to his lips, paused as if reconsidering something. "Halley."

"I can see you."

"That you can."

"Why?"

He didn't answer. Instead, we drank in silence, steam from the coffee filling the air between us, warming it until Simon himself looked warmer, his skin darker, as if the steam had melted a layer of frost.

"Are you sure you want to help me," he asked.

I nodded.

"Good." He set his cup on the table and grabbed my hand. "Because we start now."

We dashed through the coffee shop, scooting past bags of beans and boxes of supplies. I glanced back in time to see two policemen—no, two things—reach our table. Hairy, large, and shapeless one moment, dark blue, official looking, clean-cut the next. They flickered from one form to another, like a hologram of two images.

I stumbled and fought to regain my balance. "Those aren't people."

"No." Simon tugged me through the door and into the alleyway. We plunged into the shadows, the alleys behind the storefronts a labyrinth of brick walls and trashcans. Despite the cold, the stench of rotted vegetables lingered in the air.

"You're not people," I added.

Even in the dark alley, I caught Simon's raised eyebrow. "I can't be anything other than myself."

"And that self is?"

"In trouble if we don't keep moving."

And so we ran, Simon in the lead. He kept hold of my hand and tugged me around Dumpsters and over pallets that creaked beneath our boots. We crunched plastic sacks and cardboard boxes. The air felt sharp in my lungs and clouds of my breath misted my face. My neck, where I had wound my scarf, started to heat. Without breaking stride, I yanked at the wool.

At last we emerged at the far end of the alley. Up the block, people streamed in and out of the coffee shop. Even at this distance, I could taste the coffee in the air. I sucked in the scent, grateful for anything that didn't reek of water-logged wood or rancid meat.

"What are those things?" I asked.

"Something that would harm us all."

"But you won't let them."

He dropped my hand and then turned to look at me. Outside, he was more wintery than before. "No," he said. "*You* won't let them."

I touched my mittened fingers to my scarf in disbelief. How could I stop those things? I didn't even know what they were. But Simon simply nodded.

We stood in the cold forever. At least, it felt like forever. Then I noticed the world around me, people moved at a glacial pace, their breath hanging in the air. Cars inched forward, each tread squeaking the packed snow.

"What did you do?" I asked Simon.

He grinned an icy grin. "I thought we needed a breather, a little time to collect our thoughts."

"You can stop time?"

"No one can stop time. I merely . . . slowed it down, for a bit. It won't stop our friends from the coffee shop for long. They're too clever for that." He took up my hand again and tugged me forward, through the ice statue pedestrians.

"I don't understand," I said. "One minute you don't want me around, and the next I'm supposed to stop something?"

"Oh, girly ... Halley ... it's more complicated than that."

We continued our strange trek through frozen people and things, a dog with one paw raised, ready to shake; a split bag of groceries, cans hanging in midair; a shower of suspended grit from a snowplow.

"That night at the library," he said when we'd reached the bridge that spanned the river. "And in the coffee shop. You saw me. I've been waiting for the one who sees. I just didn't expect her to be so puny."

"Hey!" I pulled from his grip. "I'm not as puny as I look." That didn't sound quite right—or at least, not as right as I wanted it to sound.

"I don't know why they send me the likes of you," he continued, almost as if I wasn't even there. "You small ones who see too much and are far too fragile."

A low boom sounded behind us. It sent a jolt through me, then it resonated with how hard my heart was beating. I was many things, but fragile wasn't one of them. Simon grabbed my hands again, yanked me fully onto the sidewalk seconds before a black SUV rumbled past.

"Fragile. Like all humans."

My heart thudded even harder, and the scarf around my neck felt tight, like it was choking me, deliberately. "The world, it's—"

"Speeding up, and so should we."

We ran, again. This time, I stayed silent. This time, I kept pace with

Simon and thought about being fragile.

Maybe he was right.

❧

THE NEIGHBORHOOD CHANGED the farther we went, from old Victorians in the painted-lady style; to respectable, if smaller, houses; to un-shoveled sidewalks, cars up on blocks, and chain-link fences that looked as though someone—or something—had clawed through them.

I'd never been to this part of town before. The longer we walked (our legs had given up on running miles back), the more certain I was of one thing: this part of town didn't exist. It was another of Simon's tricks. Unless it wasn't, and it was simply one of those things people didn't want to see.

Not seeing. There was a lot of that in the world, more than I ever realized.

"If you're not human," I said to Simon, "then what are you?"

We'd moved to trudging down the center of the street, the only clear path through all the snow. The accumulation hid the sidewalk, smoothed the steps leading up to houses. All the windows were dark, and the sun was sinking, its rays and warmth obscured by the tallest buildings.

"Something old," he said to the pound of our footfalls.

"Not cold?"

"Not what?"

"That's why I—" I broke off and tried again. "When I look at you, words pop into my head," I said. Out loud, this sounded nonsensical, but I pushed on, with both my feet and my mouth. "I think: *Simon the Cold.* You don't look old to me, just . . . frost covered."

I braced for an outburst. After all, was it better to be old or cold? Either way, it wasn't much of a compliment. But Simon's laughter echoed against the buildings. For a bare second, the sun seemed to swell, glow brighter, before turning remote and winter cold.

"Oh, girly." He cleared his throat. "Halley. I am both. I am in my winter." He raised a hand, indicating the air, the snow, the ice around us. "This is like looking at my reflection."

"But it's not really your reflection," I said.

He shook his head, a smile still lingering. "No, it's not. Which is why I need to finish my work before spring comes."

At last we reached the city dump. The entrance booth was empty, the gate looped with chains and padlocked. Simon walked up to the fence, passed his hand over the locks. They sprang open, the chains swinging with their weight.

"We need to arm ourselves," he said.

"Here?" My gaze scanned the piles of discarded objects, tires and dishwashers and things that glinted in the setting sun.

"You'd be surprised what people throw away."

Simon walked through the gate, his headlamp already secured. He reached into his coat pocket and pulled out a second lamp.

Hand outstretched, he offered it to me. "Or maybe you wouldn't."

The glow of the lamp revealed treasures. And yes, I was surprised by what people threw away. In some cases, I wasn't sure it was people doing the throwing. In my hands I held a sword in finely-wrought silver. If I swung the headlamp away and peered through the dark at it, all I saw was a broom with most of its bristles missing. Simon piled odds and ends into a grocery cart, one that had no hope of plowing through all the snow—unless you viewed it by lamplight. In that case, it was a sleek sled.

My fingers lighted on a garbage can lid. I knew without even using the headlamp that it would make a perfect shield—right size, right heft, its handle made for my grip.

"Is this how you see the world?" I asked Simon.

"Most of the time. Even old Simon can fall back into lazy habits."

"So we see what we want to see and hear what we want to hear."

"And the battle rages in front of our unseeing eyes." He nodded. "Yes. There are layers to everything. People, this world, the things you hold in your hand. Most of the time, we don't need to see these things. Most people don't either."

"But now?"

"Now, things are bad. I am . . ." He hesitated, the briefest of smiles gracing his lips. "Cold, and winter is much weaker than it appears."

"And those things in the coffee shop?"

"If I'm ice—"

"They're fire?"

"In a manner of speaking, yes. They would burn this world, but not in the way you're thinking, not with flame and destruction. They spark infidelities, betrayals, revenge. Oh, there is far too much revenge in the world. Why humans have developed a taste for it, I can't say. It starts sweet but turns sour. It would fill your throat and choke you."

I clutched my broomstick sword, another question occurring to me. "That night at the library, when you turned your headlamp on me. What did you see?"

Simon was silent for a long moment. He plucked a few more items from the debris and added them to the shopping cart. Before he turned from me, he uttered one word.

"Hope."

~

WE LEFT the gates to the city dump unlocked.

"For those who might need things," was all Simon said.

The air felt warmer against my cheeks as if, somewhere, an invisible bonfire heated the city. First one, and then another snowflake floated down, big fat flakes, the sort children loved to catch on mittened fingers and on their tongues. The night filled with snow until I could barely see where we were going.

That, I realized, didn't matter. Simon knew the way. After a while, I discovered I did too. If I shut my eyes, the route we needed to take became clear, as if a map of it was on my eyelids. We were headed back toward the city center, straight into the heart of the banking and financial district.

"Why there?" I asked Simon.

"It's where they start their destruction, burning resources. Think of the crash of twenty-nine, or of o-eight for that matter."

"Will they crash the world today?"

"If not today, then someday, or somewhere. Old Simon can't be everywhere at once."

But we're here now.

I didn't say it out loud. Perhaps I only thought those words. Even so, Simon's shoulders straightened, his step quickened, and I marched alongside him. For the first time in my life, I felt like I had a mission, a purpose. I could do something—something worthwhile.

"You've always had a purpose," he said, the words soft as the snow. "Remember that."

They met us in the street, armed with briefcases and umbrellas, dressed in pinstriped suits. One woman wore high heeled shoes and yet glided effortlessly through the snow. I blinked and saw her, not as she appeared to everyone else, but her true form—a fiery beast that melted a path through the ice. Her cell phone was a weapon, something I only realized when Simon yanked me to the ground.

A lightning bolt whizzed over our heads and sizzled against the coffee shop's brickwork.

I hunkered down next to Simon, my gaze taking in the things that surrounded us. The rest of the street had cleared, the snow so heavy, it had chased everyone else inside. Streetlights bathed the night in a yellow glow, and through that glow, they approached. Bankers, police officers, firefighters—all occupations you'd instinctively trust. They circled us, each braced to attack.

"I'm going to count to three," Simon said to me, his voice calm and steady, like we were having a conversation in the coffee shop. "Then I want you to rush the one next to the fire hydrant."

The firefighter. Even in disguise, he was a good head taller than I was. He clutched a hose, which, if anyone cared to look carefully—but of course, they didn't—would be utterly ridiculous in all this snow and ice. In the world viewed through my headlamp, the creature held a coil of barbed metal. The weapon was thin, flexible, curling and uncurling like a snake. The creature stood there, unmoving, the coil undulating as if it had a mind of its own.

Simon grunted. "He's yours. I'll take care of the rest."

Mine? "But—"

"He's the one I can't fight." Simon's voice had dropped now. "That's where you come in."

"Why can't you fight him?"

"I can't even touch him. We're cut from the same cloth, as the expression goes, or in this case, the same piece of the universe."

"You're related."

"In a way. But then, so are we, Halley. So are we."

"And that's why I can see you—and them."

"She catches on quickly." This was not Simon, but the firefighter, the huge thing in front of us. "Did you also inform her of her role after today's confrontation?"

"She has no role."

"Only if you dispatch us, and dear brother, and you are not up to the task. Not now, so far into your winter."

"We shall see."

The world exploded then. The firefighter shot skyward, flames and heat evaporating the snow. The air filled with steam. As a teen, I'd taken a year of karate, but I was no fighter. I didn't know how to handle a sword. And yet, my hands knew what to do. My feet knew where to take me. I dashed not to where the firefighter had been standing, but where I knew he'd land, my sword at the ready.

His coil caught the blade seconds before his feet touched the ground. I blocked the second blow with my trashcan lid shield. But that barbed metal was pliant, and it wrapped itself around my blade, yanked the handle from my grip.

I panted, gaze darting between where my sword clattered to the road to Simon. The others surrounded him. He remained still, passive. I prayed he had a plan—for him and me.

The creature approached, barbed metal twisting this way and that, flicking toward my boots, catching strands of my scarf when I failed to lift my shield in time. I jumped back just as the coil swirled to catch me around the ankles. He advanced again, and again, I leaped. Leap, tangle, leap tangle, our movements a dance that led us away from Simon.

Keep him away from Simon. This was my only thought, even as my shield slipped from my grip and spun on the snow-slicked asphalt. *Keep him away from Simon.*

A crack reverberated. The buildings around us shook. I spun. We both did. The firefighter lowered his weapon and stared. A blizzard engulfed the other creatures, freezing them in place. At first, the rapid disintegration left me breathless, my stomach churning. A piece here, a piece there, torn apart, scattered.

The firefighter roared with so much force, I stumbled backward.

And onto my sword. With my teeth, I tore the mittens from my hands and picked up my sword. My fingers ached in the cold, but I clutched the grip, crouched low, and waited.

The firefighter twirled the coil, its barbs sparking in the air. In my mind, I saw its trajectory: toward the center of the fight, toward Simon. It would end him in a brilliant blaze of fire.

I sprang forward, caught the coil as it extended forward, the blade of my sword clanging against the metal, shaving off the barbs.

The blow sent me to the ground, sent the sword flying from my grip. The coil hung in the air and then fragmented, tiny barbs littering the ground, stabbing the snow.

The firefighter shrank. Pieces of the others broke off, scattered in the street before vanishing.

"Spring," the firefighter said, his voice weak. "Spring."

And then he, too, was gone.

I stood alone in the empty street, no sign of creatures, no sign of Simon. Nothing to show for what had just happened, only fat snowflakes that stuck to my cheeks and the broomstick I held in my hands.

MY LIBRARY BOOKS WERE OVERDUE. This was what happened when you took time out to fight creatures no one else could see. The night I returned them to the library, snow still crunched beneath my boots, but the air felt soft against my face. Most everyone went without their hats and gloves. I'd left my mittens at home.

I glanced at the garbage bin, half hoping Simon would be there. He wasn't, of course. I returned my books, paid my fine, and on the way out, stopped for a Caffeinator, making sure to stuff my pockets with sugar and those little containers of half and half. For old time's sake, I told myself.

I could never find my way back to the city dump, although I tried several times. I still had the broomstick. I hung it above my fireplace. No one ever asked me about it. I wondered if anyone could see it, and if so, how it looked to them. When I spied it from the corner of my eye, it gleamed, the handle intricately carved.

I was going to balance the cup of coffee on the edge of the garbage bin, but someone stood there, head cast downward, a glow illuminating the contents inside.

My heart sped up. I clutched the to-go cup so tightly some of the coffee slipped from beneath the lid. A flash of pain spread across my skin, then the cool air rushed in to heal the burn.

I approached, but the man didn't glance up.

"You'd be surprised what people throw away," I said.

He took a step back, as if embarrassed at being caught. My heart pounded faster. Not Simon. Not Simon.

Then, I saw his eyes.

"Simon the Cold."

"I ain't cold, girly."

"Halley."

"That's right, the comet. Here to burn another path through my sky?"

"What happened?" I asked.

"You talking about the winter? My winter?"

I nodded.

"You were there." The question was in his eyes, if not his voice.

I nodded again.

"The way it works," he said, his words slow. "I don't always remember."

And now I was cold. Simon? Not remember me?

"But it's hard to forget a comet that blazes through the sky, especially one that saves your life."

"I did that?"

"You did. But now I'm in my spring, and—"

"I'm nothing?"

"Or everything. That's the problem with spring. It's hard to tell what might grow. You can only plant the seeds."

I held out the coffee then, both hands clutched around the cup.

He shook his head. "It doesn't work that way."

"How would you know? You're in your spring."

His laugh made the temperature rise at least a degree, maybe more. Wet, heavy snow slipped from a branch and plopped on the ground. I still offered the cup, arms outstretched, until—at last—Simon the Warm took it from my hands.

Simon the Cold was first published in Frozen Fairy Tales and produced in audio by The Centropic Oracle.

INSIDE OUT

SCIENCE FICTION

The day Lexia discovered the glass wasn't fogged was the day she decided to see the outside for herself. Something swirled beneath her hand whenever she tried to wipe the condensation from the window. A few bursts of light would shine through, then the clouds reformed, opaque as ever.

Behind her, hot mineral baths churned up steam. The heated pool sent out waves of moist air. Sweat bloomed all over her skin until she glowed.

But beneath her fingers, the window was cool. Light shined behind the glass, the effect like winter on Earth—a glare to make you shield your eyes and glance away. Why? The question pinged in the back of her mind. Why would someone hide the outside?

Lexia wore her flimsy spa wrap, but didn't care. She'd see the outside, if not through the glass, then some other way. In the last year, she'd learned that there was always some other way. She cast her gaze about the spa. A group of women, her mother among them, sat at the far end, each encased to her shoulders in diamond-speckled mud. A year ago, Lexia would have sat nearby, let the women pet her, buy her trinkets from the gift shop, listen to her mother's mock protests.

"Oh, but you'll spoil her," her mother had always said, followed by a secret smile that told Lexia no amount of spoiling was ever enough.

That was before her mother embarked on another marriage—her fifth; she was a professional decorative—before their fights. Now, relaxing felt like work, pampering a chore. So Lexia turned her back on the women and went in search of something more substantial.

Like a vent. All this moist air needed to go somewhere. And somewhere had to be better than here.

With all the steam, and chatter, and strains of soothing music, no one noticed when she rounded a corner. Or almost no one. An old lady, her gnarled fingers curled around an old-fashioned book, glanced up and gave her a smile, the sort that said she knew what Lexia was up to—and highly approved. Heart thumping, Lexia dipped out of sight and confronted the nearest vent. She pried her fingers beneath its rim. To her surprise, it slipped right off. For easy cleaning, she imagined. Not that Lexia had cleaned all that much in her sixteen years.

She eased inside, replacing the cover as best she could. Lexia crawled, hiked up her wrap, and crawled some more. The change in pressure clogged her ears as she moved from one air lock to the next, through invisible filters. The air cooled, took on a metallic flavor. Churning and clanking filled her head. It was like moving through a huge metal beast, and she was somewhere deep within its innards.

One dark turn led to another until she confronted an actual door. She punched in the code she'd seen Paulo use on the gift shop register. The door slid open, revealing a grate, and beyond that, the outside.

"Oh! That worked." She laughed, the soft sound bouncing around the enclosed space.

Tiny streams of sunlight lit the backs of her hands. There was only one thing to do. She flattened her palms against the hatchwork and shoved.

The sun's glare hit her full in the face. Lexia blinked. Tears burned her eyes and streamed down her cheeks. When a shadow blocked the light, Lexia squinted, ready to bolt back inside the spa.

But wait! It was a girl. Like her! Or almost. This girl was thin, with enormous eyes. No hair. Not a single strand marred the smooth surface of the girl's head. No eyebrows, either, Lexia realized. Still, this girl looked so pretty, and so nice.

"Hi," Lexia breathed. "Do you want to come in?" She'd read that the local population was transplanted from Earth. Certainly this girl understood her.

The girl backed up, pebbles scattering in her wake, and turned from the vent's opening. Lexia threw herself forward, latched onto an ankle, her own chest scraping rocks and metal.

"Please don't go! I won't hurt you!"

The ankle in her hands stilled. Lexia unfurled her fingers bit by bit, convinced the girl would bolt. Instead, the girl turned around and crept forward until they were face to face, Lexia leaning over the vent's edge, the girl just below her.

"I'm Lexia."

The girl took Lexia's hand, turned her palm skyward, and traced lines with a finger. Puzzled, Lexia shook her head. The lines continued, up and down, over her skin, like a child learning the alphabet. Oh, the *alphabet*.

"You're Amie!" Lexia exclaimed, unsure if she should feel clever or not.

The girl, Amie, nodded.

"Well," Lexia said. "Come on inside."

Together, they crawled through the vent. At the entrance to the pool area, Lexia pressed a finger against her lips. She slipped from the opening and casually strolled around the pool area, collecting items as she went—a robe, a head wrap, someone's oversized frothy drink. Back in the vent, Aimie gulped the drink, the foam coating her upper lip in strawberry red. Lexia draped Amie in terrycloth from ankle to head, a nearly perfect camouflage for a girl from the outside.

Outside. It was almost too much.

"Come on," Lexia said when Amie set down the drink. "My room has everything we need." She took Amie's hand, and together they left the spa.

No one noticed. Or almost no one. Lexia swore that same old lady stared at them. The smile was still there, only now it was tinged with worry.

~

IN THE HALLWAY, Lexia's stomach jumped each time a guard strolled by.

They were all tall, all handsome, all with sharp eyes no amount of solicitude could hide. She led Amie through the corridors, not too fast, but not so slow someone might notice a girl who didn't belong. Only when they had reached her quarters, and the door had whooshed closed behind them, did Lexia let out a breath.

"We did it!" She grinned at Amie. "And you need a bath."

Lexia filled the tub and drained it twice, and still gray scum floated to the top of the water. But at least Amie looked clean and—more importantly—now smelled like lavender and vanilla. Even better, the girl's dark eyes glowed and although she was silent, her smile filled Lexia's heart.

It was after the bath, and a tray full of chocolates, that Amie pointed at the model on Lexia's desk.

"I get to do one every month," Lexia said, her hand lighting on the structure. It was her best one yet, a scale replica of the first station on Mars. "Since it's a hobby, I can't do more than that. I always tell myself to go slow, make it last, but I can't stop myself."

Amie cocked her head, brow furrowing.

"I wanted construction, you see. I have the test scores for it, all the spatial ability. And I love geometry." Lexia shrugged. "They keep telling me I'm too pretty, that it makes more sense to be a decorative, like my mother, and her mother. It's a better career choice—a safer one."

She leaned closer, and Amie did the same, so their noses almost met over the top of the Mars structure. "Some girls even cut themselves." Lexia drew an imaginary blade along her cheekbone. Amie jumped back and shook her head, her eyes wide and scared.

"Oh, don't worry. I won't. Besides, do you see anything sharp in here?" Lexia laughed, but it was the bitter sound she sometimes heard from her mother. She clamped her mouth shut. "Do you know how hard it is to build anything without something sharp?"

Amie's gaze went to the Mars station, then lighted on Lexia's face. Her hand moved again, first in the air, then on the table surface, like when she'd taught Lexia her name, but different.

"Oh, plans," Lexia said at last. "You're wondering if I draw plans. I can, but—"Why hadn't she considered this before? No, it wouldn't be nearly as fulfilling as building a model, but it beat waiting for her nail polish to dry or dozing through yet another facial.

She pulled up two chairs to her in-room console. She scrolled past all the social chatter, the notices for *Slam Tonight!* and the spa offering a "me" day, and dug into the educational programs. Yes! Design and Drafting, architecture, everything to teach her how to build virtual houses, cities, even stations that could be used anywhere in the galaxy, from research centers, like on Mars, to ones like they sat in now—a spa facility meant for rest and relaxation.

Lexia tore her gaze from all the potential plans and speared Amie with a look. "Did you know about this?"

Amie grinned and gave her a shrug.

"Do you need help with something, on the outside? Is that why you're here?"

Amie leaned forward and pressed the keypad. On the screen, images of makeshift dwellings appeared. Amie pointed to one and then to herself.

"You live ... there?" Lexia shook her head in disbelief. The wooden structure was little more than a lean-to. Sure, Lexia had done her time in Adventure Girls. Once, she had even slept outside, with nothing but canvas stretched over her. But at the end of the trip, the entire group had returned to a spa facility, where every pore was sucked clean, hair and nails made to shine.

Amie tapped Lexia's wrist. The girl pointed to the screen, and then to Lexia. With her hands, she mimicked building.

"Do you want my help? Want me to show you how to make it better?"

Amie gave an emphatic nod.

"Okay." Lexia pulled her hair into a loose bun at the base of her neck. "Let's see what I can do."

IT TOOK A WEEK OF DESIGNING, of visualizing, not just on the screen, but in her head, and when she could, in real time. Lexia took to collecting odd bits the spa guests left lying around. Old-fashioned books, empty containers from box lunches. These she fashioned into a small village. She learned, by watching Amie move stick figures around the structures, about life on the outside.

She knew that—somewhere—her console time was being logged.

Keeping up appearances meant venturing from her quarters. She'd loved school, but a girl destined to be a third-generation decorative spent most of her time experimenting with foundations rather than building them.

But leaving her room meant leaving Amie behind. Unless ... Her fingertips lighted on Amie's bald head. Even when the look was in fashion (and it currently wasn't), it attracted too much attention.

"Want to go somewhere?" she asked, feeling sly.

Amie's eyes went wide, but her lips curled into a smile.

"I'll get you a wig," Lexia said. "And then we can really have some fun."

IN THE GIFT SHOP, Lexia ran her fingers through the strands of a pink wig, one with spring-green highlights. A presence shadowed her steps, tall and broad. Paulo stood behind her. Paulo, who keyed in codes on the register so sloppily, Lexia often wondered if it were on purpose.

"You going to wear that to the slam tonight?" he asked.

"I might."

"Haven't seen you at one."

"My mother's been giving me fits." Actually, she hadn't seen her mother in nearly two weeks, at least not up close, but it was a handy excuse.

"Sneak out tonight." With the suggestion, Paulo winked.

"I might," she said again. *Always keep them guessing.* This was her mother's advice when it came to men. When Paulo grinned, Lexia saw that it did, indeed, work. But it was an empty sort of victory. Why build castles in the air when she could construct real places to live? Who needed boys when she had a friend—a sister—waiting for her, one who needed her help?

FROM HER VANTAGE point in the hallway, Lexia could see the wide-open door of her quarters. When her mother's voice barked commands, Lexia almost ran away. One thought kept her locked in place.

Amie.

Lexia swiped the sweat from her upper lip and considered the wig, tissue-wrapped and snug in a spa bag. Another command echoed from the room and a guard stepped out. He blinked, surprise washing across his features before he schooled them into a bland expression.

"Ah, Mrs. Mortarri? I think I've found her."

He nodded at Lexia, and she had no choice but to enter her room.

"You're not in that much trouble," he whispered as she passed.

If he thought that, then he didn't know her mother.

"There you are!" Her mother whirled, hands on hips. "Where have you been?"

"Nowhere. A walk." Her voice sounded strained, shaky. She clutched the ribbon handles of the bag and willed herself not to search for Amie. *Don't move. Don't glance around. Don't breathe.*

Her mother raised an eyebrow. "Shopping?"

Lexia cringed. Of course. No one cared if she spent hours in the educational modules on her console, but the second the charge at the gift shop went through, the system must have alerted her mother.

Her mother held out a hand. Lexia pulled the wig from the bag and dropped it into her mother's waiting palm. A year ago, she could have purchased three new wigs, and her mother would have laughed—and tried them all on herself.

"Really, Lexia? You shouldn't cheapen yourself with such trash, not to wear and not to associate with."

The words felt like a blow to the throat. No, she really didn't like Paulo—at least, not in the way he wanted her to—but the boy wasn't trash. He simply had to work and wanted to dance and drink when he wasn't. And the wig that was oh, so pretty? And would look so nice on Amie? Well, that wasn't trash either.

"And what is that?" Her mother pointed at the Mars station and the replica of Amie's village she'd built around it.

"A model," Lexia said, and how the words found their way from her throat, she didn't know. "I like building them."

"I'm not sure it's the best use of your time."

"It's just a hobby." Casual, not plaintive. *Don't let her see how much it means.*

Her mother shook her head. "You're just so ... just so ... well, I simply don't know what I'm going to do with you."

In earlier times—better times—her mother might have tried to understand. She'd sit on the floor with Lexia, both of them surrounded by building blocks, and laugh when her own constructions inevitably collapsed while Lexia's remained standing.

"You must get it from your father," she'd say, "because clearly you didn't get it from me."

Soft words no longer came from her mouth. Not since last year, since her last, awful marriage. She never spoke of Lexia's father. It was as if she wished both of them would simply fade away. They no longer shared quarters. Lexia was never invited to her mother's dinner parties; not that she wanted to eat with a bunch of adults. But eating alone, in her quarters, made everything taste the same, like salt, even the desserts. Especially the desserts.

As if she had no more words for Lexia, her mother left, without a goodbye, a kiss, a hug. Lexia stared at the shut door. Oh, that she could burn a hole into it with just her eyes.

"I'm what, Mother? Just because you don't care about the things I do, doesn't mean I'm—"

A pair of thin arms wrapped around her, a soft sigh bathing her neck. Lexia spun, mouth wide open in wonder.

"Where did you—?"

Amie pointed to the bed, or rather, the platform it sat on. Lexia knelt, rapped her knuckles against the side, and listened to the hollow sound. She eased back the panel and peered inside. Beneath the bed, there was just enough room for an Amie-sized girl.

"You're smarter than I am," she said. "I don't even have your wig, and now we can't—"

Amie pressed a finger against Lexia's lips.

"I talk too much, don't I?"

Amie simply drew her to the console. There, she scrolled through the fashion channels until the display landed on turbans.

"Oh, but those are for old ladies." Lexia wrinkled her nose. "Like my mother."

Amie opened her mouth in a silent laugh. Then she pointed to Lexia's collection of nail polish.

"Oh!" Lexia jumped up, fingers tingling like they always did before a new project. "I could make it pretty." She spun around. "I could start a trend."

She tore a strip from the bottom of her bed sheet. Around Amie's fragile head it went, then Lexia sprinkled on glitter and sparkles, and dotted the material with lime green nail polish. Lexia turned her friend toward the mirror.

"Look at you! You're gorgeous."

Amie's eyes glowed, her fingertips touching the dots that matched her nails.

Lexia clapped her hands. "Let's go have some fun."

ONLY IN SHOWING Amie the spa did the oddities strike Lexia. Why, with the sun so brilliant, was the glass perpetually fogged? Why was everything so self-contained? At the last spa, she'd gone on excursions nearly every day, took lessons in the local language, and even visited the planet's tiny moon.

Here, there was one short day trip to an island resort owned by the spa—and nothing else. The information panel talked up the splendors of the planet, the town of New Eden, the sustainable lifestyle of the local populace, and the fresh produce brought in daily to the spa.

Then she thought of Amie's lean-to and all the plans she somehow hoped to give the girl. She thought of the disease that had stolen her friend's voice as a baby. Why hide these things? The only thing on the other side of the glass was reality.

"Is it bad outside?" she asked Amie. They'd discovered the kitchens, now deserted after the formal dinner, and were working their way through a tub of berries and cream. Here was the food of New Eden. For once, Lexia was hungry. For once, things tasted sweet, and her fingers grabbed one berry after another, as if she'd never get enough.

Amie shook her head.

"But it isn't easy."

Amie shrugged and dipped a palm-sized strawberry into the cream.

"Why were you trying to get inside, then?"

Amie froze, mid-bite. Her gaze darted toward Lexia, a pleading look in the girl's eyes.

"For the same reason I was trying to get out? Just to see what was on the other side?"

Amie swallowed the strawberry and threw her head back in silent laughter.

~

MAYBE IT WAS the berry-stained fingerprints left in their wake. Maybe it was the pilfered sparkling quenchers from the walk-in refrigerator. Or maybe the guards had simply tracked their every move since they had left Lexia's quarters.

No matter. The first guard caught Lexia unaware, thick fingers around her wrist and upper arm. Amie, though quicker, fared no better. She kicked, tried to scratch, her mouth open in a silent scream.

Lexia screamed for her. Her cries brought officers and old, respected guests, and too many witnesses.

"They're hurting her," someone said, voice ringing with indignation.

An old woman hobbled into the center of the gathering. "Let the child go," she said to the guards.

The man holding Lexia released his grip on her. She rubbed his sweat from her skin and tried to wipe away the ache.

"Now the other," the old woman added.

The guards released Amie as if her skin burned them. The second her feet touched ground, she scampered off. No one chased after her, and Lexia let out a sigh that shook her whole body. She turned to thank the old woman, but froze. Yes! It was the same woman, the one in the spa, with the book and the secret smile. And now that smile bloomed again on the old woman's face. Before Lexia could say a word, a barking voice cut through the silence.

"Lexia! What have you done!"

Her mother parted the crowd with her voice and a hand—the same hand that, seconds later, cracked against Lexia's cheek.

Lexia stumbled into the guard behind her. His hands gripped her waist for longer than strictly necessary. She didn't care. Her cheek stung, her eyes watered, her heart squeezed tight in her chest.

"Mind that she is still a child," the old woman said.

"Mind your own business," her mother snapped.

"You could say I am. Is she not my granddaughter?"

Her mother paled. Lexia felt all the air leave her lungs. She focused on the old woman, her soft face, and eyes that looked both sad and kind.

"Technically, no," her mother said. "She is not."

"But as long as you're married to my son ..."

Her mother's mouth went grim. The old woman hobbled over to Lexia.

"We have not met, my dear, and I suspect we won't again. A piece of advice from an old woman, then?"

Numb, Lexia nodded.

"Don't let yourself get trapped. I did. So did your mother. That's not a sufficient reason to end up trapped yourself."

The woman kissed the bruise forming on Lexia's cheek and turned down the hall. The crowd, the guards, silent and staring, parted for her. No one spoke. At last, her mother gave a frustrated sigh, collared Lexia, and dragged her through the corridors by the spa wrap.

WHEN HER MOTHER engaged the override lock, Lexia pressed her hands against the smooth door. Her first impulse was to pound, to kick—just like a child. Instead, she leaned her forehead against the cool surface and shut her eyes. In her mind, Amie ran through the hallways, into the pool area, and crawled through the vent to freedom.

She wanted to believe the pictures in her head. An icy fist in the pit of her stomach told her it was better not to.

What had gone wrong? Why was *she* always wrong? She never sneaked out to slams, like the other girls, never even flirted with the spa workers. All she wanted was a friend. Lexia had never known that that hole inside her existed until Amie had filled the space. Now, nothing but an ache remained, that hole larger and darker than ever.

Her gaze lighted on the bed, or rather, what it sat on, its hollow platform. She crawled, wrists aching, and eased back the panel. Could she fit? She wasn't as small as Amie. Inside the space smelled old, like layer upon layer of dust and memories. Lexia eased her feet to the farthest corner, settled her hipbone near the center, and at last pressed her cheek against the floor. The bruise throbbed, but it was a handy reminder. If she was truly going to do what she planned to, she'd need that.

Lexia packed, weighing each item for its potential worth and inevitable weight. In went all the plans and designs she'd made with Amie. Although it was frivolous, she added the lime-green nail polish. From her bed, Lexia tugged the smallest blanket and rolled it tight. Then she curled into the hollow space again, belongings at her feet, blanket beneath her sore cheek.

It took a very long time to fall asleep.

In the morning, her mother's shrieks woke her.

"Where is she?"

"Sorry, Mrs. Mortarri, but there's no record at all of anyone entering or leaving her quarters."

"But she's not here."

Lexia held her breath. Would they search for her? Could anyone detect the panel, in place, but slightly off-kilter? Would anyone use an infrared detector, or for that matter, common sense?

"I suppose someone could have hacked the system," a guard ventured.

"That boy from the gift shop. What's his name?" Her mother snapped her fingers. "I don't know, but find him. Find her!"

Poor Paulo, Lexia thought. He didn't deserve this. The stomp of boots filled the room before footfalls echoed down the corridor. She squirmed, peered through the small sliver where the front panel didn't quite meet the corner of the headboard. Her mother wore a spa wrap and a wash of tears across her face. The urge to shove the panel out of the way nearly overwhelmed Lexia. In her mind, she saw the scene play out. She'd burst from her hiding spot. *Here I am*, she would say. Her mother would embrace her, kiss the bruise on her cheek, and cry even after Lexia forgave her.

She braced her feet against the wall, ready to push back the panel, but froze when the intercom buzzed.

"Mrs. Mortarri, will you be keeping your massage appointment this morning?"

"Excuse me?" her mother said. "My what?"

"Massage appointment. Under the circumstances, we can reschedule."

Lexia's chest grew tight. Her head buzzed, and the sound of it was so loud, she was afraid she'd miss her mother's next words.

"Yes, of course I'll keep my appointment," her mother said. "It's been a stressful morning."

And now Lexia couldn't breathe.

Her mother turned, the spa wrap fluttering across Lexia's field of vision before vanishing completely.

Where had her mother gone? Her real mother, not the one who had so recently swept from the room, intent on keeping a massage appointment. Where had that woman run to? Because certainly she'd gone somewhere and left Lexia behind, alone with an imposter.

She slipped from under the bed and replaced its panel, then she tore a few more strips from the bottom of her sheet. These she used to tie the blanket to her pack.

At the door, she hesitated, rocking on the balls of her feet. Would it open for her? She had shed the spa wrap, and what she guessed was the tracking device that went with it. She wore old clothes, from Earth—out of fashion, of course—but they were nondescript and sturdy. Lexia shut her eyes, inhaled a deep breath, and placed her hand on the console.

The door opened.

She grinned—couldn't help it. In a way, it made sense. Why engage an override lock on an empty room?

In the corridor, a guard passed her, the same one who had gripped her wrists and left his sweat all over her. The man stared as though he didn't recognize her. Maybe he didn't. Maybe that was part of the problem with these spas. Everyone was either a guest or a worker—no one was an actual person.

In the pool area, she rushed past the mud baths, the mineral pools, running her fingers along the fogged glass without leaving any streaks. Lexia paused near the cabana where her mother booked all her massages.

The flaps were closed.

She clamped a hand over her mouth and wished she could cry silently like Amie did. Then, she turned toward the vent.

She crawled through the structure's innards, spilled onto the pebbles outside, and scrambled to her feet. The spa sat behind her, a white blob, its own self-contained bubble in a brilliant green reality. Hills stretched for miles. Lexia ran, haphazardly at first, then with purpose toward the largest tree on the first hill.

On one of the branches, something white flapped in the wind. When she was ten feet away, she recognized it.

A strip from Amie's turban.

Lexia stood beneath the branch and peered at the path ahead of her. Another glimmer of white, there, in the distance? She slid down the hill, never losing sight of the bit of white. When she reached the second tree, she tugged the strip from the branch and tied it around her wrist. Then she ran toward the next hint of white in the distance, leaving the world of fogged glass behind.

Inside Out was first published in The Maze: Three Tales of the Future.

FLOWERS AND STONES

FAIRY TALE RETELLING

I'm standing at the self-checkout when the first pinpricks race up and down my back. I freeze, an entire cabbage clutched in my grip. For a moment, with the icy sensation against my spine, my mind blanks.

I stare at my hands. Why cabbage?

Oh, yes. Coleslaw. Homemade. It's been a long week, and I'm in the mood to shred something. Coleslaw is good for that.

I roll the cabbage between my palms like it's a basketball. With a little finesse, I could give it a spin, land a three-pointer in the open grocery sack at the checkout station across the way.

Another wash of pinpricks reminds me that I'm not the one in the family who does those sorts of things. No pickup games with vegetables or ill-advised tattoos for me. So instead, I scan the cabbage and drop it in my canvas sack—only to have the screen flash at me:

Unexpected item in bagging area.

The light above my station blinks in time with my heart. I stare at the cabbage, in the sack, with dismay. In this case, *I'm* that unexpected item.

A cashier and then a manager try to scan the cabbage. They struggle to add it manually, fingers jabbing at the screen. Then the manager sends the cashier for a price check. Even then, she can't add the amount to my bill.

I keep my lips pressed together, not daring to say a word. I know if I speak, I'll simper like some old-school Disney princess.

And that won't help.

"You know what?" the manager says, at last, her tone conveying that this is all my fault, although she can't really explain why. "It's on us."

My remaining groceries are waiting, some patiently, like the carrots. Others not so much, like the mint chocolate chip ice cream that's starting to sweat.

A third wash of pinpricks chases across my skin before the pain centers between my shoulder blades. An urge—to rush to the restroom, rush off and leave everything behind—overwhelms me. I want—*need*—to find a mirror.

At that moment, I don't care about anything else. Not my groceries, or even my purse. I'd leave everything behind all so I can yank up my shirt and glimpse the image emerging on my skin.

That urge thrums in my blood until it emerges as a compulsion. I remember to grab my purse, but I leave everything behind in my search for a restroom.

This is a high-end grocery store, with carpet and chandeliers, and enough samples on Fridays to make a meal (which is why I shop here on Fridays). The restroom is well-appointed, with a beveled mirror and infinity sinks.

I crash through the door. I don't do a stall check. I don't care if anyone else is here. I plant myself in front of the mirror and yank my shirt up and over my shoulder.

Then I spin, a slow rotation, like a dog trying to catch her own tail. The second I spot the intricate design, it slips from view. At last, I pull out my phone for a selfie.

Just as I snap a photo, a woman walks into the restroom. She halts, dark eyes panicked. Well, yes, she's just stumbled onto a bit of crazy. I wouldn't blame her if she backed out slowly, hands raised in a pacifying gesture, and then ran for the manager.

It wouldn't be the first time.

Then her expression softens. Curiosity rather than fear lights her eyes.

"Oh, hey." Her voice is low and melodic and full of appreciation. "Did you just get some ink?"

Not exactly.

But I nod. "Yeah. Sort of." As if there's *sort of* when it comes to tattoos. "Let's see."

Again, her expression is bright and friendly. So I hold still and let a complete stranger examine the tattoo between my shoulders.

"That's wicked good," she says. "Where'd you get it done?"

I have no idea.

I swallow. "A place out in San Francisco. They're fantastic."

At least, I'm pretty sure it's San Francisco. I clamp my mouth shut before I can rhapsodize about a place I've never been.

The woman pushes up a sleeve. "Great minds, huh?"

I don't know what she means, but I nod and admire the triple moon goddess tattoo on her forearm. It's really well done, and certainly there by choice rather than a surprise, like the one currently stinging my back.

The woman takes another look at my ink, her eyes squinting as if she's having trouble focusing.

"Is it ... fading?" She shakes her head. "No, now it's ..."

I slip my arm back into my shirt before this gets truly awkward. "The lighting."

Again, I press my lips shut before I can enthuse about the ambiance. Instead, I point to the chandelier above our heads (yes, *fancy*, even in the restrooms).

She accepts this with a nod. Because, really, what's her other option? Declare that my tattoo is changing before her eyes?

She heads for a stall. I take that as my cue to leave.

When I reach the self-checkout station, I discover my groceries are bagged and paid for. There's a note—a kind one, to be sure—suggesting that I find another place to do my Friday grocery shopping.

The manager won't meet my eyes. Because, yes, this has happened before.

I wait until I'm three storefronts away and tuck myself into a corner by the kiddie haircut place that's closed for the evening. It's dark and safe, and I concentrate on the brick rather than the fire against my back.

I tug my phone from my jeans pocket. The picture I took earlier is slightly unfocused. But I've done this so many times, it hardly matters. I tap and zoom, crop and enhance.

At last, an image emerges.

A triple moon goddess.

The scrollwork is intricate, and the woman in the restroom was right; it really is wicked good.

And this can't be a coincidence. Something is brewing. That much, I know. Still, as I study the tattoo, I don't know what it means.

Or what it is my twin, Alyssa, is trying to tell me.

FINDING a tattoo artist in a city the size of San Francisco isn't hard. Alyssa's found any number of excellent tattooists in any number of cities.

It's finding one who won't remember working their magic on her skin that's the issue. Another? Finding one the crone doesn't know about.

Alyssa doesn't know if an actual crone is shadowing her steps. It's simply the name she's given the thing that's haunted her and Emma since they turned eighteen. The crone knows things she shouldn't, knows things she *can't.*

Every time Alyssa thinks she's outsmarted this being, something else disrupts her life—or worse, Emma's.

Moon and Stars Tattoos is surprisingly empty for this time of day. One artist bends over the extended arm of her customer, her brow etched with pure concentration. The others appear on the verge of napping. Through the open door, Alyssa catches strains of something ancient— Fleetwood Mac, she thinks. She's never been much for music, but it sounds like something her mother would listen to.

Alyssa decides to risk it. Her card is ready, printed fresh this morning. The words: *Can't speak, acute laryngitis* should get her into a chair and inked without any issues.

As for the tattoo itself? Alyssa will let her gaze wander the artwork displayed on the walls. The right image will announce itself. If she's meant to get ink today, meant to warn Emma, that image will lead her to the right artist.

A hush falls on the space as she steps through the door. One of the male artists smirks. Another day, another time, she'd open her mouth and let him have what for. After all, *what for* is her primary skill. But not today. Today is too important.

One of the women raises an eyebrow. Yes, Alyssa knows. She looks impossibly young. They'll probably ID her, too.

"Can I help you?" the woman asks. If her eyebrow is skeptical, her voice, at least, is kind.

Alyssa doesn't mean to be rude (really, it simply happens all on its own), but her gaze is still tracking the images on the wall, searching out the one she needs, and so she barely gives a nod.

It's the scrollwork she notices first, intricate and refined. It reminds her of the very first tattoo she ever got, the one that was an apology, a love letter to her twin. With a shaky hand, she points.

"That's one of mine," the woman says.

Alyssa digs the card from her pocket, praying that the words haven't transformed into something obscene between this morning and now. Her heart thumps in her chest. Everything feels right, from the music to the tattoo to the woman waiting patiently.

She knows better than to wish too hard. It's like a beacon, sending her hopes and fears into the world where anyone might pluck them from the sky.

Like the crone.

Even so, her entire being is focused on the card and, at the same time, not. She fills her senses with everything else. Rainbows and unicorns decorating the wall, the music playing low enough the words are a mere suggestion, the scent of anticipation and blood.

The door is three steps away. Depending on what's now printed on the card, she can make a run for it. A quick break to the left, and it's all downhill. Not that anyone will chase her. At least, no one ever has. But this could be a first.

Alyssa pulls out the card and hands it to the woman and waits.

And waits.

"Oh, no problem," the woman says at last. She grins at Alyssa, and her eyes sparkle with delight. "Really, the less you say, the better my work. I'm Samantha, by the way."

Alyssa digs out her ID and hands it over.

Samantha glances at it. "Nice to meet you, and yeah, I was going to have to card you. You barely look eighteen."

Alyssa shrugs. The male tattoo artist—the one with the smirk —snorts.

And because Alyssa is feeling triumphant, she sends him a smirk of her own. When he averts his gaze, her triumph doubles.

She follows Samantha to her station. While she waits, Alyssa lets her gaze wander the art on the walls once again until it lands on the triple moon goddess.

This time, her smile is nothing but pure.

EVERYONE in the call center knows to route the worse customer calls to me. They're not supposed to. It's not an official policy. If anything, our manager would wring his hands, sweat gathering on his forehead, and insist it isn't *fair*.

No one ever listens to him. Since our center has the highest customer satisfaction rating in corporate, he never insists too hard.

At the end of each year, I get a holiday bonus and a plaque.

At the end of each year, I try not to think about the full-ride scholarship I gave up.

Sometimes I pretend I'm Snow White and each caller a dwarf, albeit ones who never made it into the fairy tale (Irate, Belligerent, Passive-Aggressive, Confused, Outraged, Lost, and Arrogant).

Repeat complainers sometimes ask for me by name. A few send me holiday cards.

I'm incapable of saying a bad word to them.

I'm incapable of saying a bad word to anyone.

To compensate, I take out my frustration on inanimate objects. Cabbage, carrots, and a fierce grater all wait for me in my kitchenette. I'm going to shred the heck out of some vegetables.

I'm going to forget about the customer who called me every foul name in the (urban) dictionary before breaking down and admitting that his wife had died. All he wanted was a pair of pants that fit, but since she did all the shopping, he had no idea what to order.

I'm going to forget about the lonely old woman who didn't want to complain so much as to talk to someone.

I'm going to forget I can still feel the residual burn of the triple moon goddess between my shoulder blades.

At this point, all that remains is a ghost of a tattoo. I've watched at least two dozen come and go over the years. Sometimes they're sophisti-cated—works of art in their own right. Sometimes Alyssa sends me nothing more than a heart, the red so vibrant you might mistake it for fresh blood.

And sometimes she sends a message.

I'm shredding and wondering what on earth I'll do with all this coleslaw. I'll never be able to eat it all on my own, and it's not like you can freeze coleslaw. My mother, perhaps. Maybe she's having a luncheon this weekend or some sort of charitable event.

A knock comes on the door of my tiny cottage. Yes, just like an old-school Disney princess, I live in an actual cottage. Although hardly anyone ever knocks on the door.

When I answer, I find my mother backlit by the big house up on the hill. Fairy lights adorn the patio, its slate gleaming as if by magic. In the yard, it's as if a celestial hand has sprinkled tiny stars along the branches of all the trees that surround what is, in truth, a mansion.

This is not the modest split-level Alyssa and I grew up in. Henry, the man who owns this mansion, is not our father. He is like a prince at the end of a fairy tale, but one with a salt and pepper goatee and round, rimless spectacles. Instead of sweeping away the maiden, Henry fell hard for the matron.

He still can't fix all that is wrong.

It's as if my thoughts have brought my mother to the cottage doorstep. In truth, they may have. Above her head, above the house on the hill, a moon rises. Not quite full, but only a few days off.

I look at my mother and blink. For a moment, the young woman from the restroom appears before my eyes. I blink again, and my mother replaces her.

Maiden. Mother.

I'm afraid to blink a third time. So instead, I say, "It's lovely to see you."

It doesn't matter if that's true or not. It's the only thing I *can* say to her. We don't talk, haven't since Alyssa and I turned eighteen. I don't mean that in a Lifetime movie sort of way, although the results are never-theless the same.

My mother stares at me, clutches her throat as if the words she wishes to speak burn.

Perhaps they do.

"I'm making coleslaw," I say, brightly, as if there aren't any number of things we should be talking about. "Could you use some? I'm always happy to share."

Something sparks in my mother's expression, something that tells me I'm on the right track.

"Are you having guests?" I venture.

"Yes." The word is no more than a whisper, but it is a word. "Guest." Relief floods her eyes. She turns, and I follow her gaze to the swollen moon rising above the house.

Guest. Singular.

A full moon.

And then I know.

~

Once upon a time, a young woman cradled two daughters inside her, her belly as round as the brilliant full moon.
When the time came, there would be three of them, three to make a family.
But the daughters were too eager, not content to stay put until the time was right. So the young woman sent her hopes, her fears, into the world.
Someone plucked them from the sky.
There would be three of them, three to make a family.
But only until the debt came due.

~

ON THE FLIGHT HOME, Alyssa pretends to sleep. Even with headphones and a book propped in front of her, the guy (and it's always a guy) next to her will want to talk.

She can't risk the altercation, the escalation, the plane making an unscheduled landing in the middle of the country, and security escorting her—and the guy—off the plane.

It's happened before.

She feels the stirrings of that impulse—to lean across the middle seat and ask the guy next to her about those three restraining orders. Oh, and some outstanding child support payments as well. It would be gratifying, absolutely, to watch this guy's complexion go from ruddy to bright red, to have half the passengers cheering him on, half applauding her.

This is how the crone tempts her. Alyssa can't know these things about this guy. But in every altercation (and there have been several), she's always been right.

Instead, she channels everything she knows and loves about her sister.

It was Emma, of course, who saved them that first day, who held fast even when Alyssa started spewing hateful words.

She hadn't meant to say them, of course. But in the last seven years, she never has. She can hear what she says warped, transformed in the air until these mutations reach the ears of the other person. A simple *I love you* becomes *I hate you—and always have.*

But the crone never counted on Emma, her sister who should've gone on to some Ivy League school, been a doctor or a scientist, or something *more.*

They say twins have their own language. If so, Alyssa and Emma had long forgotten theirs. But that didn't stop Emma from picking up on the false notes in Alyssa's tone. It didn't stop her brilliant twin from grabbing a pencil and scribbling a message across her calculus homework.

What's going on?

They spent a blissful Saturday exchanging notes until the crone caught on. It took three days before text messages were ruined, and another five for emojis.

By then, they had a plan. Alyssa would leave. Emma would stay, take care of their mother and explain the situation as best she could.

That was when Alyssa went in for her first tattoo. The intertwined *E* and *A* were so beautiful, the letters surrounded by fancy scrollwork and leaves. At the time, Alyssa didn't think to question why that bit of artwork was on the wall, at eye level, as if waiting for her.

She only knew she had to get it. Alyssa held her breath, worried that there was something too magical about the artwork. It would change before her eyes, and she'd be left with something nasty or obscene on her skin. When it remained—perfect and oh, so beautiful—she hurried home, excited to show Emma.

Alyssa found her twin clutching her ankle, pain and fear flashing in her eyes. Together they sat on the lower bunk and watched as the tattoo faded from Alyssa's ankle, bloomed on Emma's, only to vanish entirely after a few minutes.

But during all that, the image remained pure.

And Alyssa knew that no matter where in the world she was, she'd have a way to send Emma a message.

Their mother wasn't surprised to find Emma burning the goodbye note Alyssa tried to pen before she left—one filled with so many invectives it was hardly a note at all. (It was a silly attempt, but Alyssa had to try.)

Over the years, they've peeled back the layers of their story—of crones who might grant wishes but always demand their due in the end.

And, at last, they've reached the end.

Now, on this final flight home, Alyssa knows there's only so much she can channel of Emma. Her sister speaks in flowers, Alyssa in stones. Emma's words perfume the air, Alyssa's sting the ears and bite the flesh.

If Emma is often too pure for this world, then Alyssa is well suited for it. Because sometimes the guy sitting in seat 1F deserves *what for*.

Alyssa knows this, too. This fight, this final confrontation that's waiting for them, it won't be the two of them against the crone.

It's Alyssa versus Emma.

And Alyssa plans to win.

I'M CLUTCHING a gigantic bowl of coleslaw, my arms aching with the effort. With careful steps, I navigate the path to the main house. One distraction and slaw will coat everything—me, the decorative stones Henry has placed by hand, the flowers and shrubs he pampers.

Dusk shrouds the patio. My mother stands on the slate, haloed by those thousand fairy lights. On the table sits slender-stemmed glassware, an elaborate floral arrangement, with sweet, summer wine chilling in silver buckets. It's the trappings of an evening garden party, and an expensive one, too.

It will all go to waste.

My mother's hands are clutched beneath her chin, her dress billowing about her. She is as picturesque as any fairy tale princess, except her eyes are huge and wary.

Above the house, a full moon rises. There, in the twilight, the first evening star glimmers.

The night holds its breath. It's waiting, as we all are, for the crone.

I've known all along what Alyssa plans to do. How could I not? Her intent is indelible, present in each and every tattoo she sends me. Now that I've received the final one, it's as if all the pieces have fallen into place.

I know, without consciously knowing. I'm ready because she's made me that way.

I won't let her do what she plans on doing.

A ride-share pulls into the circular drive, blaring death metal and spewing exhaust. Alyssa steps out, throws a handful of bills at the driver, and then gives him the finger for good measure. Hands on hips, she surveys the backyard. Her feet are clad in steel-toe boots. Her jeans are worn through at the knees, and the collar of her gray T-shirt hangs loose.

She looks like she did the day she left, and not a minute older.

At the sight of her, my chest constricts; my heart is tender and raw.

If the past seven years don't show on my face, I feel them in my bones. Like Sleeping Beauty, I long for a hundred-year nap. I'm tired of this relentless niceness. It is false and draining, and I can't imagine another seven minutes living this way, never mind years.

That's why I plan to stop Alyssa. I will step into the void, offer myself as a sacrifice to the crone. She wants more. She wants blood.

She can have mine.

My gaze meets Alyssa's. Her tough-girl stance shifts. I wonder if she can read my intent in the same way, if it's in the blood and always has been.

The crone materializes equal distance between us.

I don't drop the bowl of coleslaw, but I let it slip through my grip. My fingers guide it to the ground, where the soil swallows it up. A cackle rings in my ears, unsettling and scornful. The slaw, of course, was a mere pretense.

I have not fooled the crone.

To my surprise, she is not the hideously-bent creature from any number of tales. She is not any one creature.

I blink and see my manager from work. I blink again, and the sales clerk from the grocery store appears before my eyes. A third time, my guidance counselor from high school, the one who urged me to apply to Harvard.

Is the crone everyone and no one at the same time? I dart a look toward Alyssa. Her eyes are narrowed, brow furrowed in confusion. I wonder what it is she sees. Missed opportunities? A truncated life, or one denied?

And because I am looking at Alyssa, I see the moment she decides. It's there in the way the soles of her boots churn the earth, the tightening of her fists. I start my run a split second before she does.

I will win.

I think this as I gain ground. I think this as I pull ever closer. What will happen when my body meets the crone's? I'm not sure. I only know I need to reach her first.

The full moon shines down on the backyard, revealing a pathway to the crone. She is everyone and everything I cannot have. She is everyone and everything Alyssa's been denied.

I'm so close, hands extended, fingertips yearning, when something white and billowing brushes past me, the figure lithe and quick.

Our mother.

She reaches the crone before I can, before Alyssa can. When the two collide, the night explodes into a million stars. A wave washes through me. There's a loosening—in my heart, my throat. I feel words, real words, in my mouth.

I want to laugh. I want to cry. I want to reach out and bring my mother back.

When those million stars fade and only the moon illuminates our backyard, nothing remains of my mother or the crone. In their wake, we discover a patch of rich earth surrounded by quartz and agates.

We stand there, me, Alyssa, and Henry, and marvel as seedlings push through the soil, sprout, and bloom as if moonlight alone sustains them. Daisies and roses, slender lilies, and flowers I don't know the names of, but certainly, Henry does.

At last, around the border, a flock of forget-me-nots blossom. Henry kneels, gathers a handful, and says:

"As if I could, my love. As if I could."

～

HENRY IS like a prince in a fairy tale.

He smooths the way for Emma to start college. When she balks, Alyssa prods and cajoles, poking her sister relentlessly until—at last—she enrolls in the honors program.

Whenever Emma falters, Alyssa says, "Don't you dare waste that brilliant brain of yours."

Henry smooths the way for Alyssa, too. She agrees—reluctantly—to take classes of her own at the community college. One each semester. She navigates the strange language of profit and loss statements, of double-entry accounting. Until she's fluent, Henry will keep the books for her, make sure the taxes are paid on time.

The first artist (other than herself) to step through the doors of *Flowers & Stones Tattoos* is Samantha from San Francisco. The first customer (other than herself) is a woman who wears a triple moon goddess on her forearm.

Her storefront is a cozy, safe place in this world. She handles the rude customers by channeling Emma. The ones who are lost, who stare at the walls until their gaze lands on the artwork they need? Those customers she tends to with care. Alyssa sends them into the world again, armed, she hopes, to fight their own battles.

When the *E* and *A* tattoo doesn't bloom on Emma's ankle, Alyssa drags her to *Flowers & Stones*. While Samantha works on Emma, Alyssa swears she feels the residual burn against her skin.

On weekends, she, Emma, and Henry gather. The garden overflows with blossoms and fragrances. The quartz and agates gleam in the sunshine. A sapling takes root, flourishes in less than a season to shade the chair where Henry rests each evening.

They are three, Alyssa thinks.

Three to make a family.

Flowers and Stones was written especially for the (Love) Stories for 2020 project. It's a contemporary retelling of Diamonds and Toads, another fairy tale that I think deserves a new twist or two.

HEART OF A PIRATE KING

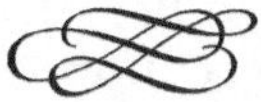

FANTASY

The first shot across the bow landed well beyond Sebastian's ship. Deliberately, it was true. Even so, in its aftermath, a mist of seawater washed his face and kissed his lips.

That was Estella, through and through, her way of fluttering her eyelashes, of casting a sultry, come-hither glance.

Sebastian wasn't falling for it. Indeed, he steeled himself against the onslaught of both cannon fire and feelings. The tiny part of his heart—the piece she hadn't splintered beyond repair—had leaped at the sight of the *Siren* and her captain coming into view.

Right up until Estella ran the Jolly Roger up the mast.

A pink Jolly Roger.

With hearts for eye sockets.

"Your wife, Captain."

His first mate had the uncanny ability of voicing the obvious without it sounding ... obvious.

"My *estranged* wife," Sebastian corrected.

He clutched the rail, grip tightening on wood worn smooth from years at sea, and licked the salt from his lips.

"She mocks me," he said, ostensibly to his first mate.

"Aye, Captain," Hadim replied. "She mocks us all."

Sebastian cast the man a look, the sort that would wilt a weaker man's soul.

"But mainly you," his first mate amended.

Again, obviously. On the other hand ...

"No." His sigh was heavy, a waterlogged thing in his chest. "She mocks us all."

When had it gone so wrong? When had Estella turned traitor? Or perhaps she'd always been one, and he'd simply failed to see the cracks in the façade, the clues to her deception.

"Captain!"

The shout came from the lookout. The boy in the crow's nest was leaning so far forward that Sebastian feared the lad might tumble to the deck below. The boy's arm was outstretched, his face a mask of fear.

Sebastian followed the trajectory and saw reason enough to put fear in his own splintered heart.

The royal navy, in battle formation, bearing down on him.

A second shot whooshed across the bow, this one closer and filled with intent.

Ah, yes. Estella as bait for this trap—a deliberate distraction, something to keep his gaze pinned in one direction while neglecting all the rest.

Still ... the *entire* royal navy? Well, he had ridiculed the pretender to the throne more than once, called out the king's corruption. Sebastian let his gaze survey the sea, count the frigates, and calculated the odds—and then immediately dismissed them.

Was he not Sebastian Black, Pirate King? Did he not captain the *Tyrant's Bane*?

"Come about!" he called, his crew snapping into action almost before the cry left his mouth.

He would take the fight to them—to Estella *and* the royal navy.

Or die trying.

WHAT WOKE HIM, Sebastian couldn't say. The gentle bob and sway of the plank beneath his chest and head? The insistent, if gentle, nudge against the small of his back every time his fingers lost their grip on the sea-soaked wood?

Or the chattering that sounded, in turns, like laughter, admonishment, and mockery.

Yes, it was the mockery that woke him.

The sun blazed hot in the sky above. Waves licked the burnt skin along his arms and back, bringing both agony and relief. His mouth was parched, his throat a dry husk.

The sight of fins circling in ever tighter loops sent his heart soaring. He strained to find purchase on the plank, its shattered and soggy edges crumbling beneath his fingers.

Then one of the creatures poked its head from the sea and filled his ears with more of that mocking chatter. A dolphin. An entire pod of them. They surrounded him, keeping him afloat, prodding the plank this way and that, like an expert navigator making minute but crucial course corrections.

"What happened?" His voice was little more than a croak. He asked the question rhetorically, certainly not to his constant companions.

Even so, a dolphin poked its head from beneath the surface. It was a tiny thing, no more than a pup. It regaled him with a stream of chatter that—if Sebastian didn't know better—was a narrative of what had happened from the time he spotted the *Siren* until he fully woke, stranded at sea.

Yes, it had been a rout from the start—the entire fleet against the *Tyrant's Bane*. Without warning, without support from any other quarter. In the past, they'd always counted on advance notice, a whisper network of fishermen and dockworkers, disgruntled guards, the townsfolk who observed comings and goings.

But for weeks now, nothing.

Other than betrayal and surprise, obviously.

Worst of all? He hadn't crossed sabers with Estella. Oh, he'd been looking forward to *that*. Not their first dual, naturally, but Sebastian had vowed to make it their last. He would've gladly gone down with the *Tyrant's Bane* if only he could have taken her treacherous heart with him.

But if the *Tyrant's Bane* had sunk, he possessed no memory of it. A concussion, perhaps? His head felt clear. When he probed his skull with careful fingertips, nothing ached, and his skin came away free from blood.

"So, where are we headed, little one?"

The dolphin chattered away in between leaping up and over waves. They were undoubtedly headed *somewhere*. Away from the trade routes, it seemed. Although, from his vantage point, here in the heart of this vast, cerulean sea, he had no true way of knowing.

Call it instinct, born from years traversing the seas. The water around him tasted wilder, salt sharp on his lips. They were heading toward the edge of the known territories and into the uncharted seas.

Which would make the odds of rescue infinitesimally slight.

Sunset brought relief to his eyes and skin, if not his worries. Even when he spotted the bump on the horizon, Sebastian shut his thoughts against the onslaught of hope. Weary, dehydrated, weak from hunger. His mind was primed to welcome a mirage.

And yet, the bump grew larger, the landscape more defined. Cliffs jutted from the sea, palm trees swayed in the breeze, and in a wide, sweeping bay, water lapped against the shore.

The dolphins' chatter increased, as did their insistent nudging against the plank. His toes touched sand the same moment the sun kissed the horizon behind him.

Before he released his grip on the wood, before he clambered to shore, the dolphin pup swooped by him one last time and bussed his cheek.

Sebastian staggered the few feet to dry land and sank gratefully into sand toasted warm by the day's sun.

A BREEZE STOLE over his skin, one cool enough to wake him but with a scent that promised heat. Sebastian rolled, sat up, and took in the quiet of the island around him.

It was time to take stock of his new home.

On his person, he possessed breeches—and nothing more. No shirt, never mind scabbard and saber. Oh, how he mourned the loss of the latter. Where was it now? At the bottom of the ocean, most likely. Or perhaps clutched in Estella's tiny—but surprisingly strong—grip.

No matter. Sebastian had battles to fight here. He doubted the immediate ones required a saber.

Fresh water. Shelter. Food. In that order. He plowed his way through the sand until he reached the tall grasses and lush vegetation beyond the shore. Once there, he discovered a path.

Overgrown, to be sure, clogged with snaking vines and underbrush that threatened to obliterate it from existence. But a path, nevertheless. Sebastian followed it into the thick, leafy interior.

Large fronds shielded him from the sun's unrelenting glare. Cool mist bathed his skin, and he licked his lips, sucked in deep breaths as if that alone might sustain him. Above the birdsong and the buzz of insects, something else babbled.

He was nearly upon it before realizing what that sound was. Water, tumbling over rocks. A waterfall, and beyond that, a wide, clear pool that looked perfect for bathing.

Sebastian knelt at the water's edge and scooped a handful, touched his tongue tentatively to the liquid already slipping through his fingers, ready to recoil at the taste of salt.

Fresh.

It was *fresh*.

He fought the urge to gulp, to greedily slurp all that he could. Control. Tiny sips. Fresh did not mean pure, necessarily. In any event, he had no wish to inhale a gallon's worth, only to regurgitate it across the jungle floor.

He ventured farther along the water's edge and inspected the pool. Was there anything lying in wait, something with teeth as sharp as sabers? He eased one foot in, and then another, and then because he was Sebastian Black, Pirate King, threw himself into the pool.

It didn't do to be overly cautious, after all.

Free of salt and sand and sweat, he continued his exploration. There were coconuts, of course, more than he had hope of consuming. All manner of tropical fruit. With each step, hope kindled in his chest. With each discovery, he moved with speed and purpose.

If he could survive, then he could be rescued. If he could be rescued?

Well, then. He could wreak revenge, for his crew, the *Tyrant's Bane*— and his heart.

The path led around the pool and back toward the sea. Before he reached the shore, Sebastian stumbled upon a shelter. In need of repair, but its bones were strong, a sleeping pallet already fashioned. And did his eyes deceive him, or was that an actual tinderbox?

The shelter was several yards up the coast from where he washed ashore, tucked in a cove that would protect him from the worst of the tropical storms. At the ocean's edge, the rocky outcroppings provided numerous tide pools filled with shellfish and crabs. The latter waved their claws as if daring him to pluck them from the sea for the day's first meal.

Sebastian shielded his eyes and surveyed his domain. He had fresh water and a means to sup whenever he liked. Here on this island, a banquet was spread before him, every last item a delicacy on the mainland. Yes, he would feast like a true pirate king.

And last, but certainly not least, he possessed a ready place to lay his weary head. Things, he mused, could be much, much worse.

It was then that he turned his attention toward the shelter and spotted the skeleton.

~

"Have I ever told you about my wife?"

The skeleton, beneath the shade of a palm tree, didn't respond. But then, it never did.

Sebastian considered his word choice and amended, "My *estranged* wife. No? Oh, my friend, I suspect you're lying to me."

He sat in front of his shelter, that evening's meal bubbling on the cook fire. In addition to the tinderbox, he'd uncovered a pot and few makeshift utensils. The rich aroma of shellfish and wood smoke laced the air. A breeze brought the scent of salt that lingered on his tongue.

He was never without salt or the slight but constant grit of sand between his molars. Such was the price of living in paradise.

"You can't possibly want to hear the story again," he said, ostensibly to the skeleton. "What? You do? Oh now, my friend, I believe you're humoring me."

At first, Sebastian thought to give this poor soul a proper burial. That meant digging without a shovel, which he was more than willing to do. It meant carrying the bones bleached white from wind and sand and sun.

This, too, didn't disturb him. As a pirate king, he'd seen—and dispensed—his share of death.

No, the simple fact was the skeleton seemed at peace where it was. As if this sailor had settled beneath a favorite palm one evening, closed their eyes, and never opened them again.

The skeleton itself was a tiny thing, and Sebastian suspected it may be a *she* rather than a *he*. With no way of knowing, he referred to his constant companion simply as *my friend*.

In any event, he felt only slightly less foolish speaking aloud. His captive audience had no way of protesting. Sebastian had no reason not to voice his woes about his current state, his shattered heart, Estella's treachery, and his ... confusion.

"It started off quite well, my friend. The way a pirate love story should."

Oh, but it had. Their courtship had been as fierce as their rivalry. Estella's *Siren* was faster, more nimble than the *Tyrant's Bane*. Sebastian commanded far more power. The sight of the Jolly Roger running up the mast of his ship struck terror in the hearts of the so-called sovereign's tax collectors, greedy merchants, and navy frigates alike.

Truth be told, the king's men were far more cutthroat than Sebastian's crew had ever been. He liked to think of it as righting wrongs, restoring what belonged to those who could not defend themselves.

And, well, yes, Sebastian and his crew certainly helped themselves to the surplus. Under King Thaddeus's reign, there was more than enough surplus to be had.

Estella had a way of getting there first, swooping in on the Siren and collecting that surplus. Her crew was small and ferocious, not a man among them. She commanded them not with an iron grip but with skill and intuition. She matched tasks to sailors, and even the unlikeliest crewmember flourished aboard her ship.

The first time Sebastian had spotted her on the bow of the *Siren*, his heart had seized. Her hair was the color of black silk and flowed like the Jolly Roger above her head. Her skin glowed in the sunshine, the exact color of damp sand.

The first time they crossed sabers, he had—to her surprise and his own—stolen an ill-advised kiss. He left that encounter with a gash along his cheekbone—and without his heart.

The first time he intercepted one of the king's frigates bearing down on the *Siren*, Estella had sent over chests of coin and barrels of wine—enough to keep his crew happy and well in their cups.

As for Sebastian himself? An invitation to sup in her cabin aboard the *Siren*.

In short order, they joined forces, joined hearts, joined in marriage.

"The rest should have been history, don't you agree?" Sebastian stirred the stew with a stick, testing the bits of meat for tenderness. "I thought we were of one mind, one heart."

Ridding the realm of King Thaddeus? Restoring order and fairness to the seven lands and their many seas? With their share of the cut, they could lower the Jolly Roger and sail into the sunset, eventually landing on an island much like this one.

"Perhaps with a few more amenities." Sebastian rubbed his chin. The beard was thick and truly magnificent. Although, in truth? He longed for a shave, for a shirt, and for a clean pair of trousers.

"And then, as you know, she betrayed me."

Possibly it was a trick of the setting sun, the light glinting *just so* off his silent companion. The skull took on a skeptical expression as if it doubted this part of the tale.

"Perhaps I am wrong."

But he *couldn't* be. With his own eyes, he witnessed Estella on the palace balcony, her arm linked with the king's. Although Sebastian stood far back in the crowd—and in disguise as well—he'd detected the possessive glint in Thaddeus's eye, the lift of the chin that spoke of triumph.

Estella herself was nearly lost in a profusion of pink silk and satin with enough lace that it was a wonder she could walk.

"If not betrayal, then what?"

He longed to know. Estella cared nothing for fancy gowns and the niceties of court life. The sea was her home, the *Siren* and its crew her heart.

If the skeleton had an opinion, certainly Sebastian would have found relief rather than fear in its words. But his companion merely stared out to sea as if the answers were there, lost among the waves.

"If not betrayal, then what?" He spoke the refrain softly, a thin sliver of smoke rising from the fire as if to capture the words. Perhaps there was no answer, at least not one he would ever know.

Sebastian knelt next to the fire and eased the stew from the flame. Yes, he would sup like a king tonight, but he would sup alone, as he had for the past month.

Without his pirate queen.

~

THE SHIP on the horizon dipped in and out of view. Behind Sebastian, at the jungle's edge, sat a stockpile of firewood. He held a fistful of kindling in one hand, the tinderbox in the other, his grip so tight, he risked slicing his palms with both.

And yet, he couldn't bring himself to start the fire.

Not yet.

Was this rescue or arrest? The sun glinted off the water, the glare stinging his eyes. He had no hope of knowing which until it was too late.

His crew wouldn't rest until they found him—dead or alive.

But then, neither would the royal navy.

And so he stood, the kindling biting into what little tender flesh remained in the center of his palm.

When he noticed the gentle gliding of the albatross, Sebastian couldn't say. It soared high above the sea unperturbed by the ship behind it or the island before it. From its beak, something swung.

He shielded his eyes against the day's brilliance and tracked the bird's progress as it drew ever closer.

The albatross released its payload with the precision of an expert artilleryman. The item tumbled from the sky, landing within feet of Sebastian. As for the bird, it looked enormously relieved to be free of its burden—and a bit cheeky, as if it knew something Sebastian didn't.

Since he'd been stranded nearly two months now, the entire realm no doubt knew things he didn't.

He dropped the kindling and pocketed the tinderbox. Armed with a slender piece of driftwood, he approached.

A satchel lay on the damp sand, close enough to the sea that the tide might steal it if he didn't move fast enough. He looped the driftwood through the strap just as a wave licked the edge of the bag.

For a long moment, Sebastian surveyed the satchel. Then he poked at it, prodded it with his bit of driftwood. The bag remained still. Besides, it was far too slender to hold much of consequence. He didn't discount poison, but then the albatross had appeared hale and healthy.

Then curiosity overrode vigilance. Sebastian drew the satchel toward him and undid the flap.

It didn't do to be overly cautious, after all.

The first item to greet him was his own image under the phrase: *Wanted: Dead or Alive.*

The likeness was passable, although it lacked the magnificent beard he now sported. Beneath his name was an outlandish reward, enough coin that Sebastian might consider turning himself in—and worry about keeping his head later.

Next was a second wanted poster, this one for the captain of the *Siren*. The artist had drawn Estella with an exaggerated hand, turning her into little more than a sea hag. The entire realm knew of Estella's beauty, and such an illustration would do little to deter treasure hunters.

His fingers shuffled the remaining contents—letters with the royal seal, battle plans for the navy, all manner of correspondence. All of it pointed to one objective. The concerted and concentrated effort to capture one man:

Sebastian Black, Pirate King.

Chatter drew his attention from the papers in his hand to the sea beyond. There, the ship on the horizon still bobbed, no closer, no farther away. Except now, a rowboat headed toward the island.

A single occupant leaned forward in the bow as if will alone could propel the boat. But no, it was the chattering pod of dolphins that took up the task, nudging and pushing the rowboat closer and closer to shore.

His gaze tracked the boat until Sebastian could make out the black hair that flowed like silk, skin the very color of damp sand, dark eyes that lit with delight at the sight of him.

Oh, yes. Quite the sea hag.

"Sebastian! My love!" Estella leaped from the boat before it fully came to rest on a sandbar.

The dolphin pup bussed her cheek as she waded to shore through waist-deep water. She held a bottle of wine aloft in one hand and pushed through the sea with the other.

"My love!" she called again. "Merry Christmas!"

Was it? Mentally, he counted the days since becoming shipwrecked, and well, yes, he was missing a day or two. But indeed, it could be Christmas.

This could also be a hallucination, brought on by a bad bit of shellfish, perhaps.

Estella halted three feet from him, soaked to the skin. She offered up the bottle of wine. When he refused it, she shrugged and set it on the sand. She unlaced her sleeves from her bodice, pulled off her boots, and placed both on the beach to dry.

"How do you like the island?" she asked.

Sebastian remained silent.

"It was my grandmother's," she continued as if he'd responded. "It's where she came to rest, in the end."

His gaze traveled up the shore, toward the shelter and his silent companion.

"Yes, exactly," Estella said.

He didn't demand. He didn't rage. He didn't kick sand or fling the wine bottle out to sea (really, the latter would be a terrible waste). Sebastian merely stood there, stony. True, after a long moment, he folded his arms across his chest. He may have tapped his foot.

Estella sighed, the light in her eyes fading to sorrow. "Oh, my love, I cannot apologize. I can only explain."

When he continued his silence, Estella grimaced.

"I suppose I deserve this." She gnawed her lip, a sign she was searching for the right words, not false ones. "Several months back, my spies brought word to me that the crown planned on marshaling their forces to capture you, convict you, and see you hanged from the neck."

She gestured toward the satchel, and he nodded. That much, he had ascertained.

"And my spies?" he said, finding his voice at last. "They brought me no word of this."

"Your spies had been infiltrated, my love. Indeed, so had members of your crew."

This? This *was* news. News he wanted to deny; news he felt the truth of deep in his bones. Had not his whisper network gone silent? Had not he detected a false glint or concealed fear in the eyes of the townsfolk and even his crew?

"And yours had not?" he countered.

"Indeed, not."

"And why is that?"

"My spies are invisible."

He barked a laugh. Yes, this was his Estella, through and through, outrageous and audacious.

"Really?" He raised an eyebrow. "How so?"

"Forgive me, my love, but how often do men notice the woman scrubbing the palace floors, or the ones sweeping the hearth and laying the fire? Do they notice the serving wench except to slap her bottom? Or think nothing of babbling to those who work in the royal pleasure houses?"

Oh, she had him there. Her network had always produced better intelligence than his own ever did.

"What are you telling me, then?" he said. "That you arranged all this?"

Some of that delight returned to her expression, those dark, soulful eyes glowing with it. "With a little help."

"Why not simply *tell* me?"

"Again, forgive me, my love, but your temperament is—" She paused again, a hint of teeth against her lip. "Legendary."

Well, *perhaps*.

"Could you have playacted the role?" She didn't let him answer. "For the plan to work, you, your crew, including the various spies, had to be convinced that I had turned traitor. There was no other way."

"And if I don't forgive you? If I strike you down here, right now?"

"I would gladly do it all again. I would lose your love and my life if only I could save yours."

It struck him then, hard and fast, like a blow to the gut. Not betrayal —at least, not the sort that mattered. But a crafty, well-executed plan that her clever mind and courageous heart put into action.

"And you fooled Thaddeus as well?" Another counterpoint, weak as it was.

Estella laughed and rolled her eyes in disdain. "You've seen my wanted poster, have you not?"

Yes, the act of a petulant child. And yet, Sebastian was still at a loss. How did they proceed? As if nothing had happened? As if his heart hadn't been splintered beyond repair?

"What is it we do now?" His words were more musing than question.

"Oh, my love." She spread her arms wide, and her smile was brighter than the midday sun. "We celebrate Christmas!"

She headed for the rowboat, turning every few steps to urge him to follow. "Come, come see what I brought."

Without recourse, Sebastian followed.

A TINY FIR tree sat well back from the cook fire. Red and gold ribbons bedecked its boughs, and all manner of gifts surrounded its trunk—lumpy parcels wrapped in brocade and tied with even more ribbons. One was definitely the size and shape of Sebastian's saber.

Estella knelt next to the fire, stirring something she claimed was fudge, although it was far too soupy for that. When he dared mention the fact, she merely eyed him.

"And when was the last time you ate chocolate?"

She had a point. He'd gladly toast the holiday with the dark sludge rather than the wine that sat cooling in the tropical shade.

"Who waits for us," he asked with a nod toward the horizon. Yes, he had also dared utter the word *us*, dared to hope, dared to believe in the schemes of this pirate queen. "Is it the *Siren*?"

"It is, with Miriam at the helm in my absence." She gave him a sly smile. "And Hadim as her first mate."

"Indeed?"

"In fact, they'd like you to marry them once you're restored to the *Tyrant's Bane*."

"Marry ... them?"

"As captain, can you not perform the ceremony?"

"I ... well, yes. Of course. But Miriam and Hadim?"

Estella glanced away. He had the distinct impression she—once again—rolled her eyes. Then another thought struck him.

"The *Tyrant's Bane*?"

"Being repaired by your crew." She removed the fudge from the fire and set it to the side to cool.

"Then it didn't sink."

"The *Tyrant's Bane*? I doubt it could."

Sebastian sat back, the onslaught of both thoughts and feelings threatening to overwhelm him.

"Estella." Her name emerged from his throat rougher than he intended. "What do we do now?" This time, his words were more question than musing.

She turned toward him, and oh, her eyes were so tender. She inched across the sand, drawing nearer to him.

"First, we celebrate Christmas. Don't you see the gifts beneath the tree?"

"I'm afraid I have nothing for you."

"Oh, I've accounted for that."

Of course, she had. "And then?"

"Then, I thought we could get reacquainted." She drew a finger along his cheekbone, the one where she'd left a scar so many months ago. "Although perhaps you could shave first."

"And perhaps I won't. Besides." He nodded toward the skeleton. "I'm not sure we should in front of your grandmother."

Estella laughed, the sound light and airy and like bells at Christmas. "And then we'll spend the week immersed in plans and strategies and tactics. On New Year's Day, we shall row out to the *Siren* prepared."

Sebastian took her chin between forefinger and thumb. It was the prelude to a kiss, and he wanted to savor the moment. "And then what, my love?"

"We take the fight to them."

He kissed her then, and it was both gentle and rough and fierce as both their rivalry and their courtship. In his chest, he felt the splinters of his shattered heart mend. They entwined together until not a single fracture remained. His heart, now whole once again, nestled securely beside that of his pirate queen.

Heart of a Pirate King was written especially for the (Love) Stories for 2020 project.

ABOUT THE AUTHOR

Charity Tahmaseb has slung corn on the cob for Green Giant and jumped out of airplanes (but not at the same time). She spent twelve years as a Girl Scout and six in the Army; that she wore a green uniform for both may not be a coincidence. These days, she writes fiction (long and short) and works as a technical writer for a software company in St. Paul.

Her short speculative fiction has appeared in *Flash Fiction Online*, *Deep Magic*, and *Cicada*.